Contemporary Issues in Canadian Drama

Contemporary Issues in Canadian Drama

edited by Per Brask

Blizzard Publishing • Winnipeg

Contemporary Issues in Canadian Drama first published 1995 by
Blizzard Publishing Inc. 73 Furby St., Winnipeg, Canada R3C 2A2
Copyright © is retained by the authors.
Foreward, arrangement and selection © Per Brask.

Cover art, *Development of the Plot III*, by Gathie Falk.
Printed in Canada by Friesens Printing Ltd.

Published with the assistance of
the Canada Council and the Manitoba Arts Council.

Caution
This book is fully protected under the copyright laws of Canada and all other countries of the Copyright Union and is subject to royalty. Except in the case of brief passages quoted in a review of this book, no part of this publication (including cover design) may be reproduced or transmitted in any form, by any means, electronic or mechanical, including recording and information storage and retrieval systems, without permission in writing from the publisher, or, in the case of photocopying or other reprographic copying, without a licence from Canadian Reprography Collective (CANCOPY).

Canadian Cataloguing in Publication Data

Main entry under title:
Contemporary issues in Canadian drama
   ISBN 0-921368-51-8
1. Canadian drama – 20th century – History and Criticism.
I. Brask, Per K., 1952–

PS8165.C65 1995   C812'.5409   C95-920036-3
PR9191.5.C65 1995

Table of Contents

Foreword
  by Per Brask 9

Text as Performance: Reading and
Viewing Djanet Sears's *Afrika Solo*
  by Susan Bennett 15

"Wisdome Under a Ragged Coate":
Canonicity and Canadian Drama
  by Chris Johnson 26

Theatre of Images: New Dramaturgies
  by Sarah B. Hood 50

The Spirit of Shivaree and the Community
Play in Canada; or, The Unity in Community
  by Edward Little and Richard Paul Knowles. 68

Change the Story: Narrative
Strategies in Two Radio Plays
  by Ann Jansen 86

Native Drama: A Celebration of Native Culture
  by Agnes Grant 103

Protest for a Better Future: South Asian
Canadian Theatre's March to the Centre
  by Uma Parameswaran 116

Theorizing a Queer Theatre: Buddies in Bad Times
  by Robert Wallace 136

The Culture of Abuse in *Under the Skin*,
This is for You, Anna and *Lion in the Streets*
  by Ann Wilson 160

Drama in British Columbia: A Special Place
  by Denis Johnston 171

Centres on the Margin: Contemporary Prairie Drama
  by Diane Bessai 184

"One Big Ontario": Nation-Building
in the Village of the Small Huts
   by Alan Filewod 208
Spiritual Resistance / Spiritual Healing:
Tremblay, Dalpé, Stetson, Champagne, Marchessault
   by Denis Salter 221
In/Visible Drama of Atlantic Canada
by Denyse Lynde 235

Acknowledgements

In putting this book together I have been blessed by these writers agreeing to participate, by Blizzard Publishing agreeing to let me pursue this project, and by my life with Carol Matas and our children.

Foreword

by Per Brask

> We cannot begin to make sense of functional attributions until we abandon the idea that there has to be one, determinate, *right* answer to the question: What is it for? And if there is no deeper fact that could settle that question, there can be no deeper fact to settle its twin: What does it mean?
> —Daniel C. Dennett, *The Intentional Stance*

The idea for this book arose when I was asked in 1992 to teach the following year the Canadian Drama course required for majoring in Theatre and Drama at the University of Winnipeg. Having worked for many years as a dramaturge with an involvement in new play development, I was very excited about the prospect. While preparing the syllabus I quickly ran into difficulties. Apart from being unable to choose from the many fine unpublished plays that characterize our history, I was also unable to offer my students good essays discussing the contemporary scene, i.e., as current as possible, without contravening copyright laws or endlessly circulating journal articles. Whatever the choice, I would not be able to construct classes which would engage in the contemporary discourse of theatre in Canada without some considerable difficulty. What was needed, I thought, was a volume which would present undergraduate students with well-written essays which could model for them a variety of interrogative strategies while at the same time introduce them to a wide range of issues intersecting along geographical, social and aesthetic lines. I developed a catalogue of issues and contacted critics

---

PER BRASK studied dramaturgy at the University of Aarhus, Denmark and is Professor of Theatre at the University of Winnipeg. His books include *Drama Contemporary: Scandinavia*; *Double Danish*; and *Aboriginal Voices: Amerindian, Inuit and Sami Theatre* (with William Morgan).

from across the country whose writing I admired. In discussions with these writers we would attempt to narrow the issue on which each would focus. It was from the outset not to be an exercise in coverage, not an attempt to be comprehensive, rather I asked the writers to zero in on what mattered to them. In other words, I asked them within the area assigned to be unapologetically selective. The result, I believe, is a volume which can be used effectively in the class room as a point from which to delve into discussion both by engaging in arguments with the writers here as well as by inspiring students to look into areas and issues in their own theatrical experience which may not have been dealt with in this book. Or, by asking students to pursue a topic perhaps touched on in a particular way in this book with reference to a certain locale or cultural milieu in their own "backyard."

That "backyard" is likely to have changed significantly during the past decade. Theatrical practice has shifted its attentions and its self-definitions over the past few years. The project of cultural nationalism which formed the ideological ground for many theatre artists during the formative 1950s, '60s and '70s seems to have lost its moral punch. Hence the "development" of the Canadian Theatre seems to have lost a discernible direction. In addition, theatre in Canada—especially theatre in English-speaking Canada—has suffered severely during the past decade or so; many theatres have disappeared due to lack of funding, many have been unable to attract sufficient audiences, and many have had to reduce their operations.

In the title essay of his insightful book on the state of Canadian theatre, *Producing Marginality* (1990), Robert Wallace has described how the confluence of the "universalist" biases of newspaper reviewers, the narrow pool of jurors for arts awards juries, the increasing influence of business ethics on the production of theatre, as enforced by boards of directors drawing their members from the business community, has created a situation in which "particularist" and innovative approaches to theatrical production automatically become marginalized.

Marlene Nourbese Philip showed in "The Multicultural Whitewash: Racism in Ontario's Arts Funding System" (1987), how jury composition, combined with an insidious distinction between the artistic community and the so-called multicultural community, reproduces the structure of the *status quo* and prevents new voices from being heard. This structural form of discrimination is also found within theatre organizations where representational aesthetics survive unchallenged and where notions of cultural nationalism are still being implemented.

That this cultural nationalism should have developed into a highly questionable practice is perhaps ironic, but it is certainly not the first time in history that an initially progressive force turned into its opposite. After all, as Alan Williams stated in an interview in *Ellipsis...* (1990) "the theatres which started in the early seventies, which built themselves up, and have grown up with a kind of rhetoric about doing Canadian plays, authentic Canadian-ness—one of the problems with that generation when they talk about this is that they mean sort of Scottish descent" (1).

In view of the radically changed and changing demographics of our country, the net result of this—at least seemingly—unicultural endeavour on the part of a large component of our professional theatre is, I believe, that this theatre has become increasingly irrelevant and decreasingly able to participate in the discourse around the story called Canada. Theatre-goers to our main regional theatres are more likely in their daily cross-cultural negotiations and conflicts to live a more immediately dramatic life than what they would see portrayed on most stages. As Douglas Arrell has pointed out in his article, "Paradigmatic Shifts at the Box-Office: Winnipeg Theatre Responds to Changing Critical Values" (1991), the time is long past when audiences, by consciously or unconsciously applying the ideals of the New Criticism, searched for messages about the universally human in plays from faraway lands. Now it seems that declining attendance records may indicate a desire for a more immediate and particular encounter with what occurs on a stage.

Performers and writers from visible minority groups are—as their numbers increase—expressing discontent at being sidelined in the theatre. In 1989 the two performers' associations ACTRA and Equity hosted a symposium on non-traditional casting in order to discuss the ways in which the lives of non-White performers could be improved. At that conference it was revealed that, whereas in the United States non-traditional casting—sometimes referred to by the unfortunate term colour-blind casting—is an established method of work in some theatres, most of the Canadian producers attending seemed to have major problems conceiving of casting, for example, a Black or Brown Juliet against a White or Yellow Romeo. With a few notable exceptions perhaps, not much has changed in this respect at our large theatres. Some may have reservations about this type of casting on legitimate semiotic grounds, but I would suggest that a theatrical production creates meaning in relation to a specific audience and not by virtue of a self-contained semiotic system. It is tempting to conjure the theory that the minimal response to this issue so far from most of our mid-sized and large professional theatre companies may be due to the (probably correct) suspicion that a theatre flourishing with non-traditional casting would soon find itself thoroughly questioning many more of its own premises, such as the very notions of performance, play, character, gender, etc.— not to mention its methods of production and the power structures associated with these. In other words the "powers that be" may well, for good reasons, see issues such as non-traditional casting as "the thin edge of the wedge," the first step on a "slippery slope."

But if the desire for non-traditional casting practices at our larger theatres cannot easily be aroused, perhaps need will eventually make it necessary. In 1988 the research firm Multifax outlined at a meeting of the Canadian Centre for Philanthropy a possible future in which by the year 2,000 less than ten percent of Toronto's five million people would be of White Anglo-Saxon Protestant descent. (Lacy, "Soul-searching in Hong-Couver"). It may mot be totally unreasonable to suggest that these trends could be projected across English-speaking Canada. If that were, indeed, a likely future then the theatre has a great deal of restructuring and rethinking to do in the next few years. Only a few professional theatres have responded to this changed and changing reality, like the Firehall Theatre in Vancouver, by presenting plays written by visible minority writers and by actively recruiting members from visible minority groups and providing training if necessary.

The increasing differentiation of Canada's cultural life, and the disappearance of a meta-narrative of what Canada is, has led important critics such as Robert Kroetsch to announce: "I am suggesting that in Lyotard's definition, Canada is a postmodern country." (*The Lovely Treachery of Words* 22). And, as Linda Hutcheon states in *The Canadian Postmodern*, "the postmodern 'different,' then, is starting to replace the humanist 'universal' as a prime cultural value. This is good news for Canadians who are not of Anglo or French origin [or any other normative nomenclature, one might add, P.B.]—that is, for a good portion of the country's population today, [...] postmodernism offers a context in which to understand the valuing of difference in a way that makes particular sense in Canada" (ix). More recently Canadian culture has also come under investigation from postcolonial perspectives such as those discussed in Donna Bennett's "English Canada's Postcolonial Complexities." Bennett ends her essay by crediting the postcolonial model of investigation with the following important insight:

> Perhaps what it finally helps us to see is that there is a collection of cultures within the *idea* of English Canada, not so much a mosaic as a kaleidoscope, an arrangement of fragments whose interrelationships, while ever changing, nevertheless serve—by virtue of their container, we might say—not only to influence what we see when we look through the glass, but also to affect the placement of the other elements in the array. (196–97)

Though the meta-narrative that produced a particular history of Canada may be crumbling, giving way to a productive and delightful polyphony, let us not lose sight of the fact that all this is happening within the context of a capitalist nation. The notions of capitalism and nationhood are both powerful shapers of narrative. Indeed, the story of capitalism in its on-goingness is in the process of subsuming and including all other narratives—becoming, if not a meta-narrative in the sense that it is the source of all legitimization, then certainly in the sense that it is able to be a source of levelling between a variety of narratives. Perhaps as an extension of Bennett's statement above we might say that the container she refers to is not only shaped by the idea of English Canada but also by the particular brand of capitalism practiced there.

Jean-François Lyotard offers both a perspective and a sense of hope in his essay "Lessons in Paganism" by stating that "history consists of a swarm of narratives, narratives that are passed on, made up, listened to and acted out; it is a mass of little stories that are at once futile and serious, that are sometimes attracted together to form bigger stories, and which sometimes disintegrate into drifting elements, but which usually hold together well enough to form what we call the culture of a civil society" (Benjamin 134). Later in the same essay he says, "But histories and policies are like cultures; they are their own references and they determine their own enemies. It may sometimes be possible to unite or even combine efforts and effects, and to both recount and implement particular narratives but it goes against reason, and reason is pagan, to totalize them on any lasting basis" (152).

If the above diagnosis of the conditions for producing theatre in Canada is even minimally correct then it is a true delight to read the essays in this volume detailing as they do a wide variety of theatrical voices who soldier on despite the odds. Of course, it is not a new situation in the cultural life of Canada that our artists continue to work in the most financially (and otherwise) unrewarding circumstances.

Indeed, the dramatic voices and gestures discussed in these essays attest to the growing polyphony and excitement that exists in pockets of theatrical life in Canada despite the lack of official encouragement, whether financially or otherwise. The essays collected here also make it clear that the essay, too, as a form of cultural intervention is thriving against the prevailing malaise.

Works Cited

Arrell, Douglas. "Paradigmatic Shifts at the Box-Office: Winnipeg Theatre Responds to Changing Critical Values." *Canadian Theatre Review* 66 (Spring 1991): 20–24.

Benjamin, Andrew, ed. *The Lyotard Reader*. Oxford: Basil Blackwell, 1989.

Bennett, Donna. "English Canada's Postcolonial Complexities." *Essays on Canadian Writing* 51–52 (Winter 1993–Spring 1994): 164–210.

Dennett, Daniel C. *The Intentional Stance*. Cambridge: MIT Press, 1987.

Hutcheon, Linda. *The Canadian Postmodern*. Don Mills: Oxford University Press, 1988.

Kroetsch, Robert. *The Lovely Treachery of Words*. Don Mills: Oxford University Press, 1989.

Lacy, Liam. "Soul-searching in Hong-Couver." *The Globe and Mail* July 8 1989: C3.

Philip, Marlene Nourbese. "The Multicultural Whitewash: Racism in Ontario's Arts Funding System." *Fuse Magazine* (Fall 1987): 13–22.

Wallace, Robert. *Producing Marginality*. Saskatoon: Fifth House Publishers, 1990.

Williams, Alan. "Tempered Nostalgia." *Ellipsis...: The Newsletter for Manitoba Playwrights* (Fall 1990): 1, 3–5.

Text As Performance:
Reading And Viewing Djanet Sears's *Afrika Solo*

by Susan Bennett

When the first audience for Djanet Sears's play *Afrika Solo* took their seats at Toronto's Factory Theatre Studio Café on November 12, 1987, the collaborative and public experience of theatre spectatorship was already well underway. For there were many different reasons why those viewers chose that night to see that particular play in that particular theatre. Perhaps they were regular attendees at the Factory Theatre. Or perhaps they had read preview materials in Toronto newspapers and magazines. Or perhaps it was as coincidental as a friend having asked if they'd like to go and see a new show. Whatever the reason, these factors had already affected how any and every spectator would view the play. In other words, the play does not ever simply begin at the moment when the first word is spoken.[1]

And in *Afrika Solo*, the play's opening has little to do with verbal discourse. Instead its first engagement with the viewer, or the reader, is "The Incantation." The stage direction reads:

> As the lights fade to black, the sound of a single drummer pounding out a Mandiani (a traditional West African rhythm), on a Djembe (a traditional West African tenor drum), is heard in the distance. The drum gets louder and is soon joined by a Djundjun (a traditional West African bass drum), a cow bell and an assortment of other percussive

---

SUSAN BENNETT is an Associate Professor in the Department of English at the University of Calgary where she specializes in theory, performance and film. Her latest book on representations of the past in/as contemporary performance will be published by Routledge in 1995.

sounds. The Mandiani overture builds to a full, sensual pulse. (15)

The description offered here by Sears (to a reader) provides a number of important clues from which an image of the play's opening frame can be constructed. It enables us to construct mentally, through the linear reading of a particularly structured collection of words, a process that the theatre audience would, of course, experience sensually and with a different sense of time. The reader, then, must make her/himself a potential director of the play in order to realize the dense and powerful impulses of Sears's opening. The cumulative effect of the increasing number of traditional West African drums suggests a soundscape which first attracts the attention of the audience and then perhaps surrounds and even overwhelms them. The effect of this is likely twofold: it more or less ensures a quiet, attentive audience; and, furthermore, it also provides a cultural context for the narrative that will subsequently unfold. This process of contextualization is further elaborated with the introduction of singing—not in English (the assumed mother tongue of a Toronto theatre-going public) but in an African dialect where the only recognizable linguistic signs might be "Mali" and "Senegal," the names of nation states which the audience would likely recognize as African. It is only after this complex orchestration of music and voice that "[t]he lights slowly fade up" (15).

Before thinking about the impact of the initial appearance of the central character Djanet, it is useful to dwell a little longer on responses to the opening sequence. The account I've provided above operates on the assumption that the gaze of the spectator is, as dominant cultural practice insists, a white Eurocentric one. That is, that the spectators would perceive the soundscape primarily as a signifier for an exotic setting for the performance. The same assumption might be seen to apply to the experience of reading the published version of Sears's play. For it is only if "The Incantation" is a performance of an exotic "other" that the various types of drums and rhythms—Mandiani, Djembe, Djundjun—require a gloss (as they are given in her text). While the experience of seeing a play tends to encourage a homogeneity in response,[2] if a spectator, or a reader, were West African or of that particular African heritage, then the effect and engagement of the play's opening would likely work very differently. It would, I think, offer a provocative and empowering sense of community, of a shared experience that might be explored in the subsequent action for both common elements and contradictions. What this points to is the necessity to remember always that any text, whether performed in a theatre space or read in the classroom, relies on the intersection of the cultural experience of the viewer, or the reader, with the cultural experience of the text itself in order to produce meaning. And that for different readers and different viewers, the experience of text will always and necessarily differ in some, many, or all areas.

The epigraph to the published version of *Afrika Solo* is the infamous line spoken by Captain Kirk in the early years of the television drama *Star Trek*, "Beam me up, Scotty"—a line which has entered popular parlance and functions as the punchline of jokes and so on. To the reader, this might signal (probably with some uncertainty) something of Sears's approach to her material: that the play is interested in science fiction, that the writer's attitude is one of disdain for the world she finds herself in, that she is interested in the effects of mass popular culture on a day-to-day lived experience. But what of the theatre audience? Is this epigraph in the theatre program? Or are they given there (or elsewhere, such as in the reviews they've read) other signals which will shape their initial responses to the performance. Perhaps a poster outside the theatre carried the extract from Vit Wagner's review in *The Toronto Star* (also printed on the final page of the published text) "Clever, insightful and devilishly [sic] humorous." This, for example, would predispose a spectator (or a reader) to expect a comic, entertaining show. In other words, both readers and viewers take account of all sorts of extra-performance materials with which to construct their first hypotheses about a play. As hypotheses are corrected, confirmed and/or amended as reading/viewing continues, those external elements continue to function in the production of response.

When Sears's play begins, the setting is "Ben's room, Cotonou, Benin, West Africa" (16). A long stage direction fills in all the details that make this geography as well as the protagonist's relation to it explicit. While the actual stage setting is clearly not intended to be realistic (it relies both on some sparse properties and a mime sequence by the performer), the amount of time elapsing before Djanet speaks allows the audience to absorb the world in which the action is about to take place. It is the reader's task to imagine the arrangement of artifacts on the stage and the actor's relation to them and to "Djanet" as character; it is the spectator's task to survey three-dimensional representations of those objects as well as the actor's mobile body: as a result of either activity, the reader or spectator will posit the collective meaning of all the various elements. At a minimum, the signs denote a departure—a deduction which is confirmed and elaborated in Djanet's opening speech. An easier task for a spectator perhaps, but both the reader of the text and the theatre audience must understand and interpret a multiplicity of meaning-generating units. This, simply stated, is the act of reading or viewing a play.

Before an audience has time to respond to this opening sequence in the action of *Afrika Solo*, the mood and, more importantly, strategy of representation shifts:

> *Suddenly, without transition, the pulsing Mandiani overture is replaced by an explosion and the sound of human 'beat boxes.' The musicians lay down a loud, sense, and heavily funky hip-hop rhythm, with their mouths. Rapping.*
>
> DJANET: I took a trip to Africa to find my root,
> Let me tell ya', what I saw did not compute.
> Not everyone was starving like they tell you on TV,
> I never met an African who lived in a tree.
> They're much more concerned with wart-hogs and
>   vultures,
> Than for African people, their history and cultures. (17)

Both the change in presentational style and the content of the rap lyrics are significant here, and it is important to consider the multivalent effects of both. In performance, the shift would be striking and much of what I describe here would be obvious to the audience confronted with the live performer. No longer is she acting as if oblivious to the presence of spectators (the convention of the fourth-wall removed[3]), but is engaging with them directly ("Let me tell ya'"). Her words, thus, are addressed to the people reading or seeing the play. In this connection, it is useful to take account of her mode of address, either in the second person "you" or in the first person plural "we." What is revealed is a number of assumptions about the reader/spectator's relationship to Africa: that s/he has no first-hand experience of the continent but draws information largely on the basis of television documentaries and dramas which are more concerned with flora and fauna than with the cultural history of African peoples (what we might think of as the National Geographic approach to the world); that s/he is assumed to be like Djanet before she made the journey that is the subject of her play; that the collective "we" have the ability to effect change ("We need to rewrite the history book" [18]).

This approach, through its oscillation between the first and second personal pronouns, presented in the context of a popular "street" form of music, makes the direct address more effective. It is not a distancing or even aggressive attack on the spectator, but instead attempts to get them involved in her narrative through the beat of the rap and a marking of their shared involvement in a Western-produced and disseminated ignorance of other cultures. The audience is made to recognize its complicity in constructing history books with gaps but also to see that Djanet herself could not, as a diasporic African, disengage herself from the same version of that history. For the reader of the text, it is perhaps harder to see the connection that is fostered in these words: it is, after all, the elaboration of rhythms created by a number of live musicians, the parameters of meaning for the spoken word and the embodiment of those words by Djanet, which produces that impact. The reader has only the most partial picture from which to construct an image of this performance.

It can be argued that the default position for any Western audience is a hegemonic whiteness. And this is a cultural condition that *Afrika Solo* addresses. It is not that this play functions here in its initial sequences or later simply as an information session for a white audience ("Let me tell ya'") or as a call to action for a black audience ("We need to rewrite the history books"). It marks as axiomatic the fact that irrespective of actual racial background, the spectators will experience the text as "white"[4]—that is to say, the apparatus of education (either officially as history has been taught in secondary and post-secondary education or unofficially as history has been disseminated in the popular media) has determined that "we" (white or black Canadians) do not know the historical and cultural specificities of African peoples. What knowledge we have has been seen through the lens of an imperialist white culture which has insisted on its superiority to countries over which it once held colonial jurisdiction. Djanet, as a woman raised in the United Kingdom and Canada—irrespective of her parents' background and her own skin color—was "white" in the way she perceived the world. And here Sears makes the point that too many plays (or, for that matter, movies or television shows, or any form of media) that we see or read, even in this contemporary moment, assume implicitly a world that is produced and received by and for white people. Other critics remind us that the same dominant perspective assumes maleness and heterosexuality. We must be vigilant, therefore, to read and view carefully for unexamined and unstated assumptions—and to position these against our own sense of self and the reality we inhabit.

Sears's play takes the form and the story of a quest, Djanet's own discovery of her roots and, as a result, her coming to terms with questions of identity. The trope of travelling is a commonly-invoked one which affords Sears the opportunity to construct her viewer or reader as someone taking the journey with the performer ("Fasten your belt, takeoff's begun, / Seven, six, five, four, three, two ... *The music explodes*" [18]). Once again, her effect is not to alienate the audience from her text, but to encourage them to learn with the protagonist something about the cultures that are Africa. The setting for "The Act" that follows "The Incantation" is also cleverly constructed to explore this trope further and to particular effect. The location of an international airport is a familiar one and precisely that place where the signifiers of identity are not only peculiarly visible but where they are regulated by the officials of state.

The climax of Djanet's story about her (white) childhood friend in England—a moving account of the inherent racism of British society—brings her to ask "Where the hell am I from?" (40). If her confusion cannot be solved in the circumstances in which the question arises, nor even by her trip as an adult woman to Africa, it is nonetheless the case that at any international airport, she must choose a nationality which must be the primary signifier of identity:

> Years later, by which time I'm the proud owner of four passports, seriously, I have a Canadian passport, a British passport, a Guyanese passport and a Jamaican passport, I again think of V.D. Where the hell am I from? (40)

In the late-twentieth-century, travel has become a commonplace and the truism that the world has shrunk is one that is heard widely in the Western world. Djanet can, it seems, choose to make her quest to West Africa and take a regularly scheduled airplane to her destination. Yet travel is not equally available to all persons. Beyond the economic accessibility of airline travel, the actual experience of negotiating the airport is bound to differ. As bell hooks reminds us, "it is crucial that we recognize that the hegemony of one experience of travel can make it impossible to articulate another experience or for it to be heard. From certain standpoints, to travel is to encounter the terrorizing force of white supremacy" (174). Djanet can choose between her various passports, one of which might accord her more or less power in certain geographies, but it is her very skin color which "identifies" her in the gaze of the authorities who would survey her and her documentation before granting access to their country. Since theatre is, for the most part, a cultural activity that is patronized by a demography of higher socio-economic groups, Sears can likely assume she shares an experience of air travel with her audience which will at one and the same time create for the reader/spectator an experience of Same/Other in their relation to Djanet.

In her description of arrival on the African continent, Djanet points to her own hybrid experience of self. As a woman, she held no power in getting easy access to the transportation office visa that she required to continue her journey on land. Her African identity had no currency even in that same continent; her gender was, in all likelihood, a liability. Her reaction—"I was so pissed off, I was sure I would boil. / And you'll never catch me dead kissing Tunisian soil!!" (44)—conveys her Western sense of efficiency, fairness and rights, a sequence of expectations clearly inapplicable in this other cultural expression. Sears is careful to make explicit the interstices of race, gender and nation that mark both a character's sense of self *and* her reception in different cultural circumstances (including performance in the theatre).

In many ways, *Afrika Solo* is a play about visibility and identity and the relationship between the two. In performance, the spectator is afforded an almost visceral response to the many theatrical elements—costume, music, sound, movement, gesture and so on—which contextualize the play's narrative line. As a spectator, the task is to hold all the on-stage signs in play and to construct responses on the basis of this complexity of meaning-generating markers. For readers of the text, the task is undoubtedly more demanding. A translation of the non-vocalized elements must take place, giving a dimensionality to their description in language, and simultaneously with their translation, the reader must imagine how this would affect comprehension of what is performed.

Special attention should be paid to the detailed and almost continuous soundtrack of the play. The question which demands an engagement with issues of identity, "Where the hell do I come from?" (40) is not a simple, singular statement of Djanet's doubt. It instead takes place against a cacophony of sound: reggae music, popular calypso and her own rendition of the British national anthem. Each kind of music signifies in a particular way, recognizable to the viewer's ear, but as they muddle over each other, they create an aural explanation for Djanet's frustration, lack of understanding, and anger. The soundscape thus represents aurally, the inner experience of the character's identity confusion.

If this attention to the non-verbal elements of Sears's text seems to impose demands on the skills of the reader, it should also be remembered that the reader enjoys the benefit of controlling the time under which the text can be received. In the experience of performance, the on-stage action proceeds at a pace determined by the director, performers and technical crew. The audience must allow themselves to be carried through that time. Should time for reflection be required, this can only be achieved by ignoring or at least giving less than full attention to the events on-stage, or in moments prescribed by the strategies of production: from brief pauses in the action, perhaps for set changes, to sanctioned breaks such as the intermission. In watching a fast-paced and often very funny play such as *Afrika Solo*, an audience would have very little opportunity to reflect on what has taken place or to separate the constituent elements of any moment in the action. It is interesting to consider to what extent an audience would register or retain the wealth of music (especially from media such as film and television) employed to facilitate levels of recognition. The reader, at her/his leisure, can unpack the various elements adopted in each segment of performance.

If *Afrika Solo* constructs a complicated negotiation of identity for the protagonist, it not only inspires the reader and spectator to engage with her struggle but to look to her/his own sense of how identity is constructed and whose interests it might be made to serve. We ask the questions "How are we seen in the society in which we live?" "What are the reasons for this?" and "How do both of these vary when we cross national boundaries?" *Afrika Solo*, then, asks its readers and spectators to be active participants in Djanet's search. At the end of the play, Djanet does not discover one answer to the problems of identity but comes to terms with her hybridity and realizes it offers a site for celebration. She discovers the beauty of herself (her self) and this releases the incantation, enabling closure. The ritualistic elements of performance frame the telling of one woman's story; they enable a translation from the particular to the general. Sears employs strategies that, though not distancing, avoid reader and spectator empathy with her protagonist. A spectator can not leave the theatre content that everything worked out for Djanet, and the ritual makes explicit the performativity of Djanet's story which reminds the reader/spectator of the larger cultural context in which her particular experience takes place.

This essay points to a few elements of a specific play to indicate the complexity of the process of reading and viewing a play at any moment in its action. I started by drawing attention to the effects of extra-textual elements on this process. It is important to recognize, too, those additions to the performance which are afforded by a printed version of the text. Since published editions of plays usually come after two or more professional productions, in preparing the script for publication the playwright often takes advantage of what she has learned in the production process. In the case of Sears's play, with the writer's additional involvement as performer, the scope for incorporating changes and/or extra information is significant.

One element, generally found in all published plays, is a brief production history. We learn that after its first Toronto presentation, *Afrika Solo* was produced at the Great Canadian Theatre Company in Ottawa some two years later. The prestige of this venue would have attracted an obviously mainstream theatre audience to this new work by a little-known woman playwright. That Sears appeared in both productions of her play is not surprising: the phenomenon of the one-woman show has characterized much work by women writer-performers in the 1980s. We're also told that *Afrika Solo* was produced by Theatre Fountainhead as a tour for the High Schools in the Metropolitan Toronto Board of Education region. This tour (no date given) assumes a very different audience from that of the Ottawa production; it begs the question what would the students "learn" (and which students) from their seeing this play.

Education also seems to be of special interest in the construction of other elements of the textual apparatus. In addition to the customary photographs (so we can glean a sense of the visual effects of performance), *Afrika Solo*, as published, includes a powerful Afterword. Part biography and part history lesson (with a useful preliminary bibliography), the playwright intervenes in our engagement with her artistic product and makes explicit many of her interests in writing the play. In this way, she connects her work to a tradition, a genealogy of black women's writing. And lest we imagine that this has little history in the Canadian theatre, Sears has elsewhere produced an important essay entitled "Naming Names: Black Women Playwrights in Canada" (Much 92–103).

In "Naming Names," Sears writes "Black women playwrights in Canada may be one group I can presume, albeit tentatively, to speak on behalf of. Tentatively, for as the colour of our skin varies in shades of Black, so do our visions, aspirations, experiences and sexual preferences" (92). Her statement is crucial. When we see or read a play, we must always ask whom does the playwright presume to speak for and, equally important, who are "we"? As a woman with some identity positions coincident with Djanet in *Afrika Solo*, but with difference marked powerfully by race, I must ask myself constantly about my own reaction to the issues provoked in this text as well as the implications of my selection of this text for discussion. I think that it is part of the education process that Sears is interested in that all of us—irrespective of race, gender, class, sexuality and so on—examine what has brought us to the expectations and assumptions we bring to bear on our realities (whether that is taking a journey across the world or to the theatre). And such an examination is never simple nor easy.[5] Michele Wallace makes the point that "black feminist creativity and analysis is forced to straddle, combine or supersede the always prior claims of white female-dominated or black male- or 'Third World'- or 'minority'-dominated cultural strategies" (216). How does this fact inflect *any* reading or viewing of any play by a black woman writer?

The critical essay is a cultural strategy which attempts to intervene in the process of reading (and/or viewing). I hope readers of this particular endeavour will realize both the differences and similarities in the acts of reading and viewing. Performance brings all the pleasure of immediacy; reading all the pleasure of reflection. The similarities between these processes bring responsibilities: each one of us must look to the assumptions we bring to our reception of any text and how or what we are prepared to learn from it.

Notes

1. See Chapter 3 (especially pp. 92–147) in my *Theatre Audiences: A Theory of Production and Reception* for a full discussion of the theatrical event.
2. See *Theatre Audiences* (163–4).
3. This convention emerges from Naturalism in the theatre where actors, usually performing in a representation of an interior space, conduct conversations and monologues as if there were no one else present. The audience-stage relationship is only acknowledged in the convention at the very end of a play: the actors taking their bows and the audience (hopefully) applauding. It is as if the actors are in a room which has had one of its four walls removed so that spectators might, rather voyeuristically, view the private, generally domestic, lives of the characters. For a careful discussion of Naturalism as a term and theatre practice, see Raymond Williams'

Keywords: A Vocabulary of Culture and Society (1981), pp. 216–219, and Glynne Wickham's *A History of the Theatre*. 2d ed., Part V (1992), especially pp. 202–214.
4. See, for example, Richard Dyer's "White" in *Screen* 29.4 (Autumn 1988), pp. 44–64 and, particularly useful, Michele Wallace's "Negative Images: Towards a Black Feminist Cultural Criticism" in *Invisibility Blues: From Pop to Theory*, pp. 241–256.
5. See the discussion on p. 96 of Sear's "Naming Names" for an account of the simultaneous and daily effects of racism and gender on black women.

Works Cited

Bennett, Susan. *Theatre Audiences: A Theory of Production and Reception.* London: Routledge, 1990.

hooks, bell. *Black Looks: Race and Representation.* Toronto: Between the Lines, 1992.

Sears, Djanet. *Afrika Solo.* Toronto: Sister Vision, 1990.

——————. "Naming Names: Black Women Playwrights in Canada." *Women on the Canadian Stage: The Legacy of Hrotsvit.* Ed. Rita Much. Winnipeg: Blizzard, 1992. 92–103.

Wallace, Michele. *Invisibility Blues: From Pop to Theory.* London: Verso, 1990.

"Wisdome Under a Ragged Coate":
Canonicity and Canadian Drama

by Chris Johnson

> Wisdome under a ragged coate is seldome canonicall.
> —H. Crosse, 1603 (one of the earliest
> uses of "canon" in its secular sense)

Selection and ranking, according to one set of values or another, are almost impossible to avoid. In the midst of working on this piece, and suspicious of canonization if not entirely convinced that it exists in Canadian drama, I answered a knock on my office door: Dr. B. N. Singh, Head of the Department of English at Arunachal University in India, was visiting; his department is adding Canadian plays to the study of Canadian literature, they'd already settled on George Ryga and James Reaney, would I choose two more for them please? There I was, canonizing, however unwillingly. For the record, I recommended David French's *Leaving Home*, not my favourite play, because it is "typical" of Canadian drama in many respects, and Judith Thompson's *White Biting Dog* because it is not "typical"—Thompson is a woman, not a realist, not mainstream, and I thought Arunachal's list needed tilting, or "destabilizing": slippery ground for both choices. I'm also aware of "canonizing" effects when I meet to consider the next season with the Prairie Theatre Exchange play development team: Michael Springate, Artistic Director and a historical materialist; Libby Mason, a feminist director; Ian Ross, Artistic Associate, a Métis and progressively nativist playwright. The values represented here are not "mainstream," but they function and select as values nonetheless. Or when I consult with the

---

CHRIS JOHNSON is the Director of the Theatre Programme and Artistic Director of the Black Hole Theatre at the University of Manitoba. He is also on the play development team at the Prairie Theatre Exchange, writes extensively about Canadian drama and theatre, was a contributor to *The Oxford Companion to Canadian Theatre*, *Canadian Drama and the Critics*, and *Post-Colonial English Drama*, directs, acts, makes masks, digs in his garden (metaphorically and otherwise), and spends a lot of time with his little boy, Zak.

annually elected students who choose the season for the Black Hole Theatre at the University of Manitoba, where the values represented change from year to year. You also select and rank when you prefer one play to another, are more engaged by some essays in this book than by others, and you do so according to your values, values of which you are conscious as well as those of which you are not.

Not long ago, "the canon of Canadian dramatic literature" was an oxymoron. In fact, conservative members of Canadian English and Drama/Theatre Departments still regard "Canadian dramatic literature" as an oxymoron. The playwrights, directors, and actors of the avowedly nationalist Canadian "alternative theatre" movement of the early '70s certainly regarded their own activities as anti-canonical, a challenge to a status quo in which canonical and fashionable American and European work dominated the stages of the Canadian regional theatre system. In the past few years, however, since the appearance of three major anthologies of Canadian plays edited by Richard Perkyns, Richard Plant, and Jerry Wasserman, the suspicion has arisen that there is indeed a canon of Canadian dramatic literature: there are those who say that there is a canon and that that's a bad thing; those who say there is, and that's good; and those who say, for a variety of reasons, that there's still no such thing.

The word "canon" used in the context of literary studies is a figure of speech derived from religion, where it refers to those writings which the Jewish and Christian faiths take to be divinely inspired, thus sacred. The human debates which determined which works were holy and which could be set aside in the lesser category of apocrypha were concluded well over a thousand years ago, and the canons of Judaism and Christianity have been constant ever since. The word was appropriated to give authority to a body of literary work regarded (by whom we'll discuss later) as essential to an understanding of the whole literature from which the works were, and are, selected: of Western thought if the canon is of the Great Books sort; of English literature as represented, say, by the Great Tradition canons proposed by T. S. Eliot or F. R. Leavis; or of various subdivided categories of literary or cultural works represented by various "canons" which choose to valorize or privilege or discriminate on the grounds of genre, period, national origin, gender of the author, sexual orientation of the author, ethnicity of the author, political opinion of the author, and so on.

> The canonical list, then, is not a two-dimensional, but a multi-dimensional, structure defining a matrix of subdivisions that may (or may not) overlap and that are not necessarily of equal importance in determining canonicity. Many of these subdivisions or subcanons are broadly generic (such as the canon of lyric poems), but they can also combine place and genre (the canon of Prairie novels) or ignore genre entirely (the canon of postmodernist writing). (Donna Bennett 135)

Canons of whatever kind operating at whatever level must exclude as well as include, and reflect a hierarchy, explicitly or implicitly: X is better than Y; or X is more important to an understanding of A than Y is; or an acquaintance with X is more important than is an understanding of Y in the education, or indoctrination, or development of an educated, or civilized, or avant-garde, or feminist, or socialist or "politically correct," or Canadian person. Or, to go right back to the beginning, X is divine while Y is secular, or at best inspirational, and is therefore more important to the development of a Jewish or Christian person. This capacity to include, exclude, and rank, and the underlying assumption that it is right and good to do so, have provoked challenges to canons of various sorts, indeed to the very idea of canon formation, from literary theorists opposed to the mind-set represented and perpetuated by the canon.

The interrogation or deconstruction of the canon, in turn, is part of a critical movement underway since the 1960s and loosely labelled "postmodernism/poststructuralism"; the ways of thought so labelled are distinguished by profound skepticism, questioning what literary studies should study, how that study should be conducted, whether it should be a separate discipline. They challenge orthodox perceptions of the nature of the text (is it unified? is it discrete? is its meaning constant? is it distinguishable from the culture of which it is part?), reinvestigate the nature of literature, and ultimately, in some cases, cast doubt on the existence of objective reality (or, as David Gardner recently put it in a speech to the Association for Canadian Theatre Research, "Ladies and gentlemen, the chairs you are sitting on do not exist"). These various schools of thought reject traditional disciplinary boundaries, and draw on the psychology of Lacan, the linguistics of de Saussure, the philosophy of Wittgenstein, Ricoeur, and Derrida, and frequently on the political theories of Marx, and/or on "the politics of identity," which valorize the perceptions of groups previously marginalized by class, gender, ethnicity, colonial status, or sexual preference, as is the case with cultural studies, feminism, Afrocentrism, subaltern studies, gay and lesbian studies (or gender studies), although it would be a mistake to characterize the views of any of these groups as monolithic.

"Canon" and "canon formation" are problematic to these new ways of thought, not least because the effects of the canon are often invisible. When unexamined, canons are often perceived as a "natural" order, a universalist expression of value transcending geography and historical period, presumably differences in gender, class, race: "Shakespeare is for all times." In this case, the likeness to holy writ invoked by the word "canon" becomes a social and intellectual force, "the materiality of metaphor." The new, opposing view is that canons, like their constituent works of art, are constructs (better understood when "deconstructed"), artifacts created in an historical moment by individuals whose opinions are influenced or even created by social groupings to which they belong, the groups in turn subject to historical forces and possessed of political ambitions and for whom, then, a canon is both a political instrument and an agenda. A canon reflects and transmits power, cultural power, and generally reinforces the values of the dominant group, in the case of our place and time: white, male, "European," heterosexual, upper or professional class. "A literary canon doubly announces the presence of cultural power. First, a canon is meant to embody the authoritative values of a culture. Second, the forces that draw up and transmit a canon (in criticism and education) have the strength to do so" (Stimpson 266). Neither an individual work of art nor a "metanarrative" like a canon can be politically neutral; when the political objective is unstated, there is implicit support for the status quo. The issue is frequently one of the marginal (or "ex-centric") versus the centre, of examining what has been excluded from the "canon" and looking for "wisdome under a ragged coate"; in Canada, the centre is, again, white, male, European, heterosexual, "educated" class, and—in the case of the canon of English Canadian drama, whose identity and existence we are exploring—Toronto. The periphery is everybody else.

How does Canada, or Canadian drama, enter into this? The national temperament, so we've been told, forbids us to think of ourselves as central to anything. Doesn't the very fact that a Canadian dramatic canon, if one exists, is Canadian disqualify it from canonical status, as the 1970's cultural nationalists thought? Furthermore, Canadian authored drama, one suspects, is still marginal to Canadian theatre, itself a marginal art form in Canadian culture by many measures. Perhaps it is the thing itself which needs interrogation: what is Canadian drama? For that matter, what is Canada and can there be a "national temperament," even assuming such a thing were socially or ethically desirable? And here, the questions raised by canonicity are helpful.

In his dauntingly eloquent and persuasive essay, "Voices (off): Deconstructing the Modern English-Canadian Dramatic Canon," Richard Paul Knowles argues that a canon of Canadian drama does exist, that it was established by a small group of men with a limited range of (self) interests, and that it consists of a limited range of plays by a limited group of writers offering a limited vision of Canada. It's a bad thing. Knowles says that the canon began to solidify in the eighties, established by the three anthologies previously mentioned (*Major Plays of the Canadian Theatre, 1934–1984*, edited by Perkyns; *The Penguin Book of Modern Canadian Drama*, edited by Plant; and *Modern Canadian Plays*, edited by Wasserman), *The Oxford Companion to Canadian Theatre*, a Canadian entry in the Longman Literature in English series with a chapter on drama, Eugene Benson and L. W. Conolly's *English-Canadian Theatre*, Conolly's *Canadian Drama and the Critics*, and a proliferation of university courses in the area.

Knowles sets out the limits of the vision of Canadian drama presented by the three anthologies and their ancillary material by mapping out the anthologized plays, then looking for the criteria behind their selection. He notes that one play, John Herbert's *Fortune and Men's Eyes*, is included in all three collections, while two plays, John Coulter's *Riel* and David French's *Leaving Home* appear in two, with French's *Jitters* in the third. (Actually the play by David French which appears twice is *Of The Fields, Lately*.) Sharon Pollock and James Reaney are also represented in all three, with different works, and Coulter, David Freeman, Michael Cook, George Ryga, George F. Walker, and Gwen Pharis Ringwood are represented in two. The playwrights who appear only once are Herman Voaden, Robertson Davies, Gratien Gelinas, William Fruet, Carol Bolt, Rick Salutin (with Theatre Passe Muraille), Aviva Ravel, John Gray (with Eric Peterson), David Fennario, Erika Ritter, Margaret Hollingsworth, and Allan Stratton. Knowles summarizes:

> The most obvious characteristic of the "canonical" plays is their conservatism. ... All of the plays collected are "main stream" efforts: all are cautiously chosen, and controversial works are avoided; ... It might be added that sixteen of the twenty-two playwrights are white males ...; all three anthology editors ... are also white males; almost all of these men

are of Anglo-Saxon or Anglo-Irish extraction; and most of the plays received their first professional production in Central Canada or in one of the "branch-plant" regional theatres. ("Voices (off)" 96–97)

(Since this article appeared, Wasserman has published a new and expanded edition of his anthology, and that does change the numbers somewhat; we'll discuss some implications later.)

Knowles then proceeds to demonstrate ways in which the collections of plays are less "eclectic and comprehensive" than they might first appear to be. Overtly political playwrights with views critical of the status quo (Ryga, Fennario) are represented by their less subversive works, as is the case with those playwrights with a feminist agenda (Pollock, Hollingsworth). The only pure collective creation in this canon, Passe Muraille's *The Farm Show* (not found in any of the anthologies, but discussed in *Canadian Drama and the Critics*) is that company's "most naturalistic script." Any tendency to the subversive or ex-centric (Herbert's gay perspective and subject matter, the regionalism of Cook, Ringwood and Bolt, or Freeman's empowerment of the disabled) is institutionalized and neutralized by Canadian drama's bias to realism, a set of conventions which reinforces a white, middle-class male vision, placing an audience in that position and locating them as voyeurs, perhaps purportedly sympathetic to, but nonetheless separate from, the underprivileged who often appear as characters. Realism emphasizes individual psychology. "The answer to any problem, then, is not to change society, but to grow up. Social problems are dramatized as personal neuroses, and as plots move towards their resolutions potential unrest is diffused" (Knowles, "Voices (off)" 100). Furthermore, the canon is "logocentric," privileging those plays whose text can be depicted more or less satisfactorily on the printed page, rather than those theatrical works making more extensive use of image, the theatrical event, improvisation, electronic media, soundscape; thus, the bias is to those plays more amenable to traditional literary scholarship and classroom practice. Knowles identifies as omissions from the canon politically activist theatre, collective work, theatricalist work, work crossing the boundaries with rock videos, television, and performance art, theatre arising from non-white cultures (notably Native theatre); one might add to that list populist theatre, theatre for young audiences, folk plays, media drama, and for the most part, plays written before 1967.

It would be difficult to argue with Professor Knowles' position that relative to the full range and richness of theatrical practice and the theatrical experience in Canada, the plays represented in the Perkyns, Plant, and Wasserman anthologies offer a limited picture. It would be equally difficult to argue that a particular group (defined by gender, class, ethnicity) is not represented in numbers disproportionate to the make up of the population at large, or even, at this time, to that portion of the population engaged in the creation and/or experiencing of theatre. The question of whether the plays in an anthology ought to be representative is a large and complex one, and is considered at length elsewhere, including in the many books cited by his and this article. I would question whether some of the plays Prof. Knowles discusses are as conservative as he says they are, but that debate is better left to the examination of specific plays in articles we will both doubtless write in the future. For the time being, I'll say that I agree to the extent that I too find more interesting and more valuable those plays which challenge received opinion (in both content and form). While I would still hold that the anthologies in question were of "unprecedented comprehensiveness and usefulness," as I said in a review of two of them in 1985 (Johnson 148), I would also question the synecdochal adequacy of a study of Canadian drama confined to the "canonical list," and agree that exclusive attention to the anthologized plays could lead to some harmful assumptions.

Instead of pursuing those debates here, however, I would rather concentrate on some unanswered questions, among them: Are the anthologies as influential as Prof. Knowles seems to assume, and is the "canon" they embody as constant? Is the identification of Canadian dramatic canon formation sufficiently inclusive, or are there opinions from additional "interpretive communities" to be considered? (And, of course, there are still those big questions with which we began this consideration.) To pursue these questions, I wrote to a number of Canadian theatres to try to determine what Canadian plays have been produced over the past three years, and to a number of Canadian universities and colleges to determine what Canadian plays are being studied. Let's find some horses and count their teeth.

There is a correlation between what plays get into a canon and what plays are being produced by professional theatres, and again, according to Knowles, the effect is the preservation of conservative values: "The theatre is an institutional practice on almost every level, and it functions as an institution in Canada, as elsewhere, to produce and circulate a specific set of values" (Knowles, "Voices (off)" 92). When the anthologizers chose their plays, their decisions were influenced by decisions made over the previous few years by the Artistic Directors of the regional theatres and of the "alternatives" which arose to challenge the regionals, for the most part, men much like themselves. Still, there is usually another step. In the case of a dramatic canon, influence is usually reciprocal and reciprocation establishes canonical momentum: once included in a canon, a play is widely produced, and stays in the national repertoire for a considerable length of time, reinforcing its claim to canonicity.

To determine whether this was the case in Canada I asked what was produced in the 1991/92, 92/93, and 93/94 seasons; this direct inquiry was necessary because the Professional Association of Canadian Theatres' published listings of annual productions go only as far as 1988, and I wanted more recent information. The canvassed theatres are all listed in the PACT Communications Centre's 93/94 guide to professional English-language theatres in Canada; they range in size from very small, developmentally oriented companies to the big theatres of the so-called regional system. I did not write to those companies which exclusively produce Theatre for Young Audiences, and I resisted the temptation to nag companies which failed to respond—the sample group, then, is to some degree self-selected. There were thirty-eight responses reporting about 640 productions.

Most of the playwrights identified as "canonical" by Perkyns, Plant, Wasserman, and Knowles were not produced in the three-year period. John Murrell, a playwright not actually in that group although many would put him there, was most strongly represented with seven productions, four of those at the Citadel Theatre in Edmonton, with which theatre and its then Artistic Director, Robin Phillips, Murrell had a working relationship—a widespread arrangement in the theatre, in Canada as elsewhere. Murrell was also produced by the Tarragon, the Vancouver Arts Club, and the Manitoba Theatre Centre (in co-production with Citadel.) George F. Walker was next, with productions of *Love and Anger* at Persephone and the Vancouver Playhouse, while Great Canadian Theatre Company in Ottawa produced *Criminals in Love* and his new play, *Tough!*. David French and John Gray were tied for third with three each, Geordie Productions in Montreal and the Globe Theatre in Regina producing *Salt-Water Moon* while the National Theatre Centre and Canadian Stage Company co-produced French's new play, *Silver Dagger*; Geordie produced Gray's *Billy Bishop Goes to War*, the Arts Club did *18*

Wheels, and NAC produced Gray's new play, *Amelia!*. Allan Stratton's *Bag Babies* was produced twice, and Pollock, Cook, Ryga and Fennario are each represented by one production. The total, then, is twenty-three productions out of six hundred and forty.

We could add in the playwrights Wasserman adds to his expanded anthology: Joan MacLeod (six productions), Judith Thompson (two), Michel Tremblay (two), Wendy Lill (two) and Robert Lepage (one). Thirty-six. Just under 6%. It would seem, then, that in Canada the national canon is not represented in the national repertoire to the extent that it is, say, in the United States, the United Kingdom, or France. In fact, the professional theatre, one of the "interpretive communities" which establishes a canon, would seem to be saying that, by some definitions of dramatic canon, there is no Canadian dramatic canon. On the other hand, the international canon is strong, even outside its fortresses at the Shaw and Stratford Festivals.

Three hundred and fifty Canadian plays, shows, festivals, collectives, and/or cabarets were produced, more than half the total, a huge shift in the status quo of twenty years ago. If Canadian theatres aren't producing Canadian "classics," what Canadian work are they doing? For one, Canadian theatre generates theatrical fads of its own (like fads for "international" plays by Brian Friel, Ariel Dorfman, and Willy Russell, with one regional after another producing *Dancing at Lughnasa*, *Death and the Maiden*, and *Shirley Valentine*). In the past, Canadian works now ranked "canonical," notably David French's *Leaving Home*, have benefitted from this phenomenon. In 91/92, 92/93, and 93/94, however, the homegrown fads were more clearly mass entertainment, commercially oriented work: according to the theatres (or the Artistic Directors) the "canonical" Canadian playwrights are Dan Needles and Norm Foster. Monodramas from Needles' Wingfield series appeared on twelve occasions at Canadian theatres, and *The Perils of Persephone* once; plays by Foster, led by *The Affections of May* and *Wrong for Each Other*, were produced twelve times.

One of the earliest challenges to canonicity questioned the distinction between "high art" and "popular culture" (for an entertaining introduction to this debate, see Harriet Hawkins' *Classics and Trash: Traditions and taboos in high literature and popular modern genres*). In brief, if an essentialist or universalist study of literature is rejected, there is a strong argument in favour of examining mass culture, as, say, sociological data, or as evidence of social values in need of deconstruction, or because the distinction between "high" and "low" is itself elitist and meaningless outside an obsolete class structure.

To take a slightly different approach, Robert Lecker uses Charles Altieri's concept of the "cultural grammar for interpreting experience" made possible by canonical literature to distinguish between curricular and canonical literature:

> In Canada, we have a shifting but identifiable curriculum that is often misread as a canon. ... By this I mean that we study works whose temporal impact is brief, whose cultural grammar is local before it is national, whose idealizations are not those we can identify with the values held by a community at large. A good way of demonstrating this assertion is to consider the popular appeal of some Canadian works that have been institutionalized and are often thought to be canonical, say, Sinclair Ross's *As for Me and My House*. While the novel may appear on course curricula throughout the country, and while much has been said about its ostensible excellence, it is not a canonical work. The average well-read person out of the academy has never heard of it. In fact, many well-read persons *within* the academy have never heard of it. ... It has no claim to public interest. It does not mediate between popular and academic demand. It transmits no cultural grammar. (Lecker 6)

And therefore is not canonical. The same can be said, of course, for the vast majority of Canadian plays, whether they're thought of as canonical or not, but plays by Needles and Foster have a stronger claim to this kind of "canonicity" than most. Their plays are a significant component of theatre practice in Canada, and, more than most, can be said to be transmitters of cultural grammar, although I would guess that the only Canadian theatrical work which could truly make such a claim would be *Anne of Green Gables* (the musical), or, shifting dramatic media, *Street Legal*, *North of Sixty*, and *Kids in the Hall*.

Needles, Foster, Peter Colley, W. O. Mitchell, a rash of Dickens adaptations, and popular revues account for about fifty productions, leaving 280 "non canonicals" proper. These constitute an astonishingly mixed bag. There are playwrights who, perhaps, could be described as "regionally canonical": Ian Weir, Morris Panych, Connie Gault, Carol Shields, Dianne Warren, Nicola Cavendish, Colleen Curran, Vittorio Rossi, Mark Leiren-Young, Janis Spence. There are many "house playwrights" on the pattern of the relationship we've noted between John Murrell and Citadel: Jim Millan and Crow's, Blake Brooker and One Yellow Rabbit, Maureen Hunter and the Manitoba Theatre Centre, Carol Shields and the Prairie Theatre Exchange, Anne Chislett and Ted Johns and the Blyth Festival, Robin Fulford and Platform 9, Sky Gilbert and Buddies in Bad Times. (The last two categories overlap; in fact, all the "boundaries" in this portion of the discussion are unstable.) There is, of course, a "cult hit," Brad Fraser's *Unidentified Human Remains and the True Nature of Love* and a strong bid for "established" status from Anne-Marie MacDonald's four productions of *Goodnight Desdemona (Good morning Juliet)*. There are many collectives, and many plays by writers and theatre workers, often young or young to the theatre, whose reputations are not, or are not yet, as "established" as those writers on the canonical list: all the above, Dean Regan, Bruce McManus, Kelly Rebar, George Seremba, Shawna Dempsey and Lorri Millan, Yvette Nolan, Sandra Shamas, Daniel David Moses, Daniel Brooks, Guillermo Verdecchia, Margaret Clark, Raymond Storey, Diana Braithwaite, Daniel MacIvor, Drew Hayden Taylor, Billy Merasty, Tina Mason, Margo Kane, Djanet Sears. Translations from Quebec: Michel Garneau, Rene-Daniel Dubois, Marie Laberge, of course Tremblay. Many of the writers come from those groups and represent those views Knowles identifies as "ex-centric," and many of their productions are mounted by companies expressly formed to present those views, circumvent exclusion, and valorize "marginality": Nightwood, Maenad, Buddies in Bad Times, Native Earth, Crow's, Platform 9, PTAM, Great Canadian, and so on. It is true that plays from this grouping are seldom to be found at the regionals, where Canadian plays of any sort are still in the minority, where if one does find a Canadian play it is likely to be "canonical." There is greater exchange between "identity" theatres and companies than I had anticipated, and greater representation on the mid-range "alternative" stages.

   The information provided by the thirty-eight theatre companies can be used in a variety of ways. The diversity of theatrical voices and languages which emerges can be read as substantiation for Prof. Knowles' contention that the Perkyns, Plant, and Wasserman anthologies present a limited vision of Canadian drama and theatre practice as a whole. Or, the 91/92, 92/93, and 93/94 seasons could be read as anthologies in their own right, anthologies in which the ex-centric and subversive are strongly represented and in which the influence of the conventions and values of realism is much reduced. It is true that much of what Knowles says about the printed anthologies can be applied to the "anthologies" represented by the playbills of the regional theatres (when, indeed, they produce Canadian plays at all), and there is certainly room for political argument about the accessibility of those Canadian institutions to the full range of Canadian voices and views. However, the very large number of productions mounted by other theatres (often theatres of the "Other" whose nature strains the definition of "institution") reach, together, a large and diverse Canadian audience, and constitute a substantial collective voice. Their collective statement regarding the nature of Canadian drama could be taken as a counter or "competing" canon, one which relocates the Canadian centre for its audience and which destabilizes the printed canon by transmitting to portions of the academic community an alternative vision of the nature of Canadian drama and influencing ideas about what ought to be taught and how it ought to be taught. Prof. Knowles' article is itself evidence of the effectiveness of the message, of the cultural power of this source of artistic authority. Or, to take the argument further still, because the capital "T" Theatre is an interpretive community which participates in canon-formation and because its value judgments so thoroughly dilute the canon put forward by the printed anthologies, the seasons constitute evidence that the "canon" is not an effective arbiter in an important area of consideration, therefore lacks canonical force, therefore is not a canon. At the very least, the dynamic created by the existence of the opposed visions embodied by these widely divergent selections of Canadian plays should be taken into account in any consideration of canonicity in Canadian drama.

It should be noted that my survey underestimates the full diversity of Canadian theatre, thus giving a diminished impression of the "ex-centricity" present in the "anthology" proposed by Canada's working theatres. Most of the conservative theatres are accounted for, as all belong to PACT and most have the resources to respond to queries from troublesome researchers; the group not accounted for includes many companies and loose groupings of people responsible for some of the most "ex-centric" theatre being produced in Canada, the community theatres Prof. Knowles discusses elsewhere in this volume, the hundreds of companies and collectives and temporary organizations producing hundreds of shows in the country's Fringe Festivals.

Furthermore, there are cultural institutions in addition to the smaller theatres at work constructing a competing canon, and/or defusing the power of the original. The Perkyns, Plant, and Wasserman anthologies are not the only Canadian play collections available. *The CTR Anthology* edited by Alan Filewod, the New Canadian Drama series published by

Borealis Press, the Theatre Passe Muraille and New Play Centre anthologies, *Newest Plays by Women*, Robert Wallace's *Making, Out* collection of plays by gay men, Colleen Curran's *Escape Acts* all depart from the "canon" and offer an economical means of expanding the range of Canadian plays studied without resorting to the usually very expensive practice of assigning to a class, say, twenty individually published plays (and, of course, the economics of publishing and distribution contribute to the commodification which favours canon-formation). Of the books mentioned, *The CTR Anthology* is the biggest and covers the longest time period, fifteen plays first published in the journal between 1974 and 1990: only three of the writers, Cook, Walker, and Lepage, could be considered canonical. *NeWest Plays by Women* includes Sharon Pollock's *Whiskey Six Cadenza* among its four scripts. None of the other collections mentioned contain canonical work.

Theatre journals played a role in constructing the "canon," and now play a role in dispersing it. There is a clear correlation between the contents of the "big three" anthologies, and those playwrights discussed, reviewed in, and contributing scripts to *Canadian Drama, Canadian Theatre Review*, and *Theatre History in Canada* in the few years preceding the publication of those anthologies. All but one of the playwrights included in the anthologies receive significant attention from the journals between 1974 and 1984, and for the most part, the amount of attention accorded in the journals coincides with whether the playwright appears in one, two, or all three anthologies. The one anthologized playwright not present in the journals is William Fruet; however, his *Wedding in White* had appeared in an anthology published by Simon and Pierre in 1973. There are other departures of other kinds. Robertson Davies' commanding lead with twenty-five points (1 point = significant attention in an article, published script, or play/book reviewed) would argue for more resounding canonization in the anthologies than he in fact received, but his years of prolific playwriting activity predate the time limits set by two of the three collections. Few playwrights who get significant attention from journals are omitted from the anthologies, Tremblay because of the English language focus, Len Peterson and Lister Sinclair because of periodization. Perhaps the most significant deviation between the canons according to the journals and the anthologies is Beverley Simons, who gets more critical attention than some anthologized writers: she is a woman, she has a limited production history, her work is decidedly not realistic and conventional. With these exceptions, which suggest that the anthologies are slightly more conservative than the journals, the correlation of hierarchical evaluations is extremely close, demonstrating that the editors' choices do arise from the values of the small scholarly group (a group within the "professional-managerial class") to which they belong; Knowles' point on the matter is confirmed.

However, a survey of the journals for the ten years since 1984 and of the relatively brash newcomer, *Theatrum*, provides an entirely different picture, an entirely different "anthology." The most recent issue of *CTR* was devoted to comedy, and includes a sociological investigation of stand-up comedy (which in years past would not have found a place in a Canadian theatre journal), an article about comedy as a political tool in the work of two Toronto Popular Theatre companies, an analysis of political strategies in the work of gay playwright Ken Garnhum, a genre consideration of the plays of Native playwright Daniel David Moses, a script from the Second City improvisational company ("mass culture"), an interview with a sketch comedian, *Shocker's Delight* by Stewart Lemoine of Teatro la Quindicina, and Tamara Bick's monodrama, *The Interview*. *Canadian Drama* 16.2, the last issue before the journal was merged with *Essays in Theatre*, is relatively staid, but its two articles on nineteenth century Canadian theatre and its semi-canonical script in translation, Marcel Dube's *Times of the Lilacs*, are accompanied by Alan Filewod's article on Canadian Popular Theatre and Cynthia Zimmerman's interview with Judith Thompson (whose canonical status is marginal and whose work is decidedly not mainstream). The fall 1993 issue of *Theatre Research in Canada* (successor to *Theatre History in Canada*) includes Patrick O'Neill's "traditional" article on a nineteenth century producer, manager, and actor, but also Reid Gilbert's article on framing gender on stage, Sara Graefe's piece on the transformation of traditional images of homosexuality in Michel Mark Bouchard's *Lilies*, and Helene Beauchamp's investigation of the relationship between theatre research and theatre practice in Theatre for Young Audiences. The April/May 1994 issue of *Theatrum* contains as "mainstream" material an interview with Monique Mercure, an article on foreign productions of plays by canonical playwrights Walker, Tremblay, and Thompson (here we'll give conservatism the benefit of the doubt), and an article on the director/designer relationship which concentrates, but not exclusively, on work at "mainstream" theatres; on the other hand, there's an analysis of voyeuristic response to on-stage scenes of torture in supposedly "liberal" plays, a long section on the Vancouver Fringe, Women in View, New Voices, New Ideas and High Performance Rodeo Festivals, and *Safe Haven*, the script of a play by

Mary-Colin Chisholm, a playwright associated with the Mulgrave Road Co-op.

A similar shift can be seen over the past few years in books about Canadian drama and theatre. Ten years ago, the bibliography for the subject was dominated by monographs about canonical playwrights, collections of interviews with canonical playwrights, and works of theatre history. While such books, like Denis Johnston's *Up the Mainstream: The Rise of Toronto's Alternative Theatres, 1968–1975*, still appear (and provide valuable service), they are greatly outnumbered by books about "ex-centric" writers and theatrical movements, and/or which treat their subjects in a manner consistent with one or more schools of the newer criticism: Robert Wallace's *Producing Marginality: Theatre and Criticism in Canada*, Alan Filewod's *Collective Encounters: Documentary Theatre in English Canada*, Yvonne Hodkinson's *Female Parts: The Art and Politics of Female Playwrights*, Judith Rudakoff and Rita Much's *Fair Play, 12 Women Speak: Conversations with Canadian Playwrights* (containing interviews with both canonical and non-canonical women writers), Diane Bessai's *Playwrights of Collective Creation*. Then there is the book you are reading at this very moment. How would you categorize its contents?

Recently, the Association for Canadian Theatre History changed its name to the Association for Canadian Theatre Research to acknowledge a shift in its members' interests and to facilitate inclusion of such work. Out of thirty-four papers delivered at the Association's 1994 conference in Calgary, only eight could be considered "mainstream" in subject and/or treatment of subject. At Ottawa in 1993 the ratio was 10 out of 22, at Charlottetown in 1992, 12 out of 24. The academy, like the small theatres, is engaged in relocating the centre, in its case through research and publication.

What about the classroom and the educational theatre? How extensively used are the "big three" anthologies, and how influential is the canon they embody on campuses across the country? Twenty-three colleges and universities reported 86 productions of Canadian plays in 91/92, 92/93, and 93/94. (Some reported *no* productions of Canadian plays.) Of the playwrights produced on campus, thirty-three, or a bit more than a third, could be considered canonical, using Wasserman's expansion of the canonical list. The problematic Judith Thompson (is she or isn't she [canonical]?) led the pack with seven: *I Am Yours* at Manitoba, Lethbridge, and Saskatchewan, *Lion in the Streets* at Cariboo and Dalhousie, *Crackwalker* at McGill, and *Tornado* (a work in progress) at Guelph, where Thompson taught and was writer-in-residence. Walker placed with six productions: *Better Living* at Guelph and McGill, *Zastrozzi* at McMaster and Saskatchewan, *Escape from Happiness* at Humber, and *Love and Anger* at UBC. A show for Tremblay with five, *Les Belles-Soeurs* at Fraser Valley and Douglas, *Bonjour la, Bonjour* at McGill, *The Real World?* at Victoria, and *Surprise! Surprise!* at UBC. Then French, Murrell, Clark, and MacLeod bunched up with two each, while there were single productions for Pollock, Reaney, Bolt, MacDonald, Hollingsworth and Stratton. The rest of the pantheon were no shows. There were many productions of non-canonical if not necessarily non-mainstream Canadian plays: *Unidentified Human Remains ...* at Humber and Waterloo, the latter also producing plays by Sheri-D Wilson and Bryden MacDonald, plays by John Mighton at Alberta, Morris Panych and Clem Martini at McMaster, Daniel MacIvor at Memorial, John Krizanc at Lethbridge, Beth Herst at Guelph, Janet Feindel at Mount Allison, David Gustav Fraser and Bryan Wade at Manitoba, and so on. Nonetheless, the Canadian canon is a much stronger presence in campus theatre than it is in the Canadian professional theatre. The international canon is an overwhelmingly strong presence, and the international fads here are Caryl Churchill and Timberlake Wertenbaker (much less conservative than the professional fads). A refreshingly large number of schools are engaged in the production of original plays, many, presumably, by students.

While roughly a third of the university/college productions of Canadian plays are "canonical," two-thirds are not, and should serve to challenge/subvert any hegemonic vision of Canadian drama offered in the classrooms. Twenty-six college and university Drama and Theatre programs responded to my queries, reporting 45 offerings of courses, either Canadian Drama courses or courses in which Canadian plays were included in significant numbers (e.g. introduction to theatre, or acting courses requiring work on scenes from Canadian plays). I did not survey English Department courses in Canadian Drama, although I now wish I had. The "big three" anthologies are widely used, as Knowles suspected, with eighteen courses using one or two of them, nearly half. Wasserman appeared most often: eleven times. Other anthologies used include Anton Wagner's *Lost Canadian Plays* series (where the course in question attempts "historical coverage"), the *CTR Anthology*, even *Five from the Fringe, Twenty Years At Play*, and *NeWest Plays by Women*. In fact, the *CTR Anthology* was called for more often than Plant, which raises the question of which anthologies should be considered when mapping out the canon: if Filewod rather than the less popular Plant were taken into consideration, we would add to the "canon" the Anna Project, Cindy Cowan, Arthur Milner, Baṉuta Rubess, Sky Gilbert, Richard Rose and D. D. Kugler among others, hardly a "conservative" list.

That still leaves a large number of courses where either the number of Canadian plays called for is insufficient to warrant the assigning of an anthology, or where instructors have elected to "teach Canadian drama" without recourse to anthologies, using single editions of plays: Guelph, where Professors Knowles, Alan Filewod, and Ann Wilson ensure a strong privileging of the newer schools of thought; Alberta; one out of two at Saskatchewan; Brock; Calgary; Erindale; one out of four at McMaster; Waterloo; UBC (where, in the courses reported over the past three years, Prof. Wasserman evidently didn't use Wasserman). Here, one does get wide deviation from the canonical list: Mulgrave Road, Carbone 14, Caravan, Dennis Foon, Daniel MacIvor, Monique Mojica, Guillermo Verdecchia, Djanet Sears, Beth Herst, Anne Chislett, Frank Moher, Michel Garneau, Hrant Alianak, Michael Ondaatje, Kelly Rebar, Beverley Simons, Timothy Findley, the Anna Project, John Krizanc, Shirley Barrie, Daniel David Moses, Norm Foster (all at universities other than or in addition to Guelph), or, revising the usual "history," Cecil-Smith *et al.*'s *Eight Men Speak* (several times) and Prof. Moira Day's attention to Elsie Park Gowan's *The High Green Gate* at Saskatchewan. Many others.

Anthologies are almost never used by themselves (maybe half a dozen occurrences). Playwrights most often required in addition to an anthology are Judith Thompson, Michel Tremblay, and Tomson Highway, none of whom were anthologized at that time. This can be read either as an instructor's attempt to make the canon more inclusive, or as what used to be called "tokenism," what Prof. Knowles calls "assimilating and often neutralizing them [ex-centric plays] in a warm but fuzzy soft-core liberal pluralism" ("Otherwise Engaged" 194); doubtless both occur. Often, plays are assigned in addition to anthologies evidently in an attempt to make the course more responsive to the region in which the institution offering the course is located: thus, Memorial adds *The Plays of CODCO*, Calgary adds John Murrell, Brad Fraser, and Frank Moher; Twenty-Fifth Street and Fringe get more attention in the West; Passe Muraille, Toronto Workshop Productions, John Krizanc in the Centre; Antonine Maillet and John Hannah in Atlantic Canada. Frequently, courses assign theatre-going, "performance as text," as a component required of their students, a notably large component at Guelph, UBC,

Manitoba, Winnipeg, Brock, Alberta (possibly others which don't specifically mention it).

At the same time, it must be admitted that the same few names do occur again and again. Very few courses (whether they use anthologies or not) omit Ryga and French, while Pollock, Walker, Thompson, and Tremblay are almost as ubiquitous. Those, incidentally, are the writers I would identify as the most likely candidates for the "real" canon, assuming for a moment its existence. They are the playwrights most likely to appear in theatre courses other than Canadian Drama, in most cases with a substantial if not overwhelming presence in the national repertoire both professional and academic, and in the cases of Walker, Thompson and Tremblay, with significant impact on theatre outside Canada, according to the *Theatrum* article I mentioned earlier (Duchesne, "Our Country's Good" 1994). Given his huge international reputation now, we should probably add Lepage, whereas in years gone by it would have been Herbert. "Well," say the unrepentant, "What's wrong with that? They're all good and interesting playwrights." (I, personally, have my doubts about French, but leave that be for now.) Furthermore, most are not excessively bound by the conventions of middle-class realism (again, French is the exception), most are suspicious of, indeed antagonistic to, received opinion, two of them are women, one of them is gay on principle as well as by personal orientation. Still, no collectives. No plays from non-white cultures.

Course content is the strongest evidence yet that something like a canon, although not a canon in all senses of the word, is in operation. If this is perceived as a problem, what is to be done? Study of a canonical work does not necessarily leave the work or its canonicity unchallenged; such a work can be deconstructed, given a reading which "points to the masks of truth with which phallocentric thought hides its fictions" in Peggy Kamuf's words quoted by James Winders (Winders 16), as Knowles does, briefly, with various plays in his article, as, say, Susan Bennett does with *The Ecstasy of Rita Joe* in her article, "Who Speaks? Representations of Native Women in Some Canadian Plays." "New historicism" is certainly the approach in some classrooms some of the time with regard to Canadian "classics."

Another obvious answer would seem to be to expand the canon and make it more inclusive, as several instructors responding to the survey have done, as Jerry Wasserman has done with his new anthology, now in two volumes, published in 1993 and 1994. The new anthology contains twenty rather than ten plays. David French's *Jitters* is replaced by *Leaving Home*, a more "canonical" play. On the other hand, Sharon Pollock's *Doc* is included in addition to *Walsh*, and, playing the numbers game yet again, she is now *the* canonical playwright, with four plays in the three anthologies. Wasserman also adds Michel Tremblay's *Les Belles-Soeurs*, Wendy Lill's *The Occupation of Heather Rose*, Joan MacLeod's *Toronto, Mississippi*, Judith Thompson's *I Am Yours*, Sally Clark's *Moo*, Marie Brassard and Robert Lepage's *Polygraph*, and Tomson Highway's *Dry Lips Oughta Move to Kapuskasing*. Wasserman thus adds the three writers course lists most often called for as additions to the "canon," and several of the writers whose omission Knowles notes. His revision of the "canon" (replacing his 1985 anthology with the two volumes published in 1993 and 1994) gives us 31 rather than 22 playwrights, 39 rather than 33 plays. The proportion of male writers falls to 20 out of 31, and the number of female authored plays rises to fourteen and a half out of 39; we gain a second play originally written in French and a play by a Native author.

Apart from the aforementioned danger of "tokenism," expanding the canon is still canon-formation, and the activity and mindset themselves trouble the new critical left. Knowles cites Alan C. Golding's contention that subversive work is rendered harmless by inclusion in a teaching anthology: "The self-conscious pluralism of so-called 'comprehensive' anthologies ... by systematizing and classifying the work, neutralizes it." He also cites Jill Dolan's analysis of ways in which Marsha Norman's *'night, Mother* was neutralized by Broadway production and Ann Wilson's account of a similar transformation of Caryl Churchill's *Cloud Nine* through its Toronto production (Knowles, "Voices (off)" 95); presumably the same thing happened to the feminist-lesbian insights of Anne-Marie MacDonald's *Goodnight Desdemona ...* when it was produced by mainstream theatres across Canada (and that was certainly my impression when viewing the MTC Warehouse production). This line of reasoning does lead to an impasse: any text list is a teaching anthology, from the perspective of the students, regardless of the source of the items included (electronic publishing, live performance, scribbled on a brown paper bag); the very fact that a work is studied in an institutional setting recontextualizes subversive work, detoxifying, "canonizing" it. There is some advantage in that such a list's nature as a construct is more obvious, and that the implied existence of an excluded "Other" is clearer, but alerting the students to the dangers of an institutional context can only ameliorate, not eliminate, the effect; struggle though he may, Prof. Knowles cannot escape the consequences of his authority.

The amelioration Prof. Knowles proposes, in the Lecker anthology and in another article, "Otherwise Engaged: Towards a Materialist Pedagogy," involves a privileging of the margins, with special attention to the work of companies such as Nightwood, Company of Sirens, and the Mulgrave Road Co-op, whose democratic structures encourage radical diversity. The theoretical position would derive from "the points at which aspects of Marxism, feminism, and deconstruction intersect. Each of these projects attacks the logocentric desire to resolve all contradictions; each is concerned with attention to gestures of exclusion and to the extent to which context determines meaning while being itself indeterminate; and each proposes a continuing process of radical heterogeneity" (Knowles, "Voices (off)" 107). The work would be facilitated by sending students to see productions, especially productions of the margins (already widespread practice, as we've seen), and through printed texts which evade the hegemonical, hierarchical power of the publishing industry through a system similar to that employed by Playwrights Co-op in its early days, when the organization published any professionally produced play submitted to it in inexpensive, staple-bound editions. In requiring professional production, we do, however, introduce the influence of institutional practice, so electronic publishing and text distribution seem to me to provide even more promising possibilities. Already, some academic journals do not appear in print, but are distributed entirely through computer networks. Chadwyck-Healey charges $16,000 U.S. for its *English Verse Drama* CD-ROM database, but the complete works of Shakespeare can already be downloaded, free of charge, from a wonderful little hidey-hole accessed through Internet; other texts in the data-base will follow in time, if indeed they're not already out there somewhere in cyberspace. New technology is an ally of new critical thought in this respect not only through doing an end-run around the publishing industry, but by joining the proponents of ex-centricity in the challenge to the very idea of authorial "ownership" of a text; this may be hard on authors and editors trying to make a living, but given the failure of attempts to control the flow of electronic data thus far, such distribution seems inevitable: "Information wants to be free," as the hackers have it.

There are still more strategies available for relocating the center and/or privileging the margins: instructors can, as I do, require each student or study group in the class to subscribe to a theatre journal (in the case of my course, *Theatrum*); they can inter/disrupt the study of "canonical" texts not only with theatre-going, but with "wild card" sessions which address whatever scripts and issues appear: as we saw earlier, this material is more likely to be non-mainstream than not.

However, admitting the editors of *Theatrum* into the process of selection, or students in the course, as Prof. Owen Klein at Windsor and Prof. Richard Plant at Queen's evidently do, does not eliminate the "canonizing" force inherent to any process of selection. Arguments against the "Canadian canon" bring up the same names, Mulgrave Road, Nightwood, post-Centaur Fennario, Monique Mojica, Djanet Sears, and an anti-canonical canon seems to take shape; the same occurs with non-mainstream anthologies, and, in the case of the *CTR Anthology* we see evidence that it is starting to replace items in the old canon thus creating a competing one. Certainly, there is a canon of anti-canonical theorists: "... many feminist critics agree that a canon constructs value as much as it reflects value; that the canon is contingent not universal; that the canon is a fiction about aesthetic and intellectual supremacy. However, every critical school must structure the culture it studies" (Stimpson 266). Thus to their credit many theorists of the new schools recognize the need for interrogation of their own practice. And that takes us back to the beginning: selection and ranking, by one set of values or another, are almost impossible to avoid. The best one can do is to be aware that this is so, and to be conscious of the activity and its implications when engaged in it; Prof. Knowles does all of us a service when he heightens that awareness.

Nonetheless, I believe he overestimates the force of the "canon" in Canadian drama, thus underestimates the sheer inquisitiveness of Canadian theatres, theatre-goers, scholars and students. Canadian drama hasn't been around long enough for the process of canonization to operate through an extended period of time, and the study of Canadian drama is an even more recent development; all canons are porous and subject to change, but the "canon" of Canadian drama changes so quickly that I would question whether it can thus qualify as a canon at all. Note how rapidly Herbert and Freeman have slipped from favour as essentially "one play playwrights" of little importance in the larger scheme, how quick the rise of Highway, MacLeod, MacDonald. Even James Reaney, who dominated W. H. New's *Dramatists in Canada: Selected Essays* in 1972, is now little written about, often omitted from Canadian drama courses (except in Ontario; he really is a regionalist after all). On the other hand, almost everyone concerned with Canadian drama and theatre now knows something about the Mulgrave Road Co-op, thanks to Prof. Knowles. Some of the things which I most admire

"Wisdome Under a Ragged Coate"   47

about George F. Walker, his immediacy, his revelling in the current vernacular, his electronic sensibility, make him very much a playwright of this time. I rather doubt he will be much produced or studied fifty years from now. Is he then canonical?

Canadian theatres do not support through their repertoire the notion of a Canadian canon, and recent criticism and analysis is so heavily concentrated on work outside the mainstream that the old canon's identity is shifting, contributing, again, to a porosity so extreme that the canonical authority of this "canon" is called into question. Very few teachers of Canadian drama accept the canon without qualification (or did, until it changed and caught up with them, probably temporarily), and a significant minority reject it entirely, in their curricular lists, or productions, or both. What Tracy Ware has to say about the canon of Canadian literature applies with even more force to the canon of Canadian drama:

> The Canadian canon has always been fluid: the available anthologies are so inclusive that no course can exhaust their possibilities, and different instructors and institutions use and even construct very different anthologies. Thus Canada has all of the uncertainty but none of the dogmatic resistance necessary for a "delegitimation crisis." Canonical interrogations "have not deconstructed the monolith in any way similar to the way it has been deconstructed in other countries" ... because there is no monolith here. (487)

While observing myself that a process of selection and ranking akin to "canonization" is almost inevitable, at least provisionally, and while conceding that trends which might be mistaken for "canonization" appear in the study of Canadian drama and that they call for wariness and interrogation, finally I don't think there is a canon, in the full sense of the word, in Canadian drama. And I think *that's* a good thing. "For Canadian literature, release from the demands of canon ought to be a liberation from the self-imposed demand that there be a defined list of accepted Canadian books. No young and vibrant literature should be burdened with the hidden requirement that it establish its own orthodoxy. ... *Canon* may describe a dead literature, it can only cripple a living one" (Fry 61–62).

Furthermore, if there definitely were a canon, one would have to choose between defending it and attacking it, and it's a lot more fun to do both at once.

Works Cited

Bennett, Donna. "Conflicted Vision: A Consideration of Canon and Genre in English-Canadian Literature." *Canadian Canons: Essays in Literary Value*. Ed. Robert Lecker. Toronto: University of Toronto Press, 1991. 131–149.

Bennett, Susan. "Who Speaks? Representations of Native Women in Some Canadian Plays." *The Canadian Journal of Drama and Theatre* 1.2 (1991): 13–25.

Duchesne, Scott. "Our Country's Good." *Theatrum* 38 (April/May 1994): 19–23.

Filewod, Alan, ed. *The CTR Anthology: Fifteen Plays from Canadian Theatre Review*. Toronto: University of Toronto Press, 1993.

Fry, August J. "Periods, canons and who wants to get into *The New Yorker* anyway." *Literature in Canada/Litteratures au Canada, Canadian Issues/Themes canadiens* 10.5. Ed. Deborah C. Poff. Ottawa/Montreal: Association for Canadian Studies and International Council for Canadian Studies, 1988. 57–65.

Hawkins, Harriet. *Classics and Trash: Traditions and Taboos in High Literature and Popular Modern Genres*. Toronto: University of Toronto Press, 1990.

Johnson, Chris. Rev. of *Major Plays of the Canadian Theatre 1934–1984* and *Modern Canadian Drama, Vol. 1. Canadian Theatre Review* 42 (Spring 1985): 147–149.

Knowles, Richard Paul. "Otherwise Engaged: Towards a Materialist Pedagogy." *Theatre History in Canada* 12.2 (Fall 1991): 192–199.

―――――. "Voices (off): Deconstructing the Modern English-Canadian Dramatic Canon." *Canadian Canons: Essays in Literary Value*. Ed. Robert Lecker. Toronto: University of Toronto Press, 1991. 91–111.

Lecker, Robert. "A Country Without a Canon?: Canadian Literature and the Esthetics of Idealism." *Mosaic* 26.3 (Summer 1993): 1–19.

New, William H. *Dramatists in Canada: Selected Essays*. Vancouver: University of British Columbia Press, 1972.

Perkyns, Richard, ed. *Major Plays of the Canadian Theatre, 1934–1984*. Toronto: Irwin Publishing, 1984.

Plant, Richard, ed. *The Penguin Book of Modern Canadian Drama*. Markham, ON: Penguin Books Canada, 1984.

Stimpson, Catharine R. "Feminist Criticism." *Redrawing the Boundaries: The Transformation of English and American Literary Studies.* Eds. Stephen Greenblatt and Giles Gunn. New York: The Modern Language Association of America, 1992. 251–270.

Ware, Tracy. "A Little Self-Consciousness is a Dangerous Thing: A Response to Robert Lecker." *English Studies in Canada* 17.4 (December, 1991): 481–493.

Wasserman, Jerry, ed. *Modern Canadian Plays.* Vancouver: Talonbooks, 1986.

———. *Modern Canadian Plays, Volume I.* Vancouver: Talonbooks, 1993.

———. *Modern Canadian Plays, Volume II.* Vancouver: Talonbooks, 1994.

Winders, James A. *Gender, Theory and the Canon.* Madison: University of Wisconsin Press, 1991.

Appendix A: Responding Theatre Companies

Arts Club, Belfry, Blyth Festival, Buddies in Bad Times, Centaur, Citadel, Crow's Theatre, Dark Horse, Firehall, Geordie Productions, Globe, Grand, Great Canadian Theatre Co., Maenad, Magnus, Manitoba Theatre Centre, National Theatre Centre, Necessary Angel, Nightwood, Passe Muraille, Persephone, Platform 9, Popular Theatre Alliance of Manitoba, Prairie Theatre Exchange, Richmond Gateway, Rising Tide, Ship's Company, Sudbury Theatre Centre, Tamanhous, Tarragon, Theatre Calgary, Theatre New Brunswick, Theatre Newfoundland Labrador, Touchstone, Twenty-Fifth Street, Vancouver Playhouse.

Appendix B: Responding Universities and Colleges

Acadia, Alberta, British Columbia, Brock, Cariboo, Dalhousie, Douglas, Fraser Valley, George Brown, Guelph, Humber, Lethbridge, Malaspina, Manitoba, McGill, McMaster, Memorial, Mount Allison, Queen's, Saskatchewan, Victoria, Waterloo, Windsor, Winnipeg.

Theatre of Images: New Dramaturgies

by Sarah B. Hood

In the beginning was the word. At least, that's how European and North American scholars usually look at theatre. The text—the script—is the basis for the study, and all the other elements, like design, movement, music, sound and light, are secondary to the spoken words. Many contemporary Canadian theatre artists, however, like artists in other parts of the world, are exploring ways of telling a story without words. In some cases, this means that theatre is moving closer to dance, with less talking and more body movement. Some stage artists are borrowing from television and film, or taking advantage of video, projected images and recorded sound. Others are using ancient theatre techniques that aren't usually found on the North American stage, like mask work, puppetry, acrobatics, juggling and stiltwalking.

For two or three years in the late '80s and early '90s, "imagistic" was the number one buzzword in Canadian theatre criticism. Used especially to describe the brilliant, inventive work of Quebec's Robert Lepage in shows like *Vinci* and *The Dragon's Trilogy*, it soon was applied to so many things that it seemed to have no more specific meaning than "very good, and visually interesting." In the context of Canadian theatre, "image theatre" can refer to Lepage, with his highly individual, always evolving theatrical style. Equally, it can be used to describe the work of this country's processional theatre artists, people who may seldom or never produce scripted plays on indoor stages. It could be applied to the dynamic dance-theatre of Quebec's Carbone 14—although the topic of

---

SARAH B. HOOD has edited both *Performing Arts in Canada* and *Theatrum* magazines. Her interest in processional performance is practical as well as theoretical, and has led her to participate in the work of a number of the companies mentioned in this essay.

dance-theatre and other cross-genre Canadian art would require an entire book unto itself. It also has a specific meaning for the disciples of Augusto Boal, the Brazilian founder of "Theatre of the Oppressed." In this context, if refers to the technique of "sculpting" a human body to create an image expressing a state or situation.

Quebec, with its exciting modern dance scene and such crossover companies as Carbone 14, sees more imagistic work than the rest of the country. Any student of Canadian theatre must try to see at least one work by Robert Lepage, although, paradoxically, he is now perhaps more involved in the world community of artists than in the Canadian theatre community. He is certainly far ahead of most of English Canada in terms of innovation.

What is remarkable about Lepage is also quite simple: he approaches the stage and the audience as though there were no rules or precedents. He does not take for granted, for instance, that gravity must apply to his actors. Scenes in some of his plays occur horizontally, with actors "walking" on walls, and elements of the set "hanging" horizontally. Like a film director, Lepage works with sudden changes from scene to scene, or from close-up to distance shot. A performer may change identities or genders in a moment; any prop or set can suddenly be used to suggest something quite different, and sound effects or projections are used to enhance the feeling of quick transformations in space, time and scale. His use of lighting is spectacular; he lights his plays with great care and attention to detail and effect. Unlike less successful artists, who may only produce a work once, Lepage has the luxury of refining his work in each new version, often over several years of reworking and revision.

It is difficult to describe fully the impact of Lepage's work in print. The live show vibrates with humour, inventiveness and intelligence. However, it is worth sketching out the bare bones of at least one show. In his *Aiguilles et opium* (performed in English as *Needles and Opium*), for example, Lepage performs solo in a monologue about a theatre director much like himself who books into a Paris hotel room that is haunted by the aura of jazz trumpeter Miles Davis and avante-garde artist Jean Cocteau. Lepage also plays Cocteau, but not Davis, who is suggested through music and slide projections only.

The set is a very large square panel of elastic fabric, built into a revolving frame that allows it to face the audience like a movie screen, or revolve into a trampoline-like surface. Lepage spends much of the play suspended like a trapeze artist on bungie cords that allow him to spin and bounce in the air. The elastic screen is used for a series of back projections of still slides, or of shadow images, like Lepage's magnified hands preparing heroin for injection into his own arm. In one sequence he acts out a pair of lovers at a restaurant table, simply by showing a live shadow projection of his own two hands holding and caressing each other, with a few props, like a wine glass. In another, the upper half of his live body above the screen matches with the projection of the lower half of a swimmer's body; a remarkable illusion. Although a more lightweight and less fully resolved piece than many of his other productions, *Aiguilles et opium* nonetheless contains more innovation and creativity than some directors bring to their entire careers.

Lepage's theatre may be characterized by the use of striking images, but his plays generally do have a scripted action that involves the telling of a story through the spoken word. There are other Canadian theatre artists, like Czech-born Jan Komarek, whose work relies almost entirely on image. Komarek uses speech as an embellishment rather than as an instrument of storytelling. His lighting verges on the work of an illusionist. He creates infinite spaces and distances in a tiny theatre area, or causes figures only a few feet away from the audience to seem to disappear entirely. He brings forth disembodied heads and ghostly, disturbing figures in half light.

Based in Toronto, Komarek has not yet assembled a large body of work in Canada. He won a Dora Mavor Moore Award for his 1993 production *The Dance of the Blue Harlequins*, staged at the Backspace of Theatre Passe Muraille. In 1994 he used the same theatre to present *Requiem for an Angel*, a work characterized by live music and the same strikingly unusual approach to light and shadow.

The Dance of the Blue Harlequins is about the approach of death, and about the act of consuming and being consumed. The set, reminiscent of a circus tent, houses a sequence of short scenes: a woman washing at a bowl of water; dancing masked harlequins; diners eating up a human being with forks. There is only one character who consistently uses spoken lines to express her character. Played passionately by Ida Carnevali, she is an aging music hall star who fears death. She appears in various scenes with a woman who might be her younger self, or a daughter (perhaps a daughter who has died, or who has never been born). Without offering a linear narrative told in words, Komarek's plays build up a series of linked images that ultimately suggest a theme or a story to the viewer who is willing to make the effort to make connections.

Other Toronto directors who explore non-linear narrative are DNA Theatre's Hillar Liitoja, who specializes in creating complex environments that allow every audience member to experience a different version of the play, and Jacquie P. A. Thomas of Theatre Gargantua, who is building on her work with Polish theatre artists to create a dramatic vocabulary of rhythmic movement and chanting.

Island Follies: Toronto's Shadowland Production Company

Shadowland Production Company is a collective group of designers who work in three ways. In some projects, they simply act as costume or props makers for someone else's stage production. For example, Shadowland has a long association with VideoCabaret's *The History of the Village of the Small Huts*, a satirical history of Canada that has run in chronological installments from 1985 through to a planned finish in 1995.

Sometimes, Shadowland stages its own productions of scripted plays. These have included a new interpretation of Aristophanes' *Lysistrata* (1990 and 1991) by Lenore Keeshig-Tobias; *Putting in Time: A Celebration of Aging* (1994) by Bonnie Ashton, and *The Handsome and Gruesome Festival* (1988), a lighthearted retelling of some of the familiar fairy tales by visual artist Barbara Klunder. However, their most characteristic work does not use a script. It falls into a genre that has several different names. Shadowland members refer to it as celebratory theatre or pageantry; others call it processional theatre, celebration theatre, interdisciplinary theatre or, in the context of Caribbean carnival arts, "mas'" (short for "masquerade").

Processional theatre, as its name implies, takes the form of a parade or street pageant. It is related to popular festival traditions all over the world; from the Days of the Dead in Mexico to Basel's Carnival in Switzerland. Yet processional theatre artists, whether they work within the context of "mainstream" European-derived theatre, or in another tradition, like that of Trinidad Carnival, may create carefully controlled work of high artistic merit. In Canada, there are two hubs of this type of work: Vancouver and Toronto. Vancouver is home to such companies as Ruby Slipper, Public Dreams Society and Vancouver Moving Theatre, while Toronto is the base for Whole Loaf Theatre, Kensington Carnival, Shadowland and others.

Image is central to the work of these companies, most of which create large-scale giant puppets, flags, masks, lanterns and other reusable parade elements. Many rely on volunteers for building. Their work deals in archetypal characters and situations: the death and rebirth of the year; the dichotomy between mind and body, or intellect and imagination, or technology and nature.

Processional theatre reaches back to carnivals and circuses for many of its effects. Stiltwalking, for example, is a skill practiced by members of Shadowland Production Company and Kensington Carnival and Vancouver's Mortal Coil, an all-female stilt company. Among the other startling techniques employed by these groups are fire-breathing and fire sculpture, dancing and acrobatics, juggling, drumming and the use of gigantic puppets, some so big that they must be manipulated by three or four people. Obviously, these techniques draw in audiences who are not used to formal theatre on a proscenium stage. But they are not only used for their sensational effect; they can also make very powerful narrative points.

The purity and simplicity of narrative through image lends itself particularly well to the transmission of political messages, whether overt or covert. Whole Loaf Theatre uses oversized masks and props to depict the combatants in their reworked mummer's play *The Deadly Wound*, about the battle between the Dragon of Light and the Knight of the Dark; a sort of reversal of the imagery of St. George and the Dragon. The company performs this play annually on New Year's eve at Toronto's edition of First Night. Its simple narrative makes a strong link between the victory of light over darkness (appropriate to the date) and the need to respect the poor and homeless rather than succumb to the sway of riches and power.

These processional theatre artists typically stage much of their work outdoors, and often in unusual venues that are not associated with "high" art. Thus, Caravan Stage Company's *The Coming*, performed on Wolfe Island, near Kingston, Ontario (1991) and on the Leslie Spit at Toronto's du Maurier Ltd. World Stage festival (1992), was a massive, musical outdoor epic that brought spectators on a five-hour journey across semi-wild terrain by bus, ferry and on foot to tell of the struggle between The Prime, a heartless master of technology, and The Coming, a ruthless Mother Nature. Kensington Carnival's *Medea* (1991), a triumph of outdoor staging, led spectators through a variety of environments, some natural and some created for the production, on the shore of Lake Ontario at Toronto's Ashbridge's Bay. Meanwhile, Whole Loaf Theatre's gigantic puppets are nowhere more at home than in a city street closed to traffic.

Also, these companies tend to create work that fits a particular day of the year. Kensington Carnival produces an annual winter solstice parade, the Kensington Festival of Lights; Public Dreams organizes an annual Hallowe'en pageant, the Party of Lost Souls.

These annual, seasonal performances are significant and consciously chosen; they recognize the roots of theatre, which lie in annual, quasi-religious or spiritual celebrations of the community, and of the relationship between humanity and nature. (Greek theatre, for example, was performed at an annual religious festival, and all levels of society were involved. Even the Santa Claus Parade is related to the seemingly universal custom of carrying a holy image through the streets in procession at religious holidays.)

The use of large, immediately recognizable images and unusual venues in the context of traditional local festivals contributes to another aspect of processional theatre: its relationship with its audience. Processional theatre implicates every individual audience member in the performance, whether by forcing people to choose to move from place to place to follow a show, or by going so far as to get bystanders into masks and headdresses, dancing along with the company. Also, many processional theatre companies enjoy a strong, symbiotic relationship with their local community. This may be the community of local artists, or, as in the case of Kensington Carnival, a particular neighbourhood (Kensington Market).

Shadowland is based on Ward's Island in Toronto Harbour. This is a unique environment, an idyllic, parklike, car-free community situated ten minutes from the heart of Canada's largest city. Because the municipal government has made serious efforts over the years to eliminate all private housing on the Islands, the residents, including government employees, media people, artists, people on welfare or UIC and many other types of residents, have gradually grown into a solid community. Originally called Shadowland Repertory Company, the group formed in 1983 after seeing the work of Welfare State International, a British processional theatre company. At first, the "principal artists" were Whitney Smith, Leida and Jerry Englar, Kathleen Doody, Brad Harley and Sarah Miller. Today, the core members are Leida Englar, Kathleen Doody, Brad Harley, Alice Norton, Joey Gladding and Anne Barber.

The company's principal artists see themselves as a channel through which groups can articulate their own important messages in parades and other celebratory theatre events. Collaboration is a key principle; the work combines theatre and direct action. With a 1984 production on

Ward's Island called *Island Follies*, Shadowland created a mythology that symbolized their own neighbourhood's struggles to survive as a community. The show was mounted with the help of over eighty volunteers, including children, and featured a huge bulldozer attacking tiny houses; while a flaming fire sculpture of the flying toad gave the Islanders a war banner that united qualities of both humility and hilarity.

From 1990 to 1992 the company carried out a three-stage project around the theme of water. In the first two years, they performed an outdoor, environmental adaptation of Aristophanes' *Lysistrata*, at the du Maurier Ltd. World Stage festival, within the Toronto Island community and at Wikwemikong Unceded Reserve on Manitoulin Island, where volunteer Native actors replaced Toronto Islanders alongside a core cast of professionals. *Lysistrata III: A Grand Celebration of Water*, was a series of parade performances involving local resident in five towns and cities along the Grand River, just west of Toronto, where the groundwater had become severely polluted by industry.

Other community-based projects have included two collaborations with Native artists: *Buffalo Jump Ahead* (1993) a metaphor for the destructive course of events relating to Native issues and the environment; and the annual *River of Fire Festival* in Big Cove, New Brunswick, where Shadowland's skills and experience in contemporary carnival techniques are put to use in both parades and pageants based on local stories and legends. As well, Shadowland lends its support to numerous processions and celebrations throughout the year, like Gay Pride Day, First Night Toronto and the Labour Day Parade.

One of the company's most important influences has been their work with Trinidad-derived carnival masquerade design ("mas'"). In 1986 Shadowland began a series of yearly visits to Trinidad to apprentice with the renowned carnival designer Peter Minshall. The art of mas' lies in the creation of an impressive and harmonic mass of moving colours and shapes that link together costumes on a single theme. Shadowland has brought Trinidad artists to Toronto to train non-Caribbean Canadian artists in carnival mas' design, especially the technique of anchoring a large metal, bamboo and/or fibreglass framework onto a light, body-fitting backpack to allow for the creation of massive costumes that can be carried by a dancing performer through intense heat for many hours.

Toronto's annual Caribana Festival, a direct spinoff from Trinidad and Tobago Carnival, is a showcase for (and a competition among) some forty masquerade bandleaders. Each one assembles work space, designs, volunteer workers and materials for a "band"—a costumed group, not a musical ensemble—that will perform once, on the day of the Caribana Parade. Their costs are recouped through the sale of costumes to the people who wear them. Montreal, Hamilton and Calgary are among other Canadian cities that now "play mas'."

Using adapted Trinidad carnival techniques and styles, Shadowland produced its first Caribana Parade band in Toronto in 1985, on the theme "Island to Island." The company brought an unbroken series of Caribana bands from the mid-'80s on. Each band included some seventy-five performers in costume, ranging from small, simple outfits to the large and elaborate "king" and "queen"; all of which depict aspects of a single theme. The theme may be political or philosophical in nature, or it may simply illustrate a pretty image such as flowers or tropical fish. Of course, Shadowland's work is always political in nature; but a great many of Caribana's other masquerade bands each year choose themes that are simply meant to entertain, amaze and please the eye.[1]

Shadowland's great strength is the ingenuity and fecundity of its creations, which are fuelled by little money but large human resources. One of the best examples of their work was the 1990 Caribana band *For the Birds*. Part of a trio about nature, with *Trees 'R' Us* and *Down To Earth*, the band featured an array of bird imagery that astonished and delighted onlookers; an environmental message was implicit. The Queen costume was "Phoenix Rising," portrayed by Joey Gladding; the king was a stiltwalking "Great Blue Heron" (Rick/Simon), which is still talked about today in Caribana circles. The free, ragged painted cloth costume gave the elevated stiltwalker a noble, mysterious quality. The band also included very large white cranes carried on poles by paraders and a drumming section with vacu-molded life-size plastic seagulls sprouting from small backpacks so that the musicians seemed to be overshadowed by a swaying flock of seagulls. In a typically Shadowlandish note of humour, the band wore black T-shirts streaked with white splatters. (The section was nicknamed the Tony O'Donahue Shithead Marching Band, a reference to a local politician who had publicly blamed Lake Ontario's pollution on fish and bird excrement.) Other members of the band included a stiltwalking flamingo in vivid pink with a puppet head on a dryer-venting hose neck; a skull-headed vulture with a gas mask, army fatigues and large, tattered ominous wings and, a crowning testament to volunteer patience and perseverance, fifty human-sized loons, with each white spot on each black wing carefully hand-painted—*twice*—with the use of stencils.

For the Birds combined a political message with creative originality. It made heavy use of "found" and recycled materials, transformed through artistic vision into animated sculptures that were individually impressive, and collectively overwhelming. These are the hallmarks of Shadowland.

As this article is being written, a continuing lack of money is drawing attention to philosophical tensions within the company. The collective is seeking ways to adapt to the needs and visions of individual members without distorting the whole. The Caribana band of 1994 was *Bare Bones*, a typically comic/ironic self reference that was, in fact, one of Shadowland's most cohesive statements ever: bodies painted in three horizontal bands of colour that blended eerily into a visual unity, broken only by models of bones and skulls dangling from the moving figures. It exemplified, as the best of Shadowland's work always does, the strength of the group, and the power of movement in the streets.

Performing the Body: Winnipeg's Primus Theatre

Whereas Shadowland's work begins with visual imagery, Primus begins with the performer and her or his voice and body. The company was founded in 1986 when Artistic Director Richard Fowler (a native of Whitehorse, raised in Edmonton) was invited to teach at the National Theatre School in Montreal. His students requested a second course the following year, after which four of them (Ker Wells, Stephen Lawson, Richard Clarkin and Karen Randoja) decided to join him and form a company based on physical training and exploration.

After some consideration, in November 1988 Primus decided to settle their work in Winnipeg. There they added two more company members (Tannis Kowalchuk and Donald Kitt) to the troupe. Over that short space of time Primus has become an important and respected component of the Winnipeg theatre scene, where Prairie Theatre Exchange (a much larger company with its own building) gave them office space from which to operate until they moved into their own offices at ArtSpace.

The work of Primus is very much based on Richard Fowler's experience with Eugenio Barba, founder of Odin Teatret in Denmark. Himself a disciple of theatre guru Jerzy Grotowski, Barba's view, put very simply, is that performers around the world have arrived at similar discoveries about the physical discipline of performance, and what makes a human being interesting to watch. Members of his company engage in daily physical training exercises together, and also carry out individual research in world performance techniques derived from such art forms as classical East Indian dance, Chinese opera or Japanese Noh plays.

Fowler learned from Barba that it is possible consciously to shape a performer's energy in order to achieve an actorly presence. It is this energy that makes a performer compelling to look at. With Primus, as in the Odin Teatret, each performer tries through the rehearsal process to discover the most potent ways of moving, standing, walking, leaping or using their hands. Gradually, these movement exercises are incorporated into a performance sequence. Meanwhile, with the director's shaping, the individual characters created in this way come together and react with one another. Music and text are added only at this stage.

Because the creative process is so intrinsic to the daily routine of the company, it is only natural that Primus offers training classes and workshops to other performers when they are at home or on tour. Also, unlike most professional theatre companies, the performers are also the company's administrators. Therefore all the money that the company raises is channelled back to the artists. This company solidarity, and the closeness it engenders, seem to be a typical feature of non text-based companies.

Primus' first production, based on the early research and rehearsal at the National Theatre School, was called *Dog Day* (performed in French as *Jour de canicule*). The show had its premiere at the Winnipeg Fringe Festival in 1989, and was sold out both there and in a later Winnipeg remount. Later the production toured to the Quinzaine international du théâtre, an important theatre festival in Quebec City, where it sold out again.

In 1991 Primus created *Alkoremmi*, a highly compelling piece of imagistic drama that has since toured to Quebec, Ontario and across the West. The Winnipeg Children's Festival saw the debut of *Scarabesque*, the company's outdoor children's performance, in 1993. *The Night Room* (1994) was the Primus' next major creation. Its setting is the semi-consciousness of a sleeping mind—or the mind of someone who cannot sleep. These three works were created through the research of the performers, shaped by the director, to reach a coherent and consistent whole.

Alkoremmi is the name of a mythical palace, with a chamber for each of the five senses. The play is about the last soul, which is waiting to be placed into a human baby. Early in the play, one character tells the audience: "... there's a place in heaven where all the souls wait in line to drop like coins into the bodies of the nearly born. ... The last soul in line is already frightened, because when he is born, all the storytellers will be dead, and that's when the end of the world will come." The rest of the play follows this theme, through the actions of various characters. There is no strict plot. The story, such as it is, exists in the connections each viewer will make for themselves between scenes.

The atmosphere of *Alkoremmi* is mysterious, dreamlike. It is well adapted for performance in alternate spaces, such as the abandoned commercial warehouse in which it played in Toronto. Audience members are led into the performance space in small groups by a woman bearing a lit candle atop a parasol. They seat themselves around the edges of a performance space with curtained areas at either end. Some sit on bleachers; others on mats on the ground. This arrangement immediately breaks down some of the traditional distance between performers and audience by forcing the audience members to choose exactly how they will sit, and to watch other audience members making the same decision. (This practice is hardly new to Primus, but it has a significant effect on the way the play is perceived.)

A stiltwalking character (Don Kitt) is one of the most striking and memorable features of *Alkoremmi*, and a reminder that the way Primus creates its shows dictates that the performance would change radically with any change in the cast. The *Alkoremmi* stiltwalker must dance, kicking up stilts behind; must rise quickly in a fluid motion from a recumbent position up to the full height of the stilts with only the assistance of his balancing stick, and must perform while carrying another actor. These are advanced stilt techniques, and need a great deal of practice to perfect. Singing and music are also integral parts of the performance. Due to the extended rehearsal process, the ensemble works together like a well-oiled machine. In another stilt sequence, the performers on the floor pass a piece of fabric over the stilt figure. It begins low down, and is caught by the stiltwalker's balance stick, then billows up and over the stiltwalker, while performers on either side pass, holding on to the fabric edges.

With Primus Theatre, the method by which shows are created dictates their form. No other company could reproduce these highly individualistic works. The skills and personalities of the performers are inseparably woven into the fabric of the piece.

Horseplay: Caravan Farm Theatre, Kamloops, B.C. and Caravan Stage Company, Kingston, Ontario

One of Canada's longest established theatre companies is the Caravan, originally formed in 1970 by Paul Kirby and Nans Kelder. The two had just fled Montreal following the collapse of their underground publication, *Logos*, which ended in a welter of legal problems after then Mayor Jean Drapeau decided a piece of political satire had gone too far. Inspired by the story of a local hero, a British Columbia train robber named Bill Miner, Kirby and Kelder conceived of a company that would allow them to express their political views while offering them independence and adventure.

The creation of the Caravan—known first as the Little People's Caravan—is a staggering testament to the vision and tenacity of Kirby and Kelder. Beginning from scratch, they taught themselves how to build touring wagons, how to maintain a team of Clydesdale horses, and how to create theatre. Overcoming one difficulty after another, the company soon lived up to its name, and by 1977 there were already five wagons in a still-growing fleet, along with horses and a fluctuating company of performers who also shared all the work of looking after the horses, cooking, making costumes and otherwise sustaining their itinerant community. Genuine and severe poverty was a way of life for many years, offset by the pleasures of community life and the joy of performing to audiences that did not otherwise see theatre. The Caravan developed its own customs, like Tabootenay celebrations (from a Salish word) that were the Caravan's gift to the communities in which they stayed; elaborate birthdays; Bill Miner Day, upon which Caravaners hang their problems in effigy on a tree; and once, a memorial of brilliant balloons for a company friend who died under the wheels of a wagon.

The Caravan travelled slowly along roads heavily travelled by impatient logging truckers, stopping in small rural communities to perform puppet plays and other productions with a larger-than-life, circus feel to them. The *Dr. Heart Medicine Show* was part of the early Caravan repertoire. An early success was the Caravan's musical show *Hands Up!*, based on the story of Bill Miner, who is credited with being the first to use the phrase. In 1976 Nick Hutchinson joined what was now known as the Caravan Stage Company as Artistic Director, soon followed by performer Peter Anderson. As a playwright Anderson has created many of the Caravan's scripts, beginning with *Coyotes* in 1978.

Coyotes was a dramatic comedy about three coyotes, played with broad comedy in expressive, painted half-masks and oversized feet, one of which, White Shadow, tries to save the last farm in Alberta from developers. A naturalistic first act gave way to a surrealistic second act, a proto-punk nightmare world of technological greed. The show, like most Caravan productions, made dramatic use of the outdoor settings: daylight changing to darkness as the drama heightened, for example. The ironic coincidences of an outdoor setting (a thundering rail line next to an idyllic pasture, for instance), were also put to use. The performance style was broad, gently bawdy, with animal characters (a Caravan staple) and lines shouted to reach across fields and over surface noise. Production values were rough, but featured robust and beautifully-made props, costumes and sets.

Anderson's *Horseplay* (1981, with Phil Savath) toured to Ontario, ending up in Toronto (where it left former Caravanner Ida Carnevali, who chose to found her Kensington Carnival in the bustle of Kensington Market). Upon returning home, the company toured *Law of the Land* (1982) and *Wagons and Dragons* (1983) through British Columbia.

Then in 1984 Paul Kirby and Nans Kelder set out on a three-year horse-drawn tour of the western United States that marked a final separation between two parts of the company. Those who chose a settled, agrarian mode of living ended up on an 80-acre farm in the Okanagan Valley, near Armstrong, B.C. Meanwhile, after a return to British Columbia for a production of Andrew Kelm's *Manifold Destiny* at Expo '86 and a tour of Vancouver and the Gulf Islands with Leon Rooke's *The Good Baby* (1987), the always restless Kirby and Kelder travelled east, eventually to come to rest in the neighbourhood of Wolfe Island, off Kingston, Ontario. Despite the geographical distance between the two Caravan theatres, a certain symmetry of actions suggests that these longtime partners share a sort of umbilical link.

In the late '80s, Nick Hutchinson took a sabbatical from the Armstrong branch of the company, finally renamed the Caravan Farm Theatre. From 1986 to 1990 he served as Director of the English section of the National Theatre School in Montreal (it was he who invited Richard Fowler to teach there, inadvertently assisting in the creation of Primus Theatre). Then he returned to the Farm.

Randy Helmers, a performer who makes regular journeys from Toronto to appear in Caravan shows, explains that the physical location of the company and the community life it engenders create a powerful blend that directly affects the work. "The land is as potent as the community," she says.

Perhaps the company's most ambitious project, beginning in 1991, was The Mystery Cycle, a multi-part adaptation of the Bible created in association with the Western Canada Theatre Company, with roots in the mediaeval Mystery Cycles of Europe. *The Creation* debuted in the summer of 1991, followed by *The Nativity* at Christmas of the same year. *The Passion* played the Farm in the spring of 1993, and then toured to churches around the Okanagan Valley.

Meanwhile, at about the same time, Caravan Stage Company mounted *The Coming* (discussed above), a massive undertaking that was staged on Wolfe Island and also, the following year, in Toronto.

With a remount of *Horseplay* at the Caravan Farm Theatre in 1993, the two companies seemed to come to yet another bend in the road. Nick Hutchinson stepped down from his position as Artistic Director (to be succeeded by a five-person team), while the Ontario Caravan sold its horses and took to the water in a new incarnation of Kirby and Kelder's vision, the Caravan Stagebarge, designed to tour shows throughout the waterways of Ontario and perhaps beyond. "An anarchist ark," as Kirby calls it, "for endangered thespians and extinct artists."

Insofar as it is possible to generalize about a quarter century of performance, the Caravan companies' plays are characterized by rich, punning language; strong visual elements, including handmade and hand-painted props and set pieces; an astounding gift for using scrounged materials (from baling wire and horsehair to railway cars) and an always lively political message that abhors the greed of capitalism and celebrates harmony among human beings, animals and the natural environment.

The Caravan Stage Company and Caravan Farm Theatre not only perform for a given community; they are a community. They are unique in Canadian theatre in that, like the traditional circus families, Caravan members and their children work side by side. Seasonally, people who might have thought they would never find themselves working on another Caravan show return to be part of it once more.

Because the Caravan companies are so separate from the urban theatre mainstream, they have often been overlooked by theatre documentarists; the early issues of *Canada On Stage*, the annual record of Canadian professional theatre from 1974 onward, make no mention of the Little People's Caravan. On the other hand, it is not uncommon for journalists who are sent to interview members of the Caravan to end up building sets or tending horses, thus ensuring that the work does not vanish as the players move on.

Implications

At the end of the second millennium, mainstage theatre is a pursuit for a relatively small portion of North America's and Europe's populations. However, processional theatre and its related forms (like Carnival mas') reach a wide and ever-growing audience. Meanwhile, both avant-garde and populist theatre artists in Canada are seeking ways to unite theatre with other forms, like dance, music and video. This tendency has brought about an increasing interest in opera among theatre directors like Robert Lepage and Richard Rose, since opera encompasses dance, music, theatre and design.

Although processional theatre is readily accepted by audiences, it is not as easily accepted by theatre critics, government funding bodies and, often, other theatre professionals. These barriers are closely related to those faced by artists working in performance traditions outside the mainstream. East Indian dance, Chinese opera and Caribbean carnival art are among the many forms that are practiced in Canada by people coming from the countries in which those forms originated, as well as by "professional," mainstream Canadian-born artists.

Theatre artists and commentators in the next millennium will be struggling with the question of what makes an art form "Canadian," and who decides what is an art form and what isn't. It may be necessary for government funding bodies to completely redesign the categories of art that they fund in order to match the shape of the art world over the next few decades. We may someday stop thinking of music, dance, theatre and film as the most accurate categories of performance.

In the meantime, image theatre, whether avant-garde or community-based, is one of the most exciting areas of Canadian theatre. After all, as they say, an image can be worth a thousand words.

Notes

1. Louis Saldenah, Eddie Merchant, Selwyn "Nip" Davis, Arnold Hughes, Noel Audain, Walter Elliot, Emmerson Myers, Whitfield Belasco

and Russell Charter are some of Toronto's pre-eminent mas' designers and bandleaders. The Caribana designers, mostly born in Trinidad, will some day be recognized as colleagues of the other theatre artists under discussion. For the moment, however, their work is little understood by the mainstream arts community, the general public, the media and the government funding agencies, so they are seldom, unfortunately considered as belonging in this context.

Suggestions for further reading:

General:

Hood, Sarah B. "Processional Theatre—Taking Over The Streets." *Performing Arts and Entertainment in Canada* (Summer 1992): 20–32.

———. "Un-Canadian Carnivals." *Canadian Theatre Review* 58 (Spring 1989): 27–30.

Wallace, Robert, ed. "Image Theatre." Special section of *Canadian Theatre Review* 50 (Spring 1987): 4–36.

Walling, Savannah T. "Crossing Over: The Interdisciplinary Experience." *Theatrum* 36 (Winter 1993-94): 13–20.

Shadowland Production Company:

Fox, John and Sue Gill. "Welfare State International: Seventeen Years on the Streets." *The Drama Review* 29.3 (Fall 1985): 117–126.

Gaysek, Fred. "Celebrating Shadowland." *Canadian Theatre Review* 58 (Spring 1989): 21–26.

———. "Shadowland: Catching the Community Beat." *Art View Magazine* (Winter 1986/87): 14–23.

Hood, Sarah B. "Caribana: The Art of Carnival in Toronto." *Performing Arts In Canada* (Summer 1990): 22–72.

———. "Mas' Appeal." *Theatrum* 24 (June/July/August 1991): 20–25.

———. "Shadowland Gathers at the River." *eye* (June 4, 1992): 35.

———. "Shadowy Existence." *Theatrum* 11 (Fall 1988): 21–25.

Jackson, Marni. "Mas' Appeal." *Canadian Art* (Summer 1987): 70–77.

Warner Keene, Susan. "Shadowland: Making Magic." *Ontario Craft* (Summer 1989): 44–46.

———. "Taking It To The Streets." *Fibrearts Magazine* (Summer 1989): 9, 14.

White, Michèle. "The History Cycle: The Parodic Seen/The Parodic Scene." *Canadian Theatre Review* 70 (Spring 1992): 50–53.

Primus Theatre:

Barba, Eugenio. "Creating the Roles." *Canadian Theatre Review* 31 (Summer 1981): 53–59.

——————. "The Way of Opposites." *Canadian Theatre Review* 35 (Summer 1982): 12–37.

Brask, Per. "The Anthropology of Performance: An Interview with Richard Fowler." *Canadian Theatre Review* 71 (Summer 1992): 81–88.

——————. "Dilating the Body, Transporting the Mind: Considering Primus Theatre." *The Journal of Dramatic Theory and Criticism* (Fall 1994): 207–219.

Buccholz, Garth. "Entering Into Intelligent Chaos: Primus Theatre." *Theatrum* 39 (Summer 1994): 9–10.

Fowler, Richard. "Grotowski and Barba: A Canadian Perspective." *Canadian Theatre Review* 32 (Fall 1981): 44–51.

McCracken, Melinda. "Primus, The Experience of an Experience." *Interchange* (January 1994): 6.

Skene, Rick. "Training for Independence." *Canadian Theatre Review* 66 (Spring 1991): 32–35.

Caravan Farm Theatre/Caravan Stage Company*:

Anderson, Peter. "Breaking All Four Walls: Open-Air Theatre at the Caravan Farm." *Canadian Theatre Review* 76 (Fall 1993): 8–12.

Bott, Robert. "The Anarchists and the Horses." *Saturday Night* (September 1979): 25–32.

Dafoe, Chris. "Theatre's Mane Man Steps Down." *The Globe and Mail* 28 July 1993: A12–13.

Henaut, Dorothy, dir. *Horse-Drawn Magic*. Documentary Film. National Film Board of Canada, 1978. 27 min.

Hood, Sarah B. "Mise-en-Green." *Theatrum* 25 (September/October 1991): 14–18.

——————. "The Mystery Cycle." *Performing Arts and Entertainment in Canada* (Summer 1991): 28–29.

——————. "Ritual Abuse." *Theatrum* 30 (September/October 1992): 18–23.

---

* The Caravan Stage Company has donated some original archival material to the Theatre Archive at the University of Guelph, Ontario. They intend to donate more at a later date.

McColm, Michelle. "Caravan Stagebarge—Trading Main for Mainsail." *Performing Arts and Entertainment in Canada* (Fall 1993): 13–16.

Reimche, Judy. "The Caravan's Nick Hutchinson: Mixing Farm and Theatre." *Okanagan Life* (Winter 1991): 15–18.

Shinnick, John. "The Caravan Stage Company." *Westworld* [Caravan Stage Company Archives, n.d.]: 20, 21, 58.

Weihs, Ronald "The Foreign Legion of Canadian Theatre." *Canadian Theatre Review* 42 (Spring 1985): 120–129.

The Spirit of Shivaree and the Community Play in Canada; or, The Unity in Community

by Edward Little and Richard Paul Knowles

The audience gathered at the old Town Hall in Rockwood, and walked from there along a tree-lined path by the river to the ruins of the Harris mill. Along the way, they saw historically costumed figures paddling canoes, emerging from caves, or haranguing them with grievances. Once at the mill, they found themselves part of a country fair, with music, crafts, refreshments, and a lively auction that began with farm implements but ended with the announcement that the township itself would be on the block at evening's end. The crowd then moved to an open space to watch moments in their township's history re-enacted on, around, under, and above surrounding platforms. Here actors mingled with, pushed through, or shouted from among the assembled crowd. The action, using styles that ranged from puppetry to polemic, focused on 1837, the Mackenzie rebellion, and the story of the so-called "Rockwood Rebels." The play granted Mackenzie himself status as an exemplary citizen and thereby connected the cause of the rebellion of 1837 to the proposed "rebellion of 1990":

EDWARD LITTLE teaches part-time at the Department of Drama, University of Guelph. He is completing a Ph.D dissertation on community plays and the relationship between theatre and community at the Graduate Centre for Study of Drama, University of Toronto and gratefully acknowledges the assistance of SSHRC.

RICHARD PAUL KNOWLES chairs the Drama Department, University of Guelph. He has published articles and chapters on Shakespeare and on Canadian Theatre in a variety of books and periodicals. He also directs and writes for the theatre.

> *a collective community response to the pressures of suburbanization and exploitative land development.*[1] *For the play's last sequence, the crowd was led deeply into the mill ruins. Here they mingled closely with the actors at a "townhall"-style debate about development, conservation, and the future of the township. The evening ended with a song.*
> —A description of *The Spirit of Shivaree*

The Spirit of Shivaree, written for and about the community of Eramosa by Dale Colleen Hamilton, a fifth-generation citizen of the Southern Ontario township, was performed by the community itself in the summer of 1990 at the site of the historic Harris Woollen Mill on the banks of the Eramosa River. It was greeted by the regional press as Canada's first community play. That the show's producers had advertised it more specifically as the first community play in Canada using the Colway Theatre Trust process, a model developed in Britain in the late 1970s and 80s,[2] made as little difference to reporters and entertainment editors as did the long history in this country of community-oriented theatre. That history extends from civic and historical pageantry in the early twentieth century through the workers' theatre movement of the 1930s to the collaborative and collective creations of "localist" theatre companies such as Passe Muraille, 25th Street, NDWT, Mulgrave Road, and the Mummers Troupe, and artists such as James Reaney, Rick Salutin, and David Fennario in the 1970s and 1980s.[3] It is ironic, but not insignificant, that in a theatrical terrain in which a sense of place, local history, and community solidarity are deeply rooted values, the first use of an imported model of this type of theatre, with its accompanying suggestion of authentication through external validation (including the participation in script development workshops of "outside" professionals such as Fennario and Salutin), should be celebrated as a landmark and focus for local pride.

Local pride is one of the things that the community play is designed to foster. This is accomplished through what Julian Hilton calls "rites of intensification" (60)—the celebration, representation, and reification of a community that demonstrates its worth both as the creator/producer of the play and as the object of dramatic representation. Community, however, often defines itself by what it excludes, and the celebration and reification of this process can also lead to an unhealthy kind of xenophobia and an entrenched conservatism. Hilton points to other aspects of community theatre, then, which he calls "rites of passage" (60), which have less to do with affirmation of the community as it is currently constituted or understood, and more with social change, cultural intervention, or community advocacy in the face of a threatening or dominant "other." In Canada this "other" often means a large metropolitan centre, as it did in the Eramosa project, where "traditional rural values" were pitted against the stereotypical unscrupulousness of developers and bankers from Toronto. It is along the continuum between an essentially conservative cultural affirmation (the solidification of community identity and values) and cultural intervention (the activist initiation of social change) that the community play locates itself as a site of negotiation in the ongoing construction of community.

* * *

The construction of community, or community understood as process rather than as stable entity, is implicated in what social theorists such as Derek Phillips describe as the difference between "territorial" communities, which are defined primarily by geo-political boundaries, and "relational" communities, which are defined by the nature and quality of inter-relationships among a membership with shared interests (12). Relational communities exist, in varying degrees, as, within, and across territorial ones. The tension between co-existing territorial and relational communities is an important factor in understanding the community play as a site of negotiation between cultural affirmation (rites of intensification) and social intervention (rites of passage). If territorial communities tend to carry with them the received values of shared history inscribed in the definition of place over time, relational communities (while often also sharing histories and values) are more likely to be concerned with issues of common interest such as shared activity, recognition, empowerment, and social change.

Distinctions between territorial and relational notions of community have other implications for the community play as well. Power in our society is often territorially defined (through land ownership, municipal and regional governments, and so on), yet apart from moving out or moving in, membership in territorial communities is non-voluntary. As Phillips points out, both membership and values in territorial communities are often "inherited" in the sense that many members will become implicated in the traditions and practices of their communities "before they are able to explicitly recognize and reflect on what they have in common" (14). Yet compared to more voluntary forms of association, the implicit hegemony of this unquestioned and unquestionable "inheritance" must also be considered against the fact that territorial communities inevitably include a much more heterogeneous membership than is usually the case for communities based on common interests. Relational communities, at least those that are not racially, ethnically, or otherwise prescribed, are more likely to be determined by voluntary participation in the *process* of community, and its actively and intentionally evolving identity.

Community participation, together with the primacy of process over product, is what best distinguishes the community play from other kinds of theatrical activity that take community as their subject, and it is for this reason that we have decided to begin our discussion with an analysis of the nature of that participation and that process, rather than with the more usual critical account of the script or performance text as product.

In Colway-style community plays, eliciting participation is a principal element in the two-year process of creation. These plays are generally rural in setting and subject, they routinely involve a "core" group of professionals, usually from outside of the community (director, designer, playwright, production manager, etc.), a cast of one to two hundred community members, plus hundreds more in various aspects of organization, administration, research, script development, and production. Colway sees its work as creating theatre not only *for,* but more importantly *with* a community. Footage from *Dignity and Grace*,[4] a documentary video about the making of *The Spirit of Shivaree*, reveals considerable concern at a meeting of the professional "core" about "letting go," and the "humbling" process of letting the community "take ownership." The rewards of the process, unlike those of more traditional theatre, are less likely to be aesthetic or artistic than social or cultural, and they are consistently articulated by the participants in the rhetoric of mutual support, solidarity, and renewal of community.

The emphasis on broadly-based community involvement in (almost) all aspects of process and performance—Colway uses the term "inclusivity"—distinguishes what we are calling "the community play," as practiced by Colway, James Reaney (in *King Whistle*), or their pageantic predecessors, from the larger body of what we have termed "community-oriented" theatre.[5] Most often in community-oriented forms a comparatively small group of theatre artists or workers create a theatrical representation of and for the larger, "host" community, holding, as it were, a mirror up to the community as a rallying point for community concern. In the Mummers Troupe's production of *Gros Mourn*, for example, the company visited a Newfoundland community in crisis over the appropriation of their land for the creation of a National Park. The company engaged in an intensive creation/rehearsal process within the community, and quickly mounted an interventionist production that served to focus and express the protests of the residents of Sally's Cove (see Brooks, 78–96). In *Gros Mourn* and similar productions that are predicated on relational notions of community beyond geo-political boundaries, cultural intervention often extends overtly to encompass community empowerment within larger social, political, and legislative structures. The Mummers Troupe in Sally's Cove, Black Rock Theatre in working-class English-speaking Montreal, Theatre Passe Muraille in Clinton, Ontario, Cahoots Theatre Projects in the "multicultural" community of Toronto, or Buddies in Bad Times in the gay and lesbian community of that city, all share an insistence that the hitherto marginalized community represented in the play gain voice and agency within the larger social structure. The theatre, to use Tony Howard's term, functions as a "mouthpiece" (43). In this regard, all community theatre workers, both as "communities" of performers and as representatives of a host community, may be seen as functioning along lines described by Raymond Williams, for whom communities and other forms of association are "the necessary mediating element between individuals and larger Society" (95). In this formulation, theatre companies, which are in, but not entirely of the community, serve as the shifting fissures, or "faultlines,"[6] around which change can be negotiated. To a lesser extent, the professional core plays this role in the Colway-style community play.

While community-oriented theatre in general tends to be situated on a shifting border between localist and nationalist concerns, then, the community play's emphasis on celebration and broadly-based community involvement makes it the most localist of the community-oriented forms. While it may *become* regionally or even nationally interventionist,[7] it is primarily concerned with relational notions of community insofar as they exist *within* the project's territorially-defined boundaries. From the perspective of the community play, Williams' "larger Society," at least initially, does not extend beyond the territorially defined community. The community play, as a "form of association," through its relatively vast size, protracted two-year process, and emphasis on empowerment through participation, situates its *participants* as the mediators in a process of publicly defining the community to be celebrated and, perhaps, changed.[8] The potential insularity of this focus on community is reflected in the words of Jon Oram, the director of the Colway Trust and of *The Spirit of Shivaree*, who says in the *Dignity and Grace* documentary that the community play process "feels a bit like a war, drawing people together. [But] in a war you know who your enemies are. In the community play you know who your friends are."

Initially, the principal elements which the community play uses to draw people together are the "inherited" notions of community—shared territory, shared history, and shared values. Once involved, the "community" of participants, both in their role as mediators, and through participation in the various structures and processes of the community play, present for their "larger society" not only a play which demonstrates behaviour and ideals that are constructed as exemplary, but also an exemplary community structure. As Hamilton herself expresses it in *Dignity and Grace*, and as the "Landscape Architect" puts it in the final scene of the play, "Eramosa Township could be a model" (Hamilton 78).[9]

To this end, in both process and product, the community play adheres to what Derek Phillips describes as the "communitarian ideal" (10). According to Phillips, this concept of community depends on four central characteristics: "a common geographical territory or locale, a common history and shared values, widespread political participation [through collective activity], and a high degree of moral solidarity" (14). The first two characteristics, because of their relationship to "inherited" elements of community, can be considered to be "conceptual" and to be implicated primarily in the *form* and *content* of the community play as product. In addition to being "inherited," however, the specific nature of these geographical and historical elements is also subject to a *process* of selection and negotiation. These conceptual elements play a foundational role as an initial rallying point for community consensus and participation, and they are a particular concern of the small group that is involved early in the process. And, as Colway points out, community support is facilitated by the early involvement of "shakers and movers." These tend to be established and influential community leaders with some history of community representation.

Territory, history, established residency, and representation (in the electoral sense) tend to present an initial image of community in preconceived conceptual terms. The community play process, however, by emphasizing the second two characteristics noted by Phillips—shared activity and moral solidarity—moderates the tendency of territory and history to control the definition of the "shared values" which the play celebrates. These last two characteristics, which can be seen to be primarily *processual*, are most directly implicated in the community play's creative and communal *process*.

On the culturally affirmative hand, solidarity, creativity, collective cultural expression, and creative play *are* constructed and celebrated by Colway as exemplary behaviour in the model community. In addition, the focus on "what best serves the play" (Oram) fosters the two elements which Phillips sees as constitutive of "solidarity": a sense of social interdependence, and a sense of belonging. On the other hand such solidarity (to the extent that it focuses on relational aspects of community) also provides the possibility for reconfiguration within the community across class and other lines. It does so through the encouragement of collective activity in the development of networks, communication, and cultural skills; through the experience of working toward common goals in groupings that may transgress the community's implicit social boundaries; and through the celebration both of personal creativity within a cultural process and pride in shared accomplishments.

In addition, the community play offers its participants various opportunities for contributing to its creative and decision making process through public meetings, community events, theatre skills workshops, and policies such as "inclusivity" and "democratization." Inclusivity insists that no one who wishes to participate is to be excluded. Democratization is implemented through a central Steering Committee and various subcommittees. The Steering Committee, principally composed of "shakers and movers," is charged with policy-making. It is the core of community representation and it largely controls the conceptual notions of community to be represented. In the interests of community empowerment and autonomy, Colway recommends that no members of the professional core sit on this committee (though in the case of *The Spirit of Shivaree*, in which the playwright was a member of the community, she did serve on the Steering Committee). The numerous subcommittees are each headed by a member of the Steering Committee, and subcommittee members are in turn encouraged to solicit additional support and membership. Subcommittees deal with results-producing functions such as historical research, fundraising, promotion, and the solicitation and coordination of volunteers. A primary goal of the committee structure is to spread the organizational and practical load of the project quickly, while encouraging the broadest possible range of community participation. The number and size of the subcommittees is limited only by the community's willingness to participate. In this regard, a primary strategy of the Colway process is to solicit support from existing community groups, clubs, and organizations which then encourage participation from their memberships.[10]

But if the community play's process lays the foundation for building "the unity in community," as well as for reconfiguring the boundaries within that community, its protracted duration and hierarchical control of conceptual elements also provide ample time for conservative forces—the status quo of community power, privilege, and stability—to organize, exercise traditional leadership skills, and assert hegemony. The possibility of cultural intervention in the community play rests in large part, then, with its processual potential for reconstruction and reconsideration of what community means. But its capacity comfortably to contain that intervention, to hold it in check, rests in large part with the degree to which the community play as theatrical product, through its focus on landscape and history, has tended to define community in terms of the historical continuity deriving from the stabilizing influence of place over time. A community play uses documented and conjectural history to tell and re-tell stories to and about its territorial community, and in the Colway model this territorial focus is seen to be an essential element in community building. On a practical level, focusing on and celebrating "the land" and associated values foregrounds "community spirit" and thus works to elicit participation and helps ensure that the play's representation of the community is non-controversial. On a fundamentally conservative pedagogical level, in telling its story a community play is involved in both remembering and constructing a collective past which, by emphasizing continuity, builds and reinforces what Benedict Anderson calls an "imagined community,"[11] or, in communitarian terms, a "community of memory."

A community of memory engenders solidarity and the continuance of "inherited" values by:

> retelling its story, its constitutive narrative, and in so doing ... offers examples of the men and women who have embodied and exemplified the meaning of the community. (Bellah *et al.* 153)

In the Rockwood case, the essential and essentially conservative values to be shared—"family and land and heritage,"—were depicted as spanning centuries and therefore as being common to exemplary pioneers and contemporary residents alike (83). Through consensus over land stewardship, preservation of farmland, and a willingness to fight for issues of control, the land was reified as a principal mediating element between old and new settler, and among heterogeneous community groups. As the character MacKenzie puts it: "It's nice to know that some things never change" (76).

The Rockwood project was first conceived as a response to issues of land control, and it is not incidental that the script of *The Spirit of Shivaree* is dedicated, not only "to those past and present who call Eramosa home," but also "to the land." Nor is it surprising that many of the most resonant moments in the community plays that have so far been mounted in Canada have had to do with this conjunction of landscape and history, in which landscape somehow (and in both senses of the word) contains history, including future histories. When the news of the MacKenzie rebellion came to the world of *The Spirit of Shivaree* by way of sentinels posted at the tops of the limestone cliffs that border the river and the playing space, it created a stir among the characters, and a chill among members of an audience for whom the historical "feel" of the occasion was immediate and poignant. Even more poignant, and more potentially constraining as the dead hand of the past, was the ghostly presence of ancestral characters—pioneer rebels and their families, including Mackenzie—looming in the windows of the mill ruins, presiding over the proceedings as the voices of history that have, in Phillips's terms, "embodied and exemplified the meaning of the community."

This documentary-style "authentication" and reification of received and reproduced (as opposed to re-created or revisionist) history and its emotional affirmation of the continuity of territorial community over time is reinforced in the play's tendency to ritualize history. *Shivaree* and the other community plays produced in Canada have engaged their audiences as participants in historical pageants, processions, and parades that have preceded and punctuated them. Each of these plays has employed evocative historical icons that again tend to function as conservative, affirmative, and stabilizing forces in the production of value and meaning. These iconic moments are often accompanied by lyrical ballads, marches, anthems, and choruses that reinforce a communal and unifying sense of shared past and present purpose, evoking, at the same time, a familiar resonance of civic boosterism and local pride.

The use of landscape as the unchanging repository of history and value is also inscribed in the historical bodies of actors who, in the case of the Rockwood play, were cast to play their own ancestors.[12] When Richard Lay played his great-great-grandfather, William Lyon Mackenzie, particularly in those scenes set in the present, in which he presided over the interpretation of his past and its meaning for the township's future, the privileging of bloodlines revealed an essentialist notion of identity and a fetishizing of ancestral descent that was essentially conservative, whatever the intentions of the show's creators. At one point in the performance, moreover, Mackenzie clearly elided past and present for the audience as well as for the "ancestrally-cast" actors, when he claimed that "I would never have made it to the border alive without the aid and assistance of country people such as *are* gathered *here tonight*" (our emphasis).[13] This, combined with the fact that the play-making process is consensual, non-contentious, and therefore generalizing, meant that, again, the interventionist potential of the process tended to be subsumed in the role of community empowerment (see Little and Sim 58).

The interventionist potential of the historical narrative of *Shivaree*—a story of armed rebellion—and of the fact that the play's central heroes—the "Rockwood Rebels" and Mackenzie himself—were advocates of violent revolution, then, was safely contained for the audience by the reassuring icons of continuity embodied in the use of familiar landscapes, faces and names. And of course neither Mackenzie nor any other of the play's rebels carried a gun.

* * *

The play's use of landscape, history, and dramatic form were not exclusively conservative, however, and if its interventionist potential was to some extent held in check, it can nevertheless be seen, even as a theatrical product, to have served in several ways as a site of negotiation for social change. Even its employment of historical narrative is less clearly or simply affirmative than may at first appear. The history on which the play most frequently draws is less the traditional, official, or national history of the acts of great men, than an explicitly revisionist and localist social history, often popular history, in which Mackenzie, for example, can cite what "the history books don't tell you" (56). Town and county histories, the records of community groups, local newspapers, Lion's Clubs and women's auxiliaries—even residents' attics—were scoured as repositories of local history. *The Spirit of Shivaree*, in fact, staged a debate at the outset of the action in which versions and ownership of history were contested. A scene in which a lecture on history by Sir Francis Bond Head, Governor of Upper Canada, speaking from what in a medieval mystery cycle would be called a *locus*, or scene-specific symbolic platform above the crowd, was interrupted by a woman who argued, speaking in French from the *platea*, or public playing area that she shared with the audience as populace, that "God doesn't only speak English and … history didn't begin when the white men came."[14] In response to her claim that Bond Head "got the story wrong," the Governor replies that he is "talking about history, not stories," to which she replies, "stories are histories and histories are stories," before she is silenced by an armed guard in an overt exercise of historical power (9). This sequence explicitly demonstrates, not only that "history" as story is ideologically constructed and coded, but also that to control history is to exercise power. The scene also works to demystify that power and render it contestable.

The site at which power is *made* contestable is the community play itself. The play's carnivalesque eclecticism of genres, styles, and voices demystifies any representational realism and gives the audience a democratic role in re-constructing the history of its own community, as opposed to a stake in the re-production of a dominant myth of "identity" (and in the suspension of its own disbelief).[15] As celebratory pageant rubs shoulders with documentary agit-prop, and as declamatory rhetoric mixes with sentimental melodrama and scenes of sit-com silliness, the audience is encouraged actively to engage in its own, purposeful, history-making, and to negotiate its past and future history in a marketplace of open debate and exchange.

History, however, is not the only fissure opened for contestation by the community play in general, or *Shivaree* in particular. Community plays tend to attract as participants a preponderance of women, and since traditional histories typically relegate women to oblivion, or at best to supporting roles, playwrights and directors must of necessity, if not by design, resort to one or more of: the examination and excavation of women's roles in history; the creation of roles for women in the plays themselves; or the cross-casting of women in men's roles. Each of these options has its own interventionist potential in a patriarchal culture, and each option was exercised in *Shivaree*. Dale Hamilton was conscious in writing the script of the job of recovering women's lives and histories. As she says in *Dignity and Grace*, "that was a very deliberate act on my part, to remind people that there were women there. And when the men were off meeting or being thrown in jail, [the women] were holding … things together." This process of recovery, in fact, extended to the invention of a non-historical character, "Ensa Cameron," who, like Hamilton herself in 1990, provides an activist voice for change in the represented community of 1837. During the scene depicting the township meeting of the "Rockwood Rebels," the men resolve to "go directly to the Centre Inn

Tavern and there within commence to mind our own business" (36). Ensa is the only woman to attend the "political meeting." It is she who objects to the resolution and proposes action, and it is she who hides the fleeing Mackenzie under her skirts when he apocryphally passes through Rockwood en route to Navy Island. "Ensa Cameron," then, plays a powerful women's role in the play, and represents an explicit example of revisionist history.

Equally effective in the revisioning of women's roles in society was the casting of women to play male roles in the play, perhaps most notably the roles of the British soldiers who patrolled the *platea*, intimidated the audience, and arrested the rebels. As actor and production coordinator Janet MacLeod said in the video documentary of the project, "for women to become the vehicles of power like that ... was quite a new experience."

The experience of empowerment for the actors, of course, was central to the play as process, but the casting of women as soldiers was part of another potential intervention effected by *The Spirit of Shivaree*. Among its most effective and disruptive devices, in fact, was the play's blurring of the lines between character and actor, and between actor and spectator. This blurring was effected in part by the use of cross-casting, masks, and emblematic costuming, in part by the mixing of contemporary and period costuming and clothing, and in part by the use of the *platea*, the temporally and spatially shifting public arena at the centre of the playing area where "the people," past and present, actors, characters, and spectators, negotiated and contested histories, values, and visions of the future. At one point the action was interrupted by an actor/character who claimed, "I don't want to be in this play anymore. I don't like the part they gave me" (64). Later, in a complex conflation of both historical time and theatrical role, a certain "Bill Mackenzie," in the "ah, fertilizer business," recognizably "played by" the historical character, William Lyon Mackenzie, in turn played by his great-great grandson, says, "I'd like to suggest that *you* hold a public meeting, right here, as soon as the play is over, and that *we* face these issues head on" (our emphasis). When the imagined "crowd" agrees, the character comments to the "real" audience, "me again. You didn't think I'd miss a good uprising, did you?" (66).

Among the most interesting and effective moments in the play, was a series of "contemporary vignettes," as they are called in the script. These are presented as public testimonials spoken from a variety of community perspectives by a seventh-generation man, a farm mother, a subdivision mother, a newcomer, a commuter, and so on, while "the characters [are] taking off costumes, applying modern makeup, accessories, etc." (60).[16]

This use of the play as a site for public and popular debate was made explicit when the action and the audience moved, physically, to the interior of the mill for the final, "town hall" sequence, which rounded out the framework initiated by the fair, auction, and marketplace of the opening sequences, and returned the play to the people. If one of the virtues of the community play process was, as Jon Oram says in *Dignity and Grace*, that it "resulted in cast members talking about the issues involved," the performance, serving as a kind of carnivalesque marketplace of contesting versions of what the play's closing song celebrates as "home," provoked the same debate within the larger community.

The fair with which *Shivaree* opened is a standard feature of the Colway-style play, but in this case it provided something more, as a framework, than the usual opportunity for broadly-based participation, some fundraising, and a smooth transition into the play proper. Culminating as it did in a theatricalized auction, the opening sequence framed the entire play within the context of community celebration as commercial exchange. Initially, items such as a communally-produced quilt (now in itself an historical artifact) were auctioned off, but capital investment (represented by the developer, "Newman," with his dark glasses and cellular phone) soon replaced "fair" dealing: "Merle and Gordon Cameron," local residents, were outrageously outbid for a much-needed pickle jar by Newman, who planned to use it as a decorative umbrella stand. The marketplace had highjacked the fair.

If *The Spirit of Shivaree* presented itself, then, as a carnivalesque and celebratory mingling of people, styles, and genres—as a fair—it did so in full consciousness that carnivalesque play occurs within a public place, *platea*, or "market square" that exists within and is dependent upon lines of economic force that are external to it. In this case these included "fair market value" for pickle jars, antiques, and agricultural land that farmers can no longer afford. In fact the fair is highjacked, as local fairs always are, by a marketplace over which the community has little control. As Peter Stallybrass and Allon White note:

> The tangibility of its boundaries implies a local closure and stability, even a unique sense of belonging, which obscure its structural dependence upon a "beyond" through which this "familiar" and "local" feeling is itself produced ... It is a place

where limit, centre and boundary are confirmed and yet also put in jeopardy. (28)

They go on to say that "it is a gravely over-simplifying abstraction ... to conceptualize the fair purely as the site of communal celebration," and they point, finally, to "the deep conceptual confusion entailed by the fair's inmixing of work and pleasure, trade and play," as a source of anxiety for "the bourgeois classes," and implicitly as a potential source of social change (30).

Among the definitions of "shivaree" (or "charivari") in the Oxford English Dictionary is "a babel of noise," and *The Spirit of Shivaree* can be seen as such a babel. As both process and product it can be seen to serve as a carnivalesque marketplace at which community celebration becomes a bargaining site for the negotiation of values. These fluid and contesting values in the community play are represented by its rites of intensification, on the one hand, and its (internally generated and externally imposed) rites of passage, on the other; by notions of community that are territorially and/or relationally defined; and by tension between cultural *affirmation* and continuity based on conservative notions of history and landscape, and cultural *intervention* based on a politics of social change. Perhaps "a babel of noise" is less accurate as a way of describing the community play, however, than a babel of voices, *sharing* a territory, and engaged in the ongoing process of imagining and *building* there a relational community of common interest.

Notes

1. Statistics Canada figures detailing overall population growth in Eramosa Township between 1901 and 1986 are reproduced in Little and Sim, (5–6). Organizers of the community play, using figures from the year-end analysis of population and households in Police Villages contained in the Ontario Assessment System "Wellington County Study," placed the population growth of the village of Rockwood between 1987 and 1988 at an unprecedented 37%.
2. The most comprehensive account of the Colway process is Ann Jellicoe, *Community Plays: How to Put Them On* (New York and London: Methuen, 1987). See also Baz Kershaw's analysis of the community play's political efficacy, (168–205).

3. Many of these plays are unpublished, there are few traces at all of many community-style plays and pageants, and where there are scripts, they are of course even more inadequate as representations of process or even of theatrical product than is usually the case in the theatre. Nevertheless, the reader is referred to Denzil Ridout, *United to Serve* (Toronto: United Church of Canada, 1927); Jessie Edgar Middleton, *A Pageant of Nursing in Canada* (Toronto: Canadian Nurses Association, 1934); Richard Wright and Robin Endres, ed., *Eight Men Speak and other plays from the Canadian Workers' Theatre* (Toronto: New Hogtown Press, 1976); Toby Gordon Ryan, *Stage Left: Canadian Theatre in the Thirties, A Memoir* (Toronto: CTR Publications, 1981); Theatre Passe Muraille, *The Farm Show* (Toronto: Coach House Press, 1976); 25th Street Theatre, *Paper Wheat: The Book* (Saskatoon: Western Producer Prairie Books, 1982); the Mummers Troupe of Newfoundland, *Buchans: A Mining Town*, *Canadian Drama/L'Art dramatique canadien* 13.1 (1987): 72–116; Chris Brooks, *A Public Nuisance: A History of the Mummers Troupe* (St. John's: Institute of Social and Economic Research, Memorial University of Newfoundland, 1988); James Reaney, *King Whistle*, Brick 8 (Winter 1980); David Fennario, *Joe Beef (A History of Pointe Sainte Charles)* (Vancouver: Talonbooks, 1991); and Robert Winslow, *The Cavan Blazers* (Ennismore, Ont.: Ordinary Press, 1993).
4. The phrase "dignity and grace" is taken from the conclusion of the James Gordon song that recurs throughout the play:
    We all know
    That this old town has gotta grow
    But can't we do it with
    Some dignity and grace.
5. This larger body includes the Worker's Theatre of Action in the 1930s, the interventionist theatre of the Mummers, Passe Muraille's collectively-created sociological documentary theatre, the revisionist historical agit-prop of David Fennario's *Black Rock*, and the increasing body of work in the 1990s by gay, lesbian, feminist, and ethnic theatre companies which relate to specifically defined relational communities. Like all community-oriented theatre, these forms originate with a localist impulse—the presentation or representation of community experience to, and for, its constituent members. In overtly seeking to expand their sphere of influence to be regionally, or even nationally interventionist, however, such forms delineate a further continuum of community-oriented theatre practice—one

concerned with issues of local, regional, or even national expression and intervention.

6. We are borrowing the concept of "faultines" from Alan Sinfield, *Faultlines: Cultural Materialism and the Politics of Dissident Reading* (Berkeley: U. of California Press, 1992).

7. The Green Paper, for example, a guide to rural land use prepared by a citizen's action group formed in conjunction with the Eramosa community play, has been cited as a model by the provincial Ministry of Municipal Affairs. For a more detailed account of the impact of *Shivaree* on local and regional planning see Little and Sim. It is also worth noting that community plays are not designed for tours or remounts outside of the community that creates them, and the remounting for a second year in the same community of the Fort Qu'Appelle community play, *Ka'ma'mo'pi' cik/The Gathering*, 1992, 1993—the first time a Colway-style play has been remounted—provoked controversy both among community play practitioners and within the community.

8. Of the three Colway-style community plays produced in Canada to date: *The Spirit of Shivaree* was conceived by Dale Hamilton as a means of provoking a localized response to increasing pressures of suburbanization (see Little and Sim); Blyth's *Many Hands* (1993), was created to celebrate a theatrical tradition in a community described as experiencing communication problems between a transient "summer theatre crowd" and the resident community; and Fort Qu'Appelle's *Ka'mo'mi'pi' cik* (1992, 1993) was designed to help reconcile differences between white and native "communities."

9. All subsequent references to the text of *The Spirit of Shivaree* are by page numbers only.

10. In Rockwood, for example, this involved groups such as the Local Architectural Conservation Advisory Committee, The Junior Farmers, two Women's Institutes, church congregations, heritage and environmental groups, the Rockwood School, the Lion's Club, the Grand River Conservation Authority, the Rockwood Recreation Committee, and eventually the township council.

11. Anderson's concern is with the construction of nationhood and nationalisms, but his concept of imagined communities applies to the micro level as well. Of particular interest to the community play's construction and authentication of historical narrative is Anderson's discussion of the construction of continuity through the remember-

ing of "forgotten" histories. See especially chapter eleven, "Memory and Forgetting" (87–206).
12. In addition to Richard Lay as Mackenzie, members of the Benham, Harris, and Hamilton families played their ancestors in *The Spirit of Shivaree*.
13. We are quoting from the videotape, The Spirit of Shivaree: *Eramosa Community Play, June 1990*. (Guelph: Hamilton/Fox). The final phrase is not included in the published script. See page 56.
14. For a political analysis of the distinction between *locus* and *platea* see Robert Weimann, *Shakespeare and the Popular Tradition in the Theater* (Baltimore: Johns Hopkins UP, 1978), 73–85 *et passim*.
15. This winning of the imaginative assent of the audience in the making of history as myths of origin is the typical technique of James Reaney in his *Donnelly* cycle and elsewhere. See Richard Paul Knowles, "Replaying History: Canadian Historiographic Metadrama." *Dalhousie Review* 67, 2.3 (Summer/Fall 1987): 228–43. The term "carnivalesque," and the concept of carnival, derive from M. M. Bakhtin, and are most fully articulated in his book, *Rabelais and his World*, trans. Helene Iswolsky (Bloomington: Indiana UP, 1984).
16. These "testimonials" mixed "actual" statements by community members with scripted perspectives prepared by Hamilton.

Works Cited

Anderson, Benedict. *Imagined Communities: Reflections on the Origin and Spread of Nationalism*. Revised ed. London: Verso, 1991.

Bellah, Robert, Richard Madsen, William M. Sullivan, Ann Swidler, and Steven M. Tipton. *Habits of the Heart: Individualism and Commitment in American Life*. Berkeley: U. of California Press, 1985.

Brooks, Chris. *A Public Nuisance: A History of the Mummers Troupe*. St. John's: Institute of Social and Economic Research, Memorial University of Newfoundland, 1988.

Dignity and Grace: The Story of the Eramosa Community Play The Spirit of Shivaree. Produced and directed by Charlie Fox and Mark Hamilton. Guelph: Hamilton/Fox, 1992.

Hamilton, Dale Colleen. The Spirit of Shivaree: *A Community Play for Eramosa Township*. Toronto: Playwrights Union of Canada, 1990.

Hilton, Julian. "The Other Oxfordshire Theatre: the Nature of Community Art and Action." *Theatre Quarterly* 9.33 (1979): 60. Quoted in Kershaw (61).

Howard, Tony. "Theatre of Urban Renewal; the Uncomfortable Case of Covent Garden." *Theatre Quarterly* 10.38 (1980): 43. Quoted in Kershaw (62).

Kershaw, Baz. *The Politics of Performance: Radical Theatre as Cultural Intervention*. London & New York: Routledge. 1992.

Little, Edward J. and R. Alex Sim. *Dramatic Action: How Eramosa Township Faced its Problems*. Guelph: Ontario Rural Learning Association in cooperation with the School of Rural Planning, University of Guelph, 1992.

Oram, Jon. "The Marriage of Two Minds." Colway publicity material. Eramosa Community Play Archives, U. of Guelph.

Phillips, Derek L. *Looking Backward: A Critical Appraisal of Communitarian Thought*. Princeton: Princeton UP, 1993.

Stallybrass, Peter and Allon White. *The Politics and Poetics of Transgression*. Ithaca, NY: Cornell UP, 1986.

Williams, Raymond. *The Long Revolution* Harmondsworth: Penguin, 1965. Quoted in Kershaw (29).

Change the Story:
Narrative Strategies in Two Radio Plays

by Ann Jansen

> Make up a story. Narrative is radical, creating
> us at the very moment it is being created.
> —Toni Morrison, *When Language Dies*

"We live immersed in narrative." So Peter Brooks states in *Reading for the Plot*, describing how "Our lives are ceaselessly intertwined with narrative, with the stories that we tell and hear told, those we dream or imagine or would like to tell, all of which are reworked in that story of our own lives that we narrate to ourselves in an episodic, sometimes semi-conscious but virtually uninterrupted monologue" (3). While concurring that lives are shaped by and into narratives, I question the necessarily "ceaseless" nature of this intertwining as well as the seemingly unmediated source of the self-made story in the above description. If we live immersed in an endless wash of narrative, it is high time to come up for air before once again diving into the wreckage.

Although we are the stories we tell, we are also the stories we are told. Even as we narrate our own lives, plotting the past and planning the future, external narratives shape our singular story-telling. Meta or master narratives, including history—the "narrative of mastery" (Wallace 139)—weigh upon our personal and collective storytelling. The weight bears more heavily on some, those on the outside fringes of the storytelling circle. Certain narratives and narrators (God's scribes) have been

---

ANN JANSEN has been a producer with the Performance department of CBC Radio since 1993. Prior to that, she was a script editor with CBC Radio Drama for five years. She has edited two anthologies of radio plays, and her academic work focusses on feminist and post-colonial drama.

privileged in shaping the validity and viewpoint, the subject and matter of any shared story. Some stories have been left out, some storytellers silenced. More telling still, most stories are presented as a complete package, with size and shape to be taken for granted. Still, some tales are structured to highlight the process and product of narrative, unwrapping the story. Radio drama in particular, with its easy allowance for various styles of narration and its fluid time-shifting, can break the usual forward momentum of a told story.

Most narrative theorizing has focused on fiction, on the narrator, whether hidden or in full view, and the narratee/receiver inscribed in the text. Drama, with its very different configuration of actors and audiences, has generally been left out of the discussion. In *A Dictionary of Narratology*, Gerald Prince states "Moreover, a dramatic performance representing (many fascinating) events does not constitute a narrative either, since these events, rather than being recounted, occur directly on stage" (58). In this approach, the narratee receives the narrative, rather than shaping her own narrative from the information presented by a variety of narrators, in turn fronting for the author (and implied author). At the very least, this approach ignores the frequent use of overt storytelling in theatre. Moreover, drama does work toward constructing narratives on three levels: the narrative shaping of the play on the part of the playwright, mediated in turn by performance; storytelling within the play, whether direct or indirect; and the narratives shaped out of that presentation by the audience.

Elin Diamond's definition of narrativity leads us to a broader, more useful understanding of the narrative process in theatre. In "Refusing the Romanticism of Identity," she describes narrativity as "the process by which a spectator of any representational medium will construct a narrative, i.e., a causal chain of events moving toward a telos or completion" (94). Process rather than product, narrativity includes the activities of the receiver of the narrative, while narrative itself is more than simply the recounting of actions by a narrator. This opens narrative to a variety of interventions on the part of the playwright and interpretations on the part of the spectator.

Narrative is a function of timing, with events ordered and placed in relation to each other. In fiction, a variety of narrative devices allow movement forward and back within the text. The stage works differently, with its eternal present informing even flashbacks and the infrequent use of narration. Diamond suggests that the tyranny of the linear plot can be loosened on stage, with the audience invited to rethink its narrativizing urge:

> Feminist artists in theatre are well placed to exploit the coercive structure of narrative, for though the theatre emphasizes one temporality—a series of "presents"—it assumes another—a story-line or narrative which is inferred by the spectator on viewing the dramatic representation. (95)

By highlighting challenges to the plot through narrative interruptions, feminist playwrights and theatre artists undermine the usual narratives ("The king died, then the queen died of grief," "They lived happily ever after").

A variety of storytelling stances and narration styles within dramas can be used to highlight and challenge conventional narrativity. The means at hand differ with the medium. If theatre is left out of much discussion about narrative, radio drama is further marginalized. This may be because of radio drama's apparent simplicity as a storytelling form; more likely, it has to do with radio drama's waning cultural importance since the advent of film and television. We live in an age driven by images, and books and radio compete with the ongoing seduction of visual media. Yet, all over the world writers and other artists are still fascinated by the possibilities of radio, whether they are creating through a conventional radio dramaturgy or experimenting in sound.

One of these writers, Angela Carter, describes radio plays as three-dimensional storytelling. While sharing a lack of visuals with traditional, oral storytelling, radio drama escapes that form's reliance on a linear line of events ("And then ... But then ..."), instead playing fruitful games with time:

> Radio may not offer visual images but its resources blur this linearity, so that a great number of things can happen at the same time. Yet, as with all forms of story-telling that are composed in words, not in visual images, radio always leaves that magical and enigmatic margin, that space of the invisible, which must be filled in by the imagination of the listener. (*Come Unto These Yellow Sands* 7)

Carter terms this open-endedness radio drama's third dimension. Radio drama invites the listener to contribute to the narrative or narratives, imagining all the visuals from the sounds and words provided on air. Given this invitation and the medium's freedom of movement, radio plays can readily be structured in ways that challenge traditional story shapes.

As on stage, there is room for a variety of perspectives, points of view or focalisations. Plays can present a number of characters, rather than one authored narrative. Beyond having her attention focused by certain directorial decisions (lighting, placement, etc.), the audience member at a theatre presentation has the freedom to gaze up, down or sideways. Radio is more akin to film in fixing a position, the microphone acting in a way similar to the camera; it also shares film's ability to move in time and space (although such manoeuvres are much less expensive in radio). Yet, unlike film, radio leaves all the visuals up to the listener. And, unlike both stage and film, the radio play lends itself to narration of all kinds, further opening the range of perspectives and allowing for differing positioning of voices.

Radio, with its reliance on the voice, varnished or unvarnished, allows for direct address, interior monologue and other narrative possibilities, mixing "telling" in with the drama's "showing" (through dialogue and sound). Audio drama ranges from the plainest storytelling, monologues, through a mingling of a variety of narrative styles and dramatic scenes to strictly dramatic, unnarrated plays. This continuum of storytelling and dramatic representation is enriched by the medium's ability to play tricks with time and space: scenes can be quickly shifted and past, present, and future shuffled easily. While radio moves forward in time—listeners do not have the luxury of turning back a page—dramatic time is malleable because of the medium's ability to replay a moment and switch tenses in a second. All this means that radio drama provides a rich opportunity for writers to interrupt the ceaseless waves of received narrative, to challenge the expected desire for a conventional beginning, middle and end.

In the two plays to be considered here, Sharon Pollock's *The Making of Warriors* and Baņuta Rubess's *No. Here Comes Ulrike Meinhof*, a number of narrative strategies are used to interpolate new stories into the apparently seamless weave of history. Pollock uses different narrative and dramatic styles to draw links between the stories of two activists from different races, classes, and centuries. Rubess refigures the actions of an infamous German terrorist in a meta-dramatic presentation, then brings Ulrike Meinhof back to life to challenge this depiction of her subversive activities. Both plays were produced for CBC Radio while I was a script editor in the Radio Drama department. Pollock's play was commissioned for "Morningside," CBC Radio's national morning program, as part of a festival of plays linked with the Second International

Women Playwrights' Festival in 1992. Rubess's play was one of two she wrote for "Adventure Stories for (big) Girls," a series she produced for the Studio '92 and '93 programs on CBC Stereo. I worked as dramaturge on the "Adventure Stories" series.

Pollock and Rubess play with the narrative and timely possibilities of drama on radio for a purpose, to reshape the histories at hand. In *The Making of Warriors*, Pollock uses multiple narrators and a combination of storytelling, fact-finding and drama to interweave two different biographies. While Rubess does not use a narrator per se in *No. Here Comes Ulrike Meinhof*, the play-within-the-play employs a variety of reportorial voices in a framing narrative. The docudrama posits first-person accounts from various witnesses, whose versions of events are in turn challenged by the ghost of a dead woman. The playwrights remake these women's stories, while focussing attention on how their narratives are being shaped and delivered.

The Making of Warriors involves the stories of three women, two historical figures and a third, fictional character, with the play focussing on two seemingly very different subjects. Sarah Moore Grimke, a nineteenth-century American suffragist, was one of the first to draw attention to correspondences between black slavery and the oppression of women. Here her story is related by means of a fairly conventional dramaturgy, aided by some narration. Anna Mae Pictou Aquash, a Micmac activist from Nova Scotia, was murdered in South Dakota in 1976. That storyline is framed in two ways: a reporting voice outlines the details of Anna Mae Pictou Aquash's life and murder, while a more personal voice angles into Aquash's death in a specific way. Both women are on the margins of history: Grimke's activities are recorded, but little known, while Aquash's murder was hushed up and her story has faded from public discourse.

Throughout the drama, Pollock uses a combination of narrative styles, storytelling, fact-finding and drama, presented through a range of subjective and seemingly "objective" voices. As the play begins, the three unnamed female narrators repeat fragments of the phrase "the making of warriors," then take turns to say "an exploration of," "a story about," "a personal reminiscence" (105). While each has a specific role in relation to a story, on occasion the three speak as a chorus or comment on events in the other story. Their subjects' lives are brought closer by this means, as well as through the use of overlapping dialogue, intercut scenes, and echoing words and phrases. All these techniques serve to highlight similarities between the two women's struggles, while building an insistent, purposeful rhythm in the play.

In one scene, Sarah's brother sets strict boundaries for his sister, who asks in dismay: "If Greek and Latin and Law are denied me ... what can I study?" The "realistic" dramatic scene is interrupted by the three narrators, who suggest:

> WOMAN ONE: A little French
> WOMAN THREE: and watercolour technique
> WOMAN ONE: white on white embroidery
> WOMAN THREE: and harpsichord lessons. (112–113)

Sarah hears these voices and responds with some bitterness, but the Sarah who speaks is not the same age as in the scene, is rather an aged woman. This lesson was clearly learned late in life. This interchange and others demonstrate how important it is for women to share their understanding, information, and stories.

Sarah's story is to some extent the expected one for her days. The early scenes portray her family's attempts to subvert her "unwomanly aspirations," to silence her protests against injustice, both personal and societal. While the strict socializing does not completely contain or control her, at various points in her life, Sarah is indeed silenced. Once, at Sunday school, she is called on the carpet for teaching slaves to read. The instructor forbids her to do anything beyond *tell* stories: "Miss Sarah, the meanin' a the word 'oral' in 'oral catechism' means 'oral'—" (109). These stories are controlled: only the rich white class is allowed first-hand access to these narratives. Similarly, Sarah is only allowed to shape her own life within limitations and as permitted by the men in charge, her father and brother. Her mother is never heard from—she is too busy raising thirteen children born in eighteen years.

After the constrictions of her early days (she is always being told to "shush"), Sarah comes into her own as an adult. She joins with her sister in speaking publicly on the rights of slaves and of women. This could seem like the climax of her story, a happy ending, but her tale is not yet finished. Instead, both women leave the public platform, Angelina because of her marriage and child-rearing responsibilities, Sarah because she is wounded by the harsh criticisms of her brother-in-law. For a time, Sarah actually disappears from the play, and her chauvinistic brother-in-law, a voice of authority, is heard holding forth on women's lot in life. Being silenced is central to *The Making of Warriors*—and silence is a powerful tool on radio, where characters not heard from or mentioned for a time disappear. Still, Sarah does rebound after this quelling. She publishes a book on women's rights and lobbies for women's votes. She makes another woman's story known through her translation of Lamartine's biography of Joan of Arc—learning more than a little French to do so. Although her sister never re-enters the public realm, Sarah will no longer be shushed.[1]

The play's other story is about someone who has been much more effectively silenced—through murder. Throughout *The Making of Warriors*, Anna Mae Pictou Aquash never appears as a character. Her voice is never heard. Rather, her struggles are conveyed through the recountings of two narrators, both white women. In scene two, all three narrators invite someone to "Come on." "Now. Now" (105). The listener is invited into the drama, but also into a car. The sound direction reads: "Car door closes; key in ignition; engine turns over; car pulls away. *We are inside*" (105 [my emphasis]). That car belongs to Woman One, who is the most personal of the narrators and the only one identified in any way.

Woman One, who describes herself as a fifty-four-year-old, slightly overweight white woman, spends the drama recounting an earlier journey, reminding us again and again of the day she drove through the Pine Ridge Reserve in South Dakota: "I didn't stop. Why should I stop? I was just ... passing through. On my way" (106). But as she drives on, she looks into her rear-view mirror to watch the men standing by the roadside, staring down at "something red":

> They no longer saw me yet I saw them, I saw them shift in the rear-view mirror, shift their ambiguous neutral gaze from the receding car to something on the shoulder of the road. (113)

Later, through the reporting of Woman Two, we understand that the bundle of red was the murdered body of Anna Mae Pictou Aquash. And later still, Woman One chooses to reverse the choice she made in that moment.

Although she did not stop that day, Woman One spends her time in the drama circling back to that place and time again and again. As she puts it, "The moment sticks" (130). She keeps describing the scene, refusing to let it go, until we all have an image of what she might have seen, of what we might as easily have driven by, just passing through. This is akin to the endless rehearsal of Wilson Harris's fiction, a means of recuperating a denied presence from the past. In Harris's words:

> I know that in unravelling the illusory capture of creation I may still apprehend the obsessional ground of conquest, rehearse its proportions, excavate its consequences, within a

play of shadow and light; a play that is infinite rehearsal, a play that approaches again and again a sensation of ultimate meaning residing within a deposit of ghosts relating to the conquistadorial body—as well as the victimized body—of new worlds and old worlds ... new stars and old constellations within the workshop of the gods. (quoted in Maes-Jelinek 232)

Similarly, Pollock's character rehearses a new response to an old situation. At the end of the play, Woman One does turn around, in a sense going back and forward at the same time. By then, she has company. The three narrators are once again together, their voices increasingly interwoven as they describe the last days of Sarah Moore Grimke alongside the murder of Anna Mae Pictou Aquash.

Buttressing Woman One's perspective is the information relayed by another of the narrators. Woman Two reports not only the facts of Anna Mae Pictou Aquash's life, but also her subject's "feelings" and attitudes. While pinning her reporting on specific dates and other verifiable details of a life, Woman Two does stray into more subjective territory: "Anna Mae Pictou Aquash is divorced. Anna Mae Pictou Aquash. Is strong" (113); "Anna Mae patrols the camp's perimeter at night. She is calm ... She misses her two girls who are with their father in Nova Scotia" (119). At times, Woman Two seems less objective than omniscient. Her tone grows more and more familiar, until she is on a first-name basis with Anna Mae. Although Pollock's directions indicate that Woman Two is a cool reporter type ("formal, neutral, factual" [104]), in the CBC Radio production the actor became more heated and involved, which may have been dictated by the growing intimacy and urgency of the details being related.

While clearly positioning Woman One as a fictional—even authorial—voice, the drama does not detail the characters or perspectives of both Woman Three and Woman Two. Woman One is everywoman, an ordinary person who represents the listener. Woman Three occupies fairly traditional narrative territory and remains quite characterless. Only Woman Two in a sense steps out of character. Her increasingly personal approach to Anna Mae Pictou Aquash's life is never clearly positioned. After using objective, reportorial techniques to build believability, she quickly shifts into opinion, as when she repeatedly remarks upon what "Some people say" in relation to Anna Mae Pictou Aquash's killing. Her dismissal of those reports benefits from the authority derived from her earlier fact-finding stance. This dissonance may work to make listeners question the similarly unidentified stance of other media authorities, displaying how difficult it is for even an "objective" reporter to remain outside a story. In a sense, a standoffish viewpoint is impossible in this drama about involvement.

The play ends with a call to action involving all three narrators and their listeners. Two of the narrators complete a declaration by Sarah, underlining the continuity of the struggle and the community of women:

> SARAH: ... But I say I am a free agent
> WOMAN ONE: gifted with intelligence
> WOMAN TWO: and endowed with immortality! (131)

Sarah insists that she will not cease her struggle: "Not till the day I die. *(Chuckles.)* Not even then" (132). The announcement of Sarah's death is followed by a statement that "Anna Mae Pictou Aquash lives" (132). Her story has not ended. Acknowledging the end of Sarah's life even as her exhortations continue, Woman One invites the listener to "get in." Two slamming doors show that the other two narrators have joined her, ready to return and play a part in the struggle. The task for the listener ("Come on") is also, in the three women's words, to "Remember," "remember," "remember" (132). Then the car pulls away.

The Making of Warriors brings far things near and draws lines between different centuries and women. In its drive to draw links among a community of women, the play may smooth out the differences *between* women and political struggles. Pollock seems to be operating on a model of inclusion as a means of compelling a community to action. Although the historical women's stories are given equal time, the manner of telling differs greatly. There are indeed correspondences between the stories. In an interview forming part of the introduction to *The Making of Warriors*, Pollock described how the language used to justify women's limited roles in the last century is similar to current usage in rhetoric that resists aboriginal rights (101). Still, the differences are also great. One woman is white, upper-class and from the nineteenth century, the other a much poorer Native woman living in the twentieth century. Sexism operated in Sarah Moore Grimke's life, but both racism and sexism worked against Anna Mae Pictou Aquash.

One might argue that although the Native woman never speaks, she is present in the drama. As well as being the focus of attention of two narrators, Anna Mae Pictou Aquash is brought to mind by the Native drumming and chanting underscoring her story. Although the chanting conveys a mood, rather than specific information, it does bring in a Native voice, one unscripted by a playwright worried about appropriation of voice. Sharon Pollock spoke of her strategy in having different narrators to convey this story:

> I thought I could have voices that are speaking directly to the listener, some of it seeming like objective news, some of it seeming like very subjective experience and some of it dramatization. Maybe I *could* tell Anna Mae's story without assuming the voice of the other, by making it objective and making evident my white perspective as much as possible. (101)

Finally, Anna Mae Pictou Aquash's absence as a character may be more powerful than her presence. Through the narrators' storytelling, we are reminded of her erasure and of the need to continue to focus attention on this story. In the end, Pollock's strategy may be to make audiences uneasy, to leave them wondering about who has access to telling stories. The drama returns to significant moments, looking back and asking listeners to turn their attention to a seemingly finished story. It paves a way for us to be able to hear this and other silenced voices in the future.

While Ulrike Meinhof has not been as effectively banished from public notice as the figures in *The Making of Warriors*, Rubess's play poses questions about the ways in which Meinhof's story has been presented by the media. Rubess also uses a strategy of juxtaposing styles and storylines in *No. Here Comes Ulrike Meinhof*. The play begins with a mock and somewhat overheated docudrama, supposedly being broadcast from a CBC studio. After being firmly established, this play is interrupted by Meinhof's materialization in studio. There she interacts with a female radio engineer, a character modelled on an actual CBC employee, Joanne Anka—who played the role in the original production. Through this meta(radio)theatricality, action shifting between "real" time and fictional time, Rubess highlights the problematic nature of retelling/reshaping history.

Meinhof has been the subject of a number of sensational books and movies in the last years. Partaking in those records' excesses, Rubess's mock play seems to assume that listeners will enjoy a similar exposé. At the beginning, this dramatic record of Meinhof's life follows a roughly chronological order, framed by interjections from a number of witnesses. No single narrator welcomes us into the story or focuses our attention. Rather, Ulrike herself arrives to denounce the docudrama's excesses.

Even then, we are left wondering about what really happened, because this character is a ghost who at times seems quite unhinged and is certainly violent. Eventually, the focus turns to the listeners, to their competing desires for a good story and for the "truth." Rubess presents an interpretation of Meinhof's life that undercuts the docudrama's "official" story, while teasing us with the voyeuristic pleasures of dramatized biography.

In the docudrama, a trio of narrative voices act as a chorus, mythologizing Ulrike Meinhof while describing elements of her public and private life. The Inspector describes Ulrike as an evil, powerful figure ("She was the toughest case of my career" [154]); Rohl's musings display his jaundiced opinion of his ex-wife; and Claudia, a socialite pal, burbles on about style and the surprises Ulrike afforded them. In addition, reports come from news readers from the BBC and the American Forces Network. The testimony, opinions, and news bulletins pile up. At one point in the drama, all these voices of authority pick up on each other's sentences, weaving a seamless, "official" version of the terrorist's activities.

In the docudrama, Ulrike herself is depicted as a journalist, though her reporting never strives for "objectivity," and is rather intensely politicized. The journalists' impersonal and anonymous radio voices are contrasted with her impassioned style. Several times she speaks publicly to rally the populace. Later she is seized, imprisoned and silenced. But the story does not end with the usual death. Instead, Ulrike is resurrected, at least in the drama. She materializes in the studio during the broadcast of this biography; in fact, her presence overrides and interrupts the drama. It is significant that she arrives soon after the docudrama "witnesses" have begun to talk about the mystery of her death: was it suicide or murder? Claudia's speech—"Eight months in isolation in a bare white cell, fluorescent lights that are never turned off, absolute silence, absolute sensory deprivation" (159)—seems to be the trigger that moves Ulrike into urgent speech.

Ulrike is wafted into being out of her silence, through her own words. As described in the sound directions, she is brought into the studio through radio technology: "Phone drops, electric sparkle of a thousand wires as Ulrike Meinhof's ghost transubstantiates in STUDIO G" (160). Throughout her time in the studio, Ulrike protests against the docudrama's version of events, even as that play returns in short bursts to override her "presence." As well as fighting against her life story, Ulrike strives to speak directly to the listening public.

> ULRIKE: Members of the oppressed. *(To JOANNE.)* Where am I?
> JOANNE: Studio G. You know. Studio G, CBC. Toronto, Ontario, Canada, planet Earth, whatever.
> ULRIKE: We address you from the colony of American imperialism, Toronto. We object to this broadcast. We have taken the studio and its workers hostage and will not release them until the truth is told. (161)

Ulrike believes she is still on a mission, and that she is not alone. Again and again, she demands that Joanne connect her with the listeners: "I have a statement to make, dammit" (162).

Rubess clearly has a purpose in foregrounding the ways in which both drama and radio operate. As explained by Stanton Garner, "Any way by which a play calls attention to its unreality, to its status as fictional construct, highlights the audience's expectation of narrative form" (183). Metadramatic techniques also interrupt an audience's desire for a completed narrative. The question of just where the drama comes from is strongly raised when one story contradicts another. Beyond this focus on the source of the drama, Rubess also challenges our trust in the medium. Should we believe all that we hear on radio? *No.* introduces us to some of the people behind the broadcast, the engineer and the maintenance man, reminding us that fallible humans make and transmit the play.

Rubess plays with other audience expectations, as when she has Joanne appeal to the audience to phone someone and save her. Presumably, no one calls. As well as working on the level of meta-radio, the play also uses conventions specific to the CBC. During Ulrike's speech about the numbing effects of consumption, the score being played is a tape supposedly left behind by another program. It is the theme from "Morningside," a welcoming piece of music heard weekdays across the nation and signalling a certain kind of down-home current affairs storytelling. During her speech to her Canadian public, Ulrike finally notices the music:

> ULRIKE: ... You don't have a life. You have a wallet. And it blinds you to the fact that people are dying in Vietnam, the Americans are bombing peaceful villages, women and children writhing from the wounds inflicted by—Change this music, bitch! Change this music! You are trying to kill me with this music! (162–163)

The normality introduced by the music (we are listening calmly to the reliable CBC) is shattered, as our expectations of the docudrama have been earlier.

The comments on radio and communications are fitting for this biography. Ulrike understands the uses of radio as a political tool for state—or terrorist—persuasion. As she says to Joanne, "I have lectured at the institute of Media Studies at the Free University of Berlin on the possibility of Agitation and Education in Radio Features and this drama is a crime" (167–168). Still, she is not successful in keeping the drama from CBC listeners. At the end, she disappears just as abruptly as she arrives, and all that remains is a drawn-out scream: "Nooooooooo!" Although not able to erase the drama, Ulrike does throw its version of events into question.

Only after the drama has run for some time does the dead Ulrike appear. By this time, the style and tone of the play about her life have been firmly established: listeners are meant to assume that this is the real play. But the apparent trustworthiness of the biography is problematized even before Ulrike's arrival. Listeners are alerted to discrepancies, given the different versions of events and the ulterior agendas of the witnesses. The scenes in the embedded play are based on the testimony of obviously biased players in Ulrike's life. Ulrike's husband is shown brutalizing her. The Inspector's comment on Ulrike's upbringing ("You see! Trained against the state from the very beginning!" [155]) follows on a scene where Ulrike's mother has just announced: "Hitler has capitulated. This means no more fear! No more lies in Germany!" (155). Does this prove that Ulrike received childhood lessons in subversion and treason, as the Inspector insists? Whose truth (story) is this?

The divergence between facts and truth is also pointed out by another patently unreliable witness, Ulrike herself. When she rails against the drama, Joanne tries to calm her.

> JOANNE: I guess the writer got the facts wrong.
> ULRIKE: Facts are irrelevant. The people need the truth.
> JOANNE: I work on so many of these dramas I don't even listen any more. It's up to the producers to check the facts.
> ULRIKE: Not the facts, the truth.
> JOANNE: But the facts *are* the truth.
>   (MUSIC: "If I Had a Rocket Launcher" stops.)
> ULRIKE: *This* is the truth. I am a prisoner of war. I am fighting a war on your behalf. (168)

Despite her volatile rage, Ulrike is unable to control the official version of her life, and the drama displaces her. It blares up several times, increasingly out of control, with chronology jumbled. Once a scene is repeated, in which Ulrike is being trained—unsuccessfully—to throw bombs in Jordan. The bomb she holds is *not* thrown twice.

While Ulrike shouts at her public (CBC listeners) to "wake up" and say "*No!*", she ignores Joanne's polite protestations. Clearly, Ulrike's version of reality is also one-sided. We are reminded that she is a fictional construct, particularly because the same actor plays Ulrike in both time frames. Also, Ulrike in the present is unable to listen to the one person in front of her. This ghost is a monologic character, unable to see anyone or anything outside the frame of her own polemic. While claiming sisterly solidarity with Joanne, Ulrike frequently threatens to shoot her. She has no recognition of the difference between their stories.

> ULRIKE: We working mothers are all the same. We know what it's like to suffocate from the children and the lies, we know how we feel when we throw plates at our husbands, when we shut the windows before we scream that we just can't stand it any more.
> JOANNE: Yeah. Um. Actually, I'm not married.
> ULRIKE: *That's a detail!* I am just like you. We are women.
> (165)

In effect, Ulrike is deaf to others, just as others have been deaf to her.

Through the interaction of the commanding Ulrike and the unassuming, kindly character Joanne, Rubess brings up questions of class and power. She shows how Ulrike's narrative actually leaves out "the people," i.e. Joanne. The play also points up the differences between women, while showing how any story is shaped in the telling. Where Pollock invites listeners into a community of women, Rubess seems interested in examining the places where women's circumstances and politics differ. She also foregrounds questions about how we listen to radio, whether factual or fictional, about how stories are formed—and deformed.

Joanne is partly won over by Ulrike's take on reality, as witnessed by her dismissal of the maintenance man, Biff, as a "lackey" when he fails to believe her story about being visited by Ulrike Meinhof (171). Also, the hostage-taking contains at least one moment of connection between the two women.[2] Ulrike briefly forsakes her obsession with her self-proclaimed platform to notice that Joanne is a human being with needs. Joanne has been complaining about the cold; finally Ulrike gives the other woman her coat. After Ulrike's disappearance, the coat is the only thing that proclaims her presence. That small action in a sense changes her story, though not in the grand way Ulrike earlier demanded.

> ULRIKE: Change it.
> JOANNE: Change what?!
> ULRIKE: I jump out the window. No one is shot. We topple the government. The stores burn to ashes. Get me new actors. I want a new script. (170)

While no change is possible in Ulrike Meinhof's actual life and death, there is always the possibility of a new script.

What do playwrights do when they long to change a previously played out story? The historical subjects in these dramas did live and die, and their biographies have taken a certain shape. As Angela Carter describes it, "Yet the end of all stories, even if the writer forebears to mention it, is death, which is where our time stops short" (2). But, as she goes on to state, we also use stories to stave off death. Both Rubess and Pollock take their characters beyond death. While it is not that any of these historical women actually live, their stories do continue. And if the playwright cannot change the outline—the murders, the suicides—she can at least get into the story, returning and remembering.

The task faced by writers interested in reclaiming lost stories is how to tell history from the point of view of the vanquished. It seems impossible to end the story on a note of victory—yet how does one stop dead and still suggest the possibility of change? The answer may be to extend past events into the future. The storytelling in *The Making of Warriors* works via repetition and return, but the narrators open the story rather than close it as the play ends. The story continues to be written, given the invitation to listeners to move forward together, or, at the very least, to remember. In *No. Here Comes Ulrike Meinhof*, Rubess brings Ulrike back to state her own confused and ultimately indefensible case, not so much to set the record straight as to highlight the shaping of stories. Her play emphasises the need to pay attention to the storytellers, to examine the methods of the record-keepers.

Both Pollock and Rubess write "beyond the ending," to use Rachel Blau DuPlessis's evocative phrase.

> Narrative in the most general terms is a version of, or a special expression of ideology: representations by which we construct and accept values and institutions ... The invention of

strategies that sever the narrative from formerly conventional structures and consciousness about women is what I call "writing beyond the ending." (x)

These plays insist that characters live on past the usual finale. Meanwhile, the two playwrights examine the beginnings and middles of their stories, working in different ways toward rewriting history and creating conscious narratives. By writing beyond the usual ending, death, the playwrights create the possibility for new beginnings. The plays also invite listeners to pay attention to the process of forming new narratives within the play, while alerting each listener to her own part in shaping the story.

Interestingly, neither play uses internal monologue, the most intimate manifestation of narration on radio. Such highly personal voices appear to give "the inside story." These two plays avoid such definitive stances, instead employing narrative techniques that throw into question how stories are told and heard. Just as the truly omniscient or anonymous narrator is of little use in these conscious narratives, so too the stories are fractured into a number of perspectives. Rather than a single point-of-view (or hearing), the plays position a variety of characters within the drama. Of course, radio drama often uses a single intimate and confiding narrator. Moving along a narrative continuum, the storytellers of radio drama whisper or speak out to listeners within and outside the drama. Other characters turn their awareness inward, allowing listeners to float along the streams of their consciousness. Depending on the intentions of the author of their thoughts, the listener may or may not be alerted to the various currents of all these stories.

Notes

1. Underscoring this movement from suppression to greater autonomy is the music associated with Sarah's drama. The brittle and polite sounds of a harpsichord, often accompanied by tinkling tea cups, segues into scenes depicting Sarah's upper-class but restrictive life. When Sarah comes into her own, the harpsichord is lost: one scene begins with her humming her own song. Her sister, on the other hand, starts learning to play the harpsichord in later life to please her husband.

2. Both story lines, the docudrama and the hostage-taking, have such a key moment, a shift in Ulrike's relationship with other players. In the docudrama, however, Ulrike is shown moving toward a more public self rather than making a personal connection with another human being. While assisting in the prison break of Andreas Baader, Ulrike makes an unexpected break for freedom herself. She leaps out a window in the library, escaping from a place where stories of certain shapes are bound and stored.

Works Cited

Brooks, Peter. *Reading for the Plot: Design and Intention in Narrative*. New York: Alfred A. Knopf, 1984.

Carter, Angela. *Come Unto These Yellow Sands*. Newcastle upon Tyne: Bloodaxe Books Ltd., 1985.

——————. *Expletives Deleted: Selected Writings*. London: Chatto & Windus, 1992.

Diamond, Elin. "Refusing the Romanticism of Identity: Narrative Interventions in Churchill, Benmussa, Duras." *Performing Feminisms: Feminist Critical Theory and Theatre*. Ed. Sue-Ellen Case. Baltimore: Johns Hopkins University Press, 1990. 92–105.

DuPlessis, Rachel Blau. *Writing beyond the Ending: Narrative Strategies of Twentieth-Century Women Writers*. Bloomington: Indiana University Press, 1985.

Garner, Jr., Stanton B. *The Absent Voice: Narrative Comprehension in the Theater*. Urbana and Chicago: University of Illinois Press, 1989.

Maes-Jelinek, Hena. "The Muse's Progess: 'Infinite Rehearsal' in J.M. Coetzee's *The Foe*." *A Shaping of Connections*. Eds. Hena Maes-Jelinek, Kirsten Holst Petersen and Anna Rutherford. Sydney: Dangaroo Press, 1989. 232–242.

Pollock, Sharon. "*The Making of Warriors*." *Airborne: Radio Plays by Women*. Ed. Ann Jansen. Winnipeg: Blizzard Publishing, 1991. 99–132.

Prince, Gerald. *The Dictionary of Narratology*. Lincoln: University of Nebraska Press, 1987.

Rubess, Baṇuta. *No. Here Comes Ulrike Meinhof. Adventures for (Big) Girls*. Ed. Ann Jansen. Winnipeg: Blizzard Publishing, 1993. 149–172.

Wallace, Michele. "Untitled." *Critical Fictions: The Politics of Imaginative Writing*. Ed. Philomena Mariani. Seattle: Bay Press, 1991. 139–142.

Native Drama:
A Celebration of Native Culture

by Agnes Grant

Native literature, that is, literature produced by Aboriginal authors, is a relatively recent phenomenon. Maria Campbell's autobiography, *Halfbreed* (1973), now considered a seminal work by many, stood as a lonely forerunner of the literature that was to follow for almost ten years. Steady production by Native writers is now filling the gaps in every genre, providing insights into Canadian Aboriginal cultures rarely glimpsed before. Nowhere is this more evident than in the field of drama.

That drama is a particularly appealing genre should come as no surprise. Love of ritual, pantomime and rich body language were integral aspects of traditional storytelling. Sanders and Peak, in *Literature of the American Indian*, point out that in traditional times poetry (songs) had four interrelated elements—words, music, body movements and the belief of the singer/dancer (43). Songs and stories, in traditional times, were much more than mere words. The facial expressions, the movements of the body whether suggested or in pantomime, were integral parts of the performance—and every storytelling event was, indeed, a performance.

Seidelman and Turner reported that among the Inuit, early collectors found the dramatic skill of the storytellers to be so great that they could

---

AGNES GRANT works for the Brandon University Northern Teacher Education Program where she teaches Native Literature courses. She is the editor of *Our Bit of Truth: An Anthology of Canadian Native Literature* (Pemmican), a co-author of *Joining the Circle: A Practioners' Guide to Responsive Education for Native Students*, and the author of *James McKay: A Metis Builder of Canada* (Pemmican).

follow the stories reasonably well even though they did not speak the language (22).

Herbert Schwarz in *Elik: And Other Stories of the Mackenzie Eskimos* explains just how dramatic the performances were:

> As I sat there and listened to his story there were times when I did not need to understand Eskimo to comprehend his tale. Felix Nuyoviak was not just a story teller, but also a superb actor who lived and acted out the various parts of the story.
>
> With expressive motion he paddled his kayak, he threw a spear, he freed his lines, he sang magic songs. Finally there was triumphant enjoyment on his face as with great effort, he hauled the whale ashore and sprayed it with water as the ancient custom demanded. (170)

West Coast Potlatches have been described as "true drama" by Diamond Jennes; they were complete with costumes, staging and sound effects (203). Much of this Aboriginal artistry was either ignored as colonizers attempted to portray the inhabitants of this land as ignorant savages, or it was suppressed by missionaries and eventually forbidden by laws. It is only in recent times that Canadians generally have become aware of the rich heritage that once existed. Contemporary Aboriginal artists are picking up the strands of this rich heritage, often producing materials which interpret the ancient beliefs and values, albeit in a foreign language and through foreign art forms. The playwright, Tomson Highway, believes Aboriginal artists have not only a unique role, but an obligation to reconstruct this suppressed heritage. He told a Brandon University audience that the little Trickster of Aboriginal mythology was so shocked and insulted when the patriarchal and conquering God of the Europeans came, that it has been passed out under a Main Street, Winnipeg bar table for 500 years. Highway believes it is the task of contemporary Aboriginal artists to "give that little man/woman one good kick in the ass so that he/she can stand up on his or her own two feet again so that we can laugh and dance again" (Address to Brandon University Students). The destruction and suppression of Native languages has made it imperative that English be the main language of communication of these contemporary artists. This is necessary both for the benefit of those members of their own cultures who can no longer communicate in their mother tongues, and serendipitously, it has made the works available to mainstream Canadians.

Though Tomson Highway (Cree) is likely the most well known Canadian Aboriginal playwright today, there are many others. Drew Hayden Taylor (Ojibway), Margo Kane (Saulteaux, Cree, Blackfoot and French), Monique Mojica (Metis) and Daniel David Moses (Ojibway) have all made outstanding contributions to the field of drama and many young, aspiring writers are waiting in the wings. The Society for the Re-Establishment of the Trickster has acted as a catalyst for much Native writing. Works of authors like Jordan Wheeler, Maria Campbell and Thomas King have been adapted for film and television and many vibrant theatre companies are exploring both creative drama and social issues using different venues. Notable in this respect are the Red Roots Theatre Group in Winnipeg, The Upisasik Theatre of Ile-a-la-Cross, Saskatchewan, the De-ba-jeh-mu-jig Theatre Group on Manitoulin Island, Ontario and the well-established Native Earth Performing Arts and Theatre Passe Muraille in Toronto.

Though each playwright brings something unique to the creation of drama many commonalities are found in all the writing. It is, first and foremost, the fact that it is *Native* drama which sets it apart from mainstream Canadian experiences. Not only are the characters in the drama Aboriginal people, but their experiences are those of Aboriginals. Consequently, issues of race, class, colonialism, discrimination, oppression, loss of culture and redefinition of culture are found in all the plays; the differences occur as each playwright brings a unique treatment to these common themes. Humour, pathos, stark realism, rage, and grief are all found in the dramas, but love, joy, optimism, pride, ritual and celebration are also found. "This," the playwrights say, "is what it is to be an Aboriginal person in Canada."

Appropriation of Native materials through literature by non-Native writers is a hotly debated topic in Canada today and "political correctness" is the butt of many a joke. One need only observe that *The Ecstasy of Rita Joe* by the non-Native playwright, George Ryga, is still included in representative Canadian literature courses in high schools and on university campuses while the works of Native playwrights languish on warehouse shelves to make the point that appropriation is an issue of serious concern. Appropriation becomes doubly important in drama as non-Natives may attempt not only to understand, but to interpret, characters from another culture to theatre audiences. *Rita Joe* is a fine play and in its time it carried a profound message to Canadian theatre goers. The message was not new, but had not been transmitted through the medium of drama before. When *Rita Joe* was first performed in

Vancouver it was a resounding success, due in large part to the "authenticity" lent it by the personality of Chief Dan George. That his speech was *not* authentic would not have been recognized, or still is not recognized by theatre goers, but this does not detract from the overall effectiveness of the play. Dan George himself said of his lines:

> My main difficulty was to combine the memory of the lines with the necessary voice tone. This means so much to an Indian. Your people speak with inflection, but our emphasis is quite different and much more subtle, for the range is limited. (Mortimer 23)

Rita Joe does not meet the cadences of the Salish language so it does not ring true for Salish people. It does not meet the style of Salish oral narrative so the metaphors of the white geese and the superb "butterfly" speech remain just that—metaphors that are satisfying for non-Native theatre goers but that do not accurately portray Native ways of being. The character of Dan George was developed to please non-Salish speaking audiences. In the play Native people were interpreted within a Western cultural paradigm but the message of the play was so important that Dan George chose to give theatre-goers what they were looking for. The play, well-intentioned as it was, is rife with stereotypes of one-dimensional Native characters suspended between two cultures, unable to cope in either. Assimilation was official Canadian government policy when Ryga wrote *The Ecstacy of Rita Joe*. Great efforts were being made to educate and mould Indians to become a part of mainstream Canadian society, though the Indians themselves had never been consulted about whether or not assimilation was also their aim. The policy was poorly thought through since racism was rampant and poorly concealed in 1967, and so, the possibility of Indians actually assimilating was non-existent. But it was generally expected that assimilation would take place and that the demise of Indian culture would accompany this assimilation. It was expected that Indians would lose all characteristics that made them uniquely "Indian" and they would become "Canadian," although even today there is no consensus on what that might be. *Rita Joe* has to be judged within that particular time frame and Ryga must be credited with portraying honestly what he knew about Indian people in the city. He was a courageous writer and if he portrayed only a part of reality, he did portray the part he knew with great integrity. Many well-intentioned Canadians were devastated by the play as they recognized their own penchant for doing good and directing the lives of others. Today, the

Native voice must be allowed to speak for itself, unfettered by another culture's interpretations. Lenore Keeshig-Tobias (Ojibway) is outspoken in her insistence that Natives be allowed to tell their own stories. Lutz, in conversation with Keeshig-Tobias points out that appropriators make colonization and dispossession disappear. They displace the whole historical process and they act as if "any culture that there is, is for the having, and can be tapped into by anyone who feels the need for that culture's spirituality, regardless of history and the politics of oppression" (Lutz 81). To understand feelings about appropriation one need only speculate on the reaction if Daniel David Moses or Margo Kane were to write dramas about a Jewish concentration camp in Poland—or on the experiences of the Irish immigrant arriving in Canada, for that matter.

Keeshig-Tobias makes her point cogently:

> I don't think that non-Natives should be telling Native stories. And, of-course, the immediate reaction is: "You are censoring my imagination!" Which makes me wonder why God has given white men such a broad all-encompassing imagination? If it's so broad why can't white men just make up their own fictional cultural society? Why draw Native society? They show us nothing new. They make no new discoveries. They simply embellish and prop up old stereotypes. (Lutz 79)

Maria Campbell supports Keeshig-Tobias' position when she says,

> I couldn't tell your people's story. And I don't need you to tell the story of our people to other white people. How can somebody interpret or tell? How can a white person tell you, another white person, about my community and my people, when he is only coming from half a place? He has to believe the other half, too. He has to believe it's there. (Lutz 58)

Daniel David Moses agrees with Keeshig-Tobias and Campbell. He cites a storyteller who went up to an Inuit community to collect stories and though he admitted to not understanding 75% of what was being told, he still felt free to pass the stories on. Moses goes on,

> And this goes into the appropriation thing. It's when people from the opposite culture try and tell these stories, they don't know what's going on. They are just going to screw them up. I mean, that's what's getting us upset. You say you want the freedom to tell our stories, and then you just screw it up.

> Freedom of the imagination shouldn't be the freedom to destroy. (Lutz 166)

The Book of Jessica: A Theatrical Transformation is a unique contribution to literature, drama and an exploration of the whole concept of appropriation. The non-Native actor, Linda Griffiths and Maria Campbell collaborated in writing the play *Jessica*. It was not an attempt to rewrite Maria's forceful autobiography, *Halfbreed*, but rather to continue with the narrative where *Halfbreed* left off. The experience was very difficult for both of them and when the play was finally completed they collaborated on the book (which includes the play *Jessica*) in order to document the process of writing and workshopping. It also deals with the difficulty an actor from one culture experiences when attempting to portray a person from another culture without misrepresenting or modifying the character to fit the actor's cultural paradigm. Appropriation and a minority group's sensitivities are serious dramatic issues; *The Book of Jessica* is invaluable reading in this area.

The themes and directions of Aboriginal writing present new foci for Canadian drama. The stark realism of Aboriginal history is not overlooked by the Native playwrights. Whether it is historical representations of Aboriginal women in *Princess Pocahontas and the Blue Spots*, the dramatization of the story of Almighty Voice by Daniel David Moses, or contemporary history like the slashing of funds for higher education for status Indians in *Education is Our Right* and the "baby-snatching" of the 1960s in *Someday*, theatre goers are reminded that the treatment of Native people in Canada has left a legacy which mainstream society is still largely ignoring. Tomson Highway stated that he has no concerns about naming people who have harmed Aboriginals in the past. Writing and talking about the past, he believes, is the right of Aboriginal artists. He says that they are no longer afraid to speak out, pointing out that "We have paid and paid" (Address to Brandon University Students). He predicts that many more of these stories will be told as Natives seek release from painful pasts through various art forms and that these artistic creations will contribute to the healing process. Mojica likely speaks for all Native artists when she dedicates her play to her son, Bear, and "towards the next generation of healing" (10). One example of the relentless destruction of culture and its lasting impact on Aboriginal people today is found in Drew Hayden Taylor's *Education is Our Right*. The Residential School teacher explains educational policy when she says, "Here at the school, we believe that in order to save the person, we must first destroy the Indian" (101). Margo Kane in *Moonlodge* also deals with this cultural destruction when she tells how she learned her first "Indian" song, "My Paddle Keen and Bright" when she was a Brownie.

The recognition that Native languages exist and have an impact on a writer's art is a fairly new phenomenon. Playwrights have to be careful to explain and interpret since it can be assumed that only speakers of the language will comprehend. Native languages have been so devalued in Canada that non-Natives have little knowledge of them, hence few clues as to meaning. Because Aboriginal cultures in Canada are so varied and each has a distinctive language, interpretations are necessary not only for non-Native audiences but for Aboriginal actors and audiences from outside the playwrights' cultures as well. Highway uses footnotes, Taylor includes the interpretations in the body of the play, Mojica largely works interpretations into her script. French appears to be her first language and a poignant clue to language loss is found when she credits "Billy Merasty for the Cree language connection" (Mojica 10). Daniel David Moses uses English only in *Coyote City* but in *Almighty Voice and His Wife* he switches to Cree with English interpretations in the script. The satisfying ending not only unites Almighty Voice and his wife, but it does so in Cree. There are others, Kane, for example, who confine themselves to the use of English only, which is also suggestive of language loss.

Native mythology plays an integral part in all Aboriginal literary productions, either directly or indirectly. Drew Hayden Taylor perhaps borrows from Charles Dickens when he introduces spirits of the past, present and future but his spirits are not ghostly apparitions dragging chains. In *Toronto at Dreamer's Rock*, Keesic, the spirit of the past, is dressed in buckskin while the spirit of the future is dressed in "undeniably futuristic garb" (Taylor 30). In *Education is Our Right* the spirits have an ethereal quality and more closely resemble the Trickster of Native mythology. The spirit of the present is dressed in a pow-wow outfit and is angry because she has to fit Indian Affairs minister, "Ebenezer Cadieux," into her very busy schedule. The spirit of the future changes clothes and occupations quickly, in typical Trickster fashion which makes the good minister's head whirl. The shape shifting in Mojica's *Princess Pocahontas and the Blue Spots* is also truly reminiscent of Trickster activities and indeed, in the character descriptions she points out that Princess-Buttered-on-Both-Sides is Coyote, one of the many faces of the Trickster (Mojica 14). The play *Jessica* differs dramatically from Campbell's autobiography both in its mythological characters and in its transformations and shape-shifting. The characters in Moses' plays move among various planes of existence which should come as no surprise to theatre goers since the title *Coyote City* is a clear indication that times and ways of being in this play will be different from those portrayed in Western literature. In *Almighty Voice and His Wife*, the two leading characters shift shapes and become a "playful" ghost and an "Interlocutor." To try to interpret the writing of Moses in terms of Western literature and theatre will only confuse and frustrate. Shape-shifting is an integral part of Native mythology and the sooner theatre goers accept it as a unique literary device, the sooner enjoyment and appreciation of the drama develop. Margo Kane's character searches for her identity in *Moonlodge*, and it is evident that she has not yet come to recognize Trickster, but there is hope that she will come to understand the roots of her cultural beliefs.

The Trickster, an androgynous figure, is integral to Tomson Highway's *The Rez Sisters* where it takes the form of a male and in *Dry Lips Oughta Move to Kapuskasing* where it is female. Highway describes the role of the Trickster for those who are not familiar with it. Though Highway uses the term "he," lacking a better term for an androgynous figure in the English language, his intention is not to suggest that the Trickster is a male.

> The dream world of North American Indian mythology is inhabited by the most fantastic creatures, beings, and events. Foremost among these is the "Trickster," as pivotal and important a figure in the Native world as Christ is in the realm of Christian mythology. ... [T]his trickster goes by many names and many guises. In fact, he can assume any guise he chooses. Essentially a comic, clownish sort of character, he teaches us about the nature and meaning of existence on the planet earth; he straddles the consciousness of man and that of God, the Great Spirit. (*Dry Lips* xiii)

English translations of Trickster mythology have always presented it as masculine. This mythology has been filtered through a patrilineal and patriarchal screen which could not fathom or accept an androgynous figure. Yet Native people have long told us that our understanding and interpretation of the Trickster is not accurate. Highway clarifies why this might be.

> In Cree, Ojibway etc., unlike English, French, German, etc. the male-female-neuter hierarchy is entirely absent. So that

by this system of thought, the central hero figure from our mythology—theology if you will—is theoretically neither exclusively male nor exclusively female, or it is both simultaneously. (*Dry Lips* 12)

The role of the Trickster is best portrayed in the scene with Marie-Adele, the sister who is dying of cancer, in *The Rez Sisters*.

> MARIE-ADELE: Go away! You stinking thing. Don't coming [sic] messing around here for nothing. Go away! Neee. Who the hell do you think you are, the Holy Spirit? Go away! Hey, but he won't fly away, this seagull bird. He just sits there. And watches me. Watches me.
> NANABUSH: Come
> MARIE-ADELE: Neee. I can't fly away. I have no wings. Yet. (19 [footnote])

Marie-Adele is facing her own mortality and she dies before the end of the play. Of course she rejects death and resents the Trickster. But in her statement, "I have no wings. Yet," we understand that it is the Trickster who will provide the strength and support for what lies ahead, as indeed happens. With his simple "Come," we see the beginning of Marie-Adele's acceptance of death.

The Trickster, in the form of the Bingo Master, holds Marie-Adele in his arms romantically as they waltz onto a different plane of existence. As Tomson predicted, Aboriginal people will indeed dance again, unfettered by religious dogma from another country, another culture. Care must be taken not to equate Marie-Adele's reference to wings with a metamorphosis into an angel. The wings are the wings of a seagull. The Trickster is concerned with neither pearly gates nor burning hellfires. The Trickster is concerned with the here and now; wings will enable Marie-Adele to leave the "real" world and join the realm of the Trickster, which could well be every bit as real as the world which theatre goers tend to view as "reality."

Whereas the women in *The Rez Sisters* accept Nanabush as a part of daily life, the men's confusion and apprehension about their spirituality in *Dry Lips Oughta Move to Kapuskasing* is best revealed in the interchange between Simon and Nanabush/Patsy where Simon is torn between the Christian doctrine of a male deity, the devaluation of women in the patriarchal, colonial system which was forced particularly upon Aboriginal men, and Cree gender-neutrality. While he admits that the crucifix has been shoved "up your holy cunt" (112) he still cannot accept femaleness in a deity until Nanabush/Patsy substitutes "womb" for the degrading cunt. This symbolizes the sacredness of the woman's power to procreate life in Aboriginal spirituality and begins to restore the understanding Simon is so desperately seeking. The androgynous character of the Trickster creates possibilities in *The Rez Sisters* and *Dry Lips Oughta Move to Kapuskasing* that are not usually found elsewhere. It is no accident that Zhaboonigan can freely describe her rape to the Trickster, that the Bingo Master is indeed the Trickster who has come to ease Marie-Adele's moment of death or that it is Nanabush/Patsy who is at last able to help Simon. Bingo and hockey are literary devices Highway uses—they are fun, they are zesty, they are real and are almost as ubiquitous in Native communities as the Trickster itself. But the plays are not about bingo or hockey. They are about Native society, about the disempowerment of Native men, the strength of Native women, the beauty, the durability and the renaissance and optimism of Native culture. Highway's plays have elevated Native literature to an unprecedented plane.

These major differences from Western theatre, which arise due to the incorporation of Native mythology, need to be recognized. Beth Cuthand, the Cree writer explains:

> There are a number of us who are going back to the old stories and using them, or they are using us, as a means of telling a contemporary story. When we use myths, then the possibilities of the use of time just broaden, because in primordial time it was *times!* It was plural. It was not just one day follows the next follows the next. It seems to me that maybe at this time in the history of the world we need to go back to these. Because I see a big change coming in the world itself, and the way humans relate to the earth, to our existence here. (Lutz 40)

Drama lends itself better to the portrayal of Aboriginal mythology than any other genre and is presenting unprecedented challenges for actors and audiences. Native people cannot be portrayed accurately without humour and laughter. Native humour is hearty and spontaneous and is often directed at misfortune turned into a joke. It is often used to deal with the pain that inevitably accompanies poverty and marginalization. Classist attitudes can contribute to a deplorable misrepresentation of the people of Highway's fictional Wasichigan Hill Reserve. Even the book cover of *The Rez Sisters* refers to life on this reserve as "tortured" and a CBC Sunday morning program (1989), referred to the "dark humour" in the play. Unique Native humour surfaces on almost every page of Highway's writing but it is by no means "dark" humour. Individual people in this play experience pain and despair, as in all cultures, but Highway's characters could be people in any poverty-stricken area, and many of the issues dealt with in the plays have nothing to do with race or economic depression. Non-Natives often feel rather uneasy with Native humour, especially when they do not recognize or understand it. When it is directed toward their culture, it often leads to anger and indignation. Kate Vangen (Assiniboine) points out three essential ingredients to good Native humour: "Keeping a safe distance (from white colonizers), seizing the proper moment, and performing the appropriate gesture" (King, Calvers & Hoy 189). Often this takes the form of "making faces" at the colonizers without the colonizers being able to retaliate or even recognizing that they are the butt of some joke.

In Highway's plays he does not "make faces" at the colonizers, though he gently lampoons Frits the Katz and Ellen's husband Raymond in *The Rez Sisters*. He shows typical Native humour when the opposing hockey team in *Dry Lips Oughta Move to Kapuskasing* is called the "Canoe Lake Bravettes," an ironic reference to the custom of giving sports teams Indian names and he demonstrates Native humour at its best when he calls the captain of this hockey team Flora MacDonald! In her discussion of Native humour Vangen points out that survival for Native people means keeping a safe distance from the colonizer and in their humour, Native writers are careful not to imitate the colonizers (King, Calvers & Hoy 203). Aboriginal playwrights keep safe distances. Cultural differences are perhaps most evident where humour is involved. Analyzing the humour in Native drama becomes very difficult in Western literary terms yet the humour is one reason why Highway's plays are so uniquely Manitoban Indian. He has captured the very essence of the culture. Non-Natives need to see these plays in the company of Native audiences in order to understand and appreciate the humour. Drew Hayden Taylor does "makes faces," especially in *Education is Our Right,* and the incongruous situations that Kane finds herself in create the humour in *Moonlodge*. The irony of Taylor's and Kane's plays lies in the fact that these situations are so true to life that non-Native audiences often fail to respond to the humour.

Western culture has long paid lip service to the "different" Native world view but little attempt has been made to understand what this might be. Through the medium of drama, Natives themselves are beginning to present a veritable smorgasbord of ideas; different concepts of time, different mythologies, a different kind of spirituality, different attitudes toward sexuality, different concepts of relationships between people where the non-interference ethic is paramount, a different attitude toward land and perhaps the most difficult for Western readers to comprehend, a gender-neutral, non-hierarchical world view. Much of the drama is yet to come; as it continues to be produced it has the potential to have a profound impact on Western modes of thinking.

Works Cited

Campbell, Maria. *Halfbreed*. Toronto: McClelland & Stewart, 1973.
Griffiths, Linda and Maria Campbell. *The Book of Jessica: A Theatrical Transformation*. Toronto: The Coach House Press, 1989.
Highway, Tomson. Address to Brandon University Students, 1992.
⸺. *Dry Lips Oughta Move to Kapuskasing*. Saskatoon: Fifth House Publisher, 1989.
⸺. *The Rez Sisters*. Saskatoon: Fifth House Publishers, 1988.
Jennes, Diamond. *The Indians of Canada*. Ottawa: Queen's Printer, 1967.
Kane, Margo. "*Moonlodge*." *An Anthology of Canadian Native Literature in English*. Eds. Daniel David Moses & Terry Goldie. Toronto: Oxford University Press, 1992.
King, Thomas. *Medicine River*. Markham: Viking Press, 1989.
King, Thomas, Cheryl Calver and Helen Hoy, eds. *The Native in Literature Canadian and Comparative Perspectives*. Oakville, ON: ECW Press, 1987.
Lutz, Harmut. *Contemporary Challenges: Conversations With Canadian Native Authors*. Saskatoon: Fifth House Publishers, 1991.
Mojica, Monique. *Princess Pocahontas and the Blue Spots*. Toronto: Women's Press, 1991.
Mortimer, Hilda. *You Call Me Chief*. Toronto: Doubleday, 1981.
Moses, Daniel David. "*Almighty Voice and His Wife*." *Canadian Theatre Review* 68 (Fall 1991): 64–80.
⸺. *Coyote City*. Stratford: Williams-Wallace, 1990.
Ryga, George. *The Ecstasy of Rita Joe and Other Plays*. Don Mills: General Publishing, 1971.

Sanders, Thomas E. and Walter W. Peek. *Literature of the American Indian*. London: Collier Macmillan, 1973.

Seidelman, Harold & James Turner. *The Inuit Imagination Arctic Myth and Sculpture*. Toronto: Douglas and McIntyre, 1993.

Schwarz, Herbert. *Elik And Other Stories of the Mackenzie Eskimos*. Toronto: McClelland & Stewart, 1970.

Taylor, Drew Hayden. *Someday*. Saskatoon: Fifth House Publishers, 1993.

——————. *Toronto at Dreamer's Rock and Education is Our Right* Saskatoon: Fifth House Publishers, 1990.

Wheeler, Jordan. *Brothers in Arms*. Winnipeg: Pemmican Publications, 1989.

Protest for a Better Future: South Asian Canadian Theatre's March to the Centre

by Uma Parameswaran

To the Beat of Drums

In India's folk theatre and its urban counterpart, the street theatre, musicians beat on the drum to get an audience together from the village and from passersby. In a classical Indian drama, the Sutradhar, (who is a stage manager or director, or both) comes on stage first and speaks to the audience. The intent of both is to introduce oneself—one's antecedents (or source of inspiration) and one's objectives—and to draw the audience into the circle of participation.

Each Canadian city has amateur drama groups that sporadically surface and sink depending on the support of their sponsors who are usually ethnic organizations. However, in the last decade four professional companies, South Asian Canadian at the core, have established themselves on firm financial and artistic ground: Vancouver Sath in Vancouver, Montreal Serai and Teesri Duniya in Montreal, and Cahoots Theatre Projects in Toronto. The core group of Cahoots consists of visible minority writers; its South Asian Canadian playwrights are Dilara

---

UMA PARAMESWARAN was born in Madras, India. She has been teaching at the University of Winnipeg since 1967. She took her Ph.D. from Michigan State University in 1972. Her fields of specialization are Post-Colonial Literatures (most of her publications are in this area), Women's Studies in Literature and Creative Writing. She is the author of *Cyclic Hope Cyclic Pain* (1972), *Rootless but Green are the Boulevard Trees* (1987); *Trishanku* (1988); and *The Door I Shut Behind Me* (1990).

Ally, Sheila James and Sonia Dhillon. Each of these theatre groups have separately declared their objectives, but the collective message is clear: protesting injustices within the ethnocentric community and among the larger community is one way of marching towards a better future.

We are in the process of forging a new national cultural identity in Canada, an identity that will be a composite of many heritage cultures. A series of metaphors (perhaps mixed, but not garbled) come to mind. The concepts of "mainstream" as a synonym for "white," and of "founding nations" for the English and French will become part of the past, as will the relegation of aboriginal culture to the peripheries. As the margins move towards the centre, the centre will perforce give way (for the instinct for survival is always the ultimate moving force) and there will be a series of mergers and divisions between the older and the newer sets of cells that will change the total configuration. Much will probably be lost by way of ethno-cultural distinctions but many ethno-cultural components will also become part of the composite culture. Perhaps that culture will be a seamless coat of many colours rather than the patchwork quilt that is today's multiculturalism. Both seamlessness and patchwork have their assets and liabilities. Nothing ever remains or should remain unchanging and monolithic. Just as political histories show the reality, indeed inevitability, of alternating movements of centralization and decentralization, imperialism (political and economic) and independent nationhood, I see seamlessness and patchwork as alternating movements.

Or, to use another analogy, the sari weavers of south Indian villages and the embroiderers of Kashmiri and Hyderabadi shawls are adept at making reversible fabrics that consist of embossed coloured dots on one side and running threads of colour on the other; I can imagine a national culture, that is both seamless and patchwork, depending on which side you display. Even as each ethno-centred group works at quilting its own identity, we should move towards the seamless phase.

Indian and Canadian Sources

In "Interrogating Identity," Homi Bhabha says, "the question of identification is never the affirmation of a pregiven identity ... it is always the production of an image of identity and the transformation of the subject in assuming that identity" (Goldberg 188). In the immigrant context, one might say that minorities, especially non-whites, have to fight for both the erasure of a negative identity pregiven by the power group and the forging of a positive identity. South Asian Canadian theatre, on its quilting side, takes both these into account and the tools available from its South Asian sources into account as well. On the seamless side, it draws from the Canadian political and literary world.

In approaching South Asian Canadian theatre, one needs to understand two historical Indian bases to the theatre of protest developed by South Asian Canadians. One, this genre owes its format to the people's theatre movement in Bengal led by Badal Sarcar and the Marxist movement in India in the earlier decades of this century. Two, it uses many of the standard stage techniques and strategies used by folk theatre in India over the centuries. Thus, we must remember that while the plots move around the problems faced by South Asians and other "visible minorities" in Canada, many of the stage techniques are a transplant from India's folk and popular traditions (which resemble morality plays of medieval England). We need to readjust our criteria and expectations accordingly, especially when assessing the quality of the dialogue and characterization. Judged by other standards, some of these plays could be summarily dismissed as rudimentary, skeletal, unrealistic.

One also needs to understand two historical bases of South Asian reality in Canada. The first concerns the pattern of South Asian immigration into Canada and is generated by forces within the immigrants' culture; the second concerns the pattern of racism in Canada and is generated by structures outside the culture.

These two sets of influences are common to most plays in this study but the degree of influence depends on historical patterns of immigration. Montreal and Vancouver are the two major centres of South Asian Canadian theatre but they are quite dissimilar because of their immigration history.

Historical Overview of South Asian Immigration

The eastern provinces saw an influx of immigrants from South Asia only in the second phase of immigration, 1960s onward. The second phase consisted of highly educated professionals trained in India or in other erstwhile British colonies. But British Columbia has had a significant South Asian presence for ninety years. A Punjab regiment that was returning from Queen Victoria's diamond jubilee celebrations in 1897 took the long way back home, through Canada. Its members saw the vast potentials of the lumber industry in British Columbia. On their return to India, they initiated the first wave of immigration (Ferguson 3).

The first immigrants, forty-five in number, arrived in 1904-05 followed by about four hundred the following year. The climate was already vitiated for Asians; whites of Vancouver had rioted, first in 1887 and then periodically, against Chinese and Japanese workers who had been brought in to complete the railway tracks. The influx of "Hindus," as anyone from India was called regardless of whether they were Sikhs, Jains, Christians, Muslims or Hindus, fanned the flames of racism. McKenzie King and Wilfrid Laurier were prime ministers who endorsed the concept of a white Canada. The Komagata Maru incident of 1914, where a shipload of Punjabi immigrants were quarantined and then turned away from Canada, put an end to immigration from India until the 1950s. But by then, there were already about three thousand, many of whom had fled into Canada from the United States after similar anti-Indian riots (Kanungo 29).

Thus, East Indians have lived in British Columbia for ninety years. They have had problems common to immigrant groups that entered Canada in the earlier half of this century. A majority were of the working classes, barely literate even in their own mother tongue; they formed self-contained communities and could prosper within them without much contact with other communities even within the same province. In addition, whereas each new ethnocentric group had its turn at the whipping post and then moved on, East Indians continued to be placed outside the pale of Canadian society because of their skin colour, religions, and heritage culture.

Not much has changed since the early years. Partly due to resistance from white Canadians and partly due to their own resistance to give up their ethnocentric culture, a large percentage of Indians in British Columbia lead ghettoized lives (and this does not mean they are not economically affluent); many of the older generation and many middle-aged women, though born in Canada, speak no English; there is no need because there are enough Indians in every profession and service to cater to their needs. The 1986 census records 66,000 East Indians of single origin and 11,000 of mixed origins in British Columbia.

The theatre groups in Vancouver focus on these realities. They deal at a very basic level with everyday problems in the lives of this particular community—intergenerational conflicts, gender-based traditional roles that are oppressive to women; the problems of aging in a sociological context, namely the break up of the traditional structure of adult children caring for their old parents; exploitation of workers in the farm and lumber industries; and the experience of racism at the hands of the larger community. Their scripts are skeletal and fluid, and the language used is usually Punjabi.

The plays are like English morality plays and Ram Lila plays of the Hindu tradition. However, instead of preaching Christian values of good and evil, or retelling epic stories with contemporary events thrown in, these Canadian morality plays deal with social, sexual, ethnic, racist and economic evils. They have some of the trappings of Eastern folk theatre: stylized spectacle, songs and music, and minimal focus on characterization and relationships. They could be called agitprop drama if their dramatic conflict, climax and denouement were more developed. As it is, they remain skits more than plays.

Vancouver Sath

Vancouver Sath is the most successful theatre group in western Canada. It is a collective. All the plays are collectively workshopped, and some are collectively written. However, Sadhu Binning and Sukhwant Hundal are the main writers. In the last five years, the collective has translated several of their plays into English, including *A Crop of Poison,* about the unconscionable horrors of pesticide; *Picket Line*, which calls on farm workers to unionize; *No Small Matter*, which deals with the rampant problem of wife battering; *Different Age Same Cage*; and *Lesson of a Different Kind*.

While all the plays deal with everyday problems, the last two are particularly painful; *Different Age Same Cage* has three scenes, each scene dealing with a specific issue—favouritism towards sons over daughters, wife-beating, and abuse of parents. In the third scene, the old mother, driven by her son to live in a farm workers' cabin so he can rent out the basement of his house, sums up the attitude:

> You need a babysitter, use your mother; you need extra money, send your mother to work in the farms; you get behind in your payments, send her to live in the cabins.

The old woman knows she has been abused, but the scene ends with her accepting that there is no reprieve for her, no penalty for him. Abuse of aging parents is a problem that is spreading in all communities, but it takes some courage to write about it because no community takes kindly to those engaged in the public washing of dirty linen.

Vancouver Sath's main playwright, Sadhu Binning, has that courage. Binning is a writer; like many Indo-Canadians, Binning has a Master's degree and like most writers he has worked at various jobs, including a very long stint as a mailman. As activist, writer and actor, he is the leading force of Vancouver Sath. He is also a key figure in *Watan*, a Punjabi-language magazine. In person, he is soft-spoken and gentle almost to the point of placidity; he reserves his fire for his writing. In *Lesson of a Different Kind*, the only published play to date (in *Ankur*, Summer 1991) Binning connects his Punjabi community with the larger community.

It is a typical non-proscenium protest drama in its theme, stagecraft and development. It is a one-act play with three short scenes. It needs seven actors, and its props and sets are minimal—a classroom and a store room. Only one character is named—Resham, a university student. Though some of the others have names (Malkit, Jasbir, Daljit) they are identified only as Old Male Worker, Old Female Worker and Young Female Worker, reinforcing the issue-oriented nature of the play.

The first scene seems purely functional for leading into the main theme: neo-colonial exploitation whereby the system employs middlemen who exploit members of their own minority community. Resham Gill's class has been asked to give an oral research report. Resham says he needs help to resolve a problem that his research has caused.

Scene two is set in a basement store room of a large office building; in addition to its realism, this setting also symbolizes that Indo-Canadians are at the bottom of the vertical mosaic that is Canadian multiculturalism. This scene deals with Resham's research experience. He has been introduced by his cousin, the boss of a janitorial service, to one of the employees, an old woman, who welcomes him in the old style—"Accha! come, son sit down, have something to eat, have a cup of tea." In the ensuing conversation between Resham, Old Woman and Jasbir, we get a view of the system. Every comment the workers make is double-edged, sometimes overtly, and sometimes ironically so that we know the implication but the speaker and listener do not. Workers can get the job only through personal recommendation—the Old Woman is the aunt and Jasbir the daughter-in-law of friends known to the Boss. Nobody gets overtime (we note the boss is contravening Canadian labour laws) and the boss treats them like family—meaning he deviously tells the worker's spouse or mother if he has a complaint about the worker. Daljit, the second female worker, is an activist who wants to form a labour union. She is aware of the neocolonialism at work. She says:

> The employers here know that the best way to exploit immigrant labour is to do it through their own people and as a result you get this contracting system. And your poor cousin is only a link in the chain. The real villains are the people who keep this system in place. (11)

The boss overhears her and she is fired.

In scene three, after submitting the report, Resham's question is: What should he do since he has been responsible for Daljit's dismissal? Binning punches home his satire of the system when he makes the teacher say that academic researchers should never get too close to their subject; they should compile data, make their analysis, but never get involved.

Lesson of a Different Kind is typical of Vancouver Sath's repertoire. It has a clear objective and it has great potential. Every line reflects a real-life situation and hints at injustices in the system and the community. The insider would instantly relate to each image and reference and would moreover associate it to other incidents. When staged, small details such as offering tea even before a visitor has sat down, or the subtext where a man in *Different Age Same Cage* invites friends to carouse every night in order to strike a matrimonial alliance that would help immigration, are very revealing of a culture.

However, the plays' shortcomings are also very clear. Mainly, the plays are too blunt and minimal; there is no leading-up, no follow-through, no nuances, no poetry. The writers are, no doubt, caught in the bind of language when they write in English, betrayed by "our tongue that stumbles over words so alien to the many places from which we've come" as I say in one of my poems. On stage and on paper, the language sounds stilted and unnatural; situations that are poignant to the point of tears become anti-climactic because the script falsifies the cadence that comes so naturally in Punjabi. There is a strong tendency among actors to be one-dimensional in their delivery, to be too loud or melodramatic. It is not easy to offer any resolutions to these problems of idiom and dramaturgy.

To give an example, what can or should one do with Punjabi colloquialisms that are often essential for building up an atmosphere or character? Vancouver Sath omits them altogether in most of its English scripts and this contributes to the stiltedness of dialogue. In one or two plays, the slangs are replaced with English slangs, but there is a dissonance in that these are often outdated English terms from England via India. Mulk Raj Anand, who wrote in India in the 1940s and '50s, used literal translations which worked well in print but will only detract on stage. To use totally Canadian street slang would not work for the Sath audience, though Serai and Teesri Duniya use them effectively because their plots and audience are multicultural.

I have my own angle on this. I believe we can transform Canadian English to reflect our multicultural realities by extending the frontiers of idioms and usages to include such standard greetings as "Accha bhai (behn), sab theek hai?" instead of its translation, "Well, brother (sister), is everything okay?" However, dramatic effectiveness must have first priority. Serai has handled this ingeniously in *Some Dogs,* where a woman shouts obscenities from time to time from the balcony of her apartment, each time in a different language. Much of the humour and symbolism lie in that she has nothing to do with the action on stage; she is just part of the backdrop which is a crowded district of apartment blocks. However, there is an overdose of four letter words, especially in the Montreal plays.

Finally, Vancouver Sath's plays highlight one of the problems faced by many minority theatres, that of being pulled in two directions on the question of fighting stereotypes. Most of the plots that have been skeletally outlined above deal with sensitive issues. The trouble with stereotyping is that on one hand there is a kernel of truth, and on the other hand harping on that to the exclusion of other qualities perpetuates inter-racial and inter-cultural tensions. The need to work for erasure of pre-given identities in the larger community conflicts with the need to raise awareness and initiate reform within the community. Serai approaches this very differently; it uses sarcasm and exaggeration when knocking the South Asian community, especially for their complacency and refusal to get involved in political and societal issues.

Montreal Companies

Getting involved is the key requirement in protest theatre. The members of Montreal Serai and Teesri Duniya are politically outspoken. For instance, Rana Bose of Serai crossed swords with Lise Payette when she produced *Disparaître (To Disappear: The Destiny of the French Nation in Quebec?)* which was aired as a two-hour French programme early in February 1989 and later condensed on CBC's *Journal*. He pointed out the incipient racism of such a stand where immigrants were being penalized in spite of being francophone. Rahul Varma of Teesri Duniya pushed for changes in immigration policy so that Indian nationals who get married to Indo-Canadians do not have to wait more than six months to get a Canadian visa. The usual wait was close to two years. The average Canadian is not aware of the many inequities meted out to non-whites. South Asian Canadian playwrights include numerous examples of such inequities in passing or between the lines in addition to highlighting one or two in the main action. Rana Bose's *Baba Jacques Dass and Turmoil at Côte des Neiges Cemetery*, is so packed with subtexts that much of it might get lost when staged.

Both, Teesri Duniya and Montreal Serai, have evolved from the second wave of immigration from India. Though East Indians have lived in British Columbia for ninety years, and in eastern provinces for thirty years, literary efforts with a Canadian setting started only in the 1980s. Indeed, my play, *Rootless but Green are the Boulevard Trees* (written in 1979 and first published in *Toronto South Asian Review* in 1984 and subsequently as a book in 1987) is the first full-length play set in Canada. The reason for this lag lies in the practical realities of any transplanted ethos. As I trace in, "Ganga in the Assiniboine," creativity is a luxury that one can afford, both at the individual and collective level, only in a late phase of immigrant life; in the first phase there is a preoccupation with nostalgia for the original homeland mixed with a sense of wonder for the new environment; in the second, one is preoccupied with climbing ladders, professional and social; in the third, one focuses on the social and social-work aspects of one's heritage culture; in the fourth phase, one (be it individual or community) looks outward towards the larger community. Only the last two phases provide the proper soil for the theatre of protest.

The theatre groups that function out of Montreal grow out of that fourth phase in the life of its major playwrights and of the East Indian community in Montreal. Unlike the Sath that is motivated by forces within the community, these companies are motivated by the patterns of racism endemic to the Canadian system and they react to forces generated by structures outside their heritage culture. Their plays consist of a multicultural cast and deal with problems common to minorities, though examples used are often from the South Asian Canadian experience.

Teesri Duniya

Teesri Duniya (Third World) was founded in 1981 by Rahul Varma and Rana Bose. Till 1985, the company produced plays in Hindi—*Julus, Ek tha Gadha, Bhanumati ka Pitara, Ghar Ghar ki Kahani, Ahsaas* and *Darwaaze Khol Do*. In 1985, they staged *The Great Celestial Cow* in English, and a year later *On the Double*, a hilarious satire of Canadian life based on an Indian production. It was about this time that there was an ideological split and Rana Bose broke away and formed Serai. Their differences are apparent in the directions each company took after 1985. Teesri Duniya has staged a major production every year. *Job Stealer* was produced in 1987; *Isolated Incident* in December 1988; *Equal Wages*, arguing for gender equality, in 1989; *Land Where the Trees Talk*, on Native Land Rights, in 1990; *No Man's Land*, and *Trading Injuries*, its radio-script, in 1993. *Trading Injuries*, like Binning's *A Crop of Poison*, is about work-place health hazards; it is about pollution in the sweatshops of the garment industry.

Teesri Duniya has a standard *modus operandi*—to target a topical controversy, work out a script, and stage a production in record time, thus capitalizing on timing and news value. The script is first written by Rahul Varma, and then workshopped and revised on a cooperative basis with other members of the company. The final scripts often bear the names of Rahul Varma and one or two others. Even when the company consisted mostly of Indo-Canadians, the *dramatis personae* were of various ethnic backgrounds, thus sending a clear message that they consider themselves spokespersons for the third world within Canadian society, namely the visible minorities who are in double jeopardy by virtue of their newness and colour. Today, Teesri Duniya (as also Serai) has almost as many non-Indo-Canadians in their core membership as Indo-Canadians. Varma endorses the principle of colour-blind casting; that is, the actors do not have to be the of the same colour or race as the characters they are portraying. In short, Othello can be played by a white actor. But can it be played without colouring his body black? Yes. A protest theatre company must protest such limitations as colour-consistent casting in order to be consistent with its mandate, and though Varma got a black actor to play the main black role in *Isolated Incident*, he places more importance on the availability and skills of actors than on surface verisimilitudes. As with most protest theatre, the aim is to protest and educate, and the louder and clearer the message the closer a play comes to achieving its goals. Thus, every aspect is simplified, starting with titles that summarize the theme, and an absence of complexity in plot and characterization.

Job Stealer reflects the vicissitudes of all immigrants who arrive without a prior job offer. They suffer hardship and humiliation in the vicious circle of "No immigration without a job and no job without Canadian experience" and by committing the sin of being overqualified. Desperate to earn something, anything, they fall prey to exploitative employers who pay them less than is legal for jobs that no Canadian would care to take up anyway. In the play Kabul, a doctor working on a sweatshop assembly line, sums it up with "Besides, if it were possible to steal a job, I would have stolen a better one." The play is fast moving and picks up on all possible aspects of the situation: army brutality in the country of origin, the callousness of medical officers assigned to check up the refugees' records, of reporters whose coverage triggers national resentment against these queue jumpers, "whose reward for short-circuiting the system is instant asylum, a work permit and social benefits," of employers who send them around in circles, and of ordinary Canadians who resent them and hold them in contempt.

There is a scene in this play that is particularly noteworthy because it preceded by several months a scene by a more famous writer, Salman Rushdie. In *The Satanic Verses*, Rushdie describes the brutality of policemen hunting down alleged or suspected illegal aliens along the coast of England. In Rahul Varma's play, the government officers in the country of origin and in Canada are ruthless barbarians who assume that all non-white refugees must be carriers of syphilis or other dreaded diseases. Their diction, gestures and actions are marshalled out with over-simplified exaggeration but on stage these ploys work very effectively. In all his plays, Varma inserts snatches from popular songs or tunes; in this play it is a line from a band that was much in vogue at the time—The Police. The immigration officer says, "Every move you make, every breath you take. Remember, until your status is decided I'll be watching you." All of Varma's plays end on a note of hope and conciliation. *Job Stealer* ends with the refugees "thanking those who accepted us. The agencies and the people, and the nations … we came with one mouth to feed but two hands to work with." That indeed is the final truth about Canada.

Teesri Duniya's Isolated Incident

Isolated Incident is one of Teesri Duniya's best scripts and productions to date. It deals with the legal system's practice of treating each case as an isolated incident. Thus, a policeman can brutally manhandle a citizen (even the same one) twenty times and be acquitted each time with a mere reprimand because action cannot be taken on the pattern of brutality but only on each single incident. The play was written for the first anniversary of the 1987 police slaying of an unarmed black youth, Anthony Griffin, in Montreal. The Griffin slaying prompted a public outcry and the Black Theatre Workshop prepared a script but stopped production for fear of a lawsuit. Teesri Duniya did not stop; it went on to get its play ready in time for the first anniversary.

In this play, Dexter Gibson, a young black accountant (the choice of a white collar job for him is significant for its rebuttal of stereotyping blacks) on his way to work is assaulted by white punkheads; instead of chasing them, the racist policeman, aptly named Savage, charges him and when he resists, fatally shoots him. The all-white jury acquits the police officer.

Anthony Griffin was not the first victim of such injustice. In the play, Jamura lists several other recent cases, showing the pattern of police brutality. He says,

> I saw Buddy Evans shot in 1978 ... I saw Albert Johnson shot in 1979 ... I saw J. J. Harper and Michael Wade Lawson shot in 1988, I saw Dexter ... and now Dexter is dead. (Varma 252)

As mentioned earlier, Varma's conclusions are conciliatory. In the last scene, Dexter's mother says, "All I wish is that something good would come out of his death ... I want to see justice done, so that everybody, even that officer, realizes what happened was wrong."

The play's strength lies in the many little details that hit home runs. It uses such elements of traditional Indian theatre as the storyteller, stage assistant, chorus, and street magician's act. It is pro-feminist in that the sutradhar (manager/director) is a woman, and there are none of the usual misogynist jokes about a woman holding power. There is balance in characterization, even if it is two-dimensional; though the play highlights police brutality and police mafia, Officer Hobly is a decent guy. Dexter is a victim, but he is also a typical Canadian youngster, cheeky and self-confident. Balwinder Singh, the only South Asian character, is generous with his hospitality, but the playwrights satirize South Asian Canadians' foibles: their communalism, as when Balwinder ignores Jamura's introductions until Jamura says, "I'm an Indian," at which he promptly invites him to stay for lunch; their propensity to watch TV all evening; their insistence on retaining their food habits ...

In *Nation and Narration*, Bhabha says that "the complex strategies of cultural identification and discursive address that function in the name of 'the people' or 'the nation' ... make them the immanent subjects and objects of a range of social and literary narratives" (292). In the characterization of Balwinder Singh, the playwright takes control of shaping the identity of his own people, and he does it in a balanced way, laughing at foibles but also drawing attention to positive "stereotyping."

The play starts on a note of slapstick comedy. Jamura says he is waiting for Ustad so they can start the play. She enters, clanging her cymbals, "I made it. The customs, the immigration, the security, and above all the traffic jam. But here I am, just in time" (Varma 231). Though she places the traffic jam "above all," we who know the racist hassle experienced by non-white Canadians every time we return to Canada from abroad, realize where the real emphasis lies.

The comedy continues as Jamura visits Balwinder Singh who is also visited by his landlord, Roach, who wants to evict him. Roach assumes Jamura is an illegal alien and calls the police who promptly leave everything else to arrest Jamura. The rapid barrage from both Savage and Roach (a strategy used in *Job Stealer* as well) show the frenzy of antagonism for non-whites. Assuming he would be hiding, they pull the place upside down etc. etc. The scene is almost silly; but victims of racial discrimination know that police efforts to weed out illegal aliens have included these and other contemptible acts, for example, bribing students to spy on fellow visa students who might be contravening the letter of the law, by holding a part-time job, for instance. The playwrights mainly satirize the police and the mafia-type brotherhood that protects them from within, but they also poke fun at the various *faux pas* that Indian immigrants make in their ignorant efforts to conform to the society around them, as in wearing a "checkered jacket."

Stage directions call for raw two-dimensional stage craft, and the play stays at the level of slapstick much of the time. Nevertheless, it succeeds in its objective.

Le groupe culturel Montreal Serai

Serai is more sophisticated than the other companies in its scripts, sets and special effects. Rana Bose, Serai's main playwright, is by profession an engineer who holds an executive position in an international company; he is an intellectual who has been influenced by the socialist ideologies of Badal Sircar and Utpal Dutt, and is widely read in literature and political science. He has written and staged nine plays. (For an introduction to his plays up to 1989, please see my article "Rana Bose and Montreal Serai.")

Each of Bose's plays is a delight to read. In *Baba Jacques*, there is a sheer exuberance of imagination; the French Canadian mystic lives in the cemetery and a stage full of characters—journalist Matt, Esther Crawford whose family owns a brewery and publishing house, bigoted Mr. Fraser—walk in and out of their vaults; the structure and stylistic techniques of the play are influenced by classical tradition and contemporary experimentation; the central thrust of the play is definitely a satirical look at South Asians' view of life in Canada and other Canadians' view of South Asians in Canada. The play is imaginative and innovative. It opens whole new worlds of Canadian consciousness as it zips around from grave to grave in the cemetery and closet to closet in society drawing out skeletons of cultural prejudices and political betrayals. His satire against his own community and Canadian multiculturalism is often virulent but always tellingly humorous. In *Baba Jacques*, Binoy's mother is the butt of this satire. She is the stereotypical South Asian woman who thinks that only doctors and engineers do real jobs, that white women are all opportunists and/or sluts, that Indian culture in Canada is in constant danger of being lost; and that the government is an endless source for grants. This perpetuation of stereotypes is problematic in many ways, but Bose's cutting edge doesn't pause for such considerations. In *On the Double*, he pokes fun at the Canadian chase for funding:

> When an Englishman has an emotion, his first instinct is to repress it; when an American has an emotion, his first instinct is to express it; when a Canadian has an emotion, his first instinct is to ask for government subsidy ... (Bose 226–227)

Five or Six Characters in Search of Toronto

Five or Six Characters in Search of Toronto was first staged in 1993, in Toronto, and again in April 1994, in Montreal. The Toronto version was written for a South Asian Canadian festival called Desh Pardesh (Country in a Foreign Country) and used references that were topical and relevant to that audience; the more recent version has used more recent events and addresses a pan-Canadian audience. The plot is the only aspect of the play that is on the surface and easy to trace. The bus in which six characters are travelling from Montreal to Toronto careens off Route 401 and the driver gets decapitated in the crash. The characters are on their way to separate conferences, all of which happen to have the acronym H.U.M.P. The bus driver resurrects, the bus enters an unending tunnel and there are no Toronto lights at the end of the tunnel; there is no Toronto any more. This is Time Zero.

The title leads one to think of Luigi Pirandello. But instead of Pirandello's concept that one wears different masks for different roles and that it is impossible for one to distinguish even in oneself the mask from the face, in this play Bose makes each character one-dimensional, mask and face being identical. Each character represents an urban tribe, as he calls it, but there are variations within each tribe and this results in the same character voicing different specifics. Thus, the pan-fundamentalist is always a bigot but at different times uses chants of different religions: "Praise the Lord, sweet Jesus," "Hare Rama Hare Krishna," "the whole nation is being taken over by minorities"[said in French], "lord have mercy, praise be with Allah," etc.

Bose's main focus is the collective, not the individual. The title could well have been chosen because of points of general intersections: Pirandello foregrounds philosophy, and so does Bose; Pirandello questions the possibility of fixity, and Bose integrates that in the title by saying "five or six"; the play was written for a Toronto festival.

More than Pirandello, Antonin Artaud might be closer to Bose's vision of theatre. Not Artaud's belief that intuition is superior to reason but his insistence that people should experience intensity; that instead of the pale imitation of a double, one must reject causal and logical action and transport the audience into an impressionistic apprehension of truths. Thus, Bose has rationally thought out his own ideas of an ideal Canada but he uses spectacle and a kind of violence (Artaud's metaphor is "cruelty") to jolt the audience into awareness.

The play uses a complex array of special effects that contribute to a surreal atmosphere in keeping with the setting of Time Zero, which also corresponds to the egotistical and fundamentalist chaos that precedes the cataclysm of the Flood in the Bible, the end of a yuga in Hinduism. This is spectacle at its most uninhibited discoesque: strobe lights, large pieces of black cloth, ominous electronic sound seemingly produced from a studio on stage complete with guitar, drums and synthesizers; headlights from Route 401, highway signs lighting up to read by turns, Valhalla, Toronto, Cite d'Ôr, Babylon, fog curling and sweeping from stage to audience. The characters are likewise flamboyantly lurid: the hockey jock with exaggerated padding on shoulder and groin, the Gen-x woman with pancake make up that glows in the dark. The language is often strident with expletives and hammers on the listener's sensibility the same way as the deafening music. But this is agitprop, agitational propaganda no holds barred.

The dialogue is so fast paced and the stage movements so caricatured that a spectator cannot catch all that is being said, but different spectators will catch on to different verbal gymnastics, and no one misses the central point of the play. It is a post-modern, deconstructionist play that deconstructs everything including deconstructionism and all the catch-words and concepts that plague the political and artistic structures around us.

The Intellectual is always politically correct and mouths academic gobbledygook. The francophone Hockey Jock is totally self-centred and oblivious of all else, like fanatic Quebecois. The Art Council Critic is cliquishly jealous of her white protégés but is tripped up by the Ethnic Writer. The Ethnic Writer is an opportunist who tells the audience how he will connive to get the Critic's favour, and does. The religious Fundamentalist, carrying a brick to build his church, believes he must raze all other churches to the ground.

The Fundamentalist, in the 1993 version, spoke in Hindi and obviously stood for the fanatics in the Hindu-Muslim clash of December 1992 in the city of Ayodhya. The play is ingenious in its use of topical satire. The April 1994 version has been updated to cover current 1994 topics and the punches are delivered sometimes with obvious emphasis, sometimes between the lines as it were:

> "the right of white people to sell cigarettes at the same price as native …";

"Toronto ... where LL.B. or not, you continue to be M.P." (re: the Indian born Jag Bhaduria whose educational degrees were questioned);

"Go west, Bill Gates" (the computer giant);

"we never get angry even though you stack all the Arts Council juries with your own people";

"wearing ladies' lawn bowling hats, painted black, which they insist is a symbol of our national heritage" (re: RCMP headgear controversy);

"No signs in English or French? Maybe then we are already on Gerrard Street" (re: Quebec language controversy and the South Asian ghetto on Gerrard);

"maybe we are caught somnambulating while history was being made on the distinct margins of two indistinct solitudes";

"I mean this conference is exclusive and only those who have a sense of exclusion can proceed to be included" (the 1994 Racial Minority Conference of The Writers' Union of Canada, which was open only to minority writers).

The man has a genius for punches and punchlines. One has to hand that to him. He makes fun of the minorities, especially his own ethnocentric group, but his most pungent satire is aimed at those at the centre, the jocks and pseudo-intellectuals who are running the country. But not for long. It is Time Zero, which "reflects the poverty of ideals at the present time." But it is also the end of a yuga (an age) and could "provide the basis for starting out all over again with a clean slate."

Response and Responsibility of the Audience

Earlier, I said that Vancouver Sath's plays highlight one of the problems faced by many minority theatres, that of being pulled in two directions on the question of portraying stereotypes from their ethnic community, and that Serai handles this conflict through sarcasm and exaggeration.

An understanding of the differences between Sath and Serai involves factors that go beyond drama and stagecraft and into social issues of class and audience; whereas Serai faces no problems when projecting and exploiting Indo-Canadian stereotypes, Sath, because of the content of its plays, faces many problems; and not only is the collective pulled in different directions, but critics and non-white audience members are even more torn in our response.

Sath and Serai are both protest repertory theatres, but they are different in many ways and a study of the content and dramatic thrust of their plays will reveal what might well be a raw edge in intra-cultural communication, namely linkages between the effects of content and class. Serai is white collar whereas Sath is blue collar, in motivation and intended audience. Like middle classes everywhere, the Serai collective have the educational background in literary canons to be clever at artistic and political manipulations as can be seen in the dexterous ways in which Rana Bose uses literary and topical allusions. A certain distancing between author/audience and the target of the satire results when Bose pokes fun at the way Indo-Canadian socialites fawn on ministers in his play *Baba Jacques*, for example, or the way sociologists pursue frivolous jargon in *On the Double*: "the psychological ramifications of sociological alienation on the siblings of second generation South Asian teenage girls living in Brossard with their parents in semi-detached condominium cottages with 2 car garages" (Bose 215). A definite, (and comforting) we-they distinction between audience members and the victimizers occurs when one deals with the issues of racism and exploitation in the larger society. The content of Binning's plays, on the other hand, are far too close for comfort: abuse within the family, discrimination within the community ...

There are two bases for objecting to writing about certain issues. One is the predictable objection to airing family (ethnic) problems outside the family; this is inspired by a false sense of "izzat" (family honour) and there is an element of hypocrisy in the objection. However, the other reason is more complex. There are already numerous pejorative stereotypes of Indo-Canadians in the larger Canadian society, some of which are based on cultural prejudices that are held without question. A common example pertains to the system of arranged marriages—time and time again, I have encountered an insurmountable block in my students when discussing novels where young men and women get married without ever having dated. From the average Canadian viewpoint this is oppression, and students seldom make the effort to consider the details, reasons, and possible advantages, of such a system. Given such a preconception, scene 8 of Bose's *On the Double*, in which parents of a young man scrutinize a prospective daughter-in-law, reinforces the stereotype with the stamp of authenticity. But the damage to the "image" of the Indo-Canadian community is not as great as it is in Binning's plays because of Bose's overt tone of exaggeration.

When Binning, on the other hand, speaks of the way some Indo-Canadians exploit their parents, his lack of dramatic sophistication and, in part the preconceived stereotyping by the reader and/or audience, do damage to the "image" of the community. Protest plays can have a positive impact on the way a group perceives itself or another group, and that is their *raison d'être*; but they can also have a negative impact. For example, at this time in Canadian politics when the Minister of Canadian Heritage is calling for input into Immigration policies, and many critics have zeroed in on allowing "sponsored parents" as not viable for the Canadian economy, a play such as Binning's *Lesson of a Different Kind* or *Different Age Same Cage* could easily be used to accelerate prejudice against Indo-Canadians, who are among the groups that more frequently avail themselves of family sponsorship provisions in the Immigration Act. If one follows Solzhenitsyn's credo that literature must consider itself an agent of societal reform, the author, and the community, might well feel the pressure of censoring themselves and their writers. When Binning shows the abusive effects of alcoholism, it reinforces the stereotype that Punjabis are prone to wife-beating; when he speaks of parents being partial to sons and strict with daughters, it adds fuel to the controversy over fetal gender-identification through amniocentesis and the termination of female fetuses in the South Asian Community.

Writers of ethnic protest plays have to resolve for themselves which forces to resist and which to draw upon. What about critics? And non-white audiences? As an Indo-Canadian critic, I have my misgivings in writing this essay. The power of the printed word can be awesome. I published my essay on Serai in *Toronto South Asian Review* in the spring of 1989. Through it, a reader in Vancouver heard of Serai's *The Komagatamaru Incident* (their production of Sharon Pollock's play) for the first time and a ball was set in motion; Serai were invited to stage the play in connection with the seventy-fifth anniversary observance of the Komagatamaru episode in Vancouver.

Am I betraying my ethnic community in foregrounding Binning instead of focusing exclusively on Bose and Varma in whose plays the we-they demarcations are clearly drawn along minorities-establishment lines? Binning, as of now, is not an accomplished playwright and I am aware that given the ground-breaking qualities of this essay and this volume, I am directing focus to certain issues that are not pleasant. But these are issues faced by all ethnic groups, just as family violence has been proven common across cultural and economic lines. I think Binning has something very significant to say and he is one of the few playwrights with grass-roots sensibilities and contacts. Time will tell.

Works Cited

Binning, Sadhu. "Lesson of a Different Kind." *Ankur* (Summer 1991): 8–13.

———. *Different Age Same Cage*. Unpublished manuscript.

Bhabha, Homi K. *Nation and Narration*. London: Routledge, 1990.

Bose, Rana. "On the Double." *The Geography of Voice: Canadian Literature of the South Asian Diaspora*. Ed. Diane McGifford. Toronto: TSAR Books, 1992. 213–227.

Ferguson, Ted. *A White Man's Country: An Exercise in Canadian Prejudice*. Toronto: Doubleday Canada, 1975.

Goldberg, David Theo, ed. *Anatomy of Racism*. Minneapolis: University of Minnesota Press, 1990.

Kanungo, R. N. *South Asians in the Canadian Mosaic*. Montreal: Kala Bharati, 1984.

Parameswaran, Uma. "Ganga in the Assiniboine." *Canadian Ethnic Studies* 17.3 (1985): 120–126.

———. "Rana Bose and Montreal Serai." *TSAR* 7.3 (1989): 37–48.

———. *Rootless but Green are the Boulevard Trees*. Toronto: TSAR Books, 1987.

Varma, Rahul and Stephen Orlov. "*Isolated Incident.*" *The Geography of Voice: Canadian Literature of the South Asian Diaspora*. Ed. Diane McGifford. Toronto: TSAR Books. 1992. 229–260.

All other scripts mentioned in this essay are unpublished.

(Research for this essay has been supported with a grant from the Social Sciences and Humanities Research Council of Canada.)

Theorizing a Queer Theatre: Buddies in Bad Times

by Robert Wallace

> ... a performative is that discursive practice
> that enacts or produces that which it names.
> —Judith Butler.

Sky Gilbert, founder and artistic director of Toronto's Buddies in Bad Times Theatre, begins a letter to the Theatre Advisory Committee of the Ontario Arts Council in March 1994 by explaining that the name of his company has become "more and more apt as the years go by." He writes: "what with AIDS, and with the plagues of various right-wing fundamentalists bearing down upon us, the mandate for Buddies in Bad Times Theatre has become curiously apt also. Our commitment to innovative/ gay and lesbian theatre is now more necessary than ever" ("Artistic Director's Letter 1994" 1).

For people not involved with the creation of innovative or gay and lesbian theatre in Toronto, Gilbert's reflection on his company's name and mandate might seem disingenuous. Quite probably, many of these would consider Buddies' current situation burgeoning, not beleaguered. In 1992, only thirteen years after its inception, Buddies was selected to organize and manage the activities of The Alexander Street Theatre Project, a large and ambitious operation that includes a 2.2 million dollar renovation of the facility that, for two decades, housed the venerated Toronto Workshop Productions. As Tim Jones, Buddies' general man-

---

ROBERT WALLACE is Professor of English at York University's Glendon College in Toronto. Editor of *Canadian Theatre Review* from 1982–1987, he has written about Canadian theatre for a wide variety of newspapers, magazines and scholarly journals as well as commented regularly on the arts for CBC television and radio for over 15 years. Since 1982, he has served as Drama Editor for Coach House Press where he has edited more than 20 volumes of Canadian plays. His own books include *The Work: Conversations with English-Canadian Playwrights* (1982, with Cynthia Zimmerman), *Quebec Voices* (1986), *Producing Marginality: Theatre and Criticism in Canada* (1990) and *Making, Out: Plays by Gay Men* (1992).

ager, explains in a submission to the Canada Council written in February 1994, the eight arts funding bodies and service organizations responsible for selecting an operator for the 12 Alexander Street facility "had the opportunity not only to view [Buddies'] renovation plans, but also to scrutinize Buddies' operational objectives of making the building accessible to alternative theatre and dance companies at heavily subsidized rental rates." Because of their decision to award the coveted operation to Buddies, Jones understandably reasons that "the will for Buddies to carry out the objectives ... [has] already received resounding approval in the community" (2).

How, then, is Buddies a theatre "in bad times," as Sky Gilbert would have it? To answer this question, one must remember that Buddies operates within a complicated matrix of social and material conditions, many of which are beyond its control. As the company enters a new phase of its development, it both reveals and reshapes this matrix. That a building undergoing renovation—the 12 Alexander Street facility—exists at the centre of Buddies (re)configuration in the mid-1990s is serendipitous inasmuch as "Buddies," as an "innovative/gay and lesbian theatre," already is an imaginative construction that has been in process since the company started to produce work in 1979. Buddies' theatrical "subjectivity," like its mandate, was not fixed with its inception; both have changed over the years, and they continue to change, partly as a result of activities and statements made by Gilbert and others connected with the company and partly by the reactions of those who observe and respond to these.

To examine how Buddies has situated itself through promotional materials such as grant applications and advertising campaigns during the last few years, as well as through its programming, and to consider how this activity has been regarded by funding bodies, the press and the theatre-going audience, is to study not only the place that the company occupies in Toronto theatre but, additionally, the ways in which this place marks the "times." This is my primary purpose in this paper. My introduction of the term "subjectivity" is meant to signal another, parallel, aim. Using ideas about identity formation offered by contemporary theorists—especially those writing under the rubric of "queer theory"[1]—I plan to interrogate the idea of gay and lesbian subjectivity itself. This is crucial, I think, if the term "gay and lesbian theatre" is to be used meaningfully. Currently, the words "gay" and "lesbian" are undergoing a process of cultural renovation or, at least, resignification, central to debates about the construction and constitution of the subject. It is not coincidental that this process intersects with the literal and figurative reconstruction of Buddies' theatrical subjectivity. If, as Gilbert argues, Buddies' name and mandate have become more apt, this is one of the reasons.

To suggest that a company or a building can demonstrate subjectivity might seem strange given that the word "subject," at least in the discourse of critical theory, usually refers to a human individual.[2] In *Discerning the Subject*, Paul Smith offers a common definition of the term by explaining its use in psychoanalysis: here "subject" signifies "the complex of psychical formations which are constituted as the human being is positioned in relation to language" (xxxiii). More pertinent to my use of the term in this essay is Brenda K. Marshall's elaboration of Smith's idea in which she explains that a subject, by being positioned in relation to language, is inescapably "subject to" ideology; indeed, it is the work of ideology to suppress the role that language plays in the construction of the subject. Working with ideas originally put forward by Louis Althusser and Jacques Lacan, Marshall is led to state that "we are each assigned a subject position according to gender, race, ethnicity, family, region, as well as according to a variety of other discourses (as a woman, as white, as Irish, as daughter, as a Midwesterner, as a consumer, etc.)" (82).

Significantly, Marshall does not mention sexual orientation in her list, a subject position particularly important to people whose same-sex sexual activities situate them outside the dominant cultural order—what Michael Warner calls the "heteronormative understanding of society" (xi). Since the mid-nineteenth century, the primary category assigned to these people was "homosexual"[3]—a clinical term that was rejected during the late 1960s in favour of "gay" and, subsequently, "gay and lesbian." The growing acceptance of these terms throughout the western world has led to their metonymic signification of group identity; terms that once applied only to sexual behaviour now are used regularly to signify "a people" or even "a nation." As Teresa de Lauretis explains in "Queer Theory: Lesbian and Gay Sexualities":

> ... male and female homosexualities—in their current sexual-political articulations of gay and lesbian sexualities, in North America—may be reconceptualized as social and cultural forms in their own right, albeit emergent ones and thus still fuzzily defined, undercoded, or discursively dependent on more established forms. (iii)

In his Introduction to *Fear of a Queer Planet*, Michael Warner argues that "In the United States, the default model for all minority movements is racial or ethnic" (xvii). I would expand his idea to suggest that this model has been used by the majority of gay activists in the Western world since the late 1960s—if only to explain why it currently weathers attack across the same terrain. For many people, certainly most heterosexual people, "sexual behaviour is clearly not the determining factor in finalizing a self-nomination" (Meyer 4), let alone in formulating a social identity. As a result, an increasingly large number of gay and lesbian people, along with others, are choosing to "renominate" themselves in other terms; the most important of these to this paper is "queer." In his introduction to *The Politics and Poetics of Camp*, Moe Meyer offers two reasons for the substitution of this word for "gay" and "lesbian":

> "Queer" does not indicate the biological sex or gender of the subject. More importantly, the term indicates an ontological challenge to dominant labelling philosophies, especially the medicalization of the subject implied by the word "homosexual," as well as a challenge to discrete gender categories embedded in the divided phrase "gay and lesbian". (1–2)[4]

Meyer goes on to present his definition of "queer," one "based on an alternative model of the constitution of subjectivity and of social identity" in which "queer" signifies "an oppositional critique of gay and lesbian middle-class assimilationism ..." (2).

While I do not wish to debate the merits of this renomination in this paper it is important to problematize the category "gay and lesbian" at its outset just as it is essential that I clarify the idea of subjectivity. For during the last few decades, the words "gay" or "lesbian" have been used not only to label social groups but also to modify *things*—films, books and plays being the examples most appropriate in this instance. Although these things are products of human creativity, they do not, of course, have a sexuality; *ergo*, buildings in which they exist—cinemas, libraries, theatres—cannot legitimately be modified by words that signify sexual behaviour. Can we then talk of "gay and lesbian" textuality of any sort? And, if so, how? What constitutes a gay film, a lesbian novel, or, more to my point, a gay and lesbian theatre?

Elsewhere, I have argued that all texts are "neutral" until a reader invests them with meaning, noting that "In this line of reasoning (which constitutes a theory of reading), the idea of a 'gay text' is problematic"

("Making Out Positions" 20). While I still maintain that a text is inherently without meaning and, consequently, that the author's sexuality, like his or her gender, does little to affect the interpretations that readers make of his or her text,[5] I now want to give more attention to the *place* of the text in the reader's "negotiation" of its meaning. In saying this, I mean to be quite literal: working with the trope of location that weaves throughout this essay, I want to consider more carefully where a text is placed—in what cinema, what bookstore and what theatre—for these sites also are texts open to interpretation.

Texts, while they may lack meaning until they are read, never exist in a vacuum but, on the contrary, operate within contexts, both literal and figurative, that seriously affect how they are read. Nor do texts simply "emerge" in contexts on their own; rather, they are positioned by their creators and those who market them, as well as by the reviewers and readers who make meaning of them in written and spoken comments. A reader approaching a text that is labelled, marketed or discussed as lesbian and/or gay will have a set of expectations that affects the way s/he reads it. In an essay titled "Reading Past the Heterosexual Imperative," Kate Davy addresses the implications of this for theatrical performance, her premise being that "the theatre as a social technology that includes its spectators is still firmly embedded in the sociosymbolic systems and discourses of the dominant culture" (166). A play that is performed in a theatre that is positioned as "lesbian" and/or "gay," is placed in a context that can't help but affect the ways it is read. Consider the fact that a spectator, just to watch a play in this context, must enter a space specifically marked as alternative to the heterosexual norm.[6]

That the context of a production space affects the meaning that a spectator makes of a performance is succinctly illustrated by a review of a Buddies' production that was published in the *Globe and Mail* in 1991. Writing about *Steel Kiss*, a play by Robin Fulford that dramatizes the social and psychological forces that lead four teen-age boys to murder a gay man in a Toronto park, critic Liam Lacey comments that in its original production at another venue, *Steel Kiss* "seemed primarily a play for straight audiences about the background to a terrible incident. At Buddies, which is a gay-oriented theatre, the play takes on a much stronger point of view: it is enraged and histrionic" (C5). A year later in *eye*, a weekly arts and entertainment newspaper, Sky Gilbert acknowledges the same idea but gives it a different spin. Gilbert states: "A lot of gay and lesbian people are frightened to set foot in a gay and lesbian theatre. Because they're not out of the closet, there are a lot of people who don't think they're defined by the term 'gay,' they think it's ghettoizing. The straight community thinks to some extent that [Buddies] represent[s] the gay and lesbian community—well, we don't. We represent a radical fringe of the gay and lesbian community ..." (Hunt 29).

Gilbert's recognition that different audience members approach his theatre (if they approach it at all) with differing expectations is based on the premise that Buddies, as both a company and a facility, has a subjectivity in which sexuality is central. His comments also imply that the "meaning" of this subjectivity is not fixed but, rather, is multiple, dependent upon the subject positions of the spectators who decide what the company "represents" and, as a result, do or do not attend one of its productions. Perhaps more important, Gilbert's comments indicate his understanding that Buddies' subjectivity is linked to its positioning—hence his concern to situate the theatre in a context of his own making, to supply it with imaginative coordinates that reject those of "the straight community."

Most certainly, Buddies does not exist in a vacuum; it occupies literal and figurative positions within Toronto culture of increasingly high profile. In the report by Tim Jones quoted earlier, Buddies' general manager suggests that the company's new space at 12 Alexander Street "holds great potential in developing a much larger audience base" than its previous location at 142 George Street. He reasons that "situated at the very heart of the lesbian and gay community, in a high traffic area, and in close proximity to subways, the location alone has given us the confidence to project growth in attendance of 5,000 people next year" (8). Gilbert, in his comments to *eye*, situates Buddies in a less literal location; indeed, by positioning Buddies on "the radical fringe of the gay and lesbian community," he not only moves the company far from the centre of Toronto's lesbian and gay neighbourhood where Jones puts it, but places it on a different map altogether.

Whereas Jones situates Buddies within geographic and economic contexts, Gilbert places it within political and aesthetic ones. This is evident not only in the example quoted above but also in Gilbert's letter to the Ontario Arts Council cited at the beginning of this essay. In his letter, Gilbert suggests aesthetic consequences of the material conditions that he considers synonymous with "bad times." Ignoring the social circumstances to which he alludes in his opening paragraph, Gilbert proceeds to isolate two trends in Canadian theatre and their results: "1. the decreasing amount of funds available for new Canadian Theatre ...

and 2. the tendency for companies on operating funding to avoid taking risks." That "new, Canadian, experimental work is relegated, at best, to the 'second' 'smaller' 'back' 'extra' or 'other' space," at least in Toronto, is the consequence to which Buddies is opposed and to which, Gilbert argues, its new facility provides an alternative. Gilbert describes the new theatre as "a 100 to 300 seat flexible black box of a space with surrounding catwalks and pit, a space which can be transformed (including its lobby, and rehearsal areas) to suit almost any environment, any approach, any theme which an imaginative director may choose." He affirms that the theatre is "totally dedicated to new Canadian work which is experimental and innovative," explaining that

> Artists at Buddies who are questioning the bounds of theatre and dance, or theatre and performance art, artists who are dealing with forbidden controversial topics, artists who wish to stage work in the audience or quite near the ceiling, will not be relegated to the "second" space. At Buddies they will have affordable space in the prime of the season with the kind of technical support which is rarely provided for this kind of dangerous work. ("Artistic Director's Letter 1994" 1–2)

Gilbert's remarks, when viewed beside Jones', indicate Buddies careful management of the strategy of "positionality"[7] which, as Jill Dolan notes in an essay published in *Theatre Journal*, is common with political activists. Dolan explains that positionality "locates one's personal and political investments and perspectives across an argument, a gesture toward placing oneself within a critique of objectivity, but at the same time stopping the spin of post-structuralist or postmodernist instabilities long enough to advance a politically effective action" (417). How does a subject utilize positionality to "advance politically effective action?" The question not only relates to subjectivity but to larger issues of power. Who governs the development of subjectivity—whether of a person or a theatre company? Who controls how the subject is named, treated and (dis)empowered?

Such questions are important to all theatre companies that regularly are "treated" to reviews and audience response. And they are especially important to not-for-profit companies whose "treatment" also includes peer evaluations for financial subsidies from the public purse.[8] The questions are not just important to companies that produce gay and lesbian work, however; they are crucial—if only because the words "gay" and "lesbian" still signify sexuality even as they become metonymies of social identity. As signifiers of sexual behaviour, "gay" and "lesbian" remain highly volatile. In Canada, as in all heterosexist cultures (are there any cultures that are not?), most gay men and lesbians cannot afford to "come out"—that is, publicly affirm their desire for same-sex sexual relations—for fear of discrimination, harassment and often violent abuse. This alone would allow Sky Gilbert to characterize the "times" as "bad" for his theatre. Indeed, given the ingrained homophobia of Canadian society, it is fair to ask what happens to a theatre company that declares its commitment to gay and lesbian work. What happens, in other words, to a theatre that "comes out?"

The answer, at least in Buddies' case, is that it operates much like the human subject who uses "coming out" as a tactic for social change: it makes sexuality a political issue. This has been Buddies' strategy since the mid-1980s when, not coincidentally, Gilbert himself came out as a gay man in public statements. While Gilbert possibly had political intentions for Buddies when he founded the company with three other graduates of York University's theatre programme, these had nothing to do with lesbian or gay subjectivity but, rather, were firmly focused on theatrical experimentation.[9] That this remained the case for some years Gilbert substantiates in an article published late in 1983 in which he states that Buddies "was formed in 1979 to explore the relationship of the printed word to theatrical image in the belief that with the poet-playwright lies the future of Canadian theatre" (Keeney-Smith 35). Certainly this was the operative principle behind Buddies' first event, a six-play festival called *New Faces of '79*, the prototype of *Rhubarb!* which the company renamed the festival the following year.[10] In an article in which he outlines the history and aesthetic of *Rhubarb!* to 1986, Gilbert notes that "'to rhubarb' is to complain, and we were complaining about Canadian theatre" from the start ("Inside the Rhubarb! Festival" 40). Explaining how he selects work for *Rhubarb!*, Gilbert links complaint to experimentation: "The criteria are these: that the piece be a half-hour or less in length and that the creators (writers, directors, whatever) are experimenting theatrically. The experiment can be for the artist, for the audience, or for both" ("Inside the Rhubarb! Festival" 42).[11]

In the mid-1980s Buddies began to rework its mandate to emphasize gay and lesbian material. Before this time, Gilbert's co-founders departed the company and Buddies joined ranks with five alternative theatres to form the Theatre Centre, an artist-run organization set up to produce work by its members and other small companies lacking space and facilities. Although Gilbert wrote and directed plays concerning gay artists during the early 1980s,[12] only with *The Dressing Gown* in 1984 did he overtly position himself as a gay playwright interested in promoting gay and lesbian work. The sold-out run of *Drag Queens on Trial* the following year raised both his and Buddies' profile. Not coincidentally, 1985 also saw Buddies inaugurate its 4-Play Festival in which the company commissioned four new plays, two by lesbians and two by gay men.

With 4-Play, Buddies officially came out as a theatre company openly engaged in the production of work by and about lesbians and gay men. While Gilbert was to write and direct a number of successful productions during the next few years—most notably, *The Postman Rings Once* (1987), the company's first mainstage production, mounted at Toronto Workshop Productions—he allowed the focus of his company to shift to other artists whose talents emerged through the company's various festivals. By 1988, when Buddies celebrated the 10th anniversary of *Rhubarb!*, work by Audrey Butler, David Demchuk, Hillar Liitoja, Ken McDougall, Marcie Rogers, Robin Fulford, Ed Roy and others had expanded the company's reputation to include not only "innovative" but "gay and lesbian" as well. But while the audience for Buddies' programming had grown concomitantly, funding had not. In an article in *what* magazine published in 1988, Gilbert connected the company's financial problems with its reorientation towards gay programming citing, in particular, difficulties in funding 4-Play. Rather than abandon the festival, however, Gilbert announced that, in 1989, Buddies would bring back 4-Play "with a vengeance" ("What's coming" 5). 4-Play, he explained, would form the centre-piece of QueerCulture, a city-wide event integrating social, political and cultural activities sponsored by gay and lesbian organizations ranging from the Canadian Gay Archives to the Inside Out Collective which annually hosts Toronto's festival of lesbian and gay film and video.

The pro-active, political stance that Gilbert assumed in 1988 has been performed by Buddies ever since. My use of the verb "perform" here is meant to connect Buddies' sexual subjectivity from this time to the present with theories of identity formation advanced in queer theory—specifically, those that view subjectivity as performance. In his introduction to *The Politics and Poetics of Camp*, Moe Meyer explains that

> Whether one subscribes to an essentialist or constructionist theory of gay and lesbian identity, it comes down to the fact that, at some time, the actor must *do* something in order to

> produce the social visibility by which the identity is manifested. Postures, gestures, costume and dress, and speech acts become the elements that constitute both the identity and identity performance. When we shift the study of gay and lesbian identity into a performance paradigm, then every enactment of that identity depends, ultimately, upon extrasexual performative gestures. Even the act of "coming out," that is, the public proclamation of one's self-nomination as gay or lesbian, is constituted by an institutionalized speech act. (4)

To develop this argument, Meyer cites the work of Judith Butler for whom categories of sex and gender are neither innate nor stable but, rather, "performatives" continually in process. Theories of identity formation that utilize such ideas invariably stress not only that sexual subjectivity is constituted in and by its performance but that its performance, by necessity, is repeated. Certainly this is true for the gay or lesbian subject who wishes to be distinguished from the heterosexual norm. As Butler explains in her introduction to *Bodies that Matter: On the Discursive Limits of "Sex"*, extrasexual gestures such as posture, dress and speech acts both cite and signify differences from heteronormative behaviour—they both repeat and refer to other and previous performatives.

Elsewhere, writing about gender identity, Butler makes a point that is useful to my argument here:

> if gender ... is an imitation that regularly produces the ideal it attempts to approximate, then gender is a performance that *produces* the illusion of an inner sex or essence or psychic gender core; it *produces* on the skin, through the gesture, the move, the gait (that array of corporeal theatrics understood as gender presentation), the illusion of an inner depth ... it is always a surface sign, a signification on and with the public body ... ("Imitation and Gender Insubordination" 28)

In her introduction to *Bodies that Matter*, Butler addresses the term "queer" directly, suggesting that "the contentious practices of 'queerness' might be understood ... as a specific reworking of abjection into political agency." She continues with a statement particularly appropriate to Buddies' evolution since the late 1980s: "The public assertion of 'queerness' enacts performativity as citationality for the purposes of resignifying the abjection of homosexuality into defiance and legitimacy" (21).

Moe Meyer also makes a statement that applies to Buddies' positioning in the 1990s, as well as to the activities of Sky Gilbert whose performances, both on-stage and off, are central to its efficacy. Meyer writes: "… queer identity emerges as self-consciousness of one's gay and lesbian performativity sets in" (4). This application is warranted given that Gilbert has performed numerous versions of "queerness" since announcing QueerCulture in 1988. In the *what* article quoted above, for example, Gilbert offered his first published rehearsal of the term:

> Growing up in a heterosexually dominated culture, the gay man or lesbian woman finds a need to express (what by necessity become) the deepest darkest secrets of their sexual and emotional lives. The result is queer culture. Just as Canada is multi-cultural, it is multi-sexual, and the encouragement of queer culture (as opposed to its oppression) encourages a lively exchange of ideas and images about our sometimes very different experiences of life. ("What's coming" 5)

Gilbert's interest in the multi-sexuality of culture and the differences that prefigure artistic expression has shaped Buddies' subjectivity during the 1990s. The company repeatedly performs its subjectivity in its marketing materials, as well as its programming. In 1992, for example, Buddies stated QueerCulture's mandate in a succinct note that also applies to queer subjectivity: "QueerCulture is a three week long celebration of alternative visions of lesbian and gay life which are sexual, brazen, radical and unconventional" (Buddies, *1992 Calendar*, inside front cover). By this time, the company was performing positionality with confidence—and for good reason: QueerCulture had grown to encompass thirty-two events at ten different venues across the city including film, theatre, visual arts, music, literary readings and dance. It also had generated controversy which, in a move that Buddies was to repeat in 1993, the company turned to its advantage.

In a speech to the Milton, Ontario, Chamber of Commerce in December 1989, Otto Jelinek, then the National Revenue Minister for Canada's Conservative government, commented on federal arts funding by saying that "it is incumbent on the Canada Council, as it is on all agencies, to be accountable to the public." Threatening that "whether the arm's-length funding policy is considered sacrosanct or not, we're going to tamper with it," he went on to single out the grant of $61,000 that

Buddies had received from the Canada Council that year. Specifically, he cited Buddies' production of *Drag Queens on Trial* and then remarked, "That's homosexuals, I take it" (Dafoe C8). Buddies, rather than simply protest the comments (which, along with many other arts organizations, it did), adopted Jelinek's off-hand remark as the title of its second QueerCulture Festival in 1990, brandishing the comment on thousands of posters which, shaped as triangles, were printed on neon-pink paper.[13] The company's ironic use of a homophobic phrase provides a clear paradigm of the performative strategies that it would develop during the 90s. In this instance, like many to follow, queer subjectivity and its homophobic context are made visible through an extrasexual sign that both signifies and cites performance. For Moe Meyer, this performative strategy—one "used to enact a queer identity, with enactment defined as the production of social visibility" (5)—is the foundation of Camp.

In 1992, the evolution of Buddies' queer subjectivity took another turn when Gilbert implied that the mandate of QueerCulture had become the mandate of Buddies' programming in general. In a letter copied to various funding organizations he wrote:

> The work that goes on at Buddies is not only new work but work which exists outside of mainstream culture and goes anywhere from poking fun at "fine art" and popular culture to seriously frightening the audience and making them sincerely angry. For a long time I have been searching for a sense of QUEER [sic] Theatre which encompassed gay and lesbian issues as well as radical art. I think we are creating this art, and these artists, at Buddies. ("Artistic Director's Letter 1992" 7)

The following year, Buddies acknowledged its evolution from a "lesbian/gay" nomination to one more specifically "queer" in a variety of promotional materials. One of the most important is Gilbert's Artistic Director's Message published in the 1993 QueerCulture Guide where he establishes that the company's queer aesthetic now is unequivocal. Because he most completely supplies his definition of the word "queer" in this message, I quote it at length:

> Let's talk about the word Queer. Because it doesn't always mean gay or lesbian. It means sexual, radical, from another culture, non-linear, redefining form as well as content. It

means power and ownership of power, images of human bondage and submission (because power is sexual and so is queer, and all good theatre is about power and the manipulations of it but that's another essay.) So. What has been happening at Buddies in Bad Times Theatre in the last two years has been the definition of an aesthetic, as people learn that one doesn't have to be gay or lesbian to get involved, when people learn that queer theatre has as its common denominator a unique relationship with the audience—you come into the theatre assured of who you are and what you believe, but you leave the theatre all shook up. We are not into explaining comfortable, politically correct moral lessons here. We are, in contrast, at Buddies, providing a space and more importantly environment where radical, sexual work can be developed ... If I was a sweeter nicer guy, I'd call Buddies in Bad Times Theatre a "gay and lesbian theatre for all people." But I'm not that nice. I'm an orgiastic poet and a drag queen, and I feel compelled to call something queer what it is. ("Artistic Director's Message" inside cover)

Earlier in this essay I suggested that the process of Buddies' reconfiguration during the 1990s parallels challenges to gay and lesbian subjectivities represented by the increased use of the word "queer." To a large part, this increase has been stimulated by Queer Nation, the movement of activists that came into political consciousness during the 1980s through the struggle against bureaucratic indifference to the fight against AIDS. While Buddies has not aligned itself with Queer Nation in any direct manner, the company's definition of the term "queer" is similar to that used by Queer Nation in the early 1990s. In their introduction to an edition of *Out/Look* that covers the "birth of a queer nation" in 1991, Allan Berubé and Jeffrey Escoffier suggest that Queer Nation calls itself "queer," not "lesbian, gay and bisexual," because the latter are "awkward, narrow, and perhaps compromised words." Their reasoning for Queer Nation's use of "queer" applies equally to Buddies' use of the term: "*Queer* is meant to be confrontational—opposed to gay assimilationists and straight oppressors while inclusive of people who have been marginalized by anyone in power" (Berubé & Escoffier 12). In acknowledging that Queer Nation's task is made extremely difficult because it is fraught with contradictions, Berubé and Escoffier could be describing

Buddies where paradoxes also make the company vulnerable to misunderstanding:

> They are trying to combine contradictory impulses: to bring together people who have been made to feel perverse, queer, odd, outcast, different, and deviant, and to affirm sameness by defining a common identity on the fringes. They are inclusive, but within boundaries that threaten to marginalize those whose difference doesn't conform to the new nation. These contradictions are locked in the name Queer Nation:
> QUEER = DIFFERENCE
> NATION = SAMENESS
> (Berubé & Escoffier 12)

In the same article in which Sky Gilbert acknowledges that Buddies represents "a radical fringe of the gay and lesbian community" (Hunt 29), he also describes an event called *Jane Goes Shopping* that was part of QueerCulture's 1992 programme. Dressed as Jane, a flamboyant drag queen who makes no attempt to disguise her gender-blur, Gilbert and an entourage of "other drag queens and leather dykes" (Hunt 29) visited the Eaton Centre, a shopping mall in downtown Toronto, where Jane shopped for a new spring frock. Gilbert explains in the *eye* article that "if people shopping in those stores are offended, they'll have to deal with it. It's an in-your-face political act ..." (Hunt 29). As part of QueerCulture the previous year, Jane led a similar group on a tour of various outdoor haunts in Toronto's gay neighbourhood where s/he had performed sex. These excursions are similar in their tactics and effects to those of Queer Nation that "play on the politics of cultural subversion: theatrical demonstrations, infiltrations of shopping malls and straight bars, kiss-ins and be-ins" (Berubé & Escoffier 14). They also illustrate Camp which Meyer argues (*pace* Susan Sontag[14]) "has become an activist strategy for organizations such as ACT UP and Queer Nation, as well as a focus in utopian movements like the Radical Faeries" (1). As Camp, Jane's performances—whether scheduled or not—provide an "oppositional critique embodied in the signifying practices that processually constitute queer identities" (Meyer 1).

The idea that the meaning of all texts and, indeed, of all contexts, depends upon the subject position of the reader is especially problematic for the Camp performance that Buddies presents. In Buddies' short history, this became most apparent during its 1993 QueerCulture festival when the company's funding was jeopardized because of public reactions to press depictions of its programming: these reactions, I presume, are what Sky Gilbert refers to, in the letter that begins this essay, as "the plagues of various right wing fundamentalists" ("Artistic Director's Letter 1994" 1). To a large degree, the reactions were incited by Christina Blizzard, a columnist with the *Toronto Sun* who, on April 1, 1993, announced that Buddies had received a grant from the City of Toronto for $58,908 in a column headed "Live sex group gets city bucks" (14). Blizzard was concerned that Buddies would use its funding to "present sado-masochism seminars as well as a 'female ejaculation Pajama Party'" ("Live Sex" 14) during its 1993 QueerCulture festival.

Despite the facts that these seminars were only three of 36 events programmed for the ten venues included in the four-week festival, and that none of the seminars was funded by Buddies itself, Blizzard used excerpts from descriptions of the seminars published in the 1993 QueerCulture Guide to represent Buddies' activities in general. In a series of columns that sustained her attack on the company, Blizzard generated enough public anxiety about Buddies' programming and funding that the budget committee of Metro Council—the body of elected politicians representing the six boroughs of Metropolitan Toronto—decided to debate its response to Buddies' annual application for a grant when it met in early July. A news story published in the *Sun* in late April, reports Alan Tonks, Chairman (*sic*) of Metro Council, as saying, "I can tell you the concerns raised by the reports that you and others have been making on this QueerCulture festival have given serious rise to a heightened concern for the manner in which public money is being expended" (Blizzard, "Hard look" 16).[15]

What interests me about this fracas, at least in the context of this essay, is that Blizzard did not need to mis-quote Buddies' descriptions of these events to incite her readers' outrage and lobbying tactics. She could rely on descriptions of the seminars to excite her readers' homophobia. Quoting the QueerCulture Guide in her column, Blizzard notes that the S/M seminars will present a "hands-on, pants down approach to SM techniques and safety." She also explains that the female ejaculation party invites participants to "bring sex toys, your pillows, your girl-friends and your sisters to a hands-on, girls-only party and learn to ejaculate" ("Live sex" 14). While such performances may not have been understood as Camp by many of her readers, they certainly were perceived as "queer."[16]

On July 7, 1993, Metro council granted Buddies its request for $26,500 after a heated debate that led to a 15–13 vote by its members.[17] Ostensibly, this debate concerned arts funding but, invariably, it focused on the sexuality of the artists applying for subsidy—or, more accurately, on the performance of sexuality enacted by descriptions of the seminars. As a result, the debate provides invaluable material for theorizing the social circumstance of queer relations in Canadian culture today. For Tim Jones, there was no need to theorize; as he said, "This was homosexuality on trial ..." ("Restore Funding" A16). Much to the chagrin of Metro politicians, Jones' claim was supported by an editorial in *The Toronto Star*; beginning with the comment that "Metro's gay and lesbian community is right to be wondering why its cultural groups were the only ones left out of the grants bonanza at Metro Hall last week,"[18] the editorial concluded: "Unfortunately, homophobia, not economic concerns, seems to have been the driving force behind the committee's decision" ("Restore Funding" A16).

To begin his 1994 General Manager's Report to the Canada Council, Tim Jones, like Sky Gilbert, refers to the "times" in which Buddies operates. After noting the "generally bleak economic climate," he comments that Buddies successfully undertook the responsibility of managing the 12 Alexander Street Project "while withstanding an ongoing assault on its freedom of expression and funding by homophobes and anti-arts funding advocates." To substantiate his belief that Buddies has emerged "profoundly strengthened as an organization," Jones cites the positive support of public organizations like the *Toronto Star*, and an impressive statistic: "... an overall growth in box office revenues of more than 30% this season" (1).

Ironically, this growth partially results from the funding fracas or, more precisely, from the ways in which Buddies responded to attacks with an aggressive performance of protest. Buddies' press releases, posters, public demonstrations and a variety of activities at its theatre galvanized a unified outcry from Toronto's arts constituencies and mobilized the anger of Toronto's gay and lesbian communities into political action. As a result, Buddies not only won its grant from Metro Council but exposed the homophobia that made its funding an issue.[19]

These, then, are the "times" that affect how Buddies operates in the mid-1990s. For many who identify with Toronto's gay and lesbian communities, the times are neither new nor unexpected; as a result they cannot celebrate Buddies' move into 12 Alexander Street without some concern. As Sue Golding, the president of Buddies' board of directors, eloquently puts it in her letter to the Ontario Arts Council in February 1994,

> Over the past three years, the artists, producers, administrators and technical staff—even the audiences—at Buddies have undergone a remarkable metamorphosis. We have transformed from being a nomadic theatre company attempting to put on the best avant-garde/experimental, gay and lesbian theatre in this city, to one which has set its sites [sic] on creating one of the most accessible, provocative and vibrant art centres in the province. Despite incredibly difficult times, including relentless attacks by right-wing media, the move has not been without its sweet victories: for we have brought together people from all walks of life—people who might not have ever rubbed shoulders with each other in different settings—and we have done this during one of the most devastating crises to hit our community. We have tried to offer, and I think for the most part succeeded, to those who have been wreaked [sic] by the untold death and destruction of HIV/AIDS, a tiny bit of respite, a "little night magic," as we've said in our season brochures; and we've tried to do this not simply by ripping apart old myths around sex and race or gender or class, but by playing with and against new forms of art itself, pitching that play at the highest professional standards available. (1)

Setting sites, citing sets, playing difference, pitching play: these are the performatives of a queer theatre.

Notes

1. One of the first theorists to introduce the idea of "queer theory" in a published text was the American academic Teresa de Lauretis who, in a special issue of the scholarly journal, *differences*, introduced a collection of essays "generated in the context of a working conference on theorizing lesbian and gay sexualities that was held at the University of California, Santa Cruz in February 1990" (iii) under the title "Queer Theory: Lesbian and Gay Sexualities." In her introduction de Lauretis explains her decision to use the term:

   > The term "queer," juxtaposed to the "lesbian and gay" of the subtitle, is intended to mark a certain critical distance from the latter, by now established and often convenient, formula. For the

phrase "lesbian and gay" or "gay and lesbian" has become the standard way of referring to what only a few years ago used to be simply "gay" (e.g., the gay community, the gay liberation movement) or, just a few years earlier still, "homosexual" (iv).

Since this early instance of sanctioned usage, many other theorists have advanced the term "queer theory" in a wide range of published texts. For recent, notable examples pertinent to this essay, see the anthologies edited by Michael Warner, R. Jeffrey Ringer, and Martha Gever, John Greyson and Pratibha Parmar listed in Works Cited.

2. Antony Easthope and Kate McGowan discuss the relationship between the terms "subjectivity" and "individual" in their introduction to "Section Three (Subjectivity)" of *A Critical and Cultural Theory Reader*. Here they explain that

> the concept of subjectivity decentres the individual by problematizing the simplistic relationship between language and the individual which common sense presumes. It replaces human nature with concepts of history, society and culture as determining factors in the *construction* of individual identity, and destabilizes the coherence of that identity by making it an *effect* rather than simply an origin of linguistic practice. (67)

3. In *Sexuality*, Jeffrey Weeks explains that

> homosexual activities are of course widespread in all cultures and there is a sustained history of homosexuality in the West. But the idea that there is such a thing as the homosexual person is a relatively new one. All the evidence suggests that before the eighteenth century homosexuality, interpreted in its broadest sense as involving erotic activities between people of the same gender, certainly existed, "homosexuals" did not. (33)

4. Perhaps because she is a lesbian, Teresa de Lauretis gives more weight or, at least, explanation to Meyer's second point. Writing about the term "lesbian and gay" in "Queer Theory: Lesbian and Gay Sexualities," she states that

> our "differences," such as they may be, are less represented by the discursive coupling of those two terms in the politically correct phrase "lesbian and gay," than they are elided by most of the contexts in which the phrase is used; that is to say, differences are implied in it but then simply taken for granted or even covered over by the word "and". (v–vi)

5. In proffering this theory of reading, I align myself with Catherine Belsey who calls for "a new critical practice which insists on finding the plurality, however 'parsimonious,' of the text and refuses the pseudo-dominance constructed as the 'obvious' position of its intel-

ligibility...." In *Critical Practice*, Belsey goes on to state that "As readers and critics we can choose actively to seek out the process of production of the text: the organization of the discourses which constitute it and the strategies by which it smoothes over the incoherencies and contradictions of the ideology inscribed in it" (129).

6. The focus of Davy's paper is *Dress Suits to Hire*, a play by Holly Hughes, an American lesbian playwright who attracted considerable attention as one of "the NEA four"—four American artists whose funding from the National Endowment for the Arts was rescinded in 1990. Davy explains that "from its inception, *Dress Suits* was made to be performed at P.S. 122, an East Village [New York] venue for new, or non-mainstream, theatre, dance, music, and performance art." As such, it represented a departure for Hughes and her collaborators who usually created work for the WOW Cafe, a theatre space in Manhattan's East Village whose address, Davy states, "is clearly lesbian" (153). Davy further explains that in the WOW context, "... artists create a theatre *for* lesbians, a theatre that responds to lesbian subjectivity" (154). She then proceeds to examine *Dress Suits* in performance at P.S. 122 and, eventually, in a university theatre in Ann Arbor, Michigan, her goal being to answer the question "What does it mean, then, when lesbian theatre is performed in venues outside of lesbian performance spaces?" (166).

7. This idea is further substantiated by a long programme note written by Sue Golding, the president of Buddies' board of directors since 1986, published in 1992 in which she overtly situates Buddies on a map of "radical geography." Because of the metaphoric intricacy of her statement, as well as its clear use of "positionality," I quote it in full:

> In the face of a cruel and relentless recession—replete with our bureaucrats proclaiming at every turn, its imminent end—a peculiar laughter refuses to be destroyed. It is a laughter filtered through the bright lights of the city and nurtured on the very anonymity of being "urban." It is not by accident that this urbanity, utterly fractured and diverse at its very core, is the strange dome to queer-ness itself. And we begin to map its routings: no longer constituted by community politics, community aesthetics, community ethics; we have here, instead, little cities: the little cities of drag; the little cities of S&M; the little cities of vanilla sex; the little cities of celibacy. We weave ourselves against and through and alongside these cities, with pleasure (and pain) being our only guides. Sometimes public, sometimes

private, sometimes underground, sometimes fictional and sometimes all or none of these at exactly the same moment, we toast to life (and death) in all its profane and impure ways.

Along the strange routings of this radical geography sits a little inn, a little roadside hut where queers of every ilk can take a rest, a drink, a joke, a fuck—and do more than simply survive. At Buddies, these kinds of urban refreshments are available to all those attracted to and propelled by the crazy throbs of the city ... ("President's Message" back cover).

8. For a fuller discussion of the relationship between marketing, reviewing and funding of small theatre companies, see my essay "Producing Marginality: Criticism and the Construction of Canadian Theatre." For a useful critique of the systems of "peer evaluation" used by Canadian funding bodies, see Ann Wilson, "A Jury of Her Peers."

9. The name of the company is taken from a lyric by French songwriter and singer Jacques Prevert.

10. This first version of *Rhubarb!* was co-produced by Buddies and Nightwood Theatre, a feminist theatre with which the company became associated as part of the Theatre Centre in 1979. By the mid-1980s, Buddies had become *Rhubarb!*'s sole producer. Exactly when, and why, Buddies assumed exclusive "ownership" of *Rhubarb!* is unclear, as are many other details about the relationship between the founding members of the Theatre Centre during its early years.

11. *Rhubarb!*'s combination of experimentation and complaint has made the festival an annual hit with artists and audiences alike—and it has more than fulfilled Buddies' mandate to produce innovative work. In an article titled "Towards a New Dramaturgy" published in *Canadian Theatre Review*, Paul Leonard comments that "Buddies' insistence that *Rhubarb!* pieces be given genuine, if somewhat undernourished productions has enabled the event to establish itself as a festival, with the characteristics of other theatre festivals—variety, concentration, and unusual fare—rather than as a developmental series for theatre insiders only" (45). For his part Gilbert argues that "by allowing artists to test their work before an audience, Buddies has engendered a unique approach to Canadian dramaturgy" (Buddies, "Supplementary Information" 2)—a statement that warrants consideration given that, by 1992 *Rhubarb!* had produced 205 different shows under its banner.

12. For example, *Cavafy* (1981), *Pasolini/Pelosi* (1983) and *Life Without Muscles or Growing Up Artistic* (1983), a play about the life and work of David Hockney.
13. A pink triangle was used by the Nazi party to signify homosexual prisoners held in concentration camps during World War II. Since the late 1960s it has been used internationally as a symbol of lesbian and gay liberation movements.
14. Meyer suggests that Susan Sontag's influential essay, "Notes on Camp," first published in 1964, complicated interpretations of the term camp "by detaching the signifying codes from their queer signified" (5). The result is that camp (Meyer distinguishes his use of the word by capitalizing it) usually is defined as "apolitical, aestheticized, and frivolous" (1), a signification he intends this book to challenge. For another "authorized account of camp" (Sedgwick 250), see Andrew Ross; also useful is Jack Babuscio's "Camp and the Gay Sensibility."
15. By late June, the grant application of the Inside Out Collective also had come under scrutiny by Metro Council. At issue in its case were descriptions that the Collective published in its Programme Guide for the 1993 festival of gay and lesbian film and video held during QueerCulture. The Collective had distributed the Guide to a large number of locations throughout Metropolitan Toronto including public libraries in mid-May. Ironically, Metro Council had made distribution of the Guide a requirement of its 1992 grant to the company.
16. At the denotative level of signification, "queer" remains pejorative in general usage. *The Concise Oxford Dictionary* defines the word as "strange, odd, eccentric; of questionable character, shady, suspect; out of sorts, giddy, faint" (Oxford 846). The *Oxford* restricts its definition of "queer" as a noun to its "slang" usage as "homosexual," noting that it is "Esp. male." The two definitions, I suggest, are intermingled in contemporary alternative or oppositional discourse where both the sexual signification of nominal use combines with the "strangely suspect" qualities signified by the adjectival form.
17. In the same meeting, Metro Council voted to reject the grant application of the Inside Out Collective in a 14-14 tie.
18. Of the 203 arts organizations that submitted grant applications to Metropolitan Toronto Council for public funding in 1993, only two were subjected to special scrutiny—Buddies in Bad Times Theatre and the Inside Out Collective.

19. A further irony ensued: in 1994, Buddies relinquished control of QueerCulture, explaining that the festival "has not only ballooned in size, it has taken on a mandate to include cultural activities which are not necessarily art. In effect, the mandate of the festival has eclipsed that of Buddies" (Jones 8). Although Buddies continues to contribute 4-Play and other performance events to the festival, QueerCulture now is managed by an independent company with its own programming committee and board to which Buddies contributes.

Works Cited

Babuscio, Jack. "Camp and the Gay Sensibility." *Gays and Film*. Ed. Richard Dyer. New York: Zoetrope, 1984. 40–57.
Belsey, Catherine. *Critical Practice*. London: Routledge, 1980.
Berubé, Allan and Jeffrey Escoffier. "Queer/Nation." *Out/Look* 11 (Winter 1992): 12–14.
Blizzard, Christina. "Hard look at grants to troupe." *The Toronto Sun* (22 April 1993): 16.
——————. "Live sex group gets city bucks." *The Toronto Sun* (1 April 1993): 14.
Buddies in Bad Times Theatre. *1992 Calendar*. Toronto: Archives of Buddies in Bad Times Theatre.
——————. "Supplementary Information." Application to the Laidlaw Foundation, 1 April 1992. Toronto: Archives of Buddies in Bad Times Theatre. 3 pages.
——————. *QueerCulture Program 1991* (6–28 April 1991). Toronto: Archives of Buddies in Bad Times Theatre. 3 pages.
Butler, Judith. *Bodies That Matter: On the Discursive Limits of Sex*. New York: Routledge, 1993.
——————. "Imitation and Gender Insubordination." *inside/out: Lesbian Theories, Gay Theories*. Ed. Diana Fuss. New York: Routledge, 1991. 13–31.
Concise Oxford English Dictionary, 7th ed. s.v. "queer."
Dafoe, Chris. "Jelinek Under Fire for Remarks on Grants." *The Globe and Mail* (2 December 1989): C8.
Davy, Kate. "Reading Past the Heterosexual Imperative: Dress Suits to Hire." *The Drama Review* 33.1 (Spring 1989): 153–70.

de Lauretis, Teresa. "Queer Theory: Lesbian and Gay Sexualities. An Introduction." *differences* 3.2 (Summer 1991): iii–xviii.

Dolan, Jill. "Geographies of Learning: Theatre Studies, Performance, and the 'Performative'." *Theatre Journal* 45.4 (December 1993): 417–41.

Easthope, Anthony and Kate McGowan. "Introduction: Section Three." *A Critical and Cultural Theory Reader*. Eds. Anthony Easthope and Kate McGowan. Toronto: University of Toronto Press, 1993. 67–70.

Gever, Martha, John Greyson and Pratibha Parmar, eds. *Queer Looks: Perspectives on Lesbian and Gay Film and Video*. Toronto: Between the Lines, 1993.

Gilbert, Sky. "Artistic Director's Letter 1994." Letter to the Theatre Advisory Committee of the Ontario Arts Council, 01 March 1994. Toronto: Archives of Buddies in Bad Times Theatre. 13 pages.

———. "Artistic Director's Letter 1992." Letter to the Theatre Advisory Committee of the Laidlaw Foundation, 01 April 1992. Toronto: Archives of Buddies in Bad Times Theatre. 7 pages.

———. "Artistic Director's Message." *Programme Guide: QueerCulture 1993* (10 April–09 May 1993). Toronto: Archives of Buddies in Bad Times Theatre. Inside front cover.

———. "Inside the Rhubarb! Festival." *Canadian Theatre Review* 49 (Winter 1986): 40–43.

———. "Rhubarb in your face." Programme for *Rhubarb!* (20 January–16 February 1992). Toronto: Archives of Buddies in Bad Times Theatre. Inside front cover.

———. "What's coming: Spring, 1989." *what* 17 (February 1989): 5.

Golding, Sue. Letter to Jan McIntyre, Ontario Arts Council, 01 February 1994. Toronto: Archives of Buddies in Bad Times Theatre. 3 pages.

———. "President's Message." Programme for *Rhubarb!* (29 January–16 February 1992). Toronto: Archives of Buddies in Bad Times Theatre. Outside back cover.

Goodwin, Joseph P. *More Man Than You'll Ever Be: Gay Folklore and Acculturation in Middle America*. Bloomington: Indiana University Press, 1989.

Hunt, Nigel. "He's here, he's queer and he's sometimes Jane." *eye* 9 (April 1992): 29.

Jones, Tim. "General Manager's Report." Letter to the Theatre Advisory Committee of the Canada Council, 01 February 1994. Toronto: Archives of Buddies in Bad Times Theatre. 11 pages.

Keeny-Smith, Patricia. "Living With Risk: Toronto's New Alternate Theatre." *Canadian Theatre Review* 38 (Fall 1983): 33–43.
Lacey, Liam. "Steel Kiss confronts audience with reality of homophobia." *The Globe and Mail* (22 Nov. 1991): C5.
Leonard, Paul. "Towards a New Dramaturgy." *Canadian Theatre Review* 49 (Winter 1986): 44–50.
Marshall, Brenda K. *Teaching the Postmodern: Fiction and Theory*. New York: Routledge, 1992.
Meyer, Moe. "Introduction: Reclaiming the Discourse of Camp." *The Politics and Poetics of Camp*. Ed. Moe Meyer. New York: Routledge, 1994. 1–22.
"Restore Funding." *The Toronto Star* 6 July 1993: A16. [Editorial.]
Ringer, R. Jeffrey, ed. *Queer Words, Queer Images: Communication and the Construction of Homosexuality*. New York: New York University Press, 1994.
Ross, Andrew. "Uses of Camp." *Intellectuals and Popular Culture*. New York: Routledge, 1989.
Sedgwick, Eve Kosofsky and Michael Moon. "Divinity: A Dossier, A Performance Piece, A Little-Understood Emotion." *Tendencies*. Durham: Duke University Press, 1993. 215–51.
Smith, Paul. *Discerning the Subject*. Minneapolis: University of Minnesota Press, 1988.
Sontag, Susan. "Notes on Camp." *A Susan Sontag Reader*. New York: Vintage Books, 1983. 105–19.
Wallace, Robert. "Making Out Positions: An Introduction." *Making, Out: Plays by Gay Men*. Toronto: Coach House Press, 1992. 11–40.
——————. "Producing Marginality: Criticism and the Construction of Canadian Theatre." *Producing Marginality: Theatre and Criticism in Canada*. Saskatoon: Fifth House Publishers, 1990. 107–76.
Warner, Michael. "Introduction." *Fear of a Queer Planet: Queer Politics and Social Theory*. Ed. Michael Warner. Minneapolis: University of Minnesota Press, 1993. vii–xxxi.
Weeks, Jeffrey. *Sexuality*. New York: Ellis Horwood, 1986.
Wilson, Ann. "A Jury of Her Peers." *Canadian Theatre Review* 51 (Summer 1987): 4–8.

The Culture of Abuse in *Under the Skin,* *This is for You, Anna* and *Lion in the Streets*

by Ann Wilson

In recent years, the sexual abuse of children looms as a horrifying social problem. This is not to suggest that the abuse of children is a phenomena particular to the late twentieth century, nor that the incidence of abuse has risen dramatically from earlier periods; rather this grotesque form of abuse, for the first time, is a topic of public discussion, including in a range of plays. What emerges from this discussion is the startling realization that in most cases, the sexual abuse of a child is not perpetrated by an assailant who is unknown to his victim but is an intimate of the child's family—a friend of the family, an uncle, a cousin, brother or father—rupturing our sense of family as a network of safe, nurturing relationships. As Gary Boire notes, the sexual abuse of children is an all too pervasive aspect of family life which collapses the boundaries "between the normal reader and discomfiting abnormal criminal. 'He' is a collective 'we.' The part *must* be the whole" (217). Boire asks, "Perhaps, just perhaps, an abusive social system is producing abusive individuals?" (217).

The culture of abuse, partially manifest as the sexual abuse of children, is explored in three plays by Canadian women: *Under the Skin* (1985) by Betty Lambert, *This is for You, Anna* (1985) by The Anna Project[1] and *Lion in the Streets* (1990) by Judith Thompson. While the action of these three plays is propelled by the deaths of girls who have been sexually molested and then murdered, none focuses on the actual

---

ANN WILSON teaches in the Department of Drama, University of Guelph. A former editor of *Canadian Theatre Review*, she currently co-edits *Essays in Canadian Theatre/Études théâtrales*. Her research interests include contemporary British and Canadian drama with a particular focus on women's writing.

event which might make it the object for an audience's voyeuristic consumption; rather each of the plays deals with the aftermath of the abuse and death, exploring the conditions under which such acts occur. In different ways, each of these plays suggests that the sexual abuse of children is not an isolated evil but the horrifyingly logical effect of ideologies which shape our understanding of gender and sexuality.

Lambert's *Under the Skin* is a domestic drama involving the lives of two neighboring families, the Bentons and the Giffords. On a spring morning, Maggie Benton, a university English professor divorced from her husband, is frantic with fear because her thirteen-year-old daughter, Emma, has disappeared. She has come to her friend, Renee Gifford, in search of comfort where none can be provided, for nothing but the safe return of a missing child can alleviate a parent's anguish. In the face of her friend's anger and despair, Renee offers what solace she can, commenting that her husband John "himself has been out every day. You've got good friends" (118).

Under the Skin evolves over a period of 181 days, ending with the police arriving, at Renee's request, to search John's workshop where we are led to believe they will find Emma's body. The action of the play charts Maggie's desperate attempt to come to terms with her daughter's disappearance which, without the resolution of the discovery of her body, is the constant tension between the rational knowledge that Emma must be dead and the unrealistic hope that she will defy the statistical average and be discovered alive. At one point, well into the summer, Maggie speaks to her missing daughter: "It's like living with a stone at your centre … I wish I could bury you and it would be finished. I want my life to start again" (150).

In this period of intense, protracted and unrelenting despair, Maggie is living a sort of death, going through the motions of living. She turns to Renee as if the contact with another person will keep her connected to life however tenuously. Renee's life revolves around her children and her husband, John, who is the third in the trio of characters in the play. What emerges in the exchanges between the three is not only a compelling portrait of a mother dealing with a missing child presumed dead, but of a woman married to a man who, as it turns out, has abducted Emma and held her captive in his workshop until she eventually dies. Not surprisingly, the memory of Emma functions as a site of contestation and negotiation between the three. For the audience, whose only knowledge of Emma comes from characters who have incompatible investments in their memories of her, the question is not which memory is accurate but what these differing perspectives on a thirteen-year-old entering a period of self-conscious awareness of her sexuality tell us about the adults who hold them.

Understandably enough, Maggie remembers a girl who is innocent, by her mother's account virtually retreating from concern with her body into a fixation on religion. When Renee suggests that Emma's behaviour towards John was flirtatiously provocative—"she was always at John, rubbing up against him" (141)—Maggie protests that Emma "was on this big religious kick. She was always quoting those last lines from Anne Frank ..." (141). Renee, trying to negotiate the differences, suggests that Emma was probably sublimating her sexuality (141). The exchange between the two women shifts focus to John when he mocks Renee by pretending that he doesn't know the meaning of "sublimation." He taunts, "I'm just an ignorant guy, Renee, I never went to no college course in psychology at night school" (142). The move is insidious, a demand by John that he be the focus of attention which he gains by mocking his wife.

John is, as Maggie notes, a bully who feels threatened by the friendship between the women. His strategy, in this instance, is to call into question Maggie's loyalty by trying to get her to betray her relationship with her friend through encouraging her to participate in his belittling of his wife. But Maggie refuses to side with him. Frustrated, John tries to humiliate Maggie by playing a game of truth. In a remarkable moment in their exchange, John asks Maggie if she finds him sexually arousing which she admits that she does. When he asks if she hates him, she responds,

> You're not important enough to hate, John. I merely despise your type ... The bully. The little bully. You push her around because she's helpless and can't do anything about it. You push her around but if anybody stands up to you you back down. (144)

What is of interest is the apparent contradiction in Maggie's attraction to a man whom she despises, for what sort of self-loathing is rehearsed in the attraction to a man who bullies and humiliates women?

The erotic economy of *Under the Skin* is complex, with attractions between the three characters, and particularly between the two women, intelligible only within the contexts of the characters' histories, which inflect their current behaviour. Early in the play, Maggie tells Renee that although the spring has brought signs of renewed life, she feels that she "should pass and the grass should wither" (134). Renee offers the banal response that "life goes on," and then provides a bit of her history, as if it parallels Maggie's. She recalls, "When Nick and I broke up, I said, That's that and I let him go," implying that the dissolution of a relationship with a man is the equivalent of the loss of a child (134). When Maggie protests, Renee explodes, saying that Maggie has never known struggle (134). "[I]f something happened to John we'd be done for," she explains and then continues to vent her resentment that Maggie is financially independent and finally concluding with the apparent nonsequitur, "I was raped once you know" (135).

What joins these apparent unrelated comments equating Maggie's loss with the break-up of Renee's marriage and her rape is the victimization of women to which they are easily susceptible because the dominant ideologies of gender in the West accord privilege to men by defining women in relation to men. In Maggie's case, John's crime against her daughter shatters Maggie's life, making her the living dead. In Renee's case, her perception of herself as inferior—to her friend and to her husband upon whom she is financially reliant—rehearse her apparently life-long feelings of victimization.

The consequences of this victimization are apparent in the lives of both women, but perhaps most obviously in that of Renee who seems to constantly try to appease a man whose response to her is fuelled by a virulent misogyny. In a marriage marked by John's ceaseless degradation of his wife, apparent in angry outbursts when he names her "cunt" and "whore," she seems resigned to unhappily making due with her situation, claiming that she "can't make it without a man!" (166). Then, as if to protect the fragile façade of her marriage, she lashes out at Maggie: "It's true what he says, you're just trying to get in between us, you're making me think things about him it's you ... (*starts to sob*) ... I can't stand it, Maggie, I can't live" (166).

In the end, Renee allows the realization that she isn't John's only victim to come to full consciousness and accepts that he was Emma's abuser and murderer. She calls the police and asks them to come to search John's workshop. When she makes the call, Maggie is standing with her, suddenly aware that her daughter's assailant was their neighbor and friend. "Forgive me," pleads Renee but Maggie says "Never" (194). Understandable though Maggie's anguish at the realization that her daughter was being held so close to home, in the space beneath the neighbor's workshop, her implication that Renee was somehow an accomplice to Emma's abuse ought not to be left unexamined, even though it does ring with a certain emotional veracity. Renee, John's other victim, is cast by Maggie as the victimizer in much the same way that earlier Renee had cast Maggie as aggressively trying to destroy her marriage.

In *Under the Skin*, the sexual abuse of children is the conflation of sexuality and subjugation which, as Adrienne Rich suggests in "Compulsory Heterosexuality and Lesbian Existence," may characterize masculine desire within our culture because the "institution of heterosexuality itself [is] ... a beachhead of male dominance" (633). In Western epistemologies, woman is secondary to man and is defined in relation to him so that sexual difference is represented as feminine lack. Man is not only the defining element, but is the primary, dominant one. This sense of woman-as-not-having-that-which-man-has is translated socially into a justification for denying woman access to power, for she who lacks cannot wield power with the same authority as man. Historically society has tended to forget that woman's secondary status is a consequence of the ways in which sexual difference are understood; instead, the relation of woman to man is naturalized, her inferiority not an interpretation of knowledge which is socially produced but an alterable fact: woman *is*— not *seems to be*—secondary to man. In the actualities of the material world, the implications of theses gender roles are legion: men enjoy economic privilege by having higher wages than women which results in women being all-too-frequently economically dependent on men. Consequently, women cultivate men's favour by subscribing to male notions of femininity. In conventional formulations of heterosexuality, the economy of sexual desire is asymmetrical: women are the objects of male desire but rarely can assert themselves as the agents of desire because acting counters the notion of passivity and powerlessness which social convention historically posits as attributes of femininity.

Rich would have us believe that heterosexuality precludes any truly equal, consensual relation between a man and woman because the social construction of masculinity demands that he exercise power over another. The sexual abuse of children is the logical effect of this configuration of heterosexuality, horrifying because of its excess: the object of male desire, a child, is so obviously not the equal, consenting partner in a relationship with an adult man. The excess of this crime occurs in another way because the impact of the abuse spills beyond the actual victim, destroying the networks of intimate social relations established to nurture the child into adulthood. By the end of *Under the Skin*, for example, not only does it seem that Maggie and Renee will never be friends but they are the secondary victims of John's crime against Emma.

In both *This is for You, Anna* and *Lion in the Streets*, the sexual abuse of children is contextualized as a consequence of dominant ideologies so that it cannot be seen as an isolated occurrence perpetrated by an abhorrent individual. *This is for You, Anna* deals with Marianne Bachmeier who walked into a German court room and killed the man who was standing trial for rape and murder of her seven-year-old daughter, Anna. Initially Bachmeier was cheered as the avenging mother who brought her child's killer to justice. Her actions, read as an expression of maternal love, drew attention to her as a mother but, as the details of her life came under scrutiny, she was found wanting because she had not been married to Anna's father, had a series of lovers and had several abortions. In short, Bachmeier's life, marked by her own sexual desire, was at odds with conventional notions of the mother as an asexual figure who selflessly devotes herself to her children. The reading of Bachmeier's action was revised in the popular press which now saw Anna's death as the consequence of inadequate mothering. *This is for You, Anna* further revises the reading of the incident by refusing to read it as narrative of individual acts, heroic or otherwise, as did the initial accounts in the popular press and the later revision. The play suggests that the conditions of Anna being raped and killed by Grabowski were the result of the intersection of three lives—Anna's, her mother's and Grabowski's—which were shaped by ideologies, including those determining gender and sexuality.

The primary focus of the play is Marianne, a woman whom we learn was born in 1950 into a family where her father was an alcoholic. She was removed from her family and sent to a children's home where she was discouraged from getting an education (254). The play suggests that her only resource for negotiating the world was her sexuality, a beauty which attracted men but left her feeling it was her sole worth (259). Bachmeier is, then, like Renee in *Under the Skin*, a woman whose sense of herself relies on her physical attractiveness but, whereas realistic techniques of Lambert's play naturalize Renee's sense of inferiority making it seem as if it were a personal pathology, The Anna Project's use of Brechtian effects, including having four actors play the role Marianne, refuses the notion that Marianne's situation as unique; rather, she is every woman and her sense of herself as a woman is produced culturally. This latter point is made clearly through the episodic structure of the play in which the story of Bachmeier does not evolve in a linear fashion but is closer to a theatrical collage: images of Bachmeier, accounts of her told not by another character but by an actor, conventional dialogues between Bachmeier and others in her life. Interspersed with these glimpses into Bachmeier's life are stories of other women living in abusive situations and tales of love, for example the story of Agate, the beautiful young woman desperately in love with a baron who forsakes her to marry a woman of his own class (252). When Agate pursues him, he orders his guards to put out her eyes. Another story is that of Lucretia who, when her husband's friend attempts to rape her, asks him to kill her to preserve her virtue but he refuses her request and rapes her, confident that shame will prevent her from speaking of this incident (265).

These tales serve as poignant reminders that children often hear stories which romanticize the suffering of women, conflating the psychological and physical cruelty of men towards women with love. Indeed, Renee's story of her rape in *Under the Skin* is startling in its parallels to Lucretia's in *This is for You, Anna*. Suffering is presented in these stories as an attribute of femininity and victimization as becoming women. If Bachmeier and the other abused women in *This is for You, Anna* are any indication, these stories of womanhood are well-learned by women who live according to these codes of femininity and, through their example, teach their daughters.

Like her mother, Anna was beautiful, a little girl who, through the circumstances of her life with her mother, had learned to negotiate the world through her attractiveness. Grabowski told "the court that Anna flirted with him" (254), a claim which John had made about Emma. These defenses alarmingly imply that female sexuality is fully developed from an early age, that the sexuality of an adult woman masquerades in the figure of a little girl and that men, faced with the allure, have no control over their responses, yielding to the temptation, violating not just the physical but also the psychological integrity of women and girls through rape. But in the scenario which represents female sexuality as the temptation which a man cannot resist, who is the victim? Clearly, the implication is that female sexuality is inherently dangerous to men, a position which does not acknowledge the degree to which society primarily defines women in terms of their bodies. Logic demands if these bodies are dangerous, then they must be subjected to submission, their potentially destructive elements controlled in a variety of ways, including in the extreme through physical abuse, perhaps even murder. In a culture which provides such fundamentally contradictory codings of femininity as rooted in the body which is to be feared and despised, women not only accept abuse in its myriad of forms, but often inflict it on themselves wanting, as Renee claims, to die.

This is for You, Anna recounts the stories of four abused women: Jenny, Eena, Maria and Marianne Bachmeier. Each is in an abusive relationship, theatrically represented through the actors gathering in a clump downstage where they move in a box-stop, suggesting that whatever movement they might make in their relationships, they are still boxed in by the culturally sanctioned patterns of abuse which they have so thoroughly absorbed. Each of the women relates the accommodations she has made to stay in her relationship. Eena, for example, remembers leaving the house and her husband one night; but she left without her purse. Finding herself "in the middle of Bloor Street without a cent," she turned around and went home (270). Although differing in detail, each of the stories is fundamentally the same: in the culture where social relations are predicated on the "institution of heterosexuality" and the power which it accords to men, in a culture which, as a consequence of that power relation, eroticizes the victimization of women thereby establishing the pre-conditions for the abuse of women and children, how can we begin to imagine women who are not victims?

As Judith Thompson's *Lion in the Streets* suggests, this culture of abuse which overdetermines our understanding of gender and sexuality results in a society in crisis. The play, as Ric Knowles notes in his introduction, eschews conventional Aristotelian structures (9) and relies on "relay" structure (8) to link the episodes which present a startling portrait of a Toronto neighborhood populated by those living in terrible personal anguish: children bullying other children; a wife whose husband publicly mocks her sexual attractiveness; a child care worker who is criticized for allowing the children to have sugar; a woman facing terminal cancer; a priest who believes he is culpable for the death of a young boy; a woman with advanced cerebral palsy whose claims of a midnight lover radically undermine conventional notions of sexuality, particularly for the journalist interviewing her; a young man trying to come to terms with his homosexuality; a young woman whose fiancé is abusive to her children. The relay structure of the play, with a character from one episode appearing in the subsequent one, not only provides a certain cohesiveness but suggests that, like the baton in a relay, cruelty and despair are transferred through the society. As Knowles notes, the play is deeply religious, seeking to discover the grace which will redeem the society caught in this violent crisis.

These portraits of local unhappiness in *Lion in the Streets* are presided over by Isobel, the ghost of a nine-year-old Portuguese girl who, seventeen years before the action of the play, had been killed by a man who had lured her into his car. Initially, in a frenzy, she cries out, "… I am lost. I am lost. I AM LOOOOOOOOOST!!" (15) and seems to be seeking the person who can take her home. But, in the course of the play's action, she shifts from wanting to be saved to presenting herself as the saviour of her community, as the person who will kill the lion in the streets (44). What is remarkable is Thompson's shifting of Isobel from a victim to an agent of salvation. In contrast to Lambert's meticulous charting of the effects of Emma's abuse and death on the lives of Maggie and Renee which ends with Renee taking action against John, a modestly positive assertion of her agency which is immediately undercut by Maggie's refusal to entertain the possibility of forgiveness, and in contrast to The Anna Project's suggestive portrait of the social production of femininity which predisposes women to be victims, Thompson boldly ventures to suggest the mechanism for healing. The political implication of her dramaturgical strategy is that women, even though victims of a particular crime, need not forever define themselves as victims. As if to amend Renee's banal comment that "life goes on," which in *Under the Skin* seems to signal a resignation to life as unjust and destructive, Isobel's determination to face the lion is a necessary step for her to reclaim control over her life. Ironic though it be, it is through her refusal to remain a victim, her insistence that she will act that the dead Isobel can enter a new life as she ascends, at the end of the play, into heaven (63).

Thompson's choice of having a little girl who was abused and murdered as the exemplar of grace is startling and perhaps contentious inasmuch as we figure children not only as innocent, but without the resources to which adults have access. But that surely, is precisely Thompson's point: if Isobel, a little girl, can seize control and refuse to be a victim by confronting the lion, then surely adults should be able to do likewise? After confronting Benjamin, her murderer, Isobel, who is now an adult says:

> I was dead, was killed by the lion in long silver car, starving lion, maul maul maul me to dead, with killing claws over and over my little young face and chest, over my chest my blood running out he take my heart with. He take my heart with, in his pocket deep, but my heart talk. Talk and talk and never be

quiet. I came back. I take my life. I want you all to take you life. I want you all to have your life. (63)

Isobel's situation is the social crisis in its most extreme: a little girl, lured into a car by a man against whom she can mount no defense. Her death, the death of child, resonates not simply as a horrible breach of a child's trust in an adult but as symptomatic of the death of the future for, without children, there can be no future. But Isobel, although physically dead, lives as the spectre haunting the play's action, kept in some form of life by her heart which refuses to die, its ceaseless talk demanding that she come back and take her life which allows her to become an adult.

As optimistic as the message of *Lion in the Streets* seems to be, Thompson can only imagine redemption through a series of religious metaphors, beginning with the Book of Proverbs which warns of "a lion at large in the streets" (26:13). The play seems to turn on an inversion, the child as the heroic agent of redemption, which echoes Jesus's promises in the Sermon on the Mount. The play ends on an obviously religious note, with Isobel's ascension into heaven. Within this context, what is at stake is faith and not a rational analysis of the social production of ideologies which reinforce and perpetuate a culture of abuse. Whatever the logical impossibility of the solution which Thompson proposes, an impossibility signalled by the fantasy of a dead child enjoying some form of life in which she can confront her abuser and continue to grow from a child to an adult, moving from limbo to the arms of God, the point of the play may be precisely in the optimism of daring to imagine salvation. While the word "salvation" carries some religious connotations, we should remember that victims need to be saved. Perhaps Thompson is right: dismantling the culture of abuse may begin with those victims who acknowledge that their victimization, while a constituent aspect of their identities, need not define them.

Notes

1. *This is for You, Anna* was created through a series of workshops, resulting in the first performance in 1983 of a twenty-minute version of the piece at the Women's Perspective Festival. The version of the script which is published dates from 1985.

Works Cited

The Anna Project. "*This is for You, Anna*. 1985." *The CTR Anthology: Fifteen Plays from Canadian Theatre Review*. Ed. Alan Filewod. Toronto: U. of Toronto P., 1993. 249–281.

Boire, Gary. "Transparencies: Of Sexual Abuse, Ambivalence, and Resistance." *Essays on Canadian Writing* (Winter 1993–Spring 1994): 211–232.

Lambert, Betty. *Under the Skin. Jennie's Story & Under the Skin*. Toronto: Playwrights Canada, 1987. 113–194.

Rich, Adrienne. "Compulsory Heterosexuality and Lesbian Existence." *Signs* (Summer 1980): 631–660.

Thompson, Judith. *Lion in the Streets*. Toronto: Coach House, 1992.

Drama in British Columbia: A Special Place

by Denis Johnston

What is British Columbia? It is "The West beyond the West," according to a recent history book (see Barman), a psychologically imposing environment which spans as much physical and human diversity as the whole rest of the country put together. If Canada can be described as a land with too much geography and not enough history, then British Columbia has more geography and less history than anywhere else.

Who are British Columbians? First, they are people who come from somewhere else. (This is true even of B.C.'s aboriginal peoples, many of whom are now engaged in rebuilding cultural homelands which effectively ceased to exist.) British Columbians situate themselves outside the mainstream of Canadian thought, and are proud to do so. Their politics are polarized, eschewing the gift for compromise which characterizes Canadian political achievement in other spheres. Because their economy has always been primarily resource-based, and hence dependent on market forces in far-away places, their economic lives have acquired a kind of earthquake mentality: long periods of progress occasionally flattened by unpredictable cataclysm. Recessions seldom hold any terror for the people of British Columbia.

British Columbians tend to be deeply suspicious of Quebec and Ontario, and simply uncomprehending of other regions of Canada. Culturally, they are not easily impressed with the work of artist-compa-

---

DENIS JOHNSTON is a writer, editor and theatre historian. He is the author of an award-winning book, *Up the Mainstream: The Rise of Toronto's Alternative Theatres*, and numerous articles on Canadian drama and theatre. After five years on the Theatre faculty at the University of British Columbia, Dr. Johnston recently joined the management team of the Shaw Festival.

triots east of the Rockies, but they can be fiercely proud of their own. In the theatre, for example, the province's most popular achievements in recent decades have been created by British Columbia's own professional performers and, occasionally, writers. Even as far back as the 1950s, when Vancouver led the country in a rebirth of locally-based professional theatre, plays by local writers occupied a special place for their audiences. The exultant response of "That's us! That's us!" which (so legend has it) new Canadian drama provoked among Toronto audiences in the early 1970s, rippled through British Columbia audiences in the preceding decades. If such achievements are forgotten now, among British Columbians as elsewhere, it is perhaps due more to Canadians' distressing capacity for ignoring their own history, than to any lack of significance in the achievements themselves.

The term "drama" generally alludes to a specialized form of literature rather than to a form of performance. Strictly speaking, then, one could discuss drama in British Columbia without ever considering what went on in the theatre. However, such a discussion would be ultimately sterile. Other forms of literature can be read, appreciated, and criticized in the privacy of one's study, but drama stumbles under this kind of treatment. The essence of drama is how it plays.

Accepting this statement—"the essence of drama is how it plays"—brings into the discussion a cluster of regrettably untidy concepts. Played by whom? *For* whom? In what kind of community, and in what kind of playhouse? (The inclusion of an audience in this discussion is the untidiest concept of all.) This essay will attempt to consider homegrown *drama* in British Columbia within the context of *theatre* in British Columbia. In other words, instead of accepting drama as a neglected stepchild of Canadian letters, it will treat drama as a written form of our theatre.

In the history of European settlement in British Columbia, as elsewhere in Canada, locally-written drama is at least as old as written history. Even in colonial days, local allusions enlivened many a comic play and variety show (see Evans 23 *et passim*). Naturally, the mainly British settlers preferred mainly British entertainments; and the higher the social class of any group, the more high-toned and anglophile was the kind of theatre which they preferred. The concept of Canadian nationalism, as something distinct from pride of British heritage, did not gather momentum until after World War I. At that time, Canadians educated in their generation's European models began to promote the founding of arts education and "art theatres" in Canada, and sometimes to introduce original plays as part of their programmes.

One early experiment, the Home Theatre near Naramata, B.C., attempted to combine theatrical training with the ideals of the art theatres of Europe. In 1922, in a chapel-like little theatre located above a new fruit-storage barn, its artistic director, Carroll Aikins, presented an original piece entitled *Victory in Defeat*, a Christian pageant staged in an avant-garde style. According to historian James Hoffman, this piece "obtained for Aikins his best reviews"; another Aikins play, *The God of Gods*, set among B.C.'s aboriginal nations, enjoyed at least one production in Toronto and two in England (see Hoffman, "Carroll Aikins" 65 et passim). Another leader of the inter-war period was Major Llewellyn Bullock-Webster, who wrote and produced a number of his own plays, initially as a private teacher of elocution and later as the provincial government's Organizer of School and Community Drama. Except for such maverick producers, however, though the "little theatre" movement did much to foster Canadian theatre between the wars, it offered scant encouragement to Canadian drama. Even the vigorous work of Aikins and Bullock-Webster now appear more as curiosities than as seminal movements.

In this inter-war period, one institution of the amateur theatre—Hart House Theatre in Toronto—produced a number of original plays. In this kind of activity, however, it had no counterpart in British Columbia. The dominant theatre company there was the Vancouver Little Theatre, but the development of original plays was not part of its agenda (see Nesbitt, chapter 2). Except for a few published plays which seem to represent a kind of "closet drama" of the 1930s, and except for an increasing amount of radio drama, few original plays survive from this period in British Columbia theatre.[1]

After World War II, professional theatre sprang to life again in British Columbia. Due probably to the long-term influence of some outstanding amateur and semi-professional organizations, Vancouver spawned a surprising number of professional companies despite, at the time, a total lack of government support for the arts. Companies such as Theatre Under the Stars, Everyman, and Totem Theatre had outstanding successes with original plays. In the emerging new world of Canadian theatre, locally written drama seemed to gain a special place in British Columbia theatre, a place it has held ever since.

Theatre Under The Stars was a popular Vancouver institution which produced operettas and musicals in Stanley Park beginning in 1940. In the years following the War, the role of TUTS as a largely amateur summer activity moved strongly in the direction of a professional year-round operation.² While most of its repertory came from Broadway, in 1952 an original musical entitled *Timber!!* shared the season's bill with such standards as *Finian's Rainbow*. Though *Timber!!* was described by Vancouver's mayor as "the first all-Canadian musical, written, produced and performed by Canadians" (quoted in Hunter 9),³ the experiment was not repeated. Perhaps the Vancouver audience preferred time-tested musical hits from elsewhere.

Named after a well-known art theatre in Hampstead, England, Everyman Theatre was founded in 1946 by the Vancouver actor-director Sydney Risk, who had worked in British repertory before the war. Comprised mainly of Risk's former students at Banff and UBC, the company soon embarked on an unprecedented winter tour through the four western provinces, before settling down to contribute to the growth of professional theatre in Vancouver over most of a decade. On its initial groundbreaking tour, one of the three plays in Everyman's repertory came from western Canada, *The Last Caveman* by Elsie Park Gowan, sharing the bill with plays by Chekhov and Oscar Wilde.⁴

A third post-war professional company was Totem Theatre, which started as a summer stock operation in a West Vancouver park in 1951. After two successful seasons of mixed programming in a rented hall in downtown Vancouver, Totem moved to a playhouse in Victoria, where it attracted much critical attention but not enough audience to survive. In its last production in Victoria (one which was then transferred to Vancouver), Totem had a signal success with *A Crowded Affair* by company member Norma Macmillan, a comedy peopled with recognizable types from Victoria. For all its success, the script of *A Crowded Affair* is apparently lost.⁵

While these three companies moved toward more commercial concerns and a more mainstream audience, the ideals of the little theatre movement persisted at the Frederic Wood Theatre. Though only a modest union of two surplus army huts, the "Old Freddie" adopted goals which ranked with those of the most prestigious art theatres. The first performance there, in December 1952, was a staged reading of a dramatic poem by the celebrated Canadian poet Earle Birney—then a faculty member at UBC—entitled *The Damnation of Vancouver* (also published as *The Trial of a City*). It was the last Canadian play at the Frederic Wood Theatre for some decades: the Art Theatre concept, internationalist in outlook, preferred European literary models to homegrown ones.

Influenced by international models such as the Edinburgh Festival, Vancouver started its own International Festival in 1958. The Festival had a great deal of success, though not all of it was financial, enabling local audiences to hear such artists as Joan Sutherland and Glenn Gould near the beginning of their international careers. Here too, a locally written play was one of the highlights of the Festival's short but starry existence. *The World of the Wonderful Dark* was the theatrical centrepiece of the first season, a blood-and-thunder melodrama by Lister Sinclair set among the coastal First Nations prior to European contact. Though critics praised the staging, music, and spectacle of the piece, their opinions varied as to the play's dramatic values. *The World of the Wonderful Dark* did not draw the same houses as the Festival's other major production, *Don Giovanni*; and like *Timber!!*, it does not seem to have ever attracted a second production.

These post-war examples took place on the verge of a revolution in Canadian theatre, brought about by a series of landmark cultural events in the 1950s. The first came in 1951 when Vincent Massey tabled the report of his Royal Commission on National Development in the Arts, Letters and Sciences. A work of conscience and conviction, the Massey Report attempted to sound the soul of what it meant to be a Canadian— and it found the arts at the core of this meaning. The second event came in 1953, with the founding of the Stratford Festival. Providing a sturdy counter-example to English-Canadians' tendency toward cultural self-effacement, the Stratford Festival proved that, with thorough planning and first-rate leadership, Canada could produce some of the best theatre in the world. The third event came in 1957, when the federal government established the Canada Council to fund the professional arts along lines recommended by the Massey Report. Finally, in 1958, the Manitoba Theatre Centre was founded, the first civic company in what was to become Canada's regional theatre network. Its progenitors designed the MTC to draw on the community support of the Winnipeg Little Theatre, on the savvy of a new generation of theatre professionals, and on a new form of funding from the Canada Council. If Stratford set the standards for professional theatre in Canada, the MTC dictated its structure: together they formed a blueprint for a new professional theatre in Canada.

This blueprint eventually resulted in three types of companies which dominate Canadian theatre to this day. One is the regional theatre, which essentially follows the pattern established by the MTC and other civic companies founded in the 1960s. A second is the summer festival, generally situated somewhere between the grandeur of Stratford and the muddling-through of summer stock. The third is the alternative theatre, which styles itself in opposition to the regional theatre and the larger festivals. I say "styles itself" because most alternative companies aspire to succeed in the same terms as these larger companies, and often their artistic leaders move on to such companies as soon as opportunities become available. For whatever reasons, what began as alternative companies in most major cities now exhibit many of the same qualities as their larger cousins (see Johnston, *Up the Mainstream* chapter 10).

In British Columbia, the flagship of the regional theatres is the Vancouver Playhouse, which produced its first play in 1963. In its first decade, the Playhouse really had no professional rival in the growing metropolis of Vancouver, nor did other theatre groups seem much interested in promoting drama written anywhere closer than New York. (Even young theatre iconoclasts emerging from universities showed more interest in plays from off-off-Broadway than in what they could write themselves.) In the '60s the Playhouse attracted a series of leaders—Malcolm Black, Joy Coghill, and David Gardner—to whom new drama was essential to the kind of enterprise they wanted to build. While the Playhouse may not have been the only regional theatre which promoted new Canadian drama, it was the most persistent in this goal, and certainly the most successful.

The first local play to be produced by the Playhouse was *Like Father, Like Fun* in 1966, a domestic comedy by the popular newspaper columnist Eric Nicol. In it, a timber tycoon attempts to liven up his too-straight-laced son, especially regarding sexual adventurousness, with predictably farcical results. The characters bore a strong enough resemblance to well-known local personalities that Artistic Director Malcolm Black sought the advice of the Playhouse's lawyer before going ahead with the production. But, Black reports, "I'll never forget the excitement of the opening night at the Playhouse; there was a howl of recognition within a minute of the curtain going up, and the laughter didn't subside until we closed the piece, with great reluctance, three sold-out weeks later." He also notes, ironically, that *Like Father, Like Fun* was "the first Canadian play to get a theatre out of a financial hole instead of the other way around" (Black 6). By the time his tenure ended in 1967, Black also brought to the stage such locally-written plays as *Countdown to Armageddon* by James Clavell (the popular novelist, then living in West Vancouver) and *How to Run This Country* by Paul St. Pierre (another newspaper columnist). He also returned to the Playhouse subsequently to direct two plays he'd had a hand in developing, Eric Nicol's *The Fourth Monkey* and Beverley Simons' *Crabdance*. Nicol's *Like Father, Like Fun*, it should be noted, went on to inglorious runs in Toronto, Montreal, and New York, where it closed on Broadway after only three performances. Though the comic issues of the play have not endured very well, Nicol's wry observations on the play's failure in New York—in his humourous book *A Scar Is Born*—still make a fascinating study of the difference between a play's local resonance and the expectations of the entertainment machinery of Broadway (see also Gray, "Preface").

Toward the end of the 1960s, three plays by George Ryga, all of which premiered at the Playhouse, quickly attained the stature of classics and causes célèbres in Canadian drama. The first was *The Ecstasy of Rita Joe*, which exploded onto the scene in 1967, Canada's centennial year. Set in the mean streets of Vancouver, *Rita Joe* tells of the martyrdom of a contemporary young First Nations woman crushed by the concrete logic of the city and its bureaucracies. Two years later the Playhouse remounted *Rita Joe* in Ottawa, where it became the first play to be performed in English at the National Arts Centre. There it was also a sensational success, and gave new Canadian playwrights a much-admired model to emulate. Ryga's next play, *Grass and Wild Strawberries*, was more controversial both critically and bureaucratically for the Playhouse. It proved acceptable to court new young audiences with a play about alienated hippie youth, accompanied live by B.C.'s best rock band; it was quite another thing, however, for the Playhouse Board to find this audience smoking marijuana in the handsome civic theatre. A still-greater controversy awaited the third Ryga play, *Captives of the Faceless Drummer*, a misunderstood poetic parable (like so much of Ryga's drama), the plot of which bore uncomfortably close parallels to the recent October Crisis in Montreal and Ottawa. Amid furious debate, the Board of the Playhouse cancelled the production and the artistic director left under a cloud. Finally presented by an alternative group in a stripped-down production at the Vancouver Art Gallery, *Captives* too attained the status of legend among Canadian plays.[6] Divisions lingered: despite their popular and critical success, almost twenty years passed before another Ryga play appeared at the Playhouse.

While Canadian plays and locally-written plays continued to form part of the Playhouse's mandate in the ensuing decade, leadership in this area passed to many smaller theatre companies which appeared in the 1970s. In British Columbia, script development was spearheaded by a company founded specifically for this purpose: the New Play Centre. The NPC began in 1970 essentially as a critiquing service for B.C. playwrights. When Pam Hawthorn became the company's first artistic director in 1972, she added play workshopping and full-scale production to its range of activities. The importance of the NPC to British Columbia cannot be overstated. As Jerry Wasserman points out in his anthology of NPC plays, *Twenty Years at Play*, in one brief period alone (1980–85) plays developed at the NPC won or were runners-up for a total of nine national playwriting awards. But awards are only part of the story. Significant too is the NPC's excellent track record in two critical tests of a script development programme: plays which receive subsequent productions elsewhere, and playwrights who progress from early efforts to greater theatrical success (Johnston & Wasserman 7). Still more important, perhaps, is an elusive contribution of the NPC: a sense of primacy given to new plays in the theatre world of Vancouver, an assurance that there is a place to which the best new scripts ought to be taken. The "stable" of writers developed at the NPC still form a solid senior corps of dramatists in British Columbia.

Like that of the Playhouse following the heady '60s, lately the prominence of the New Play Centre as a producer of new plays seems to have diminished. While it continues to contribute to BC playwriting as a critiquing service and as a unifying symbol of dramaturgical activity, the actual production of new drama has largely passed to other alternative companies. Touchstone Theatre has had a great deal of success with new plays, not only with collective creations such as *Sex Tips for Modern Girls* (1985) and *The Number 14* (1992), but also with scripted plays such as *Life Skills* (1987) by David King and *Homework and Curtains* (1990) by John Lazarus. Tamahnous Theatre in the 1980s provided opportunities for such local playwrights as Morris Panych and Peter Eliot Weiss, and has recently turned more toward performance art and poetic feminist voices such as Jennifer Martin and Sherri-D Wilson. New plays are also featured at the Station Street Arts Centre, a dynamic new alternative theatre in the seediest part of Vancouver's east side.

In other cities too, the development of Canadian plays has splintered among various theatre companies. The Nanaimo Festival has premiered several new plays about the history of Vancouver Island, especially about the robber barons of its coal-mining heritage. In Victoria, some interesting new drama has also emerged from smaller companies, though much of it has been marginalized due either to financial struggles (such as Company One in the 1970s) or to a theatre-for-young-audiences emphasis (such as the remarkably resilient Kaleidoscope Theatre). In the interior of the province, another major theatre, the Western Canada Theatre Company in Kamloops, has been as adventurous as its audience will allow. For Canadian plays, however, WCTC generally sticks to plays already proven successful in Vancouver, or those by Kamloops' favourite son Ian Weir, an accessible comic writer and a recent product of the NPC stable.

In Vancouver in the 1980s, the concept of the "hit" local play was revitalized by the far-flung success of John Gray's Billy Bishop Goes to War, which started life as a co-production of the Vancouver East Cultural Centre. This concept was taken to another level by the phenomenal local success of Talking Dirty at the Arts Club Theatre. Though the survival of the Arts Club had always depended on finding plays "with legs," Talking Dirty was its first such success from a Vancouver writer. This comedy of yuppie manners, set in Vancouver's trendy Kitsilano neighbourhood in the early '80s, went through several development workshops at the New Play Centre before opening at the Arts Club in 1981. Talking Dirty ran there for almost three years, later transferring to Toronto where it won a Chalmers award for playwright Sherman Snukal. Soon the Arts Club found yet another long-running hit, the collective creation Sex Tips for Modern Girls (1985), developed by Touchstone Theatre.[7] A third locally-written hit for the Arts Club has been Ann Mortifee's musical allegory Reflections on Crooked Walking (1982), revived in recent years for holiday audiences.

Since the mid-1980s, the rules for dramatic success have changed once again. While international hit musicals such as The Phantom of the Opera and Les Misérables re-orient theatre-going habits in Canada's larger centres, new Canadian drama has exploded once again in the anarchic setting of Canadian "fringe festivals." The fringe phenomenon has spread not only from city to city, but also through local mimesis—the Vancouver Fringe now shares its audiences with such alternative fringes as "Dancing on the Edge" and "Women in View." While the best of the fringe plays seem to be finding subsequent productions, the fringe format itself generally favours shorter scripts with smaller casts—often dramatic monologues—which seem less capable of infiltrating larger stages than the kinds of plays developed in more traditional forms of Canadian theatre.

Young actors, directors and (less often) writers use the fringe festivals to showcase their own work, not only to audiences, but also to an established theatre profession which seems to be growing slower to respond to new voices. But seasoned professionals use the fringes as well, as a means of realizing projects which have little allure for established theatres. Perhaps the best of the new scripts to be premiered at the Vancouver Fringe Festival has been *Medea's Disgust* (1991) written and performed by John Lazarus, a leading playwright who was originally trained as an actor. In this solo play, the audience is cast as an extension class attending a lecture on a popular Canadian novel. Giving the lecture is a self-absorbed English professor who is embittered and unhinged by the meteoric success of the novel's author, an exotic young woman who is also the professor's former lover and protégée.

Vancouver is still a favoured home for Canadian playwrights, for the same reasons it is a favoured home for other people: a large cosmopolitan city blessed with a mild climate, spectacular scenery, and extensive educational resources. Playwrights who gravitate to Vancouver become, over time, a part of the cultural community. Of the NPC stable developed in the 1970s, most came from elsewhere, and many still contribute to the richness of the province's dramatic fabric, for example Tom Cone, Margaret Hollingsworth and Sheldon Rosen. A second generation of playwrights is also well established here, including John Lazarus, Peter Eliot Weiss, and Ian Weir. Morris Panych continues to provide perhaps British Columbia's most distinctive voice, with such '90s plays as *Seven Stories*, *2 B Wut U R*, *The Cost of Living*, and *Diary of a Sinking Man*. Dennis Foon, for many years marginalized due to his specialization in young people's theatre, has gained recognition as an outstanding playwright for all audiences. Margo Kane's *Moonlodge* captivated audiences in Vancouver and elsewhere, as have the plays of Joan MacLeod and Sally Clark. (These last two might be considered expatriate British Columbians, the kind we always expect to return some day.) New writers continue to emerge from the theatre community, such as Gordon Armstrong (*A Map of the Senses*), Kate Schlemmer (*Iceberg Lettuce*), and Mark Leiren-Young (known for his political satires prior to his controversial radio serial *Dim Sum Diaries*). British Columbia playwrights have a profile not only through the New Play Centre and other companies dedicated to developing new scripts, but also through an annual playwriting contest sponsored by Theatre B.C. They also have a forum through the Betty Lambert Society, a professional association named after the late author of *Jennie's Story* and many other outstanding plays. The NPC's SpringRites and the fringe festivals still offer opportunities for new writers, and the recent boom in British Columbia's film and television industry presents new possibilities for economic survival (if not affluence) for full-time writers. It would be foolish to wax optimistic about playwriting in BC: our earthquake mentality teaches us not to. But for now, British Columbia is a special place to live and to work, and there is good work being done.

Notes

1. One noteworthy example is John Bruce Cowan's *Canuck,* a contemporary domestic comedy in which a young woman marries a poor Canadian over her parents' anglomaniacal objections. Surprisingly, this play remained unproduced until 1980 when it was premiered at the Shaw Festival, and received scant attention even then. Another example is a collection of one-acts by A. M. D. Fairbairn entitled *Plays of the Pacific Coast,* in which the West Coast rain forest, and particularly any native influence, is shown as sapping all energy and moral foundation from settlers of European extraction.
2. This period is documented in Richard Sutherland's *Theatre Under the Stars: The Hilker Years.*
3. See also vertical file "Theatre Under the Stars," Fine Arts Department, Vancouver Public Library.
4. For a history of this enterprise, see James Hoffman's "Sydney Risk and the Everyman Theatre." *The Last Caveman* was recently published in *The Hungry Spirit: Selected Plays and Prose by Elsie Park Gowan.*
5. I am on friendly terms with the author, the producer, and the director of the original production, but no one can tell me where a script is. What a shame that the script of such a popular indigenous play, produced at the dawning of a new age of professional theatre in Canada, should have vanished so completely! This is an important lesson for chroniclers of Canadian theatre: blessed are the publishers, the paper-hoarders, even the self-serving mythologizers. Most Canadian theatre artists, left to their own devices, will simply throw everything away.
6. For contrasting views of the controversy surrounding this play, see Christopher Innes' "The Psychology of Politics: George Ryga's Captives of the Faceless Drummer;" and Peter Hay's "The Psychology of Distortion: A Rebuttal of Christopher Innes."

7. The script, along with a description of its development, is published in *Canadian Theatre Review* 49 (Winter 1986).

Works Cited

Barman, Jean. *The West beyond the West: A History of British Columbia.* Toronto: University of Toronto Press, 1991.

Black, Malcolm. "Introduction." *Three Plays by Eric Nicol.* Vancouver: Talonbooks, 1975.

Cowan, John Bruce. *Canuck.* Vancouver: Ross, Cowan and Latta, 1931.

Evans, Chad. *Frontier Theatre: A History of Nineteenth-Century Theatrical Entertainment in the Canadian Far West and Alaska.* Victoria BC: Sono Nis Press, 1983.

Fairbairn, A. M. D. *Plays of the Pacific Coast.* Toronto: Samuel French, 1935.

Gowan, Elsie Park. *The Hungry Spirit: Selected Plays and Prose by Elsie Park Gowan.* Edmonton: NeWest, 1992.

Gray, John. "Preface." *Billy Bishop Goes to War.* Vancouver: Talonbooks, 1981.

Hay, Peter. "The Psychology of Distortion: A Rebuttal of Christopher Innes." *Theatre History in Canada* 7.1 (Spring 1986): 119–124.

Hoffman, James. "Carroll Aikins and the Home Theatre." *Theatre History in Canada* 7.1 (Spring 1986): 50–70.

———. "L. Bullock-Webster and the B.C. Dramatic School." *Theatre History in Canada* 8.2 (Fall 1987): 204–220.

———. "Sydney Risk and the Everyman Theatre." *B.C. Studies* 76 (Winter 1987–88): 33–57.

Hunter, Albert. "Loggers in Greasepaint Score Hit in *Timber!!*" *Vancouver News-Herald* 24 June 1952: 9.

Innes, Christopher. "The Psychology of Politics: George Ryga's *Captives of the Faceless Drummer.*" *Theatre History in Canada* 6.1 (Spring 1985): 23–43.

Johnston, Denis W. *Models for Drama/Theatre Education in the Secondary Schools of British Columbia.* M.A. thesis. University of Victoria, 1982.

———. *Up the Mainstream: The Rise of Toronto's Alternative Theatres, 1968-1975.* University of Toronto Press, 1991.

Johnston, Denis W. and Jerry Wasserman. "The New Play Centre: Twenty Years On." *Canadian Theatre Review* 63 (Summer 1990): 25–28.

Nesbitt, Carol Dell. *The History of the Vancouver Little Theatre Association*. M.A. thesis. University of British Columbia, 1992.

Nicol, Eric. *A Scar is Born*. Toronto: Ryerson Press, 1968.

Sutherland, Richard. *Theatre Under the Stars: The Hilker Years*. M.A. thesis. University of British Columbia, 1993.

Touchstone Theatre. "*Sex Tips for Modern Girls.*" *Canadian Theatre Review* 49 (Winter 1986): 67–110.

Wasserman, Jerry. *Twenty Years at Play: A New Place Centre Anthology*. Vancouver: Talonbooks, 1990.

Centres on the Margin:
Contemporary Prairie Drama

Diane Bessai

I

In the winter of 1994 I attended a preview at the National Film Theatre in London, England of Denys Arcand's film version of Brad Fraser's *Unidentified Human Remains and the True Nature of Love* (retitled *Love and Human Remains*). During the public discussion with Arcand which followed, the Montreal director responded affirmatively to a suggestion from the audience that this playwright is really a film writer *manqué*. Arcand, rightly bitter about his failure to obtain Alberta government funding to film in Edmonton—but as ignorant as are so many other eastern Canadians about the strength of theatre in the prairie region— off-handedly observed that in a city lacking a film-making infrastructure, it is obviously much cheaper for the writer to do his play, in his words, "as theatre in a basement somewhere." Sure enough, the last of the long list of film credits acknowledges Workshop West Playwrights Theatre, Edmonton, where, as playwright-in-residence in the mid-1980s, Fraser began to write the play. This theatre, in fact, is only one of the several

---

DIANE BESSAI is a professor of English at the University of Alberta where she teaches courses in modern drama, Canadian literature and Canadian drama. She is a founding board member of NeWest Press and the general editor of the NWP *Prairie Play Series*. She was the first theatre editor of *NeWest Review* where she has published many reviews and essays on prairie drama and theatre. She is the author of *Playwrights of Collective Creation, 1992*, a study of Theatre Passe Muraille in the 1970s.

prairie theatres over recent years that has given Fraser the opportunity to develop his craft as a now internationally-recognized playwright—as his history of production shows (Fraser, *Wolf Plays* 251–52). However, the myth of the Canadian prairie as theatrical backwater still continues and with it the assumption that fully-formed playwrights somehow emerge out of the ether.

Indeed, the strength and variety of plays by prairie playwrights in the past decade or more—-and the success of several of them both nationally and abroad—is in large measure attributable to the strength of theatre programs in the three provinces of the region devoted to the development and production of new drama. These dedicated programs characteristically come from the smaller, once designated as "alternative" theatres as opposed to "regional" civic theatres: in Edmonton, notably Workshop West, under the direction of Gerry Potter and Theatre Network, under its former artistic director, Stephen Heatley; in Calgary, Alberta Theatre Project's annual playRites Festival under Michael Dobbin; in Saskatoon, 25th Street Theatre with Tom Bentley-Fisher, and in Winnipeg, at Prairie Theatre Exchange during the directorships of Kim McCaw and subsequently Michael Springate. Dramatists of all three provinces are also actively served by their playwrights' associations with readings, workshops and other dramaturgical and professional services (Manitoba Association of Playwrights; Saskatchewan Playwrights' Centre; Alberta Playwrights' Network). In addition the various summer Fringe Festivals in three of the major prairie cities (Edmonton, where the Canadian Fringe Festival movement originated in 1981, and successively Winnipeg, and Saskatoon) have opened up new opportunities for writers as well as other theatre practitioners and new companies have emerged in consequence, for example, Teatro La Quindicina in Edmonton.

Sometimes tied to the myth of theatrical backwater is the conventional notion of "Western Canadian theatre as prairie naturalism." This particular phrasing of an often repeated but ill-defined and too-sweeping assumption comes from Vit Wagner of the *Toronto Star* in an interview in 1991 with Stewart Lemoine, Edmonton playwright, director and founder of the zany and locally much-beloved Teatro La Quindicina. The occasion was one of the company's popular visits to Toronto, in this instance with *The Glittering Heart*, an off-the-wall story of a housewife who escapes from Winnipeg to become a successful courtesan in Venice. Wagner, like so many other commentators on Lemoine, is expressing delight at his non-conformity with the standard expectations of prairie drama as regional realism. La Quindicina, named after the travelling brothel in Graham Greene's *Travels with My Aunt*, specializes in genre parody ranging from Ibsen to American movies of the 1950s to (most recently) biblical narrative of the Apocrypha. On this occasion, as always, the playwright has his response ready: "'I get asked a lot: 'Well, what's this got to do with Edmonton?' It doesn't have anything in particular to do with Edmonton, except that it's a large cosmopolitan city. We read" (Wagner J5). He seems to be rightly implying that society in this region as any other in the global village of the contemporary world can be stimulated by many kinds of imagination. By his own example, Lemoine is challenging common preconceptions about prairie drama concerning its subject matter and its form. To me this suggests that such preconceptions of prairie regional theatre and its dramatic product need revising and broadening.

II

Let me begin by categorizing "prairie drama" as the whole body of plays—no matter what the subject or theatrical form—coming from the prairie theatres that over the past fifteen years have been providing the professional environment for both emerging and established playwrights. The particular mandates of the specific theatres, tastes of individual artistic directors (or boards) and their readings of the expectations of the audiences they are cultivating are, of course, crucial to their choices of playwrights and plays. On one hand, theatres such as Prairie Theatre Exchange, 25th Street Theatre and Theatre Network have built their reputations on the presentation of regionalist themes. Initially their whole reason for being was in protest against the established theatres' failures either to provide opportunities for local writers and theatre practitioners or to offer their audiences a direct reflection of their immediate cultural environment. On the other hand, in examples such as Teatro La Quindicina or Calgary's feminist company, Maenad Theatre, the local content consists of the theatre and its artists, not the geographical subject matter commonly associated with regionalism.

In the interview already cited, Lemoine also ventures a generalization about contrasting approaches that seems apt for playwriting on the prairie: "Some people have a rage to write about something and other people look for something and, once they've found it, explore it." Although the categories are not entirely mutually exclusive, he clearly belongs to the second, as witnessed by his most ambitious exploration to date, a witty and alternately poignant epic rendering of *The Book of Tobit* (1994), Miltonic in scope, if not in tone. In addition, Lemoine is very much influenced by the strengths of the actors he knows he's writing for. Maenad Theatre, in casting about for feminist topics, decided to explore, among others, the life, work and times of Aphra Behn in their collective postmodernist medley, *Aphra* (1991). In *Transit of Venus* (1992), Winnipeg playwright Maureen Hunter, shifted from a strong regionalist emphasis (notably *Footprints on the Moon* [1988]), to research on the science and society of 18th century France for her dramatization of the life and relationships of a pioneer French astronomer. Calgarian John Murrell's much performed *Democracy* (1991) is an imaginary and heated philosophical debate between Walt Whitman and Ralph Waldo Emerson arising from the devastations of the American civil war. These idiosyncratic examples show playwrights intent on the intellectual and dramaturgical challenge of difficult, unlikely, or at least unusual material for contemporary drama, prairie or otherwise.

In prairie drama, the other kind of writer—the one with, "a rage to write about something"—may well be a regionalist with a strong urge to express his or her writer's vision by giving an explicit dramatic identity to the worlds he or she knows best, although not necessarily as a "prairie naturalist." The formally inventive Frank Moher, for example, in plays such as the satiric comedy on conservative journalism, *Prairie Report* (1988), and *Sliding for Home* (1987), a musical fantasia on early professional baseball in Edmonton, has always been committed to the importance of "telling our own story." He firmly believes that the culture of the Canadian west is different from elsewhere and that its story is best told by those who are shaped by the western experience. Even *The Third Ascent* (1988), Moher's expressionistic examination of the inside story of the 1945 atomic attack on Japan, has its seminal regional focus (with reference to the first ascent by a white man of Chief Mountain, just over the Alberta/Montana border).

A landmark play in the inauguration of indigenous modern prairie drama, 25th Street Theatre's ebullient epic-documentary collective creation *Paper Wheat* (1977), was deeply indebted to director Andras Tahn's conviction that the new professional theatre in Saskatchewan must explore the unique stories of prairie society, in this case the public story of the formation of the Saskatchewan Wheat Pool. In the new audiences for theatre he was attracting during his tenure as artistic director, he continued to cultivate that regional expectation. Playwright Don Kerr, in *The Great War* (1985) and *Talking Back* (1988), the latter on the founding of the CCF, has continued in the Tahn tradition of playfully serious representations of prairie history at 25th Street Theatre, although with a greater respect for fact and a more disciplined exploration of multiple dramatic styles. Also in the vein of public story, in this case not history, but the denial of history, is Blake Brooker's wicked musical burlesque, *Ilsa, Queen of the Nazi Love Camp* (1987). This show, revised and much performed over the years by Calgary's experimental theatre, One Yellow Rabbit, sends up the notorious James Keegstra affair. Two enraged and proud survivors of the Nazi regime confront Jim Keegstra, the mild-mannered Eckville, Alberta high school teacher who is assuring his students that the holocaust is a hoax.

In the unjustly denigrated realistic mode, recent drama has taken notable strides in two contrasting directions. One is the re-invention in contemporary terms of the rural regional tradition. Saskatchewan playwrights Barbara Sapergia, with *Roundup* (1990); Dianne Warren in *Serpent in the Night Sky* (1991) and Connie Gault with *The Soft Eclipse* (1989) are diverse examples among the several prairie women playwrights who might also come to mind, such as Conni Massing, Maureen Hunter or Kelly Rebar. The other direction, perhaps more immediately striking, is the emergence of a new prairie urban sensibility that explores, in George Ryga's suggestive phrase, the many "critical regions of social anxiety" (Wallace 73) in contemporary prairie life. From Edmonton, Brad Fraser's alternately witty, funny and horrifying *Unidentified Human Remains and the True Nature of Love* (1989) and Frank Moher's gentle *Odd Jobs* (1985) are contrastingly strong examples, as are Yvette Nolan's forthright *Blade* (1990) and Harry Rintoul's stark *refugees* (1987) and candid *Brave Hearts* (1991), from Winnipeg. Specific elements, either thematic or stylistic, are important in the new strides such works manifest as regional plays, which, paradoxically, for that very reason, may also offer windows to the wider audience. The plays by Fraser and Moher, for example, have received much attention throughout Canada and abroad, suggesting that the contemporary sensibility informing the new prairie realism resonates both within and beyond the region. With this point in mind, I now propose to examine these contemporary examples of prairie realism in more detail in order to illustrate the phenomenon of centres on the so-called margin.

III

The standard notion of doctrinaire "prairie naturalism" primarily has its roots in the earlier modern fiction of the region. The novels and short stories of F. P. Grove, Sinclair Ross, Martha Ostenso, W. O. Mitchell, and even some of Margaret Laurence, come first to mind, although in drama there are also the early plays of Gwen Pharis Ringwood, particularly *Still Stands the House* (1939) and *Dark Harvest* (1939). (Two lesser known plays of the 1930s of this order are Elsie Park Gowan's *Homestead* [1932] and Minnie Bicknell's *Relief* [1937].) This tradition evokes a view of the pioneer and early post-pioneer stages in the social development of rural prairie society. Characters are caught in a perennial struggle with a hostile wind-swept landscape that continually defies human effort to bring it under human control. They endure poverty, social isolation, personal alienation and domestic entrapment. Their spirituality is rooted in a religious fundamentalism that binds them to their relentless work ethic and destructive moral pietism. Life in the small prairie town, with its narrow-minded pretensions and cultural impoverishment, is not much better—or so the tradition goes. The pattern is one of life on the margin, most characteristically a harsh and imprisoning place, unhappily remote from some more desirable if vaguely identified centre, "east" or "south." Only W. O. Mitchell, in *Jake and the Kid*, his celebrated radio series of the 1950s, managed to turn that pattern of gloom on its head with his inimitable brand of folksy humour.

In the first phase of professional prairie theatre, the redoubtable *Paper Wheat* went some way in countering the deterministic notion of rural desperation and defeat through its themes of community co-operation and collectivity—as did Ringwood's own, slightly later, generational farm chronicle, *Mirage* (1978) or Rex Deverell's political docudrama, *Medicare!* (1980). However, recent dramatists (some of whom are themselves also fiction writers) are writing more explicitly out of a consciousness of that rural tradition in fiction, not in slavish conformity to it, but in order to re-examine it, enrich it and in some measure to subvert it through dramatic form. Recent developments in the themes and techniques of prairie realism, the dramatic depiction of life on the so-called geographical or sociological "margin" makes the "margin-centre" opposition problematical. Life on the margin, in effect, acquires cultural, social or spiritual autonomy: it becomes its own centre by convincingly insisting on its centrality to itself and its audience.

A basic expectation of the mode of realism is the authentic representation of the typical characteristics of a given society, community, or its representatives within a smaller social unit. In regional realism, the particular sense of place, its physical and cultural environment, are paramount. As already indicated, in prairie drama the conventional farm family version of this is relatively rare. Barbara Sapergia's *Roundup* is therefore useful as a contemporary text that provides a basis of comparison with two other recent, more radical, examples of rural realism. The play highlights the impact of the current "farm crisis" on a southern Saskatchewan ranching family of the mid-1980s. The characters are "as real as my experience and imagination could make them," writes Sapergia, because she wants to convey the importance for the "actual people" of agricultural life on the prairie (Preface). Balancing humour and intensity, Sapergia shows a keen eye for the details of farm labour in kitchen and corral, the ethnic and political particularities of community, and conflicts in family relationships arising from chronic financial worry. The focus is on Vera, wife and mother, whose discontents take on a slight feminist colouring in her cry for equal respect for woman's work on the farm. Thematically, the stereotypical conflict between allegiance to the land and the need to escape its tyranny takes on a positive note with the re-alignment of expectations and the recognition of individual power of choice—somewhat reminiscent of Sharon Pollock's earlier Alberta play, *Generations* (1980). The result is a solid model of conventional prairie naturalism for a present day in which choices are difficult and positive action is, as always, risky. *Roundup* is also squarely and unapologetically aimed at a regional audience who might be expected to share the play's respect for a familiar and endangered way of life in all its authentic, if predictable, circumstantiality.

At the outset of *Serpent in the Night Sky*, Dianne Warren also seems intent on the naturalistic representation of ordinary rural lives in domestic stress, although she substitutes the ordered world of Barbara Sapergia's southern ranch with a dysfunctional northern lakeside community on the edge of the bush. Here male occupation is random (taxiing visiting sportsman, poaching fish, drinking beer) and female grievance conspicuous. The catalyst for the action is the arrival of Joy, a timid young runaway from Montana whom Duff has rescued from the highway in his taxi, and now thinks to marry. Stella, his perennially angry sister who raised him from babyhood, loudly objects. Gator, her suggestively named chauvinistic bully of a husband, and the unfortunate model of macho male behavior for Duff, contrives to deflect the impressionable and irresolute younger man from any influence save his own. On the most obvious level the play seems to be setting itself up for a rather banal domestic power struggle in which the irritability level is high and self-knowledge woefully absent.

However, there are several interesting ways in which Warren departs from the conventional expectations of a realistic dramatic representation. For one, she introduces two evocative local eccentrics who live according to their own modes of reality. Twenty years before, Preacher escaped across the American border on his bicycle, driven ever since by a cosmic anxiety originating from his witnessing of an eclipse of the moon as he crossed the line. Nightly he scans the sky from the roof of his church, on guard to shoot the serpent who, according to his report of Cambodian folklore, must be prevented from swallowing the moon. Marlene, mother of Duff and Stella, has long since escaped to the bush, which she happily tramps year in and year out. Her occasional reappearance is signalled by dead rabbits on the doorsteps of her offspring. Her few words of wisdom, directed to Joy, assert the value of good "kicking boots" (61).

In another departure, the play is pure drama in the sense that its action is almost entirely defined through the immediacy of the moment. Ibsenite expositional freight, such as personal history, is minimal. We can sense but are never actually told any of the specific motives for the various flights to or from this community. In a manner somewhat reminiscent of Pinter, sudden or erratic verbal and physical outbursts or expressive interaction with physical objects (shoes, truck, rabbit skins) serve to build the play's own internal metaphoric system, with further resonance added by certain components of the geographical setting (lake, big night sky, bush, or road south). On the psychological level, *Serpent in the Night Sky* evolves into a dramatic rendering of the shifting dynamics of control. On the mythic level the parable of Preacher's quirky cosmic anxiety translates into the human terms of this immediate social environment. Thus in the penultimate scene, a communal outburst of rejection is spontaneously ritualized into a crescendo of exorcism aimed at the serpent in their own midst. Warren is transforming the circumstantial material of representational realism into a self-referential drama of symbolic gesture.

While Warren draws on a familiar astronomical phenomenon as dramatic metaphor, Connie Gault, in *The Soft Eclipse*, uses an actual eclipse of the sun as dramatic occasion. The result is an impressionistic meditation on the subtle strangeness of this hot summer day in 1965 as experienced by several women, of various ages and degrees of complexity, who are going about their daily affairs on the main street of a small prairie town. To all outward appearances the community components are commonplace: town busybody, sweet but dithering old lady, grass widow with nubile granddaughter, pregnant teenager, and temporarily discharged mental patient. The overt action is as ordinary as trips to the store, making dinner, trimming a caragana hedge, keeping bad news from a good friend, or playing hide-and-seek with the disturbed, yet unpredictably self-sufficient Lucy.

However, the playwright draws on "the disarrangement in the atmosphere" (66) during the special occasion of the impending eclipse, to revise and enrich our way of experiencing an ostensibly unexceptional small-town milieu of disparate people. The interplay of trivial activities and the oddly heightened awareness that the occasion prompts allows Gault to tease out inwardness of character through a subtext of small self-revealing or self-exposing moments that range from the banal to the oddly remarkable. Female inwardness is ultimately symbolized by the darkening of the male sun, the light of common day, by the shadow of the female moon.

A pervasive theme that refers not only to the world of the play but also, in a sense, to the possibly stereotypical expectations of its audience, is the discrepancy between the socially conditioned ideas people impose on each other—they see what they want or expect to see—and their personal sense of themselves. Through most of *The Soft Eclipse*, this creates a random and mildly discordant dramatic irony, most obviously at the expense of the narrowly judgmental and gossipy Ina, the most limited character in the play. As the time of the eclipse draws near, the accumulations of the day gather focus. Discord subsides as the older women, led by the somewhat sibylline Mrs. Currie, collectively improvise an eclipse party (complete with cherry brandy). As the moon is about to block out the sun, they are playfully inspired to mock male dominance in their lives, briefly performing a wake (for the recently deceased runaway husband of Mrs. McMillan) that sardonically transforms into a wedding march. As the light returns, they find themselves spontaneously in league with the "crazy" Lucy who has compulsively begun to tear leaves from the hitherto carefully groomed caragana hedge. In laughter and self-mockery, they accompany their hedge-stripping with recitations of their mothers' traditional recipes for the cure and preservation of the female body. For each character this brief collective act, a tiny if absurd protest against the inevitable return to what passes for female normality, takes on its own personal resonance according to her age and circumstance. But, in the words of Mrs. Currie, the ruminative old woman who serves as the concluding voice of the play, the importance is "that we came together. Once" (77–78). This suggests an affirmation of the feminine bond forged "in the moon's shadow," (71) however momentarily.

Like *Serpent in the Night Sky*, the play develops a symbolic pattern through the eclipse motif. The difference is that the characters in the former enact an eclipse-like event. In the latter the characters respond, initially obliquely and then overtly, to the actual event. In large measure the thrust of *The Soft Eclipse* is in its play of responsive language. For example, Mrs. Currie by nature speaks in a metaphoric mode (knapsacks, the jostling and mingling of atoms) in her effort to find a vocabulary to express the insights and feelings of her inner life that this day inspires, a trait she encourages in the young Alison. Only the abnormal Lucy consistently demonstrates the overt capacity to enact her elusive inner compulsions. Thus her one successful act of communication on this abnormal day—when she incites the collective stripping of the hedge—is a triumph of sorts. With this exception, however, *The Soft Eclipse* is principally reactive and reflective rather than actively self referential in the manner of *Serpent in the Night Sky*.

These three rural plays, *Roundup*, *Serpent in the Night Sky* and *The Soft Eclipse* are all authentically regional. However, the latter two include defining moments that take them beyond the straightforward representationalism of *Roundup*. In *Serpent of the Night Sky*, the important transforming sequence is deftly staged in purely dramatic terms. In the more verbally discursive *The Soft Eclipse*, the defining dramatic event is more tentative. Both, however, are landmarks in the evolution of a new prairie rural realism that incorporates and yet transcends regional authenticity.

IV

The specific identifying characteristics of a region are less easily discernible in its urban drama for the obvious reason that city life with all its problems is still city life wherever its location. Middle-class suburbs and impoverished city streets are found everywhere, as are the multicorporational office and apartment towers dominating contemporary city horizons. On the face of it, differences between cities have more to do with their degree of access to up-to-date technological amenities and money-making facilities than with regional individuality. Thus it would seem entirely incidental to the wide appeal of Frank Moher's *Odd Jobs*, in Canada and the United States, that an Edmonton audience conceivably could identify the location of the play's suburban setting within a city block. Although the bars and neighbourhoods are familiar to any youthful Edmonton audience of Brad Fraser's internationally performed *Unidentified Human Remains and the True Nature of Love*, the general interest in that play certainly has little to do with its specific rendering of local features, the particulars of Edmonton's "hostile" urban environment, for example.

Yet sensitivity to place and its social particulars provides an important filter of immediacy for the local audience. This is the first, and perhaps the best test of a play's value for others. What matters is the dramatic authority that comes from the playwright's familiarity with the shaping forces of the society he explores. The subject and treatment may also strike the nerves of a wider audience because the dramatic expression of an urban sensibility is generally accessible. For example, marginality, in its many facets—social, economic, generational and gender, as well as geographical—is itself a generic condition of urban anxiety. Prairie urban dramatists are well positioned for any or all of these, as the regional focus of plays I have selected for closer examination demonstrate. Rintoul and Nolan contrastingly examine societal issues of gender oppression; Moher reconsiders relationships between generations, while Fraser explores the estrangements of the urban young. Further, each playwright adapts or develops the techniques of realism in different ways, thereby subverting the notion of a staid or uniformly predictable "prairie naturalism."

Harry Rintoul adapts conventional naturalistic strategies to an agenda of gay sexuality. His first published play, *refugees* (1987), is a gritty, sometimes comic, and ultimately compassionate, evocation of urban underclass struggle for economic and emotional survival through a reconfiguration of the heterosexual domestic triangle. It is set in a seedy apartment in an unnamed city (most obviously identifiable as Winnipeg by its legendary cold winter) where Sydney, a male prostitute, and Patsy, a lonely waitress, are each vying for affection and refuge in the apartment of Tawe. The latter, a macho bully surviving on unemployment cheques seems unaware of his own confused sexuality. The emotional hedging of the male characters prefigures Rintoul's confessional play, *Brave Hearts* (1991). In this more forthright examination of gay gender issues, he adapts another familiar configuration of heterosexual romance: the coincidental meeting of two long lost lovers that prompts the exchange of mutual confidences on their road to reconciliation. Rafe, a querulous recovering drunk, has no memory of his earlier brief, but fulfilling encounter with the younger G.W. Now they meet as strangers at a gay house party on an acreage near Saskatoon. For half the play G.W. conceals their former connection from Rafe (and more transparently from the audience) as he makes friendly, if suspiciously persistent, overtures to discover the source of Rafe's pervasive bitterness. Yet when Rafe finally begins to respond, G.W. inexplicably backs away. In the eventual (and extended) recognition scene, Rafe's tentative anticipation of a renewed relationship is seemingly shattered by G.W.'s revelation that he is infected with HIV. In a passionate demonstration that "a brave heart does not deny" (262), Rafe resolves to share G.W.'s ill-fated destiny.

The mixed critical response to this play is instructive on the recurring issue in Canadian drama criticism of regionalism versus an avowed metropolitanism (usually located somewhere in central Canada). On one hand, reviewer Robert F. Gross roundly chastises gay playwrights from Western Canada, Rintoul among them, for their continued use of conventional realistic structures such as the confessional because the emphasis on guilt fails to make "positive statements about gay identity" (88). His comments on *Brave Hearts* are particularly scathing with reference to what I have identified as its "familiar configuration of heterosexual romance." Here Gross sees "contrivances that equal the greatest excess of 40s movie melodrama" and "too much of the deaths [sic] of the archetypal woman of pleasure, Camille, to be altogether liberating." On the other hand, other reviewers (all with connections to prairie theatre) praise Rintoul's "rigourously naturalistic drama" (Demchuk 37); his "unflinching view of the gay world" (Longfield 38); and as writing "in the traditional mode of Canadian realism and local relevance" (Arrell 34).

In short, in his use of heterosexual romance structure in combination with his particular choice of setting, Rintoul is appropriating realism (rather than subverting it, as Gross would prefer) for a specifically prairie gay agenda, directed at the prairie audience. The location of the play on an acreage property, in itself a contemporary intersecting point of rural and urban, hints that both are informed by the gay fact, whether fully acknowledged or not. The two characters in the foreground send the same signal: G.W. is a ranch man "with a working-man look" (222); Rafe is a seismologist in "designer jeans" (222). These antagonists (eventually to be reconciled as lovers) are strategically placed in the neutral ground of the backyard, equidistant from the prairie's edge, signified by a noisy thunderhead and flashing lightning, and the urbanized house, identified by the raucous sounds of a weekend party. Through the device of the confessional, we experience the full flavour of Rintoul's "unflinching view of the gay world" established in a correspondingly opposing duality: the empty degradation of anonymous sex from hazardous street pick-ups or the gathering of friends at the party in the background; the social stresses of internalized homophobia (Rafe) or the social release of self-acceptance (G.W.).

We also discover, or already recognize, the ideologically conservative nature of the whole society, rural and urban, gay and straight. When G.W. told his farmer parents he was gay, his mother insisted "it's a phase" (243) and his father, fearing ridicule in the beer parlour, kicked him off the farm. Rafe, a lingering product of middle-class heterosexual society, never did tell his late parents nor has he revealed his sexual orientation to colleagues or to straight friends. Rafe hates "faggots" (at the party he has just punched one for making a crude come-on); attending a gay party is for him an almost last resort in an increasingly sterile existence. Yet as G.W. points out, all gays do not wear their lifestyle like a badge, he for one. We also note that most of the men off-stage, like G.W. and Rafe, have traditional masculine professions or vocations. Implicitly and explicitly, Rintoul's purpose, in part, is to highlight the normalities rather than the cultivated stereotypes of gay life. His gay version of the lost and re-united lovers propelling the self-examinations of the characters contributes to the same purpose. It authenticates the emotional dimensions of gay experience for a general as well as a gay audience. Thus Rintoul's reconfiguration of an accessible heterosexual dramatic pattern reflects his effort to demarginalize an alternate way of life in prairie society: to establish its place within the society rather than outside it.

The young Winnipeg Métis playwright, Yvette Nolan, offers a more radical variation on gender issues and prairie conservatism in her brief feminist morality play, *Blade* (1990). She does so in a manner that both exploits and subverts alternate conventions of realism. Her subject is the serial murders of several Winnipeg women by a "hooker-killer," so called because his early victims were runaway native girls forced into the usual survival mode of taking to the streets (1). As opposed to Rintoul's fully extended proscenium representation, Nolan adroitly manipulates the presentational format of investigatory docudrama. Characteristically in docudrama, a first person narrator directly addresses the audience from an open, anti-illusionist stage, in this case to offer the corrective evidence of an inside story in counteraction to its misrepresented public version. As documentary realism, *Blade* becomes a critique of the investigation of one of the murders through which it targets the related issues of racism and misogyny. In a simple realistic countermovement of theatrical gesture, *Blade* also strives to implicate its audience directly in the oppressive construction of female victims into negative stereotypes.

The narrator is Angela, a university student who is the hooker-killer's latest victim. She informally paints in the background from her own perspective and tells her story up to the point when the murderer, Jack, offers her a ride in his car. For the events immediately precipitating her murder, the play shifts briefly from presentational narration into a dramatic enactment, whose validity we trust because of the youthful open-mindedness of Angela's self-presentation. The direct narration resumes when, magically, Angela re-appears, still covered in blood, to preside over the enquiries into her death—and her life. Now she addresses the audience as "a sort of after-image" who is briefly permitted to return by "the powers that be" (3). In this capacity she comments intermittently on the official enquiry and the newspaper reports or she playfully anticipates, or prompts, the words of the other speakers. These include her boyfriend, Kyle; her best friend, Connie; the eventually apprehended murderer; and her mother, Mrs. Erhart. All are witnesses or advocates, the first three speaking in dramatic monologue as if in response to the interrogations of the earthly "powers that be"—police, newspaper reporter and psychiatrist.

Like Rintoul, Nolan designs her play for a regional audience—she, initially, for a specifically Winnipeg audience. For her, the Winnipeg setting becomes an essential device of documentary authenticity for political purposes. Angela maps the scene of her murder precisely in the seedy Point Douglas district (Disraeli Bridge, Higgins Avenue, Henry Avenue). For the murderer (and the audience) this is a more likely "part of town" for street walkers than a young student who has just left her boyfriend's place in a temper (2). Winnipeg, with its high crime rate (and reactionary police force) among its large native population is also identified ideologically: a place where, in Angela's rueful understatement, "natives are sort of the low guys on the totem pole" (1). Part of the initial background is her story of the previous victim: Cindy Bear, like the others was a native girl but she also happened to be a hard working university student of Angela's acquaintance. After her murder, most students assumed that Cindy too was a prostitute, "They usually are, you know" (1). While the issues Nolan raises are not restricted to Winnipeg, her identifiable particulars (selective) of the city make them relevant to a local audience in an immediate way. In turn, the convention of direct address animates that audience by casting it into the oppositional role of surrogate for the Winnipeg public at large.

From racist attitudes towards urban natives, the distance is short to racial misogyny (Cindy Bear) and finally to misogyny *per se* when, ironically, Angela herself becomes the main object of public enquiry and judgmental speculation. Here Nolan doubly demonstrates that as far as public attitudes are concerned the medium is indeed the message. In the metaphoric sense, to be murdered by a hooker-killer is to assure the police that the victim is a whore, no matter how much protested by the people closest to her. In the literal sense, to be labeled "prostitute" by the news media is the self-perpetuating confirmation of that "truth." To Angela, these messages suggest the grim thought, "that if I *was* a hooker, then it was almost okay that I got myself killed" (3). In the same vein, but in the very last speech of the play, troubled and devout Mrs. Erhart addresses the audience ("you people ... so willing to believe the worst") on her own tentative break-through against the prevailing syndrome of blame-the-victim: "I'm beginning to think that maybe if the police had been looking for a man who was killing women, instead of a man who was killing whores, maybe he'd have been stopped a lot sooner" (5).

Since the mother's point is a Christian commonplace that only the most insensitive audience could fail to respond to at some level of recognition, Nolan tests the point on her audience more incisively. To a degree, the documentary investigation of Angela's (or Cindy Bear's) public representation or misrepresentation becomes a decoy. Whether Angela was a "good" girl, as her mother insists, or a "bad" girl as "you people" of the general public assume, is beside the point. Angela herself did not make those distinctions, which is presumably why she is "chosen" for her brief return. The fabular device of "after-image" frees her meta-dramatically from the restrictions of naturalistic necessity, maintained in the investigative monologues, and allows her to encounter the audience through a contravening physical action that begins early in her *post mortem* appearance. Her first such action is to remove the bloody sweatshirt on which she wipes her bloody hands. From here on, in total contradiction to everything that she or the others are saying in her defense, a disingenuous Angela is gradually transforming her appearance into the unmistakable image of a prostitute. At the last moment of the play, the audience is confronted by a fully altered visual representation of Angela about to re-enter the same scenario with Jack that led to her murder in the first place.

Nolan has set up her audience for a critique of the same ideological bias in its own value system that governs realistic dramatic representations of women. The issue becomes the audience's reaction to this altered version of Angela in the same dramatized context—a person it has come to know in a different, ostensibly more trustworthy documentary mode. In its surrogate role as general public, the audience is confronted with a range of possible (progressively better) reactions to Angela's deliberate transformation of herself into an image "you people" have been demonstrably projecting on her. The audience may be merely confirmed in its own bias; unsettled, at least, by the ambiguity; or fully cognizant of the irony. However, if the audience is truly persuaded by Mrs. Erhart's dawning realization, it might also recognize that not only is the so-called moral guilt or innocence of the victim ultimately beside the point, but that because she is a woman (*pace* Mrs. Erhart) Angela's murder occurs with the tacit permission of the whole society. We might now understand why the first version of the murder is dramatized as "fiction" rather than narrated as "truth." The second version, about to begin, is another "fiction." In her wry manipulation of two conventions of realism (with the help of the fabular device) into an oppositional, overtly political structure, Nolan circumvents Rintoul's more conventional strategy of appropriation.

The punning title of Frank Moher's *Odd Jobs* (1985), with its suggestions of casual and uncommon work, reflects the play's inception as an improvisational project at Catalyst Theatre, Edmonton. In the 1980s, Catalyst specialized in the interventional techniques of popular theatre for the animation of audiences on current social issues. These origins were recalled in the program of the premiere as, "a play about 'work' and the way ... we define ourselves by how we make our living." However, far from programmatic case history, or a slyly interventional play like *Blade*, *Odd Jobs* evolved into a sensitive impressionistic articulation of the growing relationship of three people who have lost their bearings in the ordinary work-a-day world. In themselves, these are an odd assortment of people: a retired and widowed mathematics professor; her handyman, a laid-off welder; and his working wife who hates her job in the complaint department of Sears. Like Connie Gault's Mrs. Currie, Mrs. Phipps is an unusual elderly woman, "a bit of a freak" (60) for her day as a woman teaching mathematics in the university instead of the usual arts subjects. Science remains her avocation but her once brilliant mind is now unpredictable. Isolated by age, her memory lapses and erratic behavior, she still finds a sense of purpose in eccentric attempts to solve a complex mathematical equation of her own devising. In lucid moments she is determined to prove the existence of an ordered universe which, in darker moments, she fears may be chaos. (Coincidentally both she and Mrs. Currie have intuitive theories of invisible matter.) The amiable Tim, made redundant on the assembly line by a robot arm, is in search of yard work. Temporary odd jobs might save his male self-respect from further diminishment in the eyes of his wife. Fortuitously, Mrs. Phipps' out-of-control garden is much in need of attention. Tim's Quebecoise wife, Ginette, is hoping to circumvent her irritation with the general public at the department store by learning computer operation at night classes. Her hobby is collecting cowboy records, a substitute for the lost ideal of the Alberta "cowboy" she thought she'd found in Tim when she first escaped to the West from the poverty of Lachine.

Moher assimilates these socially disparate human elements into an impressionistic structure, mixing fragmentary moments and more sustained encounters over a seasonally symbolic time period of early fall to spring. On an otherwise flexible and minimally furnished playing space, two stage areas are fixed: Mrs. Phipp's suburban backyard and a busy highway just down the hill. Like Warren, Moher builds his characters imagistically through patterns of physical or verbal interaction. His dominant motifs are the season, suburban location, memories of mountains, cowboy records, mathematical equations and the technological fragmentation of human endeavour. These combine into an urban/pastoral-chaos/order dichotomy variously represented in the lives of all three characters. The young couple, in their conflicting ways, grope with the pressures of dehumanizing urban employment and unemployment. The widowed Mrs. Phipps, foundering in her residual garden world of suburban pastoral, suffers from loss of community, by the physical encroachment of city on suburb in the form of the hazardous highway and by the threatening metaphysical chaos of a failed equation.

In more conventional realism, such as *Brave Hearts* and *Roundup*, the regional environment functions informationally and ideologically as fixed and unchanging background to the foreground action. The same is true of *Blade* with the difference that the audience becomes a representation of that background and, as such, is subject to change. In contrast, the regional environment of *Odd Jobs* is fluid. Moher integrates background and foreground so that, like *Serpent in the Night Sky*, the setting of the play functions literally and metaphorically in the dramatic expression of character and circumstance. The location of Mrs. Phipps' property on the edge of the city highway is a case in point. Metaphorically this signifies "hostile city" intruding into "pastoral suburb." Literally it becomes a physical danger to Mrs. Phipps in her erratic night wanderings. On such occasions she may be re-living the mountain excursions of her past, mistaking the bright lights of looming trucks for rising sun in alpine valleys. Some mornings she finds herself inexplicably at the edge of the highway, clad only in her nightgown, purse over shoulder and binoculars in hand. In these expressionistically interiorized moments, setting imagistically expresses the evanescence of a mind in distress. Here pastoral memory and urban reality collide, with the threatening highway the symbolic site of Mrs. Phipps unconscious struggle against loneliness and old age.

Although the geographical place is designated as Edmonton, Alberta, beyond a few incidental references the city is inferred rather than precisely mapped as in *Blade*. Nevertheless, some defining ingredients of character and circumstance are local and regional. Moher's sense of place emerges in his use of the popular imagery of Alberta pastoral, rural and urban. A country-and-western version drew Ginette to the West as the land of opportunity. Even in her single-minded struggle for a marketable skill, she still clings to her record collection in memory of that wistful media-inspired romantic dream of Alberta cowboys. Another version is the proximity of the mountain parks, the urban-dweller's weekend playground. This is reflected in Mrs. Phipps' fond, if occasionally wry memories of Arcadian expeditions with her husband, Wendell, and the congenial company of university friends: absurd times of skinny dipping, recorder playing and intellectual talk. In those days, the men scaled the mountains and the women remained in the valleys below, distracting themselves from worry for their safety by identifying the alpine flowers.

Closer to home, Alberta suburban pastoral is implicit in the richness of the northern summer season, made so by its brevity, now on the wane in Mrs. Phipps' garden where Tim strives to harvest and prepare for winter. He is seduced by the relaxed rhythms of these bucolic seasonal tasks and warmed by the hints of his employer's idyllic life long gone—

so different from his own and any ambitions that pragmatic Ginette (as such an intruder in the garden world) might have for their future. He comes to reject re-training, not only out of resistance to high school math (for which Mrs. Phipps would coach him), but because, in his increasing concern for his employer's well-being, he is learning to value human over push-button contact in his work. In contrast to Tim, Ginette longs for the impersonality of three walls and a computer, good money, with human relations reserved for weekends.

Tim's infatuation with the pastoral residue of Mrs. Phipps' life, which he clumsily tries to assimilate into his own (for example, he dresses up in the late Wendell's climbing gear) conflicts eventually with the urban goals of Ginette when she accepts a data-processing job in Regina. At first Tim refuses to go. To free him, Mrs. Phipps steels herself for another abandonment by initiating a determined retreat, armed only with her husband's climbing gear, to the simulated pastoral (cabins and garden plots) of an old folk's home. The eventual resolution hints of a more productive re-shaping of the pastoral/urban dichotomy in the plains city—away from memories of mountains and related associations—although not without its continuing ironies and uncertainties. For Mrs. Phipps this staves off the spectre of a retirement home or, metaphorically speaking, the despair of the failed equation. In this play, the regional setting, as defined associationally in the minds and actions of the characters, becomes a flexible dramatic metaphor for alignments and re-alignments in character relationships and circumstances in a state of flux.

While Rintoul, Nolan and Moher define their respective generic sites of acreage, inner city and suburb by their regional delineation's, Brad Fraser—a regionalist by subversion—transforms regional city into generic site. In *Unidentified Human Remains and the True Nature of Love* (1988), Fraser deliberately flouts the usual ingredients of prairie urban society, especially its conservative character, to define Edmonton as generic hostile city with just enough local detail to make his iconoclastic revision convincing. Edmonton becomes the site of boredom and desperation, make-shift employment and refuge from failure in Toronto, and most of all, sexual restlessness and violence. In its explicit sexuality, particularly in alternative forms, this version of Edmonton goes some way to challenge at least the first point of Robert Wallace's recent double-edged assertion that "[t]he dominant sensibility of Canadian culture is as anti-sexual as it is homophobic" (16). Occasional flashes of Alberta pastoral are ironic and sexually driven, for example, the participation in the role of cowboy in a S&M fantasy (46) or a camping trip that brings on a crisis of sexual orientation (44). Authentic traces of local geography refer to commercial bars, hangouts and sites of violence. The setting itself is fractured into generic locations of apartment, bar, restaurant, rooftop, park, brothel, gym etc. Like the setting of *Odd Jobs*, this functions as a fluid foreground rather than fixed background. While not symbolically integrated into character and action, as is Moher's imagistic synthesis of garden and highway, its representation as constantly shifting, fragmented environment expresses the haphazard nature of the lives of rootless characters in varying states of uncertainty.

Ideologically *Unidentified Human Remains* is light years away from *Odd Jobs*' social vision of defining ourselves "by how we make our living." For most of Fraser's characters, work is incidental or permanently temporary. The gay man, David, who once acted in a TV series in Toronto, says sardonically to his new busboy, Kane, "I find being a waiter more artistically satisfying" (15). Kane is recently out of high school, armed with credit cards, car and curfew by his rich suburban father (who collects Danby paintings and friends at the CBC). He's a willing enough worker at his low level job but is more absorbed by fantasies based on David's TV persona that lead to new, if tentative, sexual possibilities when he meets him in person. Candy, David's roommate and heterosexually disillusioned former lover, is cynical about her occasional work as a newspaper book reviewer: "How do you drag out the phrase 'It's shit' to three paragraphs?" (13). Bernie, hunter of women and partridge, and also David's life-long friend from the blue-collar neighbourhood of Beverly, works at an aimless job in a municipal office where he seems just as caged as he clearly does by marriage (50, 74). A sign of the times in Fraser's world is that the only person who is fully defined by the way she makes her living is the psychic prostitute, Benita. A specialist in S&M whose self-appointed mission is to take the sexual abuse that a client "might've forced ... on someone else—for free" (47), she is also able to "read" people's most suppressed sexual and emotional drives.

As a psychologist of violence and discontent, Fraser provides his characters with hints of uneasy histories that some of them deliberately attempt to revise or wipe out. Such is the case of Candy and her would-be suitors: Robert, a bartender from Winnipeg and the persistent Jerri, a lesbian school teacher. For others, evasion or denial predominate. David cynically denies his loving self in the guises of insatiable cruising sensualist and witty professional faggot so despised by Rafe in *Brave Hearts*.

The sexually troubled Bernie, in a psychotic version of Tawe's conflict in *refugees*, manifests his internalized homophobia in the misogyny of serial killings. In a variation on the misogynist society of *Blade*, in which some types of women matter less than others, for Bernie his victims are only "secretaries, waitresses, nurses—hairdressers, for Christ's sake" (90). Benita alone has stoically resolved her past: in comparison to her client with the cowboy fetish, she says to David, "My father was never that gentle" (48).

Fraser's hybrid stage realism explodes cinematically into multiple scenes flowing economically and without interruption on a composite set in combinations of linear, simultaneous and memory time. The characters are almost always on stage, although variously in focus. Realistic scenes are intersected by "a second score" (10), or counterpoint of background voices of characters absent from a given scene (sometimes through the device of the answering machine) who offer oblique comment on the foreground action. As an alternative to conventional dramatic exposition, intersected moments may also provide fragmentary self-revealing narratives, private ruminations or expressionistically re-lived memories. The effect is to give dramatic immediacy and density to the action and all its players.

Another type of intersection, in this case independent of the action, comes from the surreal voice of Benita. On the melodramatic level of urban thriller, her chilling camp-fire stories of ghoulish sexual violence (uncannily signaled by her singing of lines from the nursery rhyme, "Lavender Blue") suggest a gratuitous gothic figment rather than a realistic presence. Yet when actual bloody sexual violence impinges on their lives, gothic melodrama translates into real horror and disturbing suspense, for which Benita is the prescient voice. For all its darkness, *Unidentified Human Remains* is also peppered with the social humour of black comedy of manners: the persistent vacuity of the answering machine; pithy one-liners, mostly from David; and a notable comic scene where David wickedly presides over the deflation of Candy's ill-founded expectations of one suitor by the embarrassing arrival of the other. Through this radical cross-fertilization of psychological realism, expressionistic counterpoint, urban thriller and comedy of manners, Fraser offers the most comprehensive, as well as the most sensational treatment, of urban crisis.

V

Rintoul and Moher, in their different ways, work from traditional concepts of prairie society that in some way still connect urban and rural life. In *Brave Hearts*, Rintoul builds on a contemporary version of the interconnectedness of the two: the intersection of rural and urban, suggested by the acreage setting, attests to the reality of gay life in both realms of contemporary regional society. As sociological regionalism, the play dramatizes two different ways of responding to matters of gay acceptance or non-acceptance in that society, rural and urban. In a reversed emphasis, contrary to the usual stereotype of rural conservatism, G.W., the gay man from the farm who now raises horses, offers Rafe, the gay professional man from the city, the example he needs to reach a healthier self-acceptance of his homosexuality. In *Odd Jobs*, Moher creates a more complex duality by devising a cultural regionalism that interrelates regional rural myths (as preserved, for example, in the residual pastoralism of Mrs. Phipp's suburbia) and their opposing urban realities. This dichotomy not only informs the external circumstances of the three characters, but is integral to their characterization as individuals of greater or lesser complexity and the choices for change that they as individuals each make.

There is no rural presence in Nolan's *Blade* and little but ironic reference in Fraser's *Unidentified Human Remains*. In the feminist political regionalism of *Blade,* Nolan gives local definition to a wide-spread urban condition. Generically, her Winnipeg is a media-dominated world of violence and urban decay. Traditional social and moral values have hardened into racism and misogyny, reinforced by the news media as the image-makers and purveyors of public opinion. By giving local particularity to these realities, however, she is able to attribute the ironic discrepancy between general assumption and individual case to its local source, to expose the ideological foundations of what might almost be described as village malice writ large. Fraser, as a subversive regionalist, offers the local definition of contemporary Edmonton as the generic model of random and pervasive urban sexual violence. In his seven variously alienated Edmontonians, traditional prairie sexual and social patterns are subverted by their absence. Fraser, like Nolan, confronts the status quo, but he chooses a strategy of representational dramatic collage rather than face-on presentational attack.

My analysis of these four urban plays begins to isolate the varied dramatic fronts of an evolving urban "prairie naturalism." Just as the dramatic rendering of place in all four plays gives the autonomy of centre stage to characters who by circumstance are literally decentred by gender, age or social or geographical environment, so are their writers striving to centre regional urban society in the contemporary world through dramatic forms expressing that regionality.

Works Cited

Arrell, Douglas. "The Winnipeg Theatre Season." *NeWest Review* (Aug–Sept 1993): 33–34.
Bicknell, Minnie. *Relief*. Toronto: Macmillan, 1938.
Brooker, Blake. *Ilsa, Queen of the Nazi Love Camp and Other Plays*. Red Deer: Red Deer College Press, 1993.
Demchuk, David. "Queer Culture." *Theatrum* 24 (Jun–Aug 1991): 37.
Deverell, Rex. *Medicare! Showing West: Three Prairie Docu-Dramas*. Ed. D. Bessai and D. Kerr. Edmonton: NeWest, 1982. 175–259.
Fraser, Brad. *Unidentified Human Remains and the True Nature of Love*. Winnipeg: Blizzard, 1990.
———. *Wolf Plays*. Edmonton: NeWest, 1993.
Gault, Connie. *The Soft Eclipse*. Winnipeg: Blizzard, 1990.
Gowan, Elsie P. *Homestead*. *The Hungry Spirit: Selected Plays and Prose*. Ed. Moira Day. Edmonton: NeWest, 1992. 45–63.
Gross, Robert F. Rev. of *Making, Out: Plays by Gay Men. Canadian Theatre Review* 74 (Spring 1993): 86–88.
Hunter, Maureen. *Footsteps on the Moon*. Winnipeg: Blizzard, 1988.
———. *Transit of Venus*. Winnipeg: Blizzard, 1992.
Kerr, Don. *The Great War*. Unpublished, 1985.
———. *Talking Back*. Regina: Coteau Books, 1992.
Lemoine, Stewart. *The Book of Tobit*. Unpublished, 1993.
———. *The Glittering Heart*. Unpublished, 1990.
Longfield, Kevin. Rev. of *Brave Hearts*. *Theatrum* 32 (Feb–Mar 1993): 38.
Nolan, Yvette. *Blade*. *Theatrum* 31 (Nov–Jan 1992-93): S1–S5.
Moher, Frank. *Odd Jobs*. Toronto: Playwrights Canada Press, 1986.
———. *Prairie Report*. Winnipeg: Blizzard, 1990.
———. *Sliding for Home*. Toronto: Playwrights Canada Press, 1990.
———. *The Third Ascent*. Winnipeg: Blizzard, 1988.

Murrell, John. *Democracy*. Winnipeg: Blizzard, 1992.
Pollock, Sharon. *Generations: Blood Relations and Other Plays*. Edmonton: NeWest, 1981. 138–198.
Rintoul, Harry. *Brave Hearts*. *Making, Out: Plays by Gay Men*. Ed. Robert Wallace. Toronto: Coach House, 1992. 225–269.
———. *refugees*. Winnipeg: Blizzard, 1988.
Ringwood, Gwen Pharis. *Dark Harvest, Mirage, Still Stands the House: The Collected Plays of Gwen Pharis Ringwood*. Ed. Enid Delgatty Rutland. Ottawa: Borealis Press, 1982.
Sapergia, Barbara. *Roundup*. Regina: Coteau Books, 1992.
Scollard, Rose, Alexandra Patience and Nancy Cullen. *Aphra*. *Theatrum* 25 (Sept–Oct 1991): S1–S11.
25th Street Theatre. *Paper Wheat: The Book*. Saskatoon: Western Producer Prairie Books, 1982.
Wagner, Vit. "Writer's Passion is Mixing Bizarre and Banal." *Toronto Star* (6 Apr. 1991): J5.
Wallace, Robert. "Making Out Positions: An Introduction." *Making, Out: Plays by Gay Men*. Toronto: Coach House, 1992. 11–40.
———. "Writing the Land Alive: The Playwright's Vision in English Canada." *Contemporary Canadian Theatre: New World Visions*. ed. Anton Wagner. Toronto: Simon & Pierre, 1983. 69–81.

"One Big Ontario": Nation-Building in The Village of the Small Huts

by Alan Filewod

> We're going to turn this country into one big Ontario.
> —Thomas Scott in *Confederation and Riel*

The History of the Village of the Small Huts is an epic cycle of historical dramas written by Michael Hollingsworth and produced by VideoCabaret, the ultra-hip, media-cool Toronto theatre/performance art company. To date, the cycle consists of eight plays, beginning with *The History of the Village of the Small Huts, Part One: New France* in 1985, which was followed on an annual basis by *Part Two: The British* (1986), *Part Three: The Mackenzie/Papineau Rebellion* (1987), *Part Four: Confederation and Riel* (1988), *Part Five: Laurier* (1991), *Part Six: The Great War* (1992), *Part Seven: The Life and Times of Mackenzie King* (1993), and *Part Eight: World War II* (1994). Two more instalments are promised, to bring this epic re-creation of Canadian history to the present. When completed, the decalogue will stand as the largest and most ambitious dramatic treatment of Canadian history ever produced on stage. As such it is a significant contribution to the making of Canadian history, and it becomes part of the history it records. Like all national histories, it consists of intersecting ideological imperatives that argue a particular vision of the nation.

ALAN FILEWOD teaches drama at the University of Guelph. He is an editor of *Canadian Theatre Review*, and has published widely on Canadian theatre history. He is the author of *Collective Encounters: Documentary Theatre in English Canada*, and has edited two anthologies of plays: *New Canadian Drama 5: Political Drama* and *The CTR Anthology*.

Historical drama is more than a representation of history—because history itself is a product of representations made known through analyses, documents, discursive arguments and contested evidence. Every representation, every work of historical writing, is an intervention into the history it constructs. This is also the case with the historical drama, which literally *enacts* the past. In *The History of the Village of the Small Huts*, Hollingsworth enacts a vision of the nation as it proceeds through stages of colonialism towards an endlessly deferred postcolonial autonomy.

The History of the Village of the Small Huts is presented as a detached look at Canadian history—the mainstream dissected by the coolly ironic postmodern margins. But a nation is, in the final analysis, a construct of negotiated visions materialized through culture, economics and legislation, and the very success of *The History of the Village of the Small Huts* exposes its playwright as a nation-builder. The historical drama is an enactment that intervenes to revise and reconstruct the past it documents, and thus the playwright who chooses national history as the subject of enactment is by the same process contributing to the idea of the nation—even if, as is the case with Michael Hollingsworth, the history is enacted through strategies of parody and scatological satire.

Since the first instalment in 1985, the *History* cycle has become one of the most eagerly anticipated annual events in the Toronto theatre season. This success is not simply an indicator of popularity; it is also a precondition of the cycle's development as a text, because the popular reception of each instalment makes the next possible by creating audience demand and a proven track record for the funding agencies that support the project. The *History* is more than its own history: it is also an ideological expression supported by the society it scrutinizes. In that sense, the *History* cycle is the final culmination of the events it documents: the history of Canada leads to this point of retrospection, and to the material conditions of culture and economy that make the retrospection possible. Like all historical drama, *The History of the Village of the Small Huts* is a celebration of its own possibility.

Ironically, considering its provenance and theatrical idiom, *The History of the Village of the Small Huts* is the nearest we have to an "official" historical epic. That a national epic should present itself as iconoclastic and subversive is a useful comment on the way the modern Canadian state naturalizes itself in the popular imagination as a "post-national" refutation of its own power.

The first question to be posed to the cycle has to do with its popularity. If Canadians find national history as boring as we are told, why does Hollingsworth's annual installment sell out to packed houses and extended runs? There are two general reasons: the first has to do with VideoCab's unique performance style; the second has to do with the centricity of historical pageantry in Canadian culture: we may find history boring, but we're addicted to it.

The most effective description of this epic cycle is the playwright's own:

> ... scores of grotesque characters, hyperbolic costumes, 200 lighting cues an hour. The *Histories* are performed in a "black box" that is precisely perforated for light, and hinged for invisible wings. Nothing but the precise frame or sculptured space for each scene is visible—a close-up on a hand or face, the flicker of two heads conspiring, the tension of a triangle, the monumental solo with crowds at the edge of the light. Characters simply appear and vanish, fleet and insubstantial as memory, haunting as history. (Hollingsworth & Taylor 43–44)

VideoCabaret is known as a performance art collective that fuses theatrical performance with high-tech aesthetics and political satire expressed in hip Queen Street West cleverness. In fact, VideoCab, operating out of its headquarters in the Cameron House, was one of the sources of the Queen Street West idiom, which has since been widely marketed by VideoCabs' more recent corporate neighbour, CITY-TV/Much Music. With its multi-media political satires and its cross-over performances with The Hummer Sisters, VideoCab has set the tone as the epicentre of the ultra-hip in the Toronto theatre scene. And as is usually the case, the ultra-hip confers hipness on its audiences. VideoCab's audience for *The History of the Village of the Small Huts* cycle seems to have crossed demographic expectations, reaching the artistic underground, the mainstream theatre audiences, and the occasional theatre-going public, drawn by rave reviews in the daily press and on occasion by the subject matter. This shotgun appeal can also be seen in the material circumstances of the production. Because VideoCab does not have its own performance space, the cycle has been presented in rented theatres, beginning with the tiny backstage of Theatre Passe Muraille (a popular launching space for new work). For the last three instalments, VideoCab has rented the Theatre Centre, a Queen Street West space that takes pride in its hip grunginess.[1]

Throughout the cycle, VideoCab's marked ability to speak to very different audiences has worked to validate its implicit claim to historiographic authority. *The History of the Village of the Small Huts* provides a way to enjoy history without the embarrassing kitsch of patriotism.

In the black box of history, Hollingsworth replays the development of Canada as a grotesque puppet show. (This technique of ironic reduction is signalled in the title: the "Village of the Small Huts," Hollingsworth tells us in *Part One: New France*, is the original meaning of the word "Canada.") The black box and pin-point lighting direct our gaze towards a dazzling sequence of tableaux-vivants, as characters emerge out of the darkness to declare their obsessions, appetites and idiosyncrasies. Since the inception of the series, VideoCab has worked closely with Shadowland, a team of designers who have collaborated with some of the leading figures in the field of processional theatre, from Peter Minshall, the celebrated designer of the Trinidad Carnival, to Bread & Puppet and Welfare State. Shadowland's designs for the *History* cycle employ grotesque and exaggerated styles of make-up, oversize cut-out props, costumes festooned with anachronism, and pop-up set pieces. Wilfrid Laurier, as the leader of the Quebec "Rouge" Liberals, wears a bright red suit; Laura Secord carries a wooden cow by a handle on its back; pop-up landing craft ferry troops to the beaches of D-Day. Characters are identified by bold exaggerations of typifying clichés: Sir John A. Macdonald boasts a brilliantly mottled nose; Mackenzie King's constant companion, his dog Pat, is an engaging hand-puppet.

Together with the pin-spot lighting these designs transform the stage into a 3-D comic book, and the precisely drilled staging captures the antic rhythms of TV cartoon. Hollingsworth has said that his plan has been to produce each episode in the performance idiom of the popular theatre of the period under study, and at least one critic has taken this at face value, noting, for example that "*Confederation and Riel* mixes Victorian melodrama with Gilbert and Sullivan operetta." Michèle White argues that in the Queen Street West attitude,

> the artist ranges back and forth between historical precedents and the forms of the immediate present, often sharply juxtaposing them, in an attempt to house the concept in a way that both serves the idea and which will resonate with the projected audience. (53)

In fact, even postmodern performance, which claims to have the "historical precedents," the techniques of the past, available for synthesis

In fact, even postmodern performance, which claims to have the "historical precedents," the techniques of the past, available for synthesis in the forms of the present, can only *quote* the past rather than re-perform it. In each of the instalments Hollingsworth introduced elements that quote from past theatrical styles: commedia dell'arte masks and mannerism in *Part One: New France*; Punch and Judy in *Part Three: The Mackenzie/Papineau Rebellion*. But this is not to say that the plays are performed in these manners: rather they *cite* typifying theatrical gestures so that past performance techniques function as textual information. These techniques are normally superimposed on the characteristic overheated performance style. One Toronto critic, for example, noted that the "marionette-like jerky movements" in *The Mackenzie/Papineau Rebellion* helped establish "a world of cranks, puffing fools, confused idealists and pretentious twits" (Lacy D6).

In performance, *The History of the Village of the Small Huts* is an astonishing performance of theatrical virtuosity and a rigorously disciplined comic spectacle. The comic delight in parody and satire, in clever gaming, permeates the spoken text as well. The text of the *History* cycle is written in a style that might be called declarative iconography: dialogue is reduced to simple exchanges of information as characters present themselves to each other. In effect they speak their subtext—or looked at in another way, they speak cartoon captions. But simple as this may seem, the text is a dense weave of intertexts, of quotations and references from other texts, taken from historical record and popular culture. When the French explorers Radisson and Grosseilleirs meet, for example, they greet each other with the nicknames conferred on them by later generations of schoolchildren ("Ah Radishes," "Ah, Gooseberries …" [33]). In *Part Four: Confederation and Riel*, Sir John A. Macdonald parodies *HMS Pinafore*, which functions on the surface as a reference to Victorian popular culture, but also conceals an intertextual nod to the popular 19th century burlesque *HMS Parliament* (200). Throughout the cycle, historical figures speak in veiled mutations of their recorded words. In a typical example, Hollingsworth transforms a famous speech by William Lyon Mackenzie into a cartoon rant:

> Canadians, brave Canadians, loyal Canadians. Bow to your partner, bow to your friend. Put on your smile before this ends. Do you love freedom. I know you do. Who'd deny it, would you, would you? Down with the butcher, down with the baker, down with her Majesty's candlestick maker. Do

you hate oppression. I know you do. Who'd deny it, would you, would you? We all work and we all toil. The Family Compact says we're disloyal. (147)

The original speech is a classic of political rhetoric but in keeping with the intertextual structure of the cycle, it is best known as the theatrical centrepiece of Rick Salutin's *1837: The Farmer's Revolt*. Hollingsworth is concerned equally with the historical record and the popular traditions of historiography that have narrated the record.

This dense weave of intertexts is deceptive. On the one hand it rewards specialized knowledge, but on the other, that reward (a feeling of shared insight with the playwright which generates a feeling of complicity) is undermined. To catch all the references the spectator would have to have read every source Hollingsworth draws upon. The *History* cycle is a virtuoso display of learning and arcane knowledge but every reference we catch is a reminder of the many that pass us by. None of the intertexts and anachronisms is attributed, and this very lack of attribution is a device that flatters the spectator who picks up on them, and in turn reinforces the author's claim to authority. By the same token, a breach or disruption of authority has equally widespread ramifications through the text. A trivial and inadvertent error (such as Canadian troops using American drill commands and salutes in *Part Eight: World War II*) can undermine confidence in the larger structure.

The enactment of history in the cycle is a playful display of virtuosity that elicits admiration by its technical performance and laughter by its humour. These qualities explain in large part the cycle's ongoing popularity, but they are not unique. If technical skill and raucous humour were all that were needed, why pay admission to a play when we can stay at home and watch *Beavis and Butthead*? The success of *The History of the Village of the Small Huts* must in the end have something to do with the history it constructs.

Although most Canadians might dismiss the theatre as an occasional pleasure and a marginal activity, it has always served as a site for the redefinition of the Canadian nation. Canada, like the other postcolonial remnants of the British Empire, is a country that continues to obsess over its lack of an essentialist defining principle. It was brought into being at a time when nations were understood to be the incarnation of spiritual or metaphysical imperatives, usually having their source in ideas of race or history. In effect, Canada was founded for reasons of political convenience but justified by principles that no longer apply in the modern world, and we are left with a political construction that lacks an ideological imperative. It is this lack that is often explained as a quest for "identity."

Because of this ideological vacuum Canadian artists have repeatedly sought meaning through representation, to find a defining principle, a "Canadianism" in art. This was in fact the thinking that led to the founding of the Canada Council and the entire structure of arts funding in Canada today: Canada is what the artists show it to be. From Confederation to the present day, the theatre has been an important site for this showing. *The History of the Village of the Small Huts*, for all its satiric tone, falls squarely into a venerable tradition of historical pageantry in the theatre. It is the latest chapter in our ongoing national drama, and in fact it covers the same ground, for the same polemical reasons. And in the end, it makes the same arguments.

Hollingsworth's dramatic technique coincides with two popular traditions in Canadian theatre: the community historical pageant and the monumental drama. The historical pageant as we know it today was developed in England in the final years of the last century by Louis Napoleon Parker, who revived the idea of the "pageant" from its medieval sources to describe a new form of outdoor performance in which the community replays its own history. Parker's pageant technique was brought to Canada by his assistant, Frank Lascelles, who staged the 1908 re-creation of the Plains of Abraham for the Quebec Tercentenary. By the early years of this century, historical and military pageants were common across Canada.

The pageant is a celebratory form that animates iconography to justify present ideology. In performance, it is declarative—that is, it shows whatever needs to be shown to explain the past it constructs. Because of the epic scale and vast canvas, dialogue tends to be telegraphic: it signals essential information. Characters enter and explain themselves, defining their place in the sequence of cause and effect, and announcing their motives. At its simplest, this is the technique of the traditional village mummer's play:

> In comes I, St George the Bold
> T'was I who fought the dragon of old ...[2]

This same technique is one of the recurring devices that give the *History* cycle its narrative structure. In a typical example, from *Part Two: The British*:

BONTEMPS: My name, Charles Bontemps. My wife, she sleeps here, she sleeps there. Do I care? Of course not. The other seigneurs can have her. On my land I have seigneur's rights. My tenants tremble when they see me. On their wedding day their daughters run. But not fast enough. This old goat is unstoppable. Before the conquest I did not have seigneur's rights. But Carleton, he is a great man. My vassals can go dance around my Maypole forever. My eyebrows are so beautiful. A little pluck here a little pluck there. (86)

In this short speech, we learn everything we need to know about Bontemps as a man and as an actor on the historical stage. The tone is satiric and the historical argument is reductive: history is made by pigs with power. The declarative technique reveals essential and defining characteristics, and one of its problems is that it reinforces this idea of essential character.

Pageants rely on a succession of iconographic moments, and frequently substitute visual montage for interpretive narrative. There is an historical tradition in which pageantry of this kind intersects with the drama of interior character action. In Canada this occurred in the 19th century, with a genre of monumental dramas, most of which were written as poetic tragedies. These dramas were monumental in the sense that a statue in the town square is monumental: they memorialize greatness. But they also attempt to "humanize" historical figures in a way that pageants cannot, by engaging the hero in a plot designed to reveal the greatness of character.

The legacy of this tradition runs deep in Canadian drama, and few playwrights seem to escape it. This is because the monumental dramas were early attempts to locate the defining principle of Canadianism in particular historical events. By isolating certain events, the dramatists helped construct the popular tradition that continually refers to those same events as the defining points of history. It is in 19th century drama, for example, that we first see the War of 1812 and Laura Secord's journey singled out as definitive events. Every dramatist who returns to those events today is effectively following a track laid down by 19th century predecessors.

In a similar way, every episode of *The History of the Village of the Small Huts* reiterates familiar historical tropes. A trope, in this sense, is a pattern of perception, a habituation by which familiar images and narrations become "naturalized," so that we accept them as given facts. Historical dramatists tend to build on repeated patterns because our understanding of history is in fact a compilation of tropes—of narrations, historiographies and polemics that accumulate over decades. The most far-reaching trope is that of the "nation" itself, which is both the predicate and object of most historical writing. It is the predicate in that the writer of Canadian history works backwards from the present, seeking origins of the present Canada in the past; it is the object because the historian builds a rhetorical argument that shows the gradual evolution of the nation out of its various sources. This is what Hollingsworth does, and why he steps on familiar ground to make his case. To those who accept the trope of the nation as a "natural" truth, this is an entirely reasonable methodology. But to those who reject it, the defining condition of the nation may obscure rather than clarify history.

For each of Hollingsworth's installments, it is possible to identify precedents in earlier historical dramas. In 1886, for example, Charles Mair wrote a scene into his poetic tragedy *Tecumseh* in which Isaac Brock proclaims his creed to the ragtag Upper Canadians he must mobilize to repel the American invaders:

> For I believe in Britain's Empire, and
> In Canada, its true and loyal son,
> Who yet shall rise to greatness, and shall stand
> At England's shoulder helping her to guard
> True liberty throughout a faithless world. (143)

In *Part Two: The British*, Hollingsworth includes a scene in which Brock similarly announces his Imperial credo:

> BROCK: ... Gentlemen, I am not going to be liberal about this.
>   I hate the Yankee pig.
> STRACHAN: Here, here.
> BROCK: I have no use for democracy.
> STRACHAN: Here, here, well said.
> BROCK: I have a king.
> STRACHAN: And so do we.
> BROCK: That is enough for me.
> STRACHAN: Us too.
> BROCK: This land is part of the British Empire.
> STRACHAN: Well said.
> BROCK: And when the Empire calls what do we sing?

STRACHAN: Ready, aye, ready.
BROCK: Exactly. (105)

Written over a century apart for very different polemical reasons, the two scenes differ in tone. Mair's play was a celebratory attempt to propose Brock as a national hero; Hollingsworth's iconoclastic version shows Brock as simply another brutal colonial warlord in a long sequence of oppression. But this does not simply mean that Hollingsworth subverts orthodox representations, or that he is turning Mair upside down with a "counter-discourse" that refutes convention through parody. Every historical drama is an ideological intervention that expresses an historical argument, and in this Hollingsworth and Mair share a common purpose. Hollingsworth's satirical parody is not far removed from Mair's adulatory monumentalism. Both configure Brock's declaration of Empire as a significant event in the history of the nation. The difference in ideology, between Mair's Imperialism and Hollingsworth's postcolonialism, reflect the historical distance the nation has travelled in a century. In both cases, the playwright reflects and contributes to the dominant ideology of nationhood.

But what is the nation that Hollingsworth builds? According to Michèle White, the genesis of the *History* cycle was

> a single still image, the photo of the Queen handing Canada's patriated constitution to Prime Minister Trudeau in 1982. In Hollingsworth's view, it is the moment when Canada acquired nation status. (50)

The thesis of *The History of the Village of the Small Huts* is that this arrival as a nation was a natural development that advanced through stages of anti-colonial struggle, and which was retarded by a succession of self-interested twits. There are no heroes in this conception of history: even the proponents of national autonomy are driven by greed, fanatic egotism and base appetites. History proceeds through incompetence, conspiracy and obsession, but it is nevertheless progressive. As the cycle continues, Canada lurches towards some form of rational shape in which colonizing power is dismantled and redistributed—to the benefit of a new class of capitalists who buy and sell politicians. Canada arrives as a nation, the cycle implies, but the hierarchies of power remain unchanged.

The political narrative that runs through the cycle is effectively the narrative of liberalism as the term is understood in Canada.[3] The liberal ideology of postcolonial nationality is most clearly expressed by Wilfrid Laurier in *Part Five: Laurier*:

> LAURIER: ... We live in an age when each nationality will have its own state and each state will have its own nationality. And each state will include the whole nationality and nothing but the nationality. So what is one to do? The obvious. Create a new nationality. A unique nationality. A twentieth century nationality. A political nationality. A nationality that is not based on race or religion. Zoe, look at me. I will make this country a multi-national state that believes in ... Liberty. Oh liberty. What do you think of that? (246)

This is in effect the strategy of Laurier's Liberal successors. In his belief in rationality and his arrogant dismissal of the people ("The electors. And what do they do. They all moo together" [240]), Laurier anticipates Pierre Trudeau, whose conception of the nation produced the cultural policies that made VideoCab possible.

The Liberal conception of Canadian history has traditionally located the principle of nationhood in the ongoing dialectic of French-English relations. *The History of the Village of the Small Huts* reiterates this statist thesis of "founding peoples" who remain in uneasy partnership. In doing so, Hollingsworth implicitly accepts the bi-national thesis, in which the nation is configured as the negotiation of Quebec and an undifferentiated English-speaking Canada. It is for this reason that this national history is almost entirely about Ontario and Quebec. The only instalment which moves the main locus of the action from the Toronto-Quebec corridor is *Part Four: Confederation and Riel*. And even here the western scenes are presented as extensions of the Ontario-Quebec dispute.

For Hollingsworth, the experience of Ontario is metonymic of English Canada as a whole. At one point, Hollingsworth has Thomas Scott, the Ontario Orangeman shot by Louis Riel (and whose death precipitated Riel's hanging) proclaim "We're going to turn this country into one big Ontario" (182). In context, the line is a bombastic declaration of racist imperialism, but in effect it describes the historical narrative of the *History* cycle, in which English Canada *is* configured as one big Ontario.

The History of the Village of the Small Huts recapitulates the Liberal history of Canada. Much of the historical argument is familiar to the point of orthodoxy; in *Part Eight: World War II*, for example, the proposal that the Dieppe raid was launched in order to sacrifice Canadian troops on the altar of convenience and so teach the upstart colonials a lesson has been made repeatedly since the war—and in fact is the thesis of Tom Hendry's 1973 play *Gravedigger's of 1942*. What then is the relationship of this orthodoxy, this fidelity to dominant versions of Canadian history, to the satiric and parodic voice of the cycle?

To answer this we take another stroll down Queen Street West. If Hollingsworth presents Ontario as metonymic of English Canada, Queen Street West is metonymic of Ontario. Queen Street West is played across the country, via Much Music, as the epicentre of hip alterneity, as the ironic reflection of the "mainstream" it constructs through implication. But there is nothing alternative about Queen Street West; in the end it is a particularly successful commercial stretch made famous by its biggest, richest and most powerful business: CITY-TV. Queen Street West is in fact its own antithesis: the mainstream at play with itself. Moses Znaimer, the entrepreneur who runs the CITY-TV/Much Music empire, has remarked that his "interactive" TV studio ("the Much environment") at 299 Queen Street West is the "dead centre of the city, ... and therefore, in my opinion, the dead centre of the country" (quoted in Snyder 11). Liz Snyder has noted that from this vantage point, Znaimer "positions himself as a Big Brother figure, searching out the cool people who are his subjects" (11).

In this parade of corporate hipness, VideoCab's radicalism dissolves; the ironic voice flattens into a particular regional accent, which in turn imposes itself (through broadcast, through performance) as an instrument of ideological enforcement. In *The History of the Village of the Small Huts*, parody is already compromised, because the events selected for parody are contingent on the dominant cultural narratives Hollingsworth ostensibly subverts but effectively advances.

The material history of the *History* cycle embraces the historical processes it depicts and parodies. When Hollingsworth began the series in 1985 the Free Trade Agreement was still a matter of debate; the referendum crisis, the collapse of the Conservative Party, the rise of the Bloc Québécois and the resurgence of the Liberals had not yet come to pass. As *The History of the Village of the Small Huts* enacts its vision of Canada, it provides us with an index to read the history it passes through; in that sense it can be read as a populist reading of the political history of the 1980s and '90s. But as it demonstrates the recurrence of political obsessions it asserts a cyclical view of history, a cycle that parody is unable to break.

In the One Big Ontario, hip irony is a strategy of preserving power; it is the means by which orthodox historiography renews itself as the voice of cultural dominance.

Notes

1. With one exception, all the instalments have premiered in small Toronto theatres, usually in the Queen Street vicinity. The exception was *Part Four: Confederation and Riel*, which premiered in Calgary during the 1988 Olympic Arts Festival.
2. The traditional mummers play has been recorded in dozens of versions, all of which carry this common feature of declarative entrances.
3. Liberalism has usually but not always been expressed through the Liberal Party. There are exceptions: Brian Mulroney's Progressive Conservative government, with its emphasis on Free Trade and the balancing of power between English Canada and Quebec, was in effect a liberal government.

Works Cited

Hollingsworth, Michael. *The History of the Village of the Small Huts: Parts I–VIII*. Winnipeg: Blizzard, 1994.

Hollingsworth, Michael and Deanne Taylor, "VideoCabaret Chronology." *Canadian Theatre Review* 70 (Spring 1992): 43–44.

Lacy, Liam. "Historical satire highly original, funny." *Toronto Globe and Mail* 16 April 1987: D6.

Mair, Charles. *Tecumseh, A Drama and Canadian Poems*. Toronto: The Radisson Society of Canada, 1926.

White, Michèle. "The History Cycle: The Parodic Seen/The Parodic Scene." *Canadian Theatre Review* 70 (Spring 1992): 53.

Snyder, Liz. "As Much as You can Afford: Moses Znaimer and Tamara." Unpublished paper, 1992.

(I would like to thank Blizzard Publishing, who made typescript copies of the eight plays in *The History of the Village of the Small Huts* available to me in advance of publication.—A.F.)

Spiritual Resistance / Spiritual Healing: Tremblay, Dalpé, Stetson, Champagne, Marchessault

By Denis Salter

I

> A strange and powerful energy emanates from this house, as if the history of the entire world had taken place here ...
> —Michel Tremblay, *La Maison Suspendue*

"Strange," "Powerful," "Energy," "Emanates," "House," "History," "World," "Here,"—these eight densely encoded words constitute many of the recurrent stylistic and thematic issues preoccupying much of Québec dramatic literature in the last five years. It is a drama featuring characters—traumatised, brutalised, repressed, silenced, violated, abandoned, or destroyed—who experience profound epiphanies in which they discover that they *must* undertake a quest-romance in search of themselves. The first step in the quest is giving themselves permission to say "No" to the values, people, and traditions that have kept them imprisoned in a state of self-denial. This means saying "No" to folkloric mystifications of the past (*La Maison Suspendue*); "No" to patriarchy (Jean Marc Dalpé's *Le Chien*; Kent Stetson's *Queen of the Cadillac*); and "No" to self-evasion and the deceit of role-playing (Dominic Champagne's *Playing Bare*). Above all else, it means saying "No" to imaginative,

---

DENIS SALTER teaches Theatre Studies in the Department of English at McGill University. He has published on Canadian drama, Shakespearean stage history, Victorian theatre practices, performance theory, and theatre historiography in a wide variety of journals and collections.

emotional, and psychological impoverishment (Jovette Marchessault's *The Magnificent Voyage of Emily Carr* especially, but all these plays in one way or another).

In finding the courage to say "No," these characters, all of whom are artist-figures, release the kind of energy, in themselves, and sometimes in others, that can only be described as spiritual. For some of them—like Jay the romantic wanderer in *Le Chien* who returns home to murder his own father at the play's climax or Luce the actress in *Playing Bare* who can't manage to show up on opening night to play Lucky in her company's production of *Waiting for Godot*—spiritual resistance may have to become a permanent condition in which they can never stop saying "No" to the world around them in order to survive. But, for other, more blessed characters—the sometime teacher Jean-Marc in *La Maison Suspendue*, the painter Emily Carr in *The Magnificent Voyage of Emily Carr*, and the street-smart punk Erlich in *Queen of the Cadillac*—spiritual resistance may lead—however slowly, however gropingly—to spiritual healing, taking place now but just possibly lasting forever. Once they reach the healing stage, they no longer feel quite so compelled to journey through literal and figurative worlds searching for themselves. Instead, they know, if only intuitively, that they themselves are the world; and that their houses can become homes where they can perhaps answer some tough existential questions, including "Who am I, really?" and "What kind of person can I be(come)?"

Tremblay, Dalpé, Stetson, Champagne, and Marchessault: *their* quest-romance, as playwrights, has been to create the kind of dramaturgy in which the invisible world of the spirit is rendered visible; is invoked in such a way that we believe that we can actually see it as it penetrates and transforms their leading characters. How does this dramaturgy of spiritual resistance and healing work? And what are some of its larger sociopolitical implications? These are the questions that I shall explore in this paper, by considering the (symbolical) forms and functions of the houses in which these characters live; the thresholds and liminal spaces through which they need to travel in search of self-identity; their struggle to leave normal reality behind, to enter into—and yet also return from— the spiritual world; the climactic scenes of confrontation between domineering fathers and liberated children once the spiritual world has touched all of them; and the concluding scenes in which dystopian houses are either transformed, or have the potential of being transformed, into utopian homes, where the figure of the child represents a renewed family and social order.

II

The houses in all five plays are not only real places where real people live. They are also living archives for the storage of personal, family, and social memories. Like memories themselves, these houses seem to move fluidly through time and space, expanding and contracting, losing and regaining focus, and assimilating and retaining disparate impressions about the characters whose lives they record. In *La Maison Suspendue* the house —a log cabin at Duhamel—is occupied concurrently by three successive generations (1910, 1950, and 1990) of the same extended family taking their July vacation. Although the generations remain almost farcically unaware of one another's actual presence, they nevertheless respond emotionally to one another through their mutual reactions to their collective memories, carefully stored and lovingly, and sometimes neurotically, recalled at key dramatic moments. "In the hundred years that this house has stood," explains Jean-Marc (of the 1990 generation) to his lover, Mathieu, "it's my own family that has fought here, argued here, made peace, cried, tapped its feet, played the fiddle and the accordéon, sung songs and made up new jigs." When Jean-Marc discovers that the house is for sale, he has no choice but to buy it ("I bought all those memories to keep them from sinking into indifference") for he needs to revivify his own exhausted and dislocated spirit by seeking to reconcile the differences—between the rural and the urban past; between brothers and sisters; between fathers and sons—that have partly divided his family for nearly a century (28-29).

Similarly, Emily Carr in *The Magnificent Voyage of Emily Carr* feels attracted to—though also somewhat equivocal towards—the weight of her family's past history as it inscribes itself within the architecture of her house in Victoria. As she herself explains, she has "christened" it the House of All Sorts, to reflect its freedom from social constraints and its generous hospitality towards an assortment of eccentrics like herself (35 and 63). Despite its bohemian atmosphere, the house is nevertheless rooted in the traditional values of both Victoria itself (where she has often felt "buried alive" [82]) and her conservative family. It is built on land that she inherited from her father, a man from whom she had to keep her distance for, as she observes, "after eating up all the natural humanity that was in him, he was about to devour mine" (30). Yet when she thinks of the land, what she chooses to remember is not her father but rather "[t]he spirit of maternity [that] still hovers over this plot"—a spirit that comes from a cow that she and her sisters owned when they were children. For her, the house is not so much a material embodiment of her family's history but rather a shifting and evanescent state of mind, a "mystery," as she puts it, that allows her to define herself as still part of, yet also separated from, the family that has been a stubborn obstacle in her own spiritual voyage towards artistic self-expression (35). Whereas her father's house was devouring, solemn, and patriarchal, her own home is nurturing, high-spirited, and matriarchal—the very kind of home that Jean Marc wants to *re*construct at Duhamel through the selective power of memory.

In *Queen of the Cadillac*, a similar process of symbolical transformation takes place in Erlich's perspective on the world and his place within it. Scrounging a hand-to-mouth existence in the shadowy alleyways, catwalks, and underground passages of Montréal, Erlich believes that he is an orphan; but he eventually discovers that his real family lives in the green world of Culloden, P.E.I. Like Emily Carr, he, too, speaks in artistic parables, an indirect mode of speech in which life's truths are poeticised into quasi-spiritual form. A classic outsider whose role-models are Johnny Rotten and Sid Vicious ("Murder, rape, atomic bomb / death to the earth's / daughters and sons / death brought live / to everyone / on tee vee, tee vee, colour teee veee" [2]), Erlich suffers from expressionistic nightmares in which one of his former apartments literally collapses around him ("The floors begin to rot as I walk and I sink to my knees. Then I'm up past my hips, movin' slow. I stop. Trapped. Like an insect in amber" [17]). Searching in his nightmare for a stable home that he can call his own, he imagines himself travelling like an astronaut into outer space, looking back down to Mother Earth for spiritual nourishment. "I linger over Prince Edward Island. Peace. Beauty" (18): paradise at last, or so he would like to believe. But it turns out to be nothing more than a seductive illusion, polluted by his grandfather MacCulloch, a traditional patriarch who has committed incest with Erlich's mother, Hestor: "Then the earth's skin erupts in a spew of putrid lava and I'm falling toward this stinking pit. There's an old man in it and I hate him" (18). Paradise lost; it is not until the end of the play, once the destructive spirit of MacCulloch has been exorcised, that Erlich can find the family and the home that are actually his; as he does so, Montréal turns, like P.E.I., into a green world of wondrous transformations, and his "vicious" nightmares, full of postmodern *angst*, come to a permanent end.

For Erlich, Emily Carr, and Jean-Marc, as for Luce and Jay, the journey of the human spirit is indeed a series of wondrous transformations in which identity is always being placed at risk. And yet without risk, without the courage to cross over from one world to the next, spiritual healing will prove impossible. In the symbolic architecture of their houses/homes as reconfigured by memory, all these characters occupy—and are in turn occupied by—real and spiritual worlds at once; much of the time, they are positioned within liminal spaces, inside thresholds, between borders: dematerialising places where they are irradiated by the desire to become different from their normal selves. But will they in fact cross over, or will they remain transfixed, perhaps forever, on the (virtual) edge of spiritual transformation?

In *La Maison Suspendue* the house, in a mystical transfiguration, does indeed become a maison suspendue, taking its normally earthbound characters with it. Jean-Marc's great uncle (and grandfather) Josaphat-le-Violon is a fantastical storyteller-fiddler who uses the bewitching power of music (playing the aptly named "The Jig for the Devil on Vacation") to conjure up a floating canoe full of "the outcasts, the damned" (33) who pull the house through the night sky all the way from Duhamel to Montréal for "a big, big soirée" (38). For Josaphat, as for his (illegitimate) son Gabriel who thinks that Josaphat is his uncle, not his father, this journey turns the world completely upside down, reverses everyday rules and expectations, provides emotional liberation, and secretly enhances the spiritual bond between father and son. The journey is also dangerous. As Gabriel's mother (Josaphat's sister) Victoire points out, it is the dream-work of the Devil (35), a temptation to which she is especially sensitive, for Gabriel, like the canoeists, like his parents, is something of a social outcast, a child born from the incestuous passion—and love—between brother and sister. The journey is dangerous, moreover, because it ends in Montréal, a symbol in the play, as it is in much of Québec literature, of urban decay and corruption—crowded, suffocating, and poor, where the French are at the mercy of les maudits anglais.

The journey back to Duhamel, however, temporarily exorcises the influence of the Devil, as forty thousand guardian angels are now conjured by family and friends through the power of prayer. "The house shook a bit ... But it wasn't curses and drinking songs that we heard," Josaphat explains to Gabriel, "... it was hymns coming straight from Heaven ... The house rose gently into the sky, and that day, for once, it wasn't the devil who brought us home to Duhamel!" (39). Montréal, and the urban values it represents, now seems permanently left behind, although we know, especially through the perspective of Jean-Marc's generation, that the family will eventually have to leave Duhamel for Montréal, selling the house—and relinquishing the traditional rural values that it represents—for the sake of "social progress." This (violent) uprooting—a kind of religious exodus—is also the Devil's work, as the play's final tableau makes clear: "La maison suspendue, hanging from the end of a rope, hooked onto a birchbark canoe by a ship's anchor, flies over the sky of Duhamel. The canoe is guided by the Devil himself, who points the way towards the city" (101). Jean-Marc's own journey in buying and attempting to resettle in the house is therefore an exercise in nostalgic historical reversal, crossing over the threshold from the urban present into the rural past, to recuperate (perhaps forever?) the history of his family and his culture. "How often I find I miss that laugh," he recalls of his mother, La Grosse Femme. "When life gets complicated. Like it is now. She's been gone for twenty-seven years and I still miss her" (99). But, like the journeys to Montréal, Jean-Marc's journey back is also full of dangers: he may discover, as classic wanderers have throughout history, that he cannot go home again—that he cannot make his mother live again through the act of memory—no matter how much he needs to do so.

Similarly, in *The Magnificent Voyage of Emily Carr*, the House of All Sorts seems to dematerialise and become assimilated by the spiritual world with which it peacefully co-exists. "When night falls, and the men and women in the Indian villages stretch out on the ground to embark upon the magnificent voyage of sleep," Emily observes to her spiritual companion, the Soul Tuner, "suddenly in all the forests of the West Coast, the lights and the birds fall silent when she appears sparkling in the night air—the house I christened The House of All Sorts" (35). For the Soul Tuner, who moves easily between the living and the dead, the House is a liminal and primordial space that draws "everything that exists on this planet" (35) into itself; like Emily, it contains a series of thresholds, all of which must be crossed over in the never-ending search for spiritual transcendence, for what Emily repeatedly calls "aspiring" (12).

Yet sometimes Emily, her family, and her friends remain immobile, too tired, too afraid, or too confused to move well beyond the normal thresholds of their identities. Her sister Lizzie, a diffident spinster, stands literally on the threshold of the House of All Sorts near the beginning of the play, refusing to enter such an unconventional place even though she increasingly feels herself in a disorienting "state of osmosis with the innumerable fibers of the universe" (15). Near the end, however, when Lizzie is dying, she appears fully within the House, now feeling herself "young and free because the weight of time no longer weighs so heavily on me" (84). It turns out that although Lizzie is not an artist, she, like Emily, has nevertheless been on her own journey of self-discovery, rejecting Victoria and its moribund conventions, and serving as a soul mate for her sister, generously sharing what Emily describes as her "marvelous gift for healing body and soul" (83). It is Lizzie's seemingly inexhaustible spiritual power that allows her to save Emily from her incapacitating depressions; when Emily has a breakdown in England, where she has gone to paint, it is Lizzie who brings her back home. It is partly because of her sister's spiritual blessing that Emily finds herself as an artist; builds the House of All Sorts as a self-contained microcosm of the entire world; and acquires the renewed strength to make regular voyages, under the guidance of the Amerindian Goddess D'Sonoqua, through the threshold leading from everyday reality into the Old World, where, as Natalie Rewa points out, she is inspired by "a primordial female power that she tries to convey on canvas" (35).

For Jay in *Le Chien*, the threshold is literally the doorway of his family home, a mobile trailer at the end of a dirt road on the outskirts of Timmins. The visual irony is that the trailer, like Jay's family, is not at all "mobile." His family is effectively imprisoned here, slowly killing itself through incest, alcoholism, boredom, grindingly hard work, money shortages, and winter isolation. Jay is the only one who is in fact "mobile": after a fight with his father, he leaves for the U.S., where he earns a lot of money, glimpses some movie stars, rebuilds a motorcycle, and travels, in the erotically liberated spirit of *Easy Rider*, along the Interstates. Meanwhile, with all the intense concentration of a self-absorbed artist, he is preparing himself—physically, psychologically, and spiritually—for the return journey home where he plans to confront the father whom he now hates more than ever. At the start of the play, Jay walks across the dirt yard, knocks on the screen door of the mobile trailer, and calls out, "Anybody home? You there?" But no one answers. He throws a bone to the barking family dog ("Here! Shut up and gnaw on that for a while"); and as the dog stops barking and a train passes by, Jay curses, "Jesus Christ! What a fuckin' hole!" before opening a beer from the twelve pack he's carrying (3). The playwriting here is deceptively simple and economical. Within a couple of minutes, Dalpé has laid out not only his recurrent themes but also the relationship between so-called everyday reality and the disturbing spiritual forces existing within it. "Anybody home? You there?" These questions have many implications: Does anyone really live here, or are they all dead, figuratively speaking? Can this be called a home, or is it simply a silent empty space? Where is the father: is his absence a sign of his diminishing authority? confirmation that he, in effect, has always been an absent father to Jay? The barking dog, *le chien* of the play's title, is the only one to welcome Jay; like the father with whom he is associated, the dog is savage, alone, chained, and hungry—an evocative (acoustical) symbol not only of the father's character but indeed of this entire dysfunctional family. The sound of the passing train intensifies the atmosphere of isolation and imprisonment; the cursing and the beer drinking function as masculine power-rituals in anticipation of the violent struggle that will eventually have to take place between father and son.

As in classical tragedy, once Jay opens the screen door and re-enters the house to the sounds, as it were, of Cerberus guarding the entrance to the Underworld, he is making a choice from which there is no return. He will have to destroy his father, or risk being destroyed himself; he will have to sacrifice his father to secure his own deliverance. His choice, even though it exacts a high price, seems as strangely necessary as Emily Carr's voyages into the Old World for artistic replenishment, Jean-Marc's return home to Duhamel to find himself within the lost generations of his family, and Erlich's journey through outer and inner space in search of paradise lost/paradise regained. There is, however, a crucial difference. Whereas Emily Carr, Jean-Marc, and Erlich eventually achieve spiritual grace, Jay does not, for although it is a necessary act of spiritual resistance, murdering his father makes him guilty of parricide, a crime for which he will always remain accountable. Will his spirit ever be permanently healed? It is a question that the play is not prepared to answer.

The actress Luce in *Playing Bare*, like all these characters, performs a series of spiritual transformations; but for her, as for Jay, they lead to an impasse from which there may be no way out. Throughout her career, she has acted the great roles, such as Ophelia, Antigone, and Nina (in Chekhov's *The Seagull*), to escape from, rather than to encounter, herself; to create the illusion that she has not just one identity but many in which to revel. She has been doing this for so long, however, there may be no self left from which to escape; no existential base from which to invent her multiple selves; as she says, quoting from her recent performance as Nina (while holding a symbolically apt bouquet of withered flowers from opening night), "I am emptier than empty. All is dreadful. More frightening than dreadful. All is deserted. I am alone. Alone" (11).

For her, the threshold is the space between the great roles; to be herself—fully, completely—she knows that she has no choice: she must cross through the threshold, relinquishing one role, to assume the next one ... and the next one ... and the next one, world without end. But, now that she is artistically and spiritually exhausted, she doesn't have the courage to exist, however temporarily, in the spaces between. If she were to do so, she would find herself, as the play's title puts it, "playing bare," where, as she explains, "the great actress is all alone with herself once again," entrapped in a "silence" that brings about nihilistic despair (12).

What is to be done? Luce's paradoxical solution is to travel even deeper into the existential void by playing the strangely doubled role of Luce/Lucky in Beckett's *Waiting for Godot*. In being Lucky, she hopes to experience the illusion of being herself through dramatically controlled circumstances where despair is imagined, not real, symbolic, not literal, and where the responsibility for the script is Beckett's not hers. Lucky's silence will allow her to speak; Lucky's subservience will give her power ("I have to plunge down into the bottom of the great void that's engulfing me. Into the heart of the immense silence where I struggle with myself like a monster to be exorcised" [36]). As her name would suggest, Luce wants to believe that through the intensity of performance, she can illuminate the theatre—and therefore herself—so that it will again be her spiritual home, more authentic than reality itself (32); as she explains to the other actors in the deeply felt clichés that are her stock-in-trade: "I want you to get as close as possible to your souls" (49). But her strategy collapses, in part because performance will not, perhaps cannot, meet her ontological expectations. The theatre, as she discovers during the rehearsals for *Godot*, is always an exercise in simulated presence: the reality that it seeks to ensnare, through symbolic re-enactments, must always exist at one remove. "No, Victor," she says to the actor playing Vladimir, "I didn't ask you to pretend to piss, I asked you to piss" (59); and when he can't create an authentic version of the reality she needs, she suddenly cancels the rehearsal, ordering the piano player to "[k]eep on playing" (64) in the naive belief that music will succeed in creating virtual illusions when acting has failed. The next day at rehearsal, however, she again tries to force the actors to produce real emotions, but again they fail; and in a moment of Beckettian tragicomic despair, Victor opens his pants and brings out his real penis. But it is black and shrivelled from disease. How, Luce now wonders, can theatre sublimate reality into a transcendent spiritual force when reality itself is so radically incomplete? "Maybe the soul, the soul, doesn't exist," she exclaims as she surrenders to existential doubts. "The soul doesn't exist! The soul doesn't exist! The soul doesn't exist!" But, again, she orders the pianist to "[k]eep on playing" (80) so that her quasi-religious belief in the possibility of a transfigured world will remain intact.

Yet in the penultimate scene, taken up with ever more frenzied rehearsals, she at last admits that the reality that she wants to be *actually there* during performance will, like Godot himself, never come. "Why," she now asks, "do we spend all our lives chasing ghosts?" (95). Since everything now seems emptied of significance, there seems little point in staging the play. She arrives late for the opening night, just as Victor and Etienne have given up their onstage performance of Vladimir and Estragon to revert to themselves. Yet they, even as themselves, are imprisoned, like Beckett's characters, in an existential void from which there is no escape. "Let's go," says Etienne. "We're gettin' outta here"; but "*[t]hey don't move,*" (110), while Luce can be heard calling from offstage, muddling up Nina's words from the opening scene of *The Seagull*—"So many lives, all living things, so many lives have been snuffed out ..."—before the final symbolic blackout (110). Has she given up? Has she lost it? Is she drunk? Perhaps; although in becoming (a now disturbingly invisible) Nina one last time, she seems to be reasserting her belief that the theatre might still be a place where identity, however indeterminate, however precarious, can be at least partially enacted into existence. As she said earlier in the play, "I dream of the night when my soul will rise up, like in the old Greek theatres that open onto the sky. I dream that my soul starts to rise in front of the audience, higher and higher, until it carries the roof away with it, rising, rising, rising ..." (51).

In *Playing Bare* the *complete* assertion of self-identity could only come about if Luce were ready to confront and subvert the authority figures who oppress her. Paradoxically, Beckett's *Waiting for Godot* turns out to be a master-text that liberates and imprisons simultaneously: for Luce, as for Victor and Etienne, it provides a classic role in which to find herself but, since she lacks the courage to play bare, it also allows her to avoid self-knowledge. As in *Waiting for Godot*, the *mise-en-scène* for *Playing Bare* requires a tree—or what Champagne describes as "something like a tree" (vi)—that is meant to symbolise both the "tree of knowledge" and the actors' "souls" (49). Yet as a symbol, it is of course *not* the tree of knowledge nor the tree found in Beckett; it is only a diminished copy, a deformed version of the originals on which it is based. Similarly, Luce's performative dilemma is that she exists not within a primary text—

Beckett's *Waiting for Godot*—but within a metatext—Champagne's *Playing Bare*; Beckett is, in a sense, a ghostwriter who directs her every move from afar. While under Beckett's influence, she can act Lucky but she cannot really be him, so that the existential autonomy that she desires— and that she sometimes seems close to achieving—is regularly denied to her; the "tree of knowledge" is not actually hers and neither, finally, is her own soul. She can't exist with Beckett and yet she can't exist without him: at this ontological impasse, the play ends. Will Luce ever be able to separate herself from the master playwrights on whom she is so dependent? As with the problematic ending of *Le Chien*—who can Jay be now that he is guilty of the murder of his father?—this is a question that *Playing Bare* simply isn't prepared to answer.

In *Queen of the Cadillac* and *The Magnificent Voyage of Emily Carr*, Erlich and Emily Carr do in fact achieve the kind of spiritual autonomy that eludes Luce, but only after protracted struggles with their father figures, both actual and internalised. MacCulloch, the ninety-six-year-old "[v]ampire booze artist" (76) and "Celtic master" (25) in *Cadillac*, has just died when the play begins, but he nevertheless continues to exercise authority from the grave over his children and grandchildren, all of whom have reason to remain terrified of him. In a black comedy scene, as they worry that he might break out of his coffin, which he lovingly made for himself from the very best prime walnut, his daughter Katherine says, "We'll create him in the back yard. I mean cremate" (14). This is a very revealing Freudian slip. They would all like to "create him" anew, to take power away from him, and give it—including the family farm—to themselves; and just as he has once tried to destroy them by burning the house down, they would now all relish the opportunity to destroy him with fire in a collective act of revenge. It is only through revenge that they will be able to recuperate the self-esteem that MacCulloch has spent his lifetime taking away from them. "If you're after the house, me bucko," MacCulloch's son Winston says to Erlich when he suddenly turns up on the Island, "you can just forget it. I got big plans for this property …" to which Erlich, who could be speaking for all of them, replies, "Fuck the house, man. I just want to find out who I am" (64).

Throughout the play, Stetson associates MacCulloch with a Devil figure, developed from a conflation of Gaelic folklore and Christian mythology, who never seems to die but merely reappears in different forms; as Erlich's mother, Hestor, puts it, "MacCulloch's spirit is breaking down into minuscule essences that will regroup into some new being" (41). In yet another black comedy scene, MacCulloch does in fact return from the dead ("The coffin begins to rattle. Mumbles are heard from inside. Then more vigorous rattling. Then thumps and curses. Finally the lid pops up. MacCulloch appears" [42]); but only his supposedly crazy daughter Hestor can see him as he drinks Glen Fiddich and then tries to fondle her—in another revealing Freudian slip, she describes herself as "the family scrape goat" (54)—just as he used to when he was actually alive. At the end of act one, Hestor wins the first of two vividly physical battles against her Father as Devil: when he climbs back inside the coffin, she slams it shut and sits on it as he tries to break free; but she proves to be too strong for him.

At the beginning of act two, MacCulloch manages to escape from his coffin, and disappears, like a disembodied spirit, into his mystical ash grove. After the play's main recognition scenes—in which Erlich not only explains that Hestor is his real mother but also meets the other members of his P.E.I. family and learns about his grandfather's immoral character—Hestor and Erlich return to Montréal, to live together in her "home" beside a furnace in the open basement of a Westmount apartment block. Erlich has already begun to change; he now "spray paints pleasant visions … —the early violence replaced by work with a kind of twisted wisdom" (67). When Hestor sings Erlich one of MacCulloch's favourite Gaelic songs ("Fhir a' bhàta, na h-oro eile …") they suddenly feel that MacCulloch is actually there with them as a menacing if invisible presence. As the Devil himself gets ready to appear for the second battle with his daughter, the furnace, with symbolic aptness, "rattles," "thumps," "belches," "rumbles," and blasts forth with steam while the door slowly opens and "MacCulloch is spewed out" (74–75). MacCulloch eventually drags Erlich down into the furnace; but Hestor, no longer a "scrape goat," fights hard for her only son. As she recites the Gaelic proverb, "S'ann dha-fhéin a ni an cù an comhart" (literally, "The dog barks for himself," a vivid description of the soul-destroying selfishness of MacCulloch's entire life and the lives he has destroyed), MacCulloch suddenly releases Erlich, vanishes down into the furnace, then reappears briefly as Hestor pushes him back down one last time, before slamming the grate over him, saying "Go to hell where you belong" (80).

The next and final scene takes place in Montréal's Cadillac tavern where Hestor has for many years been the Queen of the play's title, fully at home, and honoured by her eccentric street-friends in a way that she had never been by her family in P.E.I. In the Cadillac, after another series of recognition scenes together with some marriages symbolising spiritual rebirth, the characters, including her real P.E.I. family and her adopted Montréal family, look upward one last time, fearful that MacCulloch might be hovering on the catwalk high above them. But no one is there: like that other "barking dog," Jay's father in *Le Chien*, the patriarch has indeed been destroyed, and mother and son can now belong without fear not only to each other but to the Gaelic culture that is rightfully theirs.

For Emily Carr, as for Hestor, the final stage in the spiritual voyage towards herself also involves an actual physical battle with her father. When her studio gets too small for all her paintings, she invents a system of cables and pulleys to hoist her parents' "sacred" furniture—as Lizzie thinks of it—up to the ceiling (65). Like Josaphat's "la maison suspendue," this arrangement gives the impression of a world in which normal values, habits, and assumptions no longer prevail: Bohemia has literally turned Victoria on its head; "suspended" it, Emily explains, "in the void" (70). As in *Cadillac*, the spirit of Emily's dead father seems actually present within the void as his armchair begins to creak just as it did whenever he sat in it when he was alive. For Emily, the chair is an object that evokes the spiritual stultification of her childhood ("Every Sunday, Father made me kneel beneath the arm of that chair while he read the morning prayers! I couldn't breathe!" [73]). Near the end of the play, once her sister Lizzie and her native Indian friend Sophie have both died, Emily is ready to confront her father within the dematerialised space high above her head. As she pulls on the cables, hoisting the armchair, she "suddenly loses her footing and is lifted off the ground;" physically, her father is much stronger than she is; the struggle—what Marchessault calls "her battle with Jacob's angel"—continues; but at the climax, Emily "is lifted off the ground one last time and falls, struck down by a heart attack" (94).

Although physically she has lost to her father, spiritually she has in effect won, because the struggle teaches her that there is no point in hating him. Through this insight, she can be her independent self *and* her father's daughter simultaneously: thus, in the last scene, we see her actually sitting in her father's armchair, recovering from a number of heart attacks, communing with the Soul Tuner, and seeking to understand where her artistic voyages have taken her. Above all, she is learning how to be another kind of artist: a writer who will seek to give voice to the infinite variety of the spiritual world ("I'll write to the dead of the human nation. And to all the beloved creatures who have disappeared into the vast, cold depths of the earth" [104]) with the kind of compassion that her former unrelenting hatred of her father had made impossible.

Works Cited

Champagne, Dominic. *Playing Bare*. Trans. Shelley Tepperman. Vancouver: Talonbooks, 1993.

Dalpé, Jean-Marc. *Le Chien*. Trans. Maureen LaBonté and Jean Marc Dalpé. Unpublished manuscript. Montréal: Centre d'essai des auteurs dramatiques, 1990.

Marchessault, Jovette. *The Magnificent Voyage of Emily Carr*. Trans. Linda Gaboriau. Vancouver: Talonbooks, 1992.

Rewa, Natalie. "Women's Art: Jovette Marchessault and Emily Carr." *Women on the Canadian Stage: The Legacy of Hrotsvit*. Ed. Rita Much. Winnipeg: Blizzard, 1992. 30–42.

Stetson, Kent. *Queen of the Cadillac*. Unpublished manuscript. 1992.

Tremblay, Michel. *La Maison Suspendue*. Trans. John Van Burek. Vancouver: Talonbooks, 1991.

In/Visible Drama of Atlantic Canada

by Denyse Lynde

In 1991/92, Bryden MacDonald wrote about his attempt to survey theatre in Atlantic Canada: "I went into overload upon realizing that tackling the East coast theatre scene in one article might be a tad ambitious" (15). Three years later, the would-be commentator's anxiety levels should be even higher. Several theatre companies are producing new work in Eastern Canada and the number of Atlantic Canadian playwrights is substantial. The situation is exacerbated by the fact that the number of plays being produced but not published is escalating. In order to suggest the range and diversity of material being written in Atlantic Canada, I will consider this rich landscape according to a three tier system: plays written and produced in the East, published and produced elsewhere; plays produced by more than one company in the East; plays produced by one company for one community. In order to respond to one local playwright's lament—"I guess I should move to Toronto too"—I will chiefly deal with the second and third levels. By choosing to do this, I realize that several playwrights will be omitted; those that, perhaps, are familiar and one would expect to see in a chapter on playwrighting in Atlantic Canada. However, rather than follow Andy Jones' inventive response to this dilemma ("Plays for Publishing" 1993) and list all of the titles of plays produced, but not published at St. John's Resource Centre For the Arts, a few specific plays will be introduced and considered.

DENYSE LYNDE is an Associate Professor of English at Memorial University of Newfoundland where she is a drama specialist. She has recently completed a full-length study of the plays of Michael Cook and is presently editing a collection of Newfoundland drama and co-organizing a theatre archival project.

236   *Denyse Lynde*

The most difficult task in writing this essay lay in selecting the work to be discussed. Choosing work from the late eighties to the present provided a framework; turning directly to theatre practitioners for recently produced work further defined the field.[1] Finally, a selection was made based on the following criteria. Each play discussed here, while reflecting its own community, speaks to a larger audience in its subject, tone or approach. These plays indicate the diversity and range of the playwrighting community of Atlantic Canada while simultaneously championing the complexity and richness of these individual artists. By discussing these plays as a group, the particular strength of each play is heightened and the resulting comparison sheds light on the sophistication of theatre in Eastern Canada.

Long characterized as rooted in the collective tradition[2], in the late eighties Newfoundland theatre begins to be dominated by an emerging new generation of playwrights who received their theatre training from the collective tradition. At the same time, Rising Tide Theatre and the Resource Centre For the Arts aggressively begin to foster and nurture these new voices. The former begins a very successful workshop series that develops several scripts[3] and the latter initiates a second space program where new work receives a much needed first try-out.

As an indication of the range and variety of drama being written in Newfoundland now, three plays will be considered, Pete Soucy's *Flux*, Janis Spence's *Catlover*, and Ed Riche's *Possible Maps*. The plays by Soucy and Spence were first produced by the Resource Centre For the Arts, L.S.P.U. Hall, St. John's, and then produced in different venues in Atlantic Canada. Ed Riche's play has only seen productions at the Resource Centre for the Arts, L.S.P.U. Hall, St. John's, as well as a fall '94 production in Toronto. When considering these three markedly different texts, two common elements emerge. All three plays work within the tradition of comic realism that defines, however loosely, much Newfoundland drama of the late eighties and early nineties. In each instance, the playwright exhibits an obvious strength in creating the comic line and situation. The characters in these three plays all share a similar dilemma: they are all attempting to redefine and reorient themselves within a shifting universe. Claude in *Flux* tries to readjust his gaze on himself, his art and his world when his girlfriend leaves him for another woman. Hester in *Catlover* finds her life turned upside down when her absent husband of nineteen years walks back into her life. The Performer in *Possible Maps* attempts to chart his way through the labyrinth of the past and his previously unarticulated relationship with his father. All three plays can be read as an attempt to adjust, rework, rechart and finally to begin a new journey of self exploration. In order to explore the shifting perspectives, each play has a central conceit. Throughout *Flux*, Claude's sculpture is assessed, adjusted, reassessed and considered. Throughout *Catlover*, the ancient cat, who remains unseen, is valued, devalued, remembered and given away. Throughout *Possible Maps*, the performer considers maps, mapping, mis-mapping and the various kinds of journeys they make possible or impossible.

In *Flux*, Claude's girlfriend moves out when she becomes attracted to a fellow activist. Joey, a welder, moves in and the odd couple relationship is established. Using Claude's sculpture as the focus, Soucy explores the resulting tensions between the two craftsmen. Joey wants Claude to tell him what it is; Claude refuses: "Well, what it means to me may not be the same thing it will mean to anyone else. I hope there'll be many interpretations" (25). Joey wants an answer and he considers the sculpture at every opportunity:

> "Joey's Music" plays as house lights fade. Music fades as the lights reveal JOEY sitting and studying the sculpture. It appears he has been doing so for some time. He finishes a can of Vienna sausages without losing his concentration. After a few moments of tilting his head this way and that, he stands to gain a higher point of view. Slowly, he circles the table, retrieving his bottle of beer from the armrest of the chair on his way around, and finally stands on the chair. With great care, he, almost as if being drawn by an unseen force, places the beer can precariously on the highest point of the sculpture. Elation. (40)

His obsession continues and he tries to explain why to Claude:

> The more I look at it. It's ... it's like when you're at a movie, and the picture is all fuzzy, because the guy running the machine ain't paying attention? You're dying for him to turn that knob, y'know, and it's taking forever. (65)

He wishes that Claude would "Just focus it" (65) so that he can read it and find the elusive "answer."

After Joey is fired from his job because he was too creative in his welding, he welds a statue of Claude as a going away present. Claude, touched by his efforts, begins to explain what his sculpture means but Joey interrupts his explanation because he can now read the art work himself: "Oh man! It's got something to do with ... (*arms back, flight-like*) ... with ... flying. Right?" (73). The play closes as the two men decide to go out for a drink to confirm their new alliance. Throughout the play, Soucy explores tensions that exist between ways of seeing and perspectives. Claude must accept his girlfriend's leave taking, the rejection of a peer art board of his bid for a show and the seeming unsympathetic voice of his new room mate. The combination of these events send him into a depression and he avoids the outer world and hibernates in the apartment. Joey's curiosity and persistence force Claude to become engaged and finally Claude realizes that Joey is not what he first thought; at the close of the play, each man leaves the apartment with a different vision of each other. What distinguishes this play is the many layered approach that Soucy chooses; *Flux* is not simply another retelling of the odd couple story. This play is a thoughtful, predominately comic consideration of the limitations of perception that we have about ourselves and others. By placing the sculpture in the centre, Soucy asks us to consider how we see and why and what we conclude.

In *Catlover*, Hester, abandoned by her husband Edwin, has cared for her father-in-law, a victim of Alzheimer's, and her husband's cat for nineteen years. Her son wants to put his grandfather in a home and have the cat put down. Hester rejects both suggestions. After Edwin returns home, she shows him his cat:

> Hester returns carrying a simple Roddie-designed post-modern cat box with a vaguely Greek temple roof-line. She places the box on the sofa and gently removes the lid. (51)

Not unlike the response of both Edwin's father and son to the unexpected return of son and father respectively, the cat bites Edwin. At the end of the play, Edwin leaves to get his belongings so that he can resume his old life with Hester. Hester, however, after a moment's indecision, quickly packs a bag and exits, leaving the house and the major responsibilities of father-in-law and cat for her husband. Unlike Edwin, however, she leaves a note saying "I'll call you. Me." (79). Here, Spence explores personal responsibilities and the idea of love.

Like Soucy, Spence's dialogue and situations are predominately comic and, while dealing with serious issues like Alzheimer's, her vision of this world is shot through with a farcical fare best illustrated by the bizarre moment of the homecoming. Edwin does not merely walk back into the lives of his family; he arrives complete with television crew and interviewer to record the tender moment for thousands of viewers. Needless to say, pandemonium breaks out in the resulting scene which has overtones of classical French farce. Other plays by Spence included *Chickens*, *Naked Bungalow* and *Walking to Australia*. In each of these texts, an apparently realistic situation is twisted and turned into a comic reflection of itself. Spence's snappy dialogue, crisply drawn characters and swiftly moving action are characteristic of her work—work that not unlike Soucy's *Flux* demands that theatre become a comic and refreshingly light reflection of life (Lynde 56).

Maps are crucial in *Possible Maps*. In the centre of the stage sits a large projection screen on which are flashed numerous slides (175). The Performer not only shows maps, pictures and black slides but also moves about the screen so that at times he is being mapped himself by the projections. His body at times frames the projections on the side, above and across. Maps and their meanings preoccupy the Performer: "Yes, the map is simply a tale, a primitive simple story—one person's version of the world" (182). However, as he tells us, different maps can offer different versions of the same geography. The Performer's father was a cartographer and he remembers his father's life through the maps he made. At one point, his father had become depressed and only recovered when he was offered a new mapping project which he eagerly accepted. However, he deliberately mis-maps the area and two fisherman get lost:

> Dad just couldn't believe that they had kept believing in the map. He had imagined that users would spot the obvious errors and then try to decode his puzzle. Where did they think they were going? They could be playing a game on the barrens, leisurely working on the crossword, searching for buried treasure. The world was too small; everybody knew everything; it was a noble project—creating a new world. (182)

His father wanted to return to a world where maps could be created; failing that he tries to offer a new view of the world.

When his father has another crisis, the Performer visits him in his study where he is shown another map, this time of his father's life. He is now, he tells his son, in the "Labyrinthine canyons of despair" (197). The father decides he must scale the canyon walls. His son acknowledges how his own life, too, is a map: "I choose to leave the expedition before the Despairs. These lands are mine. They are anything but featureless. The journey seems as perilous as my father's. Many times I've thought of turning back ... but ... I might get lost and ... what would I find" (199).

At the end of the play, the Performer records his father's death and his father's legacy to him:

> Though he seemed in good health, I guess the Despairs and the difficult climb had taken the good out of him. He left this.
> *He holds up a piece of paper.*
> A last navigational aid. It reads simply ...
> *The lights fade. On the floor of the stage, an X-shaped pool of light appears. The performer steps into it.*
> "You are here." (199).

The Performer's legacy from his father is perhaps the most important map, confirming where he is and opening up the possibility for future maps. These three plays all share positive conclusions in which the central figures find themselves renewed, refreshed and at the brink of a new passage.

Ray Guy, another Newfoundland playwright and brilliant satirist, has delighted St. John's audiences with several plays. Perhaps his most successful, *Young Triffie's Been Made Away With*, is a fiercely comic tale of Newfoundland domestic life where no member of this society escapes the playwright's biting tongue. As in his other works, Guy goes beyond the comic realism characteristic of the other works discussed here to explore a kind of black comedy. Here, a local girl is found murdered and by the end, not only is the murderer exposed but also incest, alcoholism, drug addiction, rape and all other manner of sins are exposed. Guy leaves no stone unturned. In all these Newfoundland plays, playwrights are responding to their rapidly changing world with a resilient and essentially positive statement of survival. Maps, changing responsibilities, new perceptions and comic outlook can be found and survival will continue.

In the mainland maritime provinces, there is likewise an incredible variety of plays being written and produced; here, however, what immediately becomes apparent is the many different approaches and genres being explored. Rather than fully exploring the vast varieties of comic realism, mainland playwrights often explore heightened versions of realism or other, more self-consciously serious forms than that characteristic of Newfoundland drama. In order to illustrate some of the different approaches, four very different texts will be briefly considered. *The Summer of Piping Plover* by Catherine A. Banks was first produced by Upstart Theatre, Halifax, in 1991. *Safe Haven* by Mary-Colin Chisholm was commissioned and workshopped by the Mulgrave Road Company and first produced by them in Spring 1992. *Adrift* by Sheilagh Hunt was first produced by Empty Mirrors Productions at the 1993 Atlantic Fringe Festival. *Honey and White Blood* by Wanda Graham was produced at the 1992 Atlantic Fringe Festival by Fools for Love.

Safe Haven is a truly moving play dealing with the painful subject of AIDS. Cassie, divorced mother of Katie, discovers that her ex-husband has infected her with the HIV virus and she must come home to tell her family and friends. The first person she must tell is Kevin, a one time sexual partner. Cassie's closest childhood friend, Hannah, is a local physician who does Kevin's test and, concerned with Cassie's behaviour, soon realizes that her friend is infected. Because Hannah, like Cassie, had a single sexual encounter with Kevin, she, too, has herself tested. Once the test results of Hannah and Kevin are returned negative, they must offer whatever support they can to Cassie and her plans for the future of her child. *Safe Haven* calls for a variety of locales that can be realized in either a realistic manner or a more fluid style as the stage directions in the performance text from Mulgrave Road indicates: "in general we were able to avoid blackouts and long scene changes, the scenes flowed into each and the transitions seemed integral" (iii). By centering the play on those who surround Cassie, the focus immediately becomes deeply personal and, consequently, curiously poignant.

Cassie's unwed mother, Mamie, died shortly after her birth and her aunt, Mamie's older sister, Fay, raised her as her own. When Cassie comes home to tell Kevin, she wants Fay to talk to her about the mother and birth. Fay brings out several old photos and Cassie offers to sort them out:

> CASSIE: Maybe I could see what kind of albums I can find, and bring them down the next time I come, because I don't think we'll get through all these others this weekend.
> FAY: No, I don't suppose we will, what a jumble. It's an awful big job getting things straightened out, isn't it? (28)

Of course, there is a lot of "straightening" Cassie must do and she is determined to do what she must do. As soon as she is alone with Kevin, she tells him. Not surprisingly, he is angry and frightened and leaves her immediately. The scene closes with Cassie alone with her fears and anxieties:

> I'm the one who's got it, I'm going to ... oh christ please take this away, let me wake up sweet jesus, let me wake up ...

> somebody take the night away, oh jesus sweet jesus, I just
> want things to go back, let me go back, I want them the way
> they were, dear god, sweet jesus, dear jesus. (35)

Once Hannah and Kevin find they are not HIV Positive, they must comfort their friend the best way they can by offering support.

Safe Haven is a beautifully written play which delicately and compassionately explores the issue of AIDS in modern society. Betrayal, anger and fear give way to comfort, friendship and love as these four adults come to grips with what AIDS means for them and their loved ones. The play ends with Hannah and Cassie watching the offstage child play ball with Hannah's dog. This ending, with the women discussing guardianship of the child while the child runs and splashes, brings the strengths of this play into clear focus. Chisholm allows her characters to respond to this crisis with dignity and strength and through this response, *Safe Haven* becomes a hauntingly memorable text. The carefully crafted characters and clear point of focus lift *Safe Haven* from the sensational to the universally memorable. In Soucy, Spence and Riche, a predominately comic response to a shifting world prevails; Chisholm, centering her text on the AIDS crisis, personalizes and humanizes the epidemic with compassion. In all cases, the plays are deeply rooted and reflective of their own community but, due to the universal nature of their themes, each play in turn speaks to a larger audience.

The Summer of Piping Plover by Catharine A. Banks explores the conflicting demands of self, family and community when a local government considers the creation of a campground and theme park on a secluded beach property. Eric, a former draft dodger, and Pam had moved to an idyllic maritime retreat following Eric's release from jail in an attempt to get back to nature. Following a period of roughing it, the birth of his daughter forces Eric to get a job, leaving Pam with the responsibility of the farm. When the play begins, the daughter, Sacha, now fourteen, has been educated at home by Eric but Pam has decided that she must be integrated into society. In order to achieve this, she invites Edna, a local woman, to their home to help her complete a quilt she discovered in her attic. When the plan for the development is announced, Eric resolves to stop it at any cost. Pam, who is against it as well, looks for a compromise. Sacha becomes preoccupied with the fate of a maimed sea gull she tries to nurse back to health while a visiting university student, Marnie, alerts Eric to the importance of the area as a nesting ground for piping plovers. Banks works this plot through to its but what lifts this realistic piece of slice-of-life drama out of the mundane is her poetic use of the quilt, damaged gull and nesting birds to support and enhance the more overt plot.

Eric seizes on the plight of the piping plover to validate his personal struggle against the proposed development. They become merely an empty slogan for him to use against everybody and anybody who supports the development. He has no concern for the community and finally for his family. Sacha struggles to keep the maimed bird alive despite her father's insistence that it should be left to die. Her mother moderates between the two, insisting that Sacha can try to save the bird if she wishes. As tensions in the family increase, the bird deteriorates and Sacha becomes increasingly distressed. In order to keep the bird alive, Sacha needs Marnie to help her. Eric also wants Marnie's help initially because of her knowledge of the plovers and, then, personally, to help him in his stand. The death of the gull clearly underlines Eric's failure with his daughter and perhaps marks his first step away from the family. The cause will override the concerns of the community and those of his family.

In the centre of the action, like the eye of a hurricane, sits Pam and her quilt. The quilt, "Storm at Sea," symbolizes Pam's function in her family and her community. She creatively takes the pieces and puts them together into a work of art just as she creates the solution whereby the nests and the development are able to live together. It is characteristic of Pam that she will finish someone else's work and it is significant that she finishes the work of someone from the heart of this community. The act of completing the quilt marks her movement into the community from her previously isolated position. At the close of the play, Eric, like the dead gull, is absent but the completed quilt hangs bravely on the kitchen wall while Pam begins a new quilt for her daughter. This new quilt will mark her daughter's entrance into the community; the two women will establish new ties.

The Summer of Piping Plover mingles the social issues found at the heart of *Safe Haven* with the interior journeys explored by Spence, Soucy and Riche. Here the quilt functions as did the cat, sculpture and map but here the public and private worlds appear to be on the verge of collision. Compromise and a reordering allow a new journey to begin as the play closes; at this moment, the compassion and understanding of *Safe Haven* is fully integrated with the confidence and cockiness of *Cat Lover*. It is this integration that pushes *The Summer of Piping Plover* beyond a local issue play and allows it a voice on the national arena; the text becomes specific but universal.

The poetic realism of *The Summer of Piping Plover* is in sharp contrast to the abstract absurdism of *Adrift*. Using Erwin Schrodinger, the physicist who formulated the equation of quantum mechanics and his famous paradox as a starting point, Sheilagh Hunt explores the intricacies of a relationship as A and B paddle a boat. There only companion is a Ghost that they may or may not see:

> A third character, the ghost, enters and exits. He or she is the devil's advocate reminding 'A' & 'B' of the things they hide from each other, intentionally or not. Certain topics are interjected into the dialogue by the ghost in trying to coax the characters to take a stand on philosophical and personal differences. (1)

The action takes place in and around the row boat which is set on a revolve that allows it to move at specific moments. The play opens with a discussion of the box that A says contains a cat named Schrodinger. Although B wants the box opened, A refuses stating that the "Uncertainty keeps us alive" (4). Under discussions of progress, weather, time and the box, A and B explore the demands that people place on each other, the nature of relationships and on our sense of self.

Issues become more heated when the Ghost presents them with a note in a bottle announcing that war has been declared. A and B argue, then, on the course of action, finally, of course, remaining *Adrift* with the box between them. At the end of the play, B demands that the box be opened, an action that B believes will allow them to proceed, to move on. With reluctance, A agrees and the play ends with the ribbon being untied as the Ghost speaks:

> And so the box was unsealed.
> Were the wounds of our players thus healed?
> Was the cat live or dead?
> Ah—why not tell me instead.
> Was the secret obscured or revealed? (33)

Adrift, clearly indebted to Beckett, stands on its own, depicting how two individuals find themselves *Adrift* in relationships. The necessity to open the box clarifies the need for action, to seize the challenge, to ask and answer the question, whatever the cost. By opening the box, the relationship in the boat is irrevocably changed. To what degree, must remain hidden, but the action must be taken. Although Hunt chooses a very different style, again characters come to a turning point where options must be reexamined and assessed. Claude, Hester, the Performer, Cassie and Pam are joined by A and B; all are at a crossroads where decisions must be made and a new journey begun. In this case, Hunt places the emphasis on the ability to act; the opening of the box becomes an act of defiance and hope.

Honey and White Blood by Wanda Graham is a feminist play that explores the politics of sex, identity and writing. The structure of the play is deliberately fluid; a series of short scenes labelled by colours "To be played in any order" (i). These scenes involve a play and a play within a play in which characters are doubled. One scene that gives a glimpse of the complexity of the text is "Purple" where many of its various threads are exposed. In this scene, He, She, Waiter and June with the only lover she trusts, Bruga, a marionette, engage in a stylized duel of sorts, where individuals carefully approach and probe each other, exploring sexual tensions and artistic values. He clearly wants a conventional approach:

> HE: Where is the beginning?
> JUNE: He hates you, but he's jealous.
> SHE: What is beginning?
> BRUGA: I am a very distinguished Count.
> HE: A point of take-off, a touch of reality.
> JUNE: Because he can't figure out what we do.
> SHE: Reality! Poetry.
> JUNE: Val's too "orderly" to be a poet.
> HE: WHERE DOES IT BEGIN. (Purple 2)

He wants order, precision, clearly a phallocentric style. She offers alternatives:

> SHE: (*Gives them a look*) It moves from her dreams outward into space, time.
> HE: Gives us fact about her. Like I do.
> JUNE: Your kisses are paradise. (*Kissing him*).
> SHE: Perhaps I should weed your new novel.
> JUNE: What new novel?
> HE: And that journal ... it's poisonous, makes you lazy ...
> SHE: Someday it will be a great human document. (Purple 3)

June finds herself trapped between the two modes of thought and begins to collapse physically:

> SHE: I see. I fail ejaculatory writing.
> HE: You need English lessons.
> JUNE: I'll never marry again.
> SHE: Follow me into the ephemeralness of subconsciousness ... (Purple 5)

It is She who clarifies June's position, her version, and the underpinning of the play: "Her portrait is a mobile. Images float freely in the atmosphere ... dancing in the little winds ... taken in any order ... the outcome remains the same ..." (Purple 5). The entire play explores these different attitudes and perspectives in each scene which is characterized by a specific colour. *Honey and White Blood* confidently and adroitly explores politically charged issues within a framework that succinctly reflects its themes. Here, sculpture, cat, map, quilt, box are again transformed; the mobile, fully integrating structure and substance, dances freely with the same comic mayhem of Spence and occasionally with the biting satire of Guy.

There are several other playwrights writing in Atlantic Canada. Mary Vingoe has written several plays and her *Living Curiosities* was recently published. Greg Dunham and Michael Hennessey have both had work produced in Prince Edward Island. Dunham's most recent, in 1992, *Island Smoke* and *A Man Looking Out The Window*, are available through Playwrights Union of Canada. Michael Hennessey's work, produced on the Island and elsewhere, includes *The Trial of Minnie McGee* and *Young Maud*. Playwrights Harry Thurston and Gregory M. Cook turned to history in their play, *Black River Miracle*, first produced in 1992 and dedicated to the memory of Nova Scotian miners and their families. Jack Sheriff, working out of Nova Scotia, continues as a writer, director and playwright with Playwrights Canada listing his catalogue of plays. A major force as playwright and mentor is, of course, Christopher Heide who has worked with several companies on different projects. Presently he is associate director for young theatre with Mermaid Theatre of Nova Scotia where a writing workshop for students is held each summer, resulting in *Summer Pickings* and *World Without Adults* in 1991, a play about vandalism in 1992, a collective in 1993 and *Growing up in Nova Scotia* in 1993.

Playwriting in Atlantic Canada is a serious business. With several companies dedicated to original work, plays are being nurtured, developed and produced, frequently at more than one theatre. Unfortunately, two factors keep these works shrouded from the general public. First, the chronic lack of national arts coverage tends to tie play and production to separate and often discreet communities. When plays and/or productions move, there is generally some specific connection between individuals involved; the artistic communities tend to remain isolated from each other in the main. Secondly, plays are not being published, and even when they are, they remain unknown and unread. The quality of drama being written in Atlantic Canada is impressive. This partial commentary is offered as a challenge to readers and producers of drama; look beyond the various canons of Canadian drama, beyond the commentary of national systems and explore this rich and unknown terrain of drama written in Atlantic Canada.

Notes

1. Many people helped me get the word out to playwrights across this region. Particularly I would like to thank Pete Soucy, Jenny Munday, Artistic Director, Theatre New Brunswick, Allena MacDonald, Artistic Director, Mulgrave Road Co Op Theatre, Chris Heide, Lee Lewis, Derek Martin, Jane Buss and all the playwrights who sent me their work.
2. Michael Cook, Tom Cahill, Al Pittman, Grace Butt, and others, are among the small group of working Newfoundland playwrights from the 60s and 70s.
3. *The Painful Education of Patrick Brown* by Michael Cook, *Woman in a Monkey Cage* by Berni Stapleton as well as scripts by Des Walsh and Kevin Major among several others.

Works Cited

Hunt, Sheilagh. *Adrift*. Unpublished.
Jones, Andy. "Plays for Publishing." *Newfoundland Theatre Research*. St. John's: Memorial University, 1993. 177–178.
Lynde, Denyse. "Janis Spence: Chickens, Cats and the Responsibility of Love." *Canadian Theatre Review* 69 (Winter 1991): 49–56.

MacDonald, Bryden. "Not Leaving Home." *Theatrum* (Winter 1991): 10–13.
Riche, Ed. *Possible Maps* in *Solo*. Ed. Jason Sherman. Toronto: Coach House Press, 1994. 173–200.
Spence, Janis. *Catlover*. Unpublished.
Soucy, Pete. *Flux*. Playscript. Toronto: Playrights Canada Press.

For Further Reading

Banks, Catherine A. *The Summer of Piping Plover*. Playscript. Toronto: Playwrights Canada Press.
Blackmore, Jenni. *Walking With Beothuk*. Unpublished.
Brookes, Chris. *A Public Nuisance*. St. John's: ISSER, 1988.
Chisholm, Mary-Colin. *Safe Haven*. *Theatrum* 38 (April/May 1994): 51–55.
Cochran, Lisa. *Shawna*. Unpublished.
Dunham, Greg. *Island Smoke*. Playscript. Toronto: Playrights Canada Press.
———. *A Man Looking Out a Window*. Playscript. Toronto: Playrights Canada Press.
Graham, Wanda. *Honey and White Blood*. Unpublished [draft three].
Guy, Ray. *Young Triffie's Been Made Away With*. Unpublished.
Heide, Chris. *The Promised Land*. Playscript. Toronto: Playwrights Canada Press.
Hennessey, Michael. *The Lesser Man*. Unpublished.
———. *The Trial of Minne McGee*. Unpublished.
———. *Young Maud*. Unpublished.
Hyrtle, Kevin. *A Gift for Buford*. Unpublished.
Hoyt McGee, Arlee. *Stone Silence*. Unpublished.
Majka, Christopher. *Dear Faith*. Unpublished.
Peters, Helen, ed. *The Plays of Codco*. New York: Peter Land, 1993.
Sheriff, Jack. *Catalog of Jack Sheriff's Plays*. Toronto: Playwrights Canada Press.
Spence, Fara E. *The Errors of Her Ways*. Unpublished.
———. *Love in a Microwave Oven*. Unpublished.
Thurston, Harry and Gregory M. Cook. *Black River Miracle*. Unpublished.

Townshend, Adele. *For the Love of a Horse.* Ottawa Little Theatre Workshop 'Ranking' Play Series, 1962.

Vingoe, Mary. *Living Curiosities. Adventures For (Big) Girls.* Ed. Ann Jansen. Winnipeg: Blizzard, 1993. 25–49.

———. *Holy Ghosters 1776.* Unpublished.

[Note: Some of the above unpublished plays are among those being prepared for publication by Denyse Lynde with the support of the Newfoundland and Labrador/Canada Cooperation Agreement on Cultural Industries. Through a similar arrangement, a number of collective creations are being prepared for publication by Helen Peters. Both volumes are to be published in Fall 1995 by Breakwater Press.]